I0611322

HOUSE OF BROKEN BONES

HOUSE OF BROKEN BONES

EDGAR J HERN

Second Edition: September 2025

10 9 8 7 6 5 4 3 2

Printed in the United States of America.

Publisher's Cataloging-in-Publication Data

Names: Hern, Edgar J., author.
Title: House of broken bones / Edgar J. Hern.
Description: Includes bibliographical references. | Las Vegas, NV: Amazon KDP, 2025.
Identifiers: LCCN: 2025905076 | ISBN: 979-8-9928840-0-5 (hardcover) | 979-8-9928840-1-2 (paperback) |
979-8-9928840-2-9 (paperback/pocketbook) |
979-8-9928840-3-6 (ebook)
Subjects: LCSH Fantasy fiction. | Science fiction. | Horror fiction. | Short stories. | BISAC
FICTION / Science Fiction / Action & Adventure | FICTION / Psychological | FICTION / Horror /
General | FICTION / Fantasy / Urban | FICTION / Political | FICTION / Fantasy / Dark Fantasy,
Classification: LCC PS2608 .E76 H68 2025 | DDC 813.6--dc23

Other than a few shared life experiences approved for publication, this book is a work of fiction. All incidents, dialogue, and characters, except for some well-known historical figures, are products of the author's imagination and are not to be construed as real. Where real-life historical persons appear, if any, the situations, incidents, and dialogues concerning those persons are entirely fictional and are not intended to depict actual events. In all other respects, any resemblance to living or deceased persons is entirely coincidental. While some facts and statistics are real, their usage in this story is entirely fictional.

The medical definitions provided in the glossary are intended solely to assist readers in understanding the context of the story. While care has been taken to provide clear and accessible explanations, these definitions are not meant to serve as comprehensive medical references or substitutes for professional medical advice. Readers are encouraged to consult medical literature or a healthcare professional for detailed information or guidance on medical terms and concepts.

DEDICATION

For my daughter, Lana, whose laughter brightens my days and whose dreams inspire my heart. May you always chase what sets your soul on fire, and know my love will forever be your guiding light. Thank you for your valuable input in this book. Your insights helped shape what lives within these pages.

Special Mention

LA BRUJA MALDITA

Thank you, Ellen Guinan and Samantha Garibay-Hernandez, for sharing your embarrassing moments, and Donna Lynn, for sharing your views on John Lennon's death anniversary.

TABLE OF CONTENTS

AS CLEAR AS NIGHT

Wednesday, March 17, 2004. 1:35 a.m.

The silence in the opulent study was stifling, broken only by the faint rustle of gloved hands rifling through a sea of documents. Moonlight filtered through the grand arched window, casting a pale glow on the mahogany desk and the walls lined with leather-bound books. Behind the black ski mask, Alex Blackwell's piercing blue eyes darted from one sheet to the next until, at last, a slip of paper seemed to glow beneath his touch—the elusive bank lockbox number belonging to a New Jersey lottery winner. His lips curled into a wicked smile as he scribbled the information onto a notepad. Then, without a sound, his body began to shimmer and dissolve, fading into the shadows as if he had never been there at all.

Reappearing in the driver's seat of his car, Alex cast one last glance at the millionaire's Villa Grande, its grandeur bathed in ethereal moonlight. The engine roared to life, and he shifted into gear. Feeling the thrill pulse through him, he pulled off the mask to reveal a cunning smile. With his plan now in motion, the promise of a life-changing fortune lay just within his reach.

* * *

The air was cold enough to warrant fuzzy wool gloves and scarves that wrapped around twice. Swaying gently like a lullaby in the breeze, the trees tickled the black clouds to a gentle rumble. Light rain fell across central Long Island as a storm raced through the East Coast states. Alex parked his white coupe at the intersection of Jerusalem and Eastern Avenues, across from Province Security Bank. Its proximity to the Seaford-Oyster Bay Expressway was ideal, serving as a quick getaway route.

Having slipped his fingers into thin, nonslip leather gloves, he pulled the ski mask over his head and peered through an 80-millimeter angled spotting scope. The scope's objective lens let in 77% more light than a standard 60-millimeter, delivering sharper resolution through the gloom. From the strip mall parking lot, he could see the vault through the bank's glass doors. After waiting for a teller to exit, he watched as she carefully closed the heavy door without letting it latch before clearing. In an instant, the scope gave way to gravity and bounced twice before settling onto the car's red leather seat.

Alex materialized safely inside the vault in a sitting position, relieved he hadn't landed on the pelvic injury from his last job. It was chilly, and the teller's perfume lingered in the air. He stood quickly, moving toward the appropriate lockbox as ringing phones and distant voices filtered through the partially closed door. Ignoring the blinking red light on the surveillance camera, Alex reached into his leather jacket pocket and pulled out a pouch with a ball-peen hammer and a center punch. But before he could punch the double-lock mechanism, the door behind him slid open again. Shocked at the interruption of what should have been a swift in-and-out job, he glanced over his shoulder and dropped both tools.

The manager gasped at the sight of him, her tattooed eyebrows arching above thick-framed glasses. For a moment, they locked eyes, frozen in mutual hesitation. Then a bulky key chain slipped from her trembling fingers, clattering against the tile. Fear seized her throat, stifling a scream. Her legs buckled as the masked man bolted toward the door. She slammed against the wall and collapsed in a heap onto the cold tile. Whether he shoved her or she fell on her own was never clear.

Alex's heart raced as he vaulted over the counter and sprinted past the customers lined up between him and freedom. *This was not part of the plan,* he thought, his thudding footsteps echoing off the marble walls.

"It's a bank robber!" A woman's piercing scream shattered the sudden silence, triggering a wave of panic. Every eye turned toward the masked man.

To create a diversion, Alex shoved a few startled patrons against the divider ropes. Brass posts clanged as several people toppled while he made a beeline for the glass doors.

Slumped over a check desk, the security guard leaped into action. "Stop!" he shouted, drawing his gun as he darted across the lobby. At the sight of a brandished weapon, more customers screamed and dove for the relative safety of the floor.

Thinking he could reach his car without having to clear, Alex dashed out of the bank, his heart tripping in his chest. Several customers walking up the sidewalk ducked and ran for cover as he bolted past.

The guard flung the glass door open and aimed his gun, one delicately quivering finger on the trigger.

Rain pounded the asphalt as Alex ran mindlessly into the street. A blast from a truck's horn drained the blood from his face. He froze—staring at a fuel tanker bearing down on him. His breath caught. Spotting his car across the street, he quickly envisioned himself behind the steering wheel. With a deafening roar, the truck surged forward, missing his face by mere inches before he cleared.

With adrenaline surging, the security guard's trembling finger tightened—jerking the trigger before thought could intervene. The bullet pierced the truck's front tire, unleashing 105 PSI in a deafening blast that shattered the calm.

Instinct took over as the driver slammed on the air brakes and yanked the steering wheel hard left, sending the tanker careening sideways. It growled like a slain dragon, grinding through traffic and gouging deep ruts into the asphalt. With a violent crack, a utility pole snapped under the truck's onslaught and sent live wires snaking onto the pavement. Two cars that skidded into the tank ripped through the metal body, spewing hundreds of gallons of fuel onto the street. One of the fallen power lines swayed like a cobra dancing to the tune of a pungi, spitting sparks each time it hit a puddle.

The driver hauled himself through the window, gripping the side-view mirror for support. A trickle of blood from a cut on his forehead ran down his nose, but he didn't notice. The door panel bent under his weight. As he stood gasping for air, his heart raced like a wild stallion. Fuel thickened the air, its sharp scent mixing with the sight of twisted wreckage below. His thoughts scattered as he assessed the damage, trying to figure out what to do next. It had all happened so fast. He was sure he'd struck the man. And those eyes! Those panic-stricken eyes were an image he would never forget! An icy chill ran down his spine when he noticed sparks flying from a severed power line.

Still locked in its territorial dance, the cobra plunged into the rushing gasoline stream. "Holy shit!" he cried. The explosion rattled the entire block. A civilian who jumped out of his car to help was blasted backward twenty feet. Windows shattered in adjoining buildings as metal fragments from the tanker skewered nearby brick walls, vibrating to a standstill.

When Alex peeled off his ski mask, his normally confident face was pale and damp. His head whirled, and his hands trembled. Breath tore through his burning lungs, each inhale scraping like gravel.

Disturbed by the havoc he had caused, Alex watched the inferno in the rearview mirror as he drove down Jerusalem Avenue. This near-death incident served as a stark reminder of his many brushes with death. Yet, none were as terrifying as when he first discovered his ability to clear.

* * *

Saturday, July 1, 1972.

Alex peered into the freezer, then the refrigerator, his throat parched. The glass of milk did nothing to quench his nagging thirst, leaving him craving something cold enough to freeze the sweat on his brow. He imagined icy water cascading down his body, a chilling waterfall from a towering cliff. His mother's voice echoed from the living room as he rummaged for the perfect drink.

"Try the orange juice. It's fresh!" Melissa called out.

Or was it refreshing? He dismissed the uncertainty, focusing on his mission, and reached down for the orange juice. Noticing the dewy carton, he tightened his grip as he lurched up—forgetting the freezer was still open. His skull struck the door with a bone-jarring crack, shaking the refrigerator to its core. Searing pain ripped through him as the refrigerator wobbled violently, both doors swinging in protest.

"Ahh!" Alex shrieked. Glittering sparks blinded him just before the kitchen vanished into a black abyss. As the carton hit the floor, juice fanned out in shimmering streaks across the linoleum.

* * *

The hospital's noise swelled into a chaotic blur, loudspeakers blaring over frantic voices. Nausea twisted in his gut as fluorescent lights flickered overhead, vanishing into streaks as the gurney sped forward. Disoriented, Alex shut his eyes against the pulsing brightness. After a sharp left turn, the world lurched sideways, slamming into the sharp bite of lingering disinfectant. Urgent voices swarmed around him, but the world was already slipping away.

"Young man, can you hear me?" the doctor asked.

Alex struggled to open his eyes. Words felt thick in his throat, each letter clinging to his tonsils, blocking his speech and fogging his mind. Someone opened the basement door and shone a light down into the dank cavern, waving it around in search of the lost boy.

His mind screamed at the penlight.

Yes, I'm here!

The doctor diagnosed Alex with a closed-head injury and placed him on observation for acute symptoms: vomiting, incoherent speech, headache, dizziness, and confusion. A head X-ray revealed no internal bleeding, nor did it detect the slight swelling in the brain compressing the nervous system.

"A concussion usually requires seven to ten days to heal. We see this all the time. Ramming your head into the freezer door is more common than you think. We'll stanch the bleeding and monitor your son until I authorize his release," the doctor explained, her posture still sharp after hours on her feet.

Hunter Blackwell consoled his wife with a gentle pat on the shoulder. His lips pressed thin, the lines on his forehead etched deep with concern.

"Are there any other tests you can do?" he asked, clearing his throat. "You know, something besides an X-ray?"

"There was a recent publication about a new three-dimensional X-ray machine that uses computed axial tomography. It would give us a better view, but it's still several months away from general use." The doctor shifted her feet, certain this was not what Mr. Blackwell wanted to hear. "Our staff is committed to your son's care," she said, sliding her right hand into her coat pocket to fidget with her pen. "Alex will need plenty of bed rest for a few days. I'll prescribe medication to help with nausea and headaches, if needed. Your son should be up and running in a few days."

* * *

Back home in the comfort of his room, Alex avoided the grinning cat clock with its glossy black finish. Every tick, every twitch of tail and eyes in unison made the room spin. As the days passed, he progressed to walking without assistance and forming coherent sentences, much to his mother's relief. By the fourth day, he had returned to his old routine of waking at pitch-black o'clock, a habit he'd picked up from his father. "Early to rise makes for significant changes and a productive man," his father always said. "It develops the mind and soul, giving you an edge over everyone else." Alex took all his father's advice to heart, down to his love for fashion and a well-groomed appearance.

The lid on the styling gel opened with a soft pop. Alex inhaled the scent before dipping two fingers into the jar. Rubbing the gel between his palms, he smoothed his hands over his head and worked his fingers through his thick, jet-black hair.

Alex winced when his fingernail scraped his head wound, releasing a new flood. A sharp, rhythmic throb pulsed through the wound, flaring when he glanced into the light. He felt as though his heart would burst out of his head. Short, deep breaths escaped him as he tried to hold back the tears.

Instantly, chemicals seeped into the gash and spread beneath the skin, weaving into his bloodstream. The blue gel contained triethanolamine, which interacted with his brain cells, making them more receptive to external stimuli. His skin prickled as if lightning danced beneath it, and his thoughts scattered like ash in a windstorm. A second compound, iodopropynyl butylcarbamate, intensified the effects. They triggered an unorthodox transformation; electrons rearranged, molecules formed cells, and radical bridges sparked across billions of nerve endings—his body no longer his own, but something newly wired.

That night, a fever took hold, ravaging his already fragile state. Melissa stayed by his side, applying wet towels to his forehead and constantly changing the sweat-drenched bedsheets.

* * *

Several days later, Alex recovered and resumed his daily squabbles with his brother, Bart. He returned to his after-school job at Jonathan Gerstein's mini-mart. Old man Gerstein was pleasant and cheerful, unlike most of the grumpy men his father associated with in Massapequa. *Living in cold weather most of your life is enough to make anyone grumpy,* was his father's axiom. With his sandy blond hair graying at the temples, Jonathan was a great storyteller, prone to stomping the floor at the story's climax. His wild narratives left listeners laughing more at his idiosyncrasies than the tales themselves. Not a day went by without him whistling a tune from his favorite musical, where one dances joyfully through the neighborhood in the rain.

While replenishing the stockroom, Alex heard the bell above the front door chime. Two sets of footsteps—one heavier than the other—entered, followed by a brief, muffled chat and the sound of a closing door. After stacking a few cases against the wall, he was struck by the stillness—the kind of silence he would expect on an evening stroll through a cemetery. When the ancient floor groaned beneath his feet, the hairs on the back of his neck bristled. He listened for chattering or bursts of laughter, but the silence thickened, pressing against his ears until curiosity clawed its way forward.

Alex crept to the register counter as cautiously as a white-tailed deer venturing into a meadow. He scanned the store for the proprietor, but a glance at the convex mirror revealed nothing but empty aisles. Heart pounding, he stepped around the cylindrical comic book rack to check the register. To his dismay, it was open, the bill compartments empty except for a few stray pennies left behind. He bit down on his knuckles, thinking fast. *Something's wrong. Mr. Gerstein would never leave the register open, not even for a second!* Alex had seen movies like this and knew the likely outcome. Someone usually ended up hurt or dead.

"Mr. Gerstein?" he whispered, the hollows under his eyes darkening with fear. Overhead, the ceiling fans' banana-frond blades spun in rhythm with the ominous throb of the refrigerators. He noticed that the welcome sign at the front door had been turned over to read Sorry, We're Closed.

"Mr. Gerstein, are you here?" he whispered again.

Crack!

A sharp pop of gunfire jolted him. His heart raced as he dashed blindly toward the manager's office. Flinging open the door, he saw Mr. Gerstein's body lying in a pool of blood, still twitching beside the wooden desk. The proprietor's mouth gaped, his eyes transfixed in desperation, but Alex's attention snapped to the two men standing over him. One wore a black leather jacket stretched tight over his belly, failing to conceal the revolver in his hand. His partner held a canvas bag, bulging with cash. Behind them, the steel door of the safe stood wide open.

The rotund thief stared. "What the fuck? Louie, I thought you checked the back."

"Get him!" shouted the other.

Alex stumbled as he turned to run. Air rushed past his face as the chubby one lunged for him. Barely out of reach, he seized the comic book rack and hurled it into his path. The crash sent glossy pages skidding across the floor like autumn leaves. Alex glanced back just in time to see the giant fall, then bolted toward the canned food aisle.

Straining to rise, the hefty man grunted, wobbling as comic books slipped beneath him.

"Chenco, you idiot!" cried Louie. Leaping over his fallen comrade, he rushed down the nearest aisle.

Alex's heart was pounding, his lungs on fire. Louie's head bobbed ahead of him in the next aisle, then rounded the turn to cut him off. Dread coiled in his stomach. With Chenco right behind him, escape was impossible. All he could think about was Mr. Gerstein's lifeless, horror-stricken eyes and how he might soon share the same fate.

Praying the rack would hold his weight, he jumped for the second shelf and reached for the aisle's supporting wall. His left foot hit the next shelf, sending a shower of goods careening to the floor. Amid the clattering cans, Alex shrieked at the sudden jolt, but his fingers found the rim. Arms straining, he thrust himself over the supporting wall and swung his feet onto the top shelf. Boxes of cold medicine scattered into the air. *No time to rest!* He rolled off the shelf and landed on all fours, crushing the boxes beneath him.

Purple high-tops screeched to a halt where Alex had been just seconds earlier. Louie's face turned bright red and the veins at his temples throbbed. "Lucky bastard!" he shouted, breathing heavily through his narrow nose and kicking several cans in frustration. The overhead light shadowed his squinting eyes, distorting his face into a dreadful mask.

Chenco, still panting from the chase, managed to grab Alex's left shoe before the boy cleared the aisle. He slammed it against the broken shelf, sending down another cascade of cans.

"Come on!" Louie shoved Chenco aside and led the way into the next aisle, where his sneakers again squeaked to a sudden stop. The boy was gone. Instead, small boxes littered the floor like confetti, crushed from his landing. Inching ahead, Chenco followed the barrel of his gun down the aisle. His brown eyes shone with fierce determination. Since the kid had seen their faces, getting him was imperative. Even if that meant shooting the punk at point-blank range, just like Mr. Gerstein.

Convinced they would find the boy, Louie was already plotting diabolical ways to dispose of the body. He stood quietly by the stockroom, his eyes wild and his bony jaw clamped tight. "Flush him out!" he barked, his eyes squinting into the dimness. He used so few words when he spoke that his sentences were often as short as those in cheap telegrams. After a few tense minutes, Chenco reappeared, empty-handed and puzzled. Louie slammed the wall with his fist. *I'm sick of this game. We should've ended this already!* He gritted his teeth in silent fury and focused on the last remaining door. His chapped lips curled into a snarl.

Perched on the sink, Alex pictured himself dead on the bathroom floor, wide-eyed, blood pooling beneath him. His heart thudded as he fought for air. After a futile tug at the window, he leaped off the sink. Even if he could squeeze through the narrow opening, the rusty security bars would stop him cold. Powerless, he wondered if his death was inevitable. Maybe they'd let him go if he just waved his T-shirt in surrender. *Isn't that how it's done in movies? Or is that only between friends playing cops and robbers?*

Alex panted, knowing he had to keep fighting. He ran into the stall and locked the wooden door, his eyes squeezed shut.

Outside, Louie grinned and rapped on the bathroom door. "Come out, come out, wherever you are."

Annoyed, Chenco pushed him aside and yelled, "That's enough with the fuckin' horseplay. I'll show you how it's done!"

A forceful kick sent the strike plate ripping off the door frame. Chenco drew his gun and stepped into the bathroom, kicking the metal plate with his heavy boot. It scraped across the floor and struck the toilet with a clatter. Startled by the noise, he fired blindly. The bullet tore through the thin partition, whizzed past Alex's head, and pierced the brick wall. Debris sprayed his neck, yet he remained still. His dry mouth tightened, and his aching legs trembled from squatting on the toilet seat cover. There was no shame when the tears welling in his eyes finally spilled over. Had he stayed home today, he'd be running in the park with his dog instead of running for his life. Taking a deep breath, he twisted his torso and placed his trembling hands against the cool brick wall. He shut his eyes tightly, wishing he could be where the birds fly free, bask in the sun's warmth on his bare back, and stand beside his arrogant older brother—though that last thought left a bitter taste.

Suddenly, a wave of tingling sensations washed over him, as if every molecule inside him was being ripped apart like grains of sand tumbling in an hourglass, as though God's massive lungs had blown a mighty blast of air through him. He stifled a scream when his hands and arms disappeared. Then a gust of fresh air whipped through his hair, and before he realized it, his body had rematerialized on the other side of the brick wall. Confused and frightened, Alex huddled in the same position with the sun warming his sweat-drenched back. Examining his body for gashes or oozing blood, he struggled to make sense of his ordeal.

Am I delusional?

He ran home, not even missing the lost shoe, feeling lucky to be alive.

* * *

Days later, Alex explained his newfound ability—what he called clearing—to his parents and siblings in the garage. He preferred not to use the word disappear; clearing involved erasing all thoughts except for the location where he wanted to rematerialize.

"Dream on," said Bart with a snigger. "Now that you have all of us together, are you going to lay a gasser?"

Elizabeth and Walter laughed.

Melissa looked at her husband, who leaned forward in response to her pleading eyes and said, "Be cool, guys."

Bart sighed heavily and rolled his eyes. "Dad, you know he's only trying to psych us out!" he said, stomping his foot.

"Nevertheless, let's give him our undivided attention," his father said, one brow raised in warning.

Bart challenged his younger brother, hoping to turn the tables. "Why don't you 'clear' into that empty freezer before I dip out, you spaz?" he sneered, his nose creasing.

Determined to put his brother in his place, Alex cleared his mind and concentrated on the vacant space inside the chest freezer. He pictured himself inside, snickering at their stunned expressions. Ignoring the junk accumulated on the hinged lid, he stared intensely at the freezer. Liz erupted into giggles at his contorted face, her braces glinting in the harsh overhead light cradled in cobwebs. Then, pressing her hands to her mouth, she watched her brother concentrate, anticipation flickering in her eyes.

Suddenly, he was gone. Vanished. Liz, Bart, and Walt stood agape. Stunned, no one, especially not Bart, dared move a muscle. Then Liz screamed, "Far out!"

The avocado-green freezer sat askew against the wall, secured with a padlock to prevent the children from getting trapped inside and suffocating. Despite the distractions, Alex had successfully teleported into the freezer. The stale air weighed on his lungs. Even worse, he hadn't counted on the small space triggering awful memories of his trauma in the bathroom stall. In the pitch black, he shut his eyes and focused on the cool garage floor just outside. After several tense seconds, he opened his eyes. He thought Bart had turned off the garage light, but his head bumped against the lid when he leaned forward. Realizing he was still confined, he concentrated even harder on the garage floor, but still nothing happened.

Now panicked, he bellowed for help, fists hammering the walls.

"Somebody *please* do something!" Melissa pleaded hysterically, but no one knew where the padlock key was kept. Alex's faint screams continued, and the more he cried for help, the more distressed his mother became.

"Out of the way!" Hunter shouted, charging toward the freezer with an ax hoisted over his shoulder. He swept aside the accumulated junk on the lid and swung at the padlock with such ferocity that everyone recoiled as the ax struck the lock with a sharp clang. Sparks flew on the sixth attempt, and the padlock burst open. With the pop of suction releasing, Alex heaved the lid up and leaped out, his burning lungs gasping for air, his thin arms flailing.

After a few supervised experiments, Hunter determined that his son's ability to clear only worked in the presence of light, either natural or artificial. He explained that life is dependent on light. "It says so in the Bible," he boasted. "Genesis 1:3: 'And God said, "Let there be light!"' From then on, life took form: plants, trees, and living creatures." He stressed that Alex should never attempt to clear in total darkness, a precept not to be taken lightly.

* * *

Hunter didn't know how his son acquired this ability to vanish and rematerialize, and he preferred it to remain a mystery. He was certain that revealing the secret would bring relentless media scrutiny. Their life as a close-knit family would end. The thought of jeopardizing precious family time sent shivers down his spine. *The kids would love that*, he thought, his aging blue eyes darkening with despair. Worse, their private affairs would be splashed across every television show and tabloid nationwide. Reporters would embellish Alex's story with idiotic headlines like Disappearing Boy Visits Earth from Faraway Galaxy! Dodging hundreds, possibly thousands, of people vying for prized snapshots with their zoom lens cameras was not the life he wanted for his wife and four children: Alexander, the gifted one; Bartholomew, the proud one; Elizabeth, the sweet one; and Walter, the quiet one.

Never revealing Alex's secret became the new family rule. Though it pained his heart, Hunter ensured compliance by periodically lecturing his son on safety and prohibiting him from playing with the neighborhood kids.

* * *

Despite his father's best efforts to instill a moral center, Alex chose the path of corruption. His appetite was avaricious, and no amount of seasoning could alter his taste for wealth. He soon discovered that objects could clear with him, provided none carried an electrical current. Without considering the consequences, clearing stolen goods became a daily habit. After a few weeks of perfecting his skills, he craved bigger risks—first cleaning out cash registers in neighborhood stores, then moving on to more valuable prizes. It took several years before he thought to carry a 3-liter canister of oxygen if things went wrong.

By age thirty-two, Alex focused exclusively on high-end jewelry stores, seeking gold bracelets, ropes of pearls, and diamond earrings. Clearing gave him power beyond anything he'd ever known. He funded a lavish lifestyle for years by selling premium articles to a loyal out-of-state broker. His biggest haul: two sacks of Russian diamonds, lifted from an international distributor and sold to a famous retail chain specializing in engagement rings. The sale included the declaration, Kimberley certificate, and altered origin and ownership paperwork.

Alex closed the deal at the buyer's bank, offering exclusive watches to James Jaramillo and his associate, Donald Kennings, thereby securing their confidence. Back at the office, James settled comfortably in his chair, his face riddled with wrinkles that resembled dried-out, cracked mud. When others spoke, he often pressed his index finger over his upper lip. Alex couldn't help thinking he looked like the kind of guy who would loudly suck on a wooden toothpick at dinner.

Beside him, Donald's thin lips gave him a serpent-like impression when he smiled. He knew everything about raw-cut diamonds and was well aware these had been stolen. Still, the considerable savings were enough for him to overlook the fraud. A smirk formed on his lips: curling with the sly unease of an Eastern garter snake. *Who gives a fuck where he got them? The company's already ahead of the game, so I'm fine with it.*

Men like James and Donald were fixtures in Alex's world—where charm was just lacquer over rot, and every handshake came with a whisper.

Later that week, Alex slipped into a different role—this time for his father. Though unemployed, he claimed to be managing a high-profile corporation in Manhattan. "You should see the office," he said smugly. "From the thirty-sixth floor, I can see the baseball fields in Central Park."

"Bet you can see every game on a clear day," his father said, giving his son's shoulder a congratulatory pat.

Alex's ego swelled at the pride in his father's eyes. If he played his cards right, he could go on forever. He pushed aside the curtain and gazed out into his father's yard. "Sometimes I can hear the crack of the bat on a home run," he said, and they both burst out laughing.

Alex spent his days casing stores in Wantagh, Seaford, Amityville, Oyster Bay, and Massapequa for valuables he could turn over for quick profit. Clearing into bank vaults was easier than drilling holes into the lockboxes, using mirrors to study the lock's wheels, or messing with nitroglycerin to blow the vault door. "Eat your heart out, John Dillinger!" he would cry when clearing from a vault.

Still, he faced problems, particularly with determining the safest altitude for materializing. With a miscalculation, he might reappear anywhere from three inches to three feet above the floor, sending him tumbling. A few bruises were nothing. His arrogance and neglect did the real damage.

* * *

Thursday, March 18, 2004.

The day after the incident with the fuel tanker, Alex decided to deposit his ID and credit cards in a bus depot locker. Eventually, he recognized the need for a lookout and picked his girlfriend, Stacey Foster, as the perfect accomplice. To his chagrin, his request astounded her. She could not fathom how a man with such an extraordinary gift could think only of corrupt ends.

"This God-given power should be used for the good of the people. You should be saving lives and helping police apprehend criminals!"

she argued, her body planted firmly in front of him. "Find a way to save our world from corruption instead of adding to it." But her pleas meant nothing. When he shrugged off her concerns, she rolled her eyes and stalked out in a huff.

Stacey wanted nothing to do with his power. She insisted she wasn't interested in money, a claim supported by her wealthy background. Despite the tension, she knew she could always rely on her mother, Kathryn, for a quick loan in a crisis. As a registered nurse, she earned enough to support her lifestyle.

Two years after Stacey's father, Bradley, passed away, doubts lingered about the circumstances of his death. Though she hated to admit it, Stacey suspected her mother of killing him to control the $85 million empire.

Worsening the betrayal, her brother, Erik, seven years her senior, had been pushed out of the family pharmaceutical business after a bitter dispute with their power-hungry mother. As CEO, Kathryn stripped her son of his lucrative executive role. The board of directors saw it as a family disgrace, but they said nothing, relieved it was him, not one of them.

Erik cut all ties with their rapacious mother, refusing to speak to her again. But Stacey couldn't afford to ignore Kathryn. Not yet. If she wanted answers about her father's death, she had to dig deeper.

* * *

During successive visits to her mother's house, Stacey secretly installed and retrieved an apparatus between the keyboard and computer to record keystrokes, letting her retrieve stored data without loss. Wearing a pink robe and a towel wrapped around her head, she pulled the floral curtains aside, letting the sun's warmth fill her room. Two lamps centered on a royal-blue accent wall highlighted the landscape oil painting. An elegant chess storage box with gold and silver pieces rested on a wooden lift-top coffee table. Stacey and Alex had spent countless hours locked in strategic battle, though he could only claim victory in one of their many games.

Settling into her desk chair, Stacey installed the keystroke device and booted up her computer without disturbing the towel on her damp hair. Her gaze settled on a photo of her and Alex at a local ice-skating rink, and she quickly looked away. Despite her feelings for him, she wasn't sure she could accept his criminal tendencies. Until she sorted through those tangled emotions, seeing him again would come with its challenges. Blinking away the tears, Stacey set her jaw and activated the device, downloading her mother's keystrokes.

* * *

With Kathryn away for the long Independence Day weekend, Stacey took an extra vacation day to search for evidence about her father's death. After easily hacking into Kathryn's computer, she pecked at the keyboard with her manicured fingers. Shock morphed into revulsion, then anger as she scrolled through business documents that detailed the firing of four board members and a 10 percent reduction in the workforce. Her father would have been livid. Then she paused over a cryptic entry in Kathryn's daily planner:

May 23, 2002, 1:35 a.m.

The Spanish software was successfully installed.

Strange. Especially considering her hatred of Spanish. How could she have installed a program the night dad passed away? Clicking more slowly, she found an entry mentioning a dust-like substance. A quick search brought up a page describing Spanphyx in disturbing detail. Stacey grimaced. The name's resemblance to *Spanish* couldn't be a coincidence.

Stacey learned that the powder, typically sold on the Asian black market, caused suffocation. She read aloud: "In a moist environment, the microscopic particles expand to one thousand times their original size. If inhaled, they cause death by asphyxiation."

"Oh!" Stacey cried, then hit print.

* * *

After successfully clearing into the jewelry store, Alex stood before a U-shaped counter, its glass surface veiled by a pristine white sheet that hid a cache of riches. On the wall, mirrored displays held opulent necklaces, glimmering under the security lights like constellations in the desert sky. Silent as a shadow, Alex scowled beneath his ski mask, defying the watchful cameras as he whisked the sheets away to reveal the coveted jewels. Mindful of the ticking clock and the threat of silent alarms, he withdrew a ball-peen hammer from the pouch at his waist and shattered the glass in swift, surgical strikes. Ornate watches, gleaming diamond rings, and shimmering pearl necklaces were each in turn tucked carefully into the pouch.

The sound of a low growl made him freeze in mid-grab.

A glance over his shoulder confirmed his fear. A pair of gleaming eyes fixed on him, above a row of wicked teeth. Before he could blink, the black Rottweiler lunged. Alex flung himself over the counter just as powerful jaws clamped onto the heel of his left shoe, ripping it off his foot. As he sailed over the shattered glass, he sliced his hand on a jagged shard before plunging down the far side. With a menacing growl, the Rottweiler dropped the shoe and pounced after him.

Alex's body slammed onto the floor with a sickening thud, knocking the wind out of him. He had to clear out before the police arrived. *I must get the coordinates to clear!* Breathing in painful gasps, he forced himself to all fours and started to stand up, but the Rottweiler's weight flung him to his back.

Teeth bared, the Rottweiler loomed over him.

Alex flailed, trying to keep it at bay, flinching as drooling jaws snapped shut. A flurry of punches landed, but the dog barely flinched. The beast lunged again, claws raking his chest. Holding the dog's neck with his left hand, he shielded his face with the other.

Then he saw it coming.

The bite caught flesh first, then only air. He pulled his hand back just in time.

His knee struck a forceful blow to its belly. *Yelp!* Bloodied but free, Alex scrambled to his feet and drove a series of kicks to its groin until it lay motionless.

Sweat clung beneath the mask, stinging his eyes as his lungs burned with every wheeze. The wail of sirens assaulted his ears. Leaping back over the counter, he reached for his mangled shoe just as a police car screeched to a halt in front of the jewelry store. The dispatcher's voice crackled through the two-way radio, like static tearing through a storm. Without hesitation, Alex snatched up the jewelry pouch, fixed his eyes across the intersection, and cleared, leaving the shoe behind.

The serene night sky glittered with stars and the moon shone through the low clouds, casting a soft glow over the landscape below. Rematerializing next to his parked car, Alex gingerly climbed in wearing only one shoe and pulled off his ski mask. For a fleeting moment, he watched the swarm of police cars converge before pulling away. The night's haul would have to wait until he dressed his wounds.

* * *

Stacey parked behind the others in the circular driveway of her mother's two-story colonial home. With a passing look, she noticed the perennial flowers on the island hadn't returned, but the burning bush and liriope, nestled around the lampposts, were thriving. Alex stood in front of the graceful steps, waiting. As she approached, she took a deep breath, unsure whether calling him had been the right choice. Yet the way he moved with such ease, paired with that enchanting smile, brought her a sense of comfort and led her to clasp his hand.

She gasped, pulling his hand closer to inspect it. "How on earth did this happen?"

"It's nothing to worry about." He dismissed her concern blithely. "I cut myself on some broken glass."

"Alex, I see the cuts from the glass, but these," she ran her finger over the still-raw gashes, "these are puncture wounds. Either a snake or a dog did this."

He waved off her concern. "It's fine. I've cleaned and disinfected them thoroughly, but if you insist, I promise to see a doctor first thing tomorrow morning." His uninjured hand gave a cocky three-fingered salute.

Stacey's eyes narrowed. Something about his tone didn't sit right, but here and now wasn't the place to press him, so she let it go.

He offered his elbow with exaggerated charm and said, "Now, let's go meet your mother."

They entered the reception hall, where the polished marble floors gleamed under the chandelier's soft light. Alex was captivated by the foyer, particularly its Renaissance-style domed ceiling. A quiet presence approached to take their coats. She was a tall woman with a hawk-like nose and shoulders as rigid as a wooden clothes hanger, her thin-framed glasses perched precariously on the bridge.

"When you said your family was well off, you didn't mention they were filthy rich," he remarked as Stacey led him under the imperial staircase toward the gathering room, his eyes on the sway of her hips.

"I don't like to talk about my parents, especially not since my father passed away two years ago. This was his empire. Unfortunately, my mother and I have . . . drifted apart since the funeral," she said carefully.

Stacey pushed open the glass doors, revealing an exquisite Goertz grand piano and an eight-piece ensemble performing Tchaikovsky's *Variations on a Rococo Theme,* based on Fitzenhagen's arrangement. The cellist's eyes were closed as his fingers danced effortlessly across the fingerboard. His body swayed in time to the music, mirroring the strings' emotional resonance.

Impressive, thought Alex.

The limestone walls radiated warmth, reflecting off the black marble flooring. Olive-green sofas sat slightly askew, accompanied by a bronze sculpture of a naked man sitting in quiet contemplation atop a black marble end table. Behind the ensemble, a sleek glass wall framed a panoramic view of a Japanese garden, complete with a koi pond framed by cherry and bonsai trees.

Kathryn had never appreciated this style. It had been her husband's vision for the gathering room, which he had enjoyed for several years. If it were up to her, she would recreate an early 1800s European salon, featuring French Empire-style furniture, a Georgian armoire, and long drapes in shades of morel-mushroom brown, palm-leaf green, and island-sand beige.

"Stacey, my dear," Kathryn said, extending her arms and gliding across the floor with spurious affection and a gleam in her eye for Stacey's handsome companion. Her ostentatious display of rings and bracelets dimmed against the necklace draped above her plunging neckline—a single 18-carat Colombian emerald, its rich spruce green encased in a sunburst of diamonds. Each facet caught the light with mesmerizing fire.

The two women leaned forward, lips puckered, and exchanged successive air kisses. "This is Alex," Stacey said, her smile wavering as her mother's eyes lingered on him. "I told you about him a while back, remember?"

"I can't remember what I did yesterday, Stacey. How do you expect me to keep track of *all* your boyfriends? You change them like your underwear." She sounded a little tipsy. "You *do* wear underwear, don't you, dear?"

Alex took her outstretched hand, cupping it in his, and kissed the spot just above her knuckles to break the tension. His gaze lingered on the glittering rock on her right middle finger, quietly estimating its worth. He straightened, meeting her piercing gaze, making him feel both vulnerable and captivated. Her gaze brimmed with desire, yet left no room for submission. She was in control, and no man would ever take that away from her. Her short, sandy hair and radiant skin dazzled under the ambient light. His body responded to her touch as he imagined the feel of her geranium-pink lips and the firm curves accentuated by her dress.

A smirk spread across Kathryn's face as she assessed him, admiring his square jaw and full lips. The warm lighting cast soft shadows on his brows, deepening the mesmerizing blue of his eyes. His sharp taste in clothes emphasized broad shoulders and a ramrod-straight posture, the embodiment of quiet confidence. For a fleeting moment, she imagined him hovering ecstatically over her trembling form, reveling in the touch of her smooth skin. With a confidence born of her own desirability, Kathryn slid her arm through his and led him away, eager to display him to the guests.

Stacey expected this behavior from her mother, but that didn't make it easier to accept. It was why she'd distanced herself . . . yet she always came back for more. Ever since Kathryn had expunged Erik from the family trust, Stacey had endured her mother's mistreatment in hopes of helping him regain his rightful control.

Her loyalty to Erik ran deep, shaped by moments long before trust funds and betrayals. She remembered one moment vividly—grammar school, and a girl named Antoinette Stoltzfus. Plump, with medium-length strawberry blonde hair and bulging brown eyes, Antoinette looked as if she were hoarding mothballs in her cheeks. She fancied herself both brilliant and tough, crediting books for her brains and baseball for her right hook. Socially, she was a disaster.

"I don't like how you comb your stupid hair," Antoinette sneered at Erik, her gelatinous cheeks jiggling with each poke into his skinny chest.

Stacey rushed over before Antoinette could lay another hand on him. She stepped in front of Erik, crossed her arms, and declared, "I'm tired of you bullying other kids, Antoinette!"

"So-o-o?" Antoinette drawled, expelling her foul breath with every syllable. A cluster of boys appeared, anticipating a scuffle, or better yet a full-on catfight. Antoinette placed her hands on her hips, challenging Stacey with a raised brow. "And just what are you going to do about—"

Stacey's fist collided with Antoinette's soft, chubby cheek, sending her plummeting into the two boys behind her while the other three stood, mouths agape. After that, neither Erik nor Stacey ever heard from Antoinette again.

* * *

"You strike me as a man who knows exactly what he wants," Kathryn purred, stopping next to her full-size replica of Michelangelo's *David*. The statue, made of white resin, stood brazenly beside the bar, gathering strength before facing Goliath. At the other end of the bar stood a copy of Donatello's version of David, graceful and relaxed after his monumental battle.

Alex ordered a drink, surreptitiously glancing at David's genitalia, measuring up, grateful he wasn't born in the same era. "Depends what I'm after," he said with a grin, raising the glass to his lips. He could feel Kathryn's calculating stare, stripping away the layers of his confidence with quiet precision. There was no need for games here. He wanted her just as much as she wanted him.

* * *

Stacey chatted with her grandfather, whose short white hair resembled a cockatoo's ruffled feathers. Bushy brows leaped out from his round, red face, and the corners of his eyes drooped. His mouth popped open whenever he looked up, giving him a constant air of surprise. In between their stilted comments, Stacey stole glances at Alex, still intensely focused on her mother. Even from across the room, she could see the glimmer of amusement and lust in her lover's eyes. Shifting uncomfortably in her seat, Grandpa Fred rambled on about overcoming alcoholism, his words falling on deaf ears while she nodded along politely.

"I woke up in the park, not knowing where I was or even who I was," said Fred, his mind trailing off. Then he resumed, tapping her shoulder. "That was when I realized I needed help. And look at me now!" He hopped up joyfully, maintaining his balance as Stacey reached out to steady him with a laugh.

"Yes, I can see you've been saved, Grandpa." To her relief, Fred excused himself to use the bathroom. Smiling, she watched him shuffle lightly across the almost liquid floor, which only seemed to increase his desire to urinate. As Stacey turned to reclaim Alex, an older woman with wrinkled, insistent fingers tugged at her sleeve. Though her movements were slow and deliberate, she muttered something about the ensemble's final and most challenging variation, an allegro vivo.

"Do you like classical music, my dear?" the woman asked, her voice tinged with nervous eagerness to connect.

Stacey shot her a glare, her patience worn thin. *This is a nightmare. Why must I deal with all these annoying people?* Rolling her eyes, she said, "Actually, I'm into rap."

Startled, the woman nearly spit out her champagne, but Stacey was already walking away.

* * *

Over the next few months, Stacey noticed a shift in Alex's behavior. Subtle changes, yet obvious to someone in love. Weak excuses replaced intimacy. Promises crumbled as romantic dinners became hurried fast-food stops, mere conveniences for his so-called evening obligations. At 4:35 one morning, he pulled up in front of Stacey's house after spending the night with Kathryn. With the engine and heater running, he stripped off his clothes, stuffed them into a drawstring sack, and shoved it beneath the driver's seat. Ripping open a packet of unscented moist towelettes, he dragged one briskly over his body to erase any trace of Kathryn. Then he slipped into a spandex T-shirt, wool pants, and leather moccasins designed to minimize friction and noise.

Having mastered stealth over his years of burglarizing homes and stores, Alex stood quietly on the terrace. Flexing his feet, he popped his ankles—ensuring they wouldn't crack as he crept through the house. Slowly, he inserted the key and turned the handle to retract the latch before exerting pressure on the door. A slight upward tug kept the hinges from squeaking as he slipped through the narrow opening. Pushing the door against the frame, the bolt quietly slid into place. With slow, measured breaths, he stayed near the walls, where the wooden floors had less play, and avoided shifting his weight until his lead foot was firmly planted. When he reached Stacey's bedside, he stood listening for several minutes before surreptitiously easing into bed.

She feigned sleep, her silent tears soaking into her pillowcase.

* * *

Stacey didn't need a fortune teller; she already suspected Alex had been sleeping with her mother from the beginning. Even so, she needed to see it for herself. One windy evening, she followed his car east on Sunrise Highway but lost sight of him when he turned right onto Farmingdale Road. She scanned the streets for any sign of him. Just as he turned onto Main Street, she caught sight of his car again and tailed it to the Travelin' Horseman Restaurant.

Brittle maple leaves swarmed across the intersection, pitter-pattering like hundreds of hermit crabs scrambling across a sunbaked pier. Three bicyclists sliced through the cascade while the wind whipped up the fabric of one rider's unbuttoned shirt, streaming behind him like a ribbon of melted chocolate.

Bundled up in a beige fur coat and matching hat, Stacey's mother stood by the entrance, cigarette in hand. Alex stepped out of his car, draped in the black leather trench coat Stacey had given him for his birthday. She burned with rage, remembering the hours spent locating the style he'd seen in a magazine. And now he was showing it off to another woman—her mother, no less!—flashing that bemused smile as if nothing were wrong. He even had the audacity to kiss Kathryn in public. Stacey's lips tingled as she wondered whether her mother felt that same electric thrill. Casually, Alex slipped his arm around Kathryn. The low hum of live jazz spilled into the night as he pulled open the door, and they disappeared inside.

Stacey had promised herself she would never shed tears for any man, especially those who cared only about their egos, but she was so overcome with rage that breaking down was therapeutic. She pulled out sharply from the curb and cut off a young man, who missed clipping her car by inches.

"Hey, bitch! Watch where you're fuckin' going," the other driver shouted, adding a rude gesture and a few choice insults about female drivers. But his cries were in vain, for Stacey had already vanished.

* * *

Three days later, on a Sunday afternoon, Stacey paid her mother an unannounced visit, primed for a woman-to-woman talk. She took a deep breath and looked her mother square in the eyes. "I know about you and Alex, Mother."

Kathryn sipped her tequila, savoring the burn as it slid down her throat. "I was starting to wonder if you had the balls to confront me." She set the glass on the end table beside the grand piano and walked to the bar where her designer bag lay. With practiced ease, she dug through the depths for a cigarette and lighter. Before the flame lit, the glass whizzed past her head and shattered against the wall, staining the limestone with tequila and barely missing a 10-foot abstract wall sculpture. Kathryn looked at the broken glass serenely. "My, you really *do* have balls."

"Now you listen to me, mother dear," Stacey said, getting in her face. "You have no idea what you're getting yourself into. Alex is dangerous! I'd advise you to stay clear of him."

Kathryn lit her cigarette, took a drag, and blew the smoke into her face. "You know what your problem is, Stacey," she said with a twitch of her nose. "You don't know how to hold on to a man. You never have."

Stacey struggled to control her anger, her jaw clenched, a vein bulging at her temple. "I know all about how you ensnare your men. I'm ashamed to be the daughter of a slut like you!"

The slap came fast and hard, leaving a burning red mark. Stacey squeezed her eyes shut as pain shot down her spine. In disbelief, she brought a trembling hand to her throbbing face. "Don't you *dare* lay a finger on me ever again, or so help me—"

"What do you intend to do, Stacey?" asked Kathryn, inching closer. "Cry like the little pathetic girl you—"

Stacey's fist smashed into her mother's startled face, sending her tumbling backward into *David.* The imitation hit the floor with a sharp clatter and sent shards skittering across the hard surface. Dazed, Kathryn sat up and felt her bloodied lip, then reached with an unsteady hand to pick up a broken piece. Her features twisted as she realized the piece was David's scrotum and shriveled-up penis. Embarrassed, she tossed it back into the pile.

Kathryn stood up, teetering on her stilettos, and shrieked, "Get out of my house!" Her hair was in disarray, and her bloodshot eyes bulged with fury. Tension twisted her face. "First thing Monday morning, I'm writing you out of the will! Do you hear me? Just like your pathetic brother. You'll never have any of this! And you'll never lay a hand on my jewelry!"

"Don't worry, Mother. I'll make sure you're buried with your jewels."

Stacey left without another word.

"You are out, I tell you!" Kathryn's final battle cry rang out, a lock of hair straggling over her left eye.

* * *

A single cell vibrated into existence, followed by trillions more. If slowed to a crawl, they could be seen agitating the air as they bonded into intricate patterns. Yet in a fraction of a second, Alex materialized, dressed in his tight-fitting all-black outfit and ski mask.

Silence hung in the air like a woolen blanket. The men's department store was empty, but Alex was used to the eerie stillness. He moved quietly down the aisle, passing neatly stacked dress shirts on wall shelves and carefully arranged sweaters on display tables. Mannequins showcased expensive suits in calculated poses.

Alex picked up the calf-length burgundy coat with blue-and-gold paisley lining he'd been eyeing for a few days. Standing before a large mirror, he tried the coat on even though he'd already done so while casing the place. The coat gave him an air of finesse, and he knew the color alone would set him apart from the black or gray most men typically wore.

"I must say, that is one very stylish coat," a thin, breathy voice said from behind.

Alex spun around, his eyes widening and his heart shifting into second gear.

An older man with prominent rosacea smiled up at him. Bone degeneration had humped his spine, and his arms were covered in intricate Navy tattoos. Untidy snow-white hair reminded Alex of a cockatoo's ruffled feathers.

"Didn't mean to startle you," the man said with a chuckle as he stepped up to smooth out the shoulder pad. "Quite dapper indeed."

The man didn't seem threatening, so Alex's heart shifted back to first. Still, he remained alert.

The stranger's eyes narrowed. Concentrating, he cocked his head to one side and said, "I've seen you before." He placed a forefinger to his lips to breathe life into his elusive memory. "Can't remember where, but I recognize those eyes. I never forget eyes, my friend."

Alex shifted his gaze to avoid further scrutiny. "I've never seen you before in my life."

"From afar," replied the man, nodding. He leaned closer, showering Alex with his hot breath and locking eyes in a moment of shared understanding. "Like two ships passing in the night." He turned to walk away, assuming the stranger would follow. "How did you get in here anyway?" he asked in a raspy voice.

"I have my ways," replied Alex, keeping pace behind him.

"That's quite all right. You don't have to tell me," the man said. "I don't stick my nose in other people's business." Stopping next to a square pillar, he stooped to retrieve a brown paper bag and slid into a sitting position. "Come, sit down." He flexed his fingers twice, the joints cracking. "Have a drink with me."

"Thanks, but I must be going."

"You don't know what you're missing. Look," said the man, pulling down the brown bag to reveal a bottle of high-end whiskey.

Alex raised an eyebrow at the label. Definitely not the kind of bottle you'd find in a paper bag. "On second thought, I suppose I can spare a few more minutes."

With a chortle, the man said, "I knew you could be bought." He untwisted the cap, handed Alex a glass, and poured out a generous measure of liquid gold. They clinked the bottle and glass together. The old man wriggled against the post with a contented sigh and said, "My youth adventurer ID says my name is Fred."

"Nice to make your acquaintance, Fred." Alex held out his hand. With no intention of removing his mask, he said, "My name is . . . Misterio." They shared a laugh. As the whiskey flowed down his throat, Alex closed his eyes, savoring the warmth that spread through him. "If you don't mind me asking, how did *you* get in here?"

"I'm an adventurer!" said Fred, raising his bottle to toast his achievement.

"That's a funny way of saying homeless."

The man laughed heartily. “Young man, I’m far from homeless. And it’s true, I *am* an adventurer.”

“Pray tell.”

Fred smiled, reminiscing. “I’ve always wondered what it would be like to stow away on a pirate ship. To sail the deep blue seas in search of monsters and sirens that sing enchanting songs from rocky shores. To be caught up in a sea battle with cannons blazing, the mast shivering, a pirate banner snapping overhead.” He leaned forward, wielding an imaginary sword between his arthritic fingers. “This is the last time you and your crew will sail the West African seas, Duque de Misterio!” he shouted, waving Alex into the scene.

Picking up on his cue, Alex crawled forward and faced the one-eyed scourge of the great Atlantic.

“You will pillage and kill no more, Captain Frederick!” the Duque de Misterio shouted, ordering his fervent crew to fire the cannons. Plumes of smoke billowed into the air, obscuring the once-clear sky as a cannonball pierced the ship’s wooden hull.

Many projectiles splashed into the sea, spattering frigid waters over the wooden deck. Captain Frederick stood his ground fearlessly, wishing he could make the Duque eat his words as a main course in the mess hall. He pointed his sword at the Duque. “Swing ‘er round and fire!” he ordered his crew of bloodthirsty savages. Cannonballs bombarded the ship. One struck the mast and splintered it into toothpicks, sending sailors scrambling. Another hit the hull with a boom, spraying debris across the deck. The Duque’s ship lay in ruins, engulfed in flames and sinking into the ocean’s depths.

“You haven’t heard the last of me, Captain Frederick!” shouted the Duque de Misterio. “Mark my words. I’ll defeat you if it’s the last thing I do! Full sail ahead!”

Fred sat back, confused. “Did you just say ‘Full sail ahead’?”

“Ah, yeah.”

“You do know you’re sinking, right?”

Laughing at his own ignorance, Alex returned to the pillar and sat beside Fred, whose hysterical guffaws shook his body.

When they finally calmed down, Fred took another swig from the bottle. "As a child, I wondered what it would be like to do anything. Now, I do everything I once dreamed of. Since I can't stow away on a pirate ship, I stow away in department stores. Sometimes I hide in the bathroom with my feet up on the toilet seat and wait for the store to close. Once the coast is clear, I wander around, trying on whatever catches my eye. I enjoy this newfound freedom and the adventures I conjure up in my crafty little head." Swirling the whiskey around in the bottle, he took a long, slow whiff and allowed the aroma to ferment in his brain. Then he asked, "Have you ever been in jail?"

"Never," replied Alex, "Nor do I plan to."

"I've been thrown into the slammer twenty-seven times," Fred admitted.

"You're shitting me."

"I shit you not," Fred replied with a smirk. "I've been in jail so many times, the police chief shakes his head whenever he sees me. He knows my kids' phone numbers by heart. Within an hour or two, I'm back home . . . right where I *don't* want to be." He gazed at Alex, who stared back, processing his words. "I run in the rain and splash in the puddles naked because that's what I want to do. Daring things no one considers doing in a zillion years." He turned and looked Alex squarely in the eyes. "Have you ever gone skydiving?"

"Can't say that I have."

"It's exhilarating! The wind wraps around you, pulling you down and in seconds, you're plummeting toward the Earth at a terminal velocity of a hundred and twenty miles an hour!" Fred exclaimed. He extended his arms, rocking back and forth as if gliding through turbulent winds. His right hand brushed against Alex's face, forcing him to look away. Then, he batted his eyelids, puffed out his cheeks, and swished the air side to side to simulate free fall. Turning to Alex, he shouted, "You ought to try this! It's like a forty-four-hundred-watt hairdryer blowing in your face, whipping up your locks to slap your handsome features a trillion times!"

Alex's eyes sparkled as he doubled over with laughter. Hopping to his feet, he said, "You mean like this!" Alex crouched and extended his arms, flapping them against the rushing air. His face contorted as he puffed out his cheeks and batted his eyes to avoid the strong current. "Oh no!" he shouted, looking over his shoulder. "I forgot my parachute!"

They ended the skydive with a hearty round of laughter. Fred's eccentricity captured Alex's imagination. He sat back down and leaned into Fred's shoulder, laughing until his muscles ached. Eventually, they subsided into a soft chuckle and a sigh of relief.

Later, Fred stood with great care, mindful not to wake the joint pains that had gone into hibernation.

"Where are you going?" asked Alex, surprised.

"I gotta tinkle. Back in a flash, scrotum rash." Fred walked away gingerly to avoid releasing the floodgates.

Alex nodded with amusement. "Great, now I have a new name."

Pouring himself another glass of whiskey, Alex reflected on his life. Just a few days ago, he was in the powerful jaws of a Rottweiler, fearing for his life and desperately fighting for the upper hand, a violent struggle that felt endless. And today he was enjoying drinks with a stranger and listening to his charming tales. He lifted the glass to his lips, but before he could take another sip, he heard Fred hollering. Fearing for his new friend's safety, he jumped up and ran to the aisle, his heart pounding with alarm.

"What the fuck," said Alex. His eyes widened as the old-timer ran down the aisle toward him, his arms extended like a great white pelican about to take flight—naked as a newborn rodent on a warm summer's eve.

Hair disheveled and a wide grin on his weathered face, Fred shambled down the aisle in a burst of energy. His steps were unsteady, but his eyes sparkled as he tottered forward, his arms flailing for balance. Despite his age, his spirit seemed youthful and carefree, his whoops echoing off the walls.

Alex laughed so hard his sides ached. "Now, why would you want to do something like that?" he asked, catching his breath.

"Because I can!" exclaimed Fred. He launched into a waltz routine that quickly turned into a cha-cha, his flabby body wiggling to a Latin beat only he could hear. Then he stopped abruptly. "Oh, no!" he cried in alarm.

"What's the matter now?"

"I think I just soiled myself."

Alex lowered his head sympathetically.

"I'll be right back." Fred shuffled off, head down.

"And don't forget to put your clothes back on!"

When Fred returned, he found Alex sitting against the pillar, sipping whiskey. "Follow me. I know where you can stay until the store opens tomorrow morning."

Alex followed, quietly considering whether to clear.

"I don't know how you plan on walking out of here tomorrow with that fancy coat, but I strongly advise against it. Maybe it's time to shape up and be a good soldier," Fred said, wagging his finger in the air. Their footsteps echoed off the walls in the absence of a reply. Abruptly, he stopped and snapped his fingers. "I know where I've seen those eyes. You were at my daughter's party!"

Fred spun around, but Alex was gone. A moment later, he heard a car engine roar to life outside, tires screeching away.

* * *

Monday, August 23, 2004.

Once she was sure Alex was sound asleep, Stacey tiptoed out of the bedroom. Driving north on Cedar Swamp Road to Glen Cove, the lavish homes lining the street by Old Tappan Park blurred past her window, unnoticed. Just after two in the morning, she let herself into Kathryn's house and disarmed the alarm. Quietly, she proceeded up the staircase, gripping a canvas bag in one hand.

Stacey had had enough of sleepless nights from suppressing her anger and bitterness. Although she knew it was unhealthy, she refused to tell Erik the truth, preferring that he continue believing their father had died of natural causes. If it had not been for her acquisitive mother, Bradley would still be alive today, sharing his life and contagious laughter. Kathryn had stripped away her daughter's joy in life. *Miserable bastards, they deserve each other! And as far as Alex is concerned, he can rot in hell along with her!*

Stacey's actions had nothing to do with his infidelity. She'd let go of that easily enough. What truly bothered her was his avaricious nature and his refusal to reject his life of crime. Her nose twitched with pride. Something it had never done before.

Her heart jumped when the bedroom door squeaked, and she held her breath as her eyes adjusted to the dim light. Kathryn sprawled on the bed with the satin sheet pushed aside, her face faintly illuminated by the nightlight. The reek and empty bottle on the nightstand suggested her mother had indulged in shots of tequila before calling it a night. Stacey crept deeper into the dragon's lair. She placed the canvas bag at the foot of the bed, pulled out a gas mask, and slipped it over her face, pulling the straps taut. A four-ounce squeeze bottle came out next. The warning beneath the skull and crossbones read: Danger. Do not handle without a respirator mask. Do not operate in a ventilated area. Do not inhale.

After her practice with a foam mannequin head, Stacey thought administering the lethal dust would be quick and easy. But the sight of Kathryn's face rekindled all her childhood fears and insecurities. Her hand trembled as the memory returned. She was sneaking into the kitchen for a cookie from the ceramic rooster jar, only to freeze at the sound of her mother's foot tapping in time with those caustic words:

What are you doing? Since that day, Stacey had despised surprises. Even more so, her inability to respond to the relentless barrage of her mother's vitriolic questions.

Newly resolved, Stacey held the small bottle up to her mother's nose, squeezed on the inhale, and quickly pulled it away to prevent the fine particles from becoming airborne on the exhale. As she repeated the process, the dust penetrated her mother's lungs and clung to the moist lining of the bronchioles.

Fighting down the urge to leave before her mother woke up, Stacey's fingers slackened. As if at her mother's behest, the cap slipped from her fingers and landed on Kathryn's chest with a small bounce. Stacey held her breath, her eyes wide with fear behind the mask. A bead of sweat trickled down her back as her mother stirred in her sleep. Her first instinct was to bolt, but she remained frozen, listening to her own muffled breathing and trying to still the rising terror. Oh so gently she lifted the cap and resealed the container, breathing a sigh of relief. With the mask and empty bottle stuffed back into the canvas bag, she turned to make her escape.

"What are you doing?"

Stacey's heart jumped. *What do I say?* There was no excuse for being in her mother's bedroom at three in the morning.

Kathryn turned on her side, stretched one arm across the bed in her sleep, and murmured, "Aren't you staying tonight, Alex?"

Stacey left without a second thought.

* * *

Kathryn's death stunned the community. No one was more surprised than Alex. Not because of her untimely end, but because he hadn't yet located her jewels. Slumped in his leather chair, he slammed his fist against the armrest and seethed, cursing himself. "I should've looked harder," he said aloud. He stared at the ceiling light, searching for a solution.

Kathryn was more intelligent than she looked. She always seemed to be one step ahead.

Alex stroked his chin and bit his lip. If not for her bulldozer-like resolve, he would have lifted the emerald necklace by now. Oblivious to the monochrome movie flickering in the background, he stood up and began pacing back and forth, fists clenching and unclenching. *That necklace alone must be worth a quarter of a million dollars!* His eyes gleamed, and a wicked grin spread across his lips. "I'll have it soon enough," he said, nodding confidently before sinking back into the chair.

* * *

Kathryn never had the opportunity to exclude her daughter from the will. As a result, the eight-bedroom estate, the pharmaceutical company, and her precious stones were still bequeathed to Stacey, with Erik Foster left empty-handed. She trusted Stacey to look after her brother after the inheritance. Her rift with Erik was simply a power struggle she intended to win.

Just as her mother had surmised, Stacey was already preparing to transfer the company's majority ownership to him. And true to her word, she would allow Kathryn the dignity of being buried with her precious gems. When she described the extra-wide casket required to accommodate the extraordinary burial dress and jewels, Alex flipped.

"That's ridiculous! Everyone and their mother will try to dig up the grave! Look at what happened to King Tut!" Alex said, waving his arms.

"I'm having a special metal shell made that will be welded shut once the casket is put in. It'll be impossible for anyone to break in without heavy equipment."

Alex grimaced, then took a deep breath. The plan sounded credible, but still . . . "Where are the jewels now?" he asked casually.

"Safe in an undisclosed location," she said with a knowing smirk. She had to give him credit for asking.

* * *

Tuesday, September 7, 2004. 11:00 a.m.

The funeral united the rich and powerful, including Fortune 500 executives and the governor of New York, with his lovely wife, who had visited the estate on multiple occasions while Bradley was alive. Guests had traveled hundreds of miles to see Kathryn and her spectacular gems laid out for the viewing.

Alex waited for a chance to slip a flashlight into Kathryn's casket. His chance came when a middle-aged woman dropped her glasses and accidentally kicked them toward the security guard standing by the open casket. The guard leaned over with a wince and slowly straightened to return them. *Probably a herniated disk*, Alex thought as he stepped forward and leaned over the casket. *Thank you, Lady Luck!*

"Excuse me, sir," the security guard said, flexing his double-jointed finger.

Alex's heart skipped a beat as he gave the guard a blank stare.

"You're not allowed to cross the viewing ropes. Please stay put while I take inventory," the guard said, his nasal voice turning several heads.

Alex shrugged at the group now staring in his direction and gave a sheepish chuckle. "Certainly, my man. Be my guest. You can even frisk me if you wish. I just wanted to pay my respects properly." He lifted both arms, letting his black coat spread open to reveal his designer deerskin belt.

"That won't be necessary, sir," the guard said apologetically, shuffling in hurried emperor penguin steps.

Alex casually shifted his gaze from one curious mourner to the next, wondering if any of them had seen him drop the flashlight. He could see the polished chrome handle next to her thigh. If the guard lifted the right lid, he might discover the addition and ruin Alex's only chance to get to the jewels.

Focusing on Kathryn's hands, the guard counted the extravagant display of tennis bracelets and rings. Next, he turned his attention to the ruby earrings, emerald necklace, and profusion of jewelry arrayed at her sides. Alex's jaw was so tense he swore he could have bitten through steel chains. His teeth gleamed as his lips parted in a grimace, eyes fixed on the slender flashlight.

"The only thing remaining is the anklet," the guard said, placing his hand on the lid that shrouded Kathryn's legs. "This will only take a moment." The flashlight shifted when he partially raised the lid.

"Do you actually believe I could reach her ankles from here?" Alex asked.

"Oh, of course not," the guard said, letting the lid slip from his grasp. "I'm only doing my duty, sir."

"You take your job very seriously." Alex slung an arm around the guard's shoulders and gave a conspiratorial squeeze. "I'll make sure the family knows how competent and efficient you are."

Leaning askew to ease the pressure of his herniated disc, the guard resumed his place at the casket's head, then glanced at his watch when the funeral director strode in. "Viewing is over and the casket will now be closed. Please move to the chapel, just through that door," said the director, pointing. "The service will begin in fifteen minutes."

Sunlight filtered softly through long, sheer golden drapes that hung from ceiling to floor. About 250 guests entered quietly and packed the plain wooden pews facing the old, dejectedly silent organ. Stacey and Erik stood in the vestibule, receiving hugs and condolences from people they had never met. He was pleased to see the board of directors, who also shared their enthusiasm for his long-awaited return. "I'm sure Erik wouldn't have a problem leaving his prestigious teaching position," Stacey said, smiling for the first time that day. She left him with the directors and approached Alex, who walked in from the viewing room like a cat that had just eaten the canary.

“I think everyone’s here, and the eulogy is about to begin,” she said, a slight blush rising in her cheeks. “Everyone except my grandfather, that is.”

“Is he okay?”

“Believe it or not, he’s in jail right now. Of all moments to pull one of his stunts,” she said, shaking her head. “He likes to push the limits. The problem is, he always gets caught, and this time I refused to bail him out to teach him a lesson.”

Alex nodded with a sly smile. “Maybe it’s time for your grandfather to shape up and become a good soldier.”

Her jaw tightened at the asinine comment. “Really, Alex? Coming from you?”

He shrugged, wishing he could take it back, knowing full well she had every reason to be upset.

Disappointed, Stacey shook her head again. “I suppose you should take a seat up front with Erik. I’ll join you after I gather the pallbearers,” she told him as she stalked off.

Alex nodded and moved through the room, charming each person he passed, though his thoughts were fixed on Stacey. *Something’s different about her.* Those impassive eyes, the hard line of her jaw, that little twitch in her nose unsettled him. Now that Stacey had inherited everything, she reminded him of . . . Kathryn. Even her walk suggested wealth and power. *How far will she take it?*

* * *

Pastor Jim Atkinson looked out into the congregation, his smile widening as he greeted them. He was a well-dressed, well-mannered, handsome Black man who comforted friends and loved ones with his whimsical sermons. "She liked to go shopping at high-end department stores on weekends. Oh, and on Mondays, Tuesdays, Wednesdays, and Thursdays as well.”

Alex didn’t care for his jovial tone and shifted in his seat as he calculated his next move. *How am I going to clear into Kathryn’s casket with Stacey hanging over me? I can't take any chances with so many people standing around. I'll have to clear from my car, away from prying eyes, so I can focus on the distance and safely clear back. Can I clear once the casket is covered with dirt? I'd better go before then.*

"Are you OK?" Stacey whispered.

"Huh?" Alex felt stupid for not noticing when she sat down.

"You should pay attention," she said softly. "It doesn't look good to daydream in front of the pastor."

Alex looked up at the pastor, who had apparently finished his homage to Kathryn and was now advocating for a revolution of values and ideas. "I challenge each of you to go out and practice the joy of brotherhood," Pastor Jim said, his tone serious. "Random acts of kindness create a good foundation for living and help eliminate loneliness and sorrow. We must live in faith and love to generate hope. Look to the world with an open heart and reach out to those who cannot stand on their own two feet." Pausing to sweep his gaze out over the crowd with satisfaction, his eyes fell on Alex, who squirmed under the scrutiny. "While we live in a world where money is king, evil will always exist. The least we can do is look after those less fortunate than ourselves . . .

"Let me repeat the sage words a friend once told me . . ."

A hush settled.

Jim raised his hands—not in spectacle, but in conviction—and let the silence speak.

Then, with quiet authority and the weight of a promise, he said, "It is time."

Stacey gave Alex a sharp nudge.

After the service, a man in a black trench coat and rugged cowboy hat held the reins on a pair of majestic black Friesians that led the way, their hooves clip-clopping a somber beat. The six pallbearers sat solemnly on the stagecoach's narrow seats. Each time the coach hit a bump or pothole, their bodies jerked in unison, and the wheels squeaked in protest, as if echoing the complaints of an aging door in desperate need of oil. Following the hearse to White Blossoms, a private woodland garden cemetery, a line of stretch limousines and luxury cars crept in a procession reminiscent of the death of a U.S. president.

As the mourners crowded around the gravesite, a trio of bagpipers played "Amazing Grace." Lowering the bulky casket from the carriage, the pallbearers trudged to the graveside in slow formation. Even more impressive than the elaborately carved casket was the six-ton excavator required to lower it into the custom-built metal sarcophagus. The grave had been dug wide and deep to accommodate the container's oversized dimensions. Welders lowered their masks and fired up their blowtorches, sealing the metal container in a cascade of flickering light. As the last sparks faded, the excavator let out a throaty snort, expelling a thick plume of black smoke from its upturned steel nostril. A beast of precision and power, it steadied its grip. Then it lowered Kathryn into the earth, her final resting place.

"This is the part I don't like about funerals," Alex whispered, kissing Stacey on the head and slipping out of his seat. He hoped she would not follow him during the critical part of the interment and was relieved, upon reaching his car, to see she had remained seated. *I worried over nothing. This will be easy after all. No different from when I cleared into the old freezer as a teen.* But this time, he was prepared. With the aid of his trusty flashlight, he could confidently clear in and out without raising suspicion.

Moments later, Alex concentrated on Kathryn's location, now eight feet below ground level. One second, he was in his car. The next, he was gone. Inside the pitch-black casket, the silence of the dead was different from the silence of the living. Being eight feet under entailed a level of self-awareness he'd never experienced, a sensation only the dead might understand. He became acutely aware of his breathing and heartbeat from a new perspective.

Struggling in the confines of the coffin, Alex's hand brushed against Kathryn's cold face. Wasting no time, he shoved her body aside and then felt along the silky lining, searching for the flashlight. His fingers grazed it, but just as he reached for it, he accidentally knocked it further from his grasp. His breath came slow and deep, shaky but determined. *Stay calm. Start from the beginning, slow and easy.* Pushing against the cushioned board above his head, he inched himself down, enabling him to grasp the flashlight.

He exhaled in relief.

Salivating, he brought the flashlight to his face and clicked the switch.

Nothing.

Shock swept through his body, quickly followed by violent trembling. He took a moment to calm down and tried the switch again.

Still, nothing.

"What the fuck?" he whispered, his hands now shaking in dismay. His heart pounded, echoing in his ears like an unrelenting drumbeat.

Alex flicked the switch rapidly several times, but the blackness remained undisturbed. "Wait, keep calm. Stay *calm!*" he blithered. "Check the batteries. Maybe they're in backward."

Beads of sweat rolled down his neck, soaking his already-stained shirt. With shaking fingers, he pulled off the battery cover and found an empty chamber. His heart sank—deeper than Kathryn's grave. Something had gone terribly wrong!

"It's not possible!" he screamed, tears stinging his eyes. "I put fresh batteries in last night!" He shoved against the casket lid and scrabbled wildly—first at the satin padding, then the unrelenting mahogany—but it didn't budge. Desperation tethered him to his post. He was a permanent prisoner in Kathryn's cold tomb, trapped with her rotting body. Alex screamed again and again, but the only answer was the thud of dirt being shoveled above him.

Let me out of here!

Someone let me out! I can't breathe!

Can anyone hear me?

Let me OUT!

Pleeeeeease!

* * *

Family, friends, and strangers offered their last condolences, dwindling until Stacey stood alone by the mound, reflecting on the events of the past two weeks. Losing herself among the twittering of birds and the fragrant scent of massed flowers, she smiled wryly at life's unexpected quirks. *Survival requires action, even if that means cutting people off or brushing them aside.*

Stacey held her purse firmly and walked down the slope. The gentle breeze ruffled her hair as she paused next to a trash can and watched a cherry blossom tree's delicate petals drift by her. In the coolness of its shade, she reached into her bag and took out two AA batteries—the same ones she'd removed from Alex's flashlight while gathering the pallbearers.

The batteries lingered in her hand for a moment as she allowed memories of Alex to flit through her mind. Then she let them all go. They hit the bottom of the trash can with a kerplunk, an appropriate end to that chapter in her life. *Two problems solved with flawless execution*, she thought. *It's all over. I've learned my lessons well. I'm ready to move forward.*

Heartache from the past had oppressed and challenged her, but also shaped her into who she was now. Guilt and remorse were for the weak and foolish. As she headed to her car, a lingering group of young men eyed her, their thoughts unmistakable. She saw the dollar signs in their eyes and, in the style of her deceased mother, gave them a callous stare as a warning, her nose twitching. *Don't fuck with me or my emotions unless you want to end up in a suitcase somewhere deep in Death Valley.*

THE CLOWN AND THE CAREGIVER

Thursday, August 19, 2004. 8:46 a.m.

As the Texas sun beat down, a caravan of colorful circus trucks rumbled down Highway 83, their engines roaring in unison. The pulse of circus life reverberated through the North College district, miles from their destination. A storm of gravel coated everything in dust. Inside the trucks, the animals grew restless, their instincts bristling with anticipation. Lions paced with low growls that shivered through the air. Elephants trumpeted with excitement, their calls piercing the cacophony outside.

At the rear of the caravan, Susan, the bearded lady, navigated a long-bed pickup truck hitched to a 27-foot fifth-wheel RV. Her braids frayed into baby hairs, clinging like ground ivy to her damp skin. Hot breeze stirred her wild beard, itching her chin. Susan gripped the steering wheel, her focus unwavering as country music blared over the engine's rumble. The truck jolted over a pothole, its tires slamming against the wheel wells. She reached for a cup of iced soda, finding its chill a soothing break from the heat. Just as she raised it, another jolt sent soda splashing across her vintage harlequin blouse.

"Ugh, seriously?! Not again!" she exclaimed, glancing down at her blouse. With a frustrated sigh, she grabbed some napkins from the center console and dabbed futilely at the spill before it set.

On the bank of Elm Creek, a red-eared slider stood tall, its head raised. Its resolute stare fixed on the fast-approaching truck towing the fifth wheel. As the vehicle barreled down the highway, the turtle scurried away, yielding to the looming presence of the metallic beast that, like itself, carried a home on its back.

The clatter of the fifth-wheel hitch grating against the kingpin went undetected for miles under the cover of blasting music and roaring engines. A soft ping, barely audible, echoed with the drumbeat as the safety pin swung back and forth, rhythmically striking the locking bar with each jolt of the truck bed. The pin, which should have been locked in place, dangled precariously . . .

Dmitri, the strongman, and Lev, the little person, were inside the fifth wheel preparing breakfast. Lev set plates and flatware on the table while Dmitri, his muscles stretching the fabric of a white muscle shirt, called out, "How do you want your eggs?"

"Over easy, smothered in green chili sauce, please," said Lev, pulling a chair back.

Dmitri lifted the lid from a small bucket of lard and spooned some into the hot frying pan. It sizzled as he added a generous slab of bacon.

With a comical grimace, Lev asked, "Why must you use that stuff? Are you trying to turn me into a walking lard ball?"

Gingerly swirling the lard in the pan, Dmitri raised an eyebrow. He quickly turned, flexed his free arm, and said with a mischievous grin, "You see these muscles? I grew up eating lard all my life in

Mother Russia, and this is how I turned out. If you eat lard, you can grow as big and strong as I am. Imagine the sheer power!"

"It's a little late for that," said Lev, gesturing to his short stature with a wave. "Now that you mention it, I sure miss Mother Russia."

"Да, я тоже," agreed Dmitri, adding eggs to the sizzling bacon.

Blissfully unaware of the calamity ahead, Susan roared past Lowden Street, singing along to her favorite tune. A slight left curve loomed ahead, its several waterlogged potholes waiting in quiet ambush. Taking another swig of her drink, she dropped the cup in the holder, tightened her grip on the steering wheel, and leaned into the turn. The kingpin heaved within the jaw coupling, unlocking the bar like a jail cell door.

The truck's front wheel plunged into a gaping pothole, unleashing a torrent of water and severing the kingpin from the jaw coupling. As the vehicle turned, the camper's loft slammed against the driver's rear quarter panel. Teetering precariously, the fifth wheel scraped against the asphalt before flipping. Susan's face was etched with agony as she watched the catastrophe through the rearview mirror.

"What the hell?" Dmitri's mind raced to comprehend the unfolding disaster.

"Aaagh!" Lev cried, paralyzed with fear.

The camper tilted ominously to the right. Dmitri desperately clutched the frying pan as the RV's sharp slope sent flames spilling into the hot lard. Grease burst into a wild inferno, flames lapping ferociously. Dmitri lost his balance and instinctively hurled the burning pan. It flew like a fireball, splattering grease across the sofa, which ignited in a burst of flames . . .

The screech of twisting metal and cracking fiberglass pierced Lev's eardrums, adding to the mounting chaos. He clung to the table as the world tilted and then flipped, his eyes widening with panic and mouth contorting in terror. The refrigerator doors swung open, sending the contents plummeting over him. Frozen in disbelief, he watched as leftover food in plastic containers, liter bottles of soda, and fruit bombarded him. The most dangerous were the beer bottles. They rained like giant hailstones, one striking his temple. The refrigerator plunged toward him, hitting the table with a loud thud, shearing it in two and pinning him against the wall.

"Help me!" he screamed as the cramped space darkened with smoke. He could feel the heat of fire behind him, roaring as it found more fuel, and filling his straining lungs with smoke . . .

Dmitri was thrown toward what had been the foot of the sofa, now the topside. Instinctively, his hands shot out to soften the impact, but one arm plunged into the searing flames. He recoiled, letting out a howl that tore through the mangled room. The fire raged, saturating the air with the stench of burning fiberglass. A metallic screech made him look up, just in time to see the range hurtling toward him. He leaped aside as it smashed into the door. Hearing Lev's pained cries, Dmitri sprang over the range, keeping his head low, dodging the smoke. His powerful arms wrapped around the refrigerator, lifting it clear off the table.

"Get out!" Dmitri yelled, veins in his temples popping.

Lev scurried out from underneath the unit, and the strongman dropped it back onto the table.

"There's no way out!" Lev shouted, his eyes wild as he coughed black smoke. "The camper landed on the exit side!"

Dmitri sprang onto the range, reaching up to open the sliding window. The opening wasn't large enough for his bulky body, so he ripped the tempered glass off their tracks. In the background, the fire popped and crackled menacingly as it advanced. Adrenaline surged, numbing him to the blackened burn on his arm.

"Get up here!" he called. Lev clambered up the range to where the strongman crouched, bracing himself. Dmitri grabbed Lev by the seat of his pants with his right hand. In one swift movement, he pushed off with his muscular legs and hurled his partner through the window like a shot put.

Arms flailing, Lev landed with a thump on the side panel of the fifth wheel, surprised by how hot the metal already was. He scrambled to his feet in time to see Dmitri push himself out through the window, swing his legs around, and jump off the vehicle.

"Time to fly like an eagle, little buddy!" Dmitri cried.

Lev took one step back and sucked a determined breath before hurling himself toward his friend. He soared through the air with his eyes shut and teeth clenched, landing in the waiting arms of the strongman, where he burst into tears. His heart beat against his smoke-filled lungs. *Damn, we almost died.*

Susan rushed toward them, her long braided hair swinging behind her, sobbing with relief. "Hurry! We have to get away from the camper!" she exclaimed, tugging at Dmitri's arm, Lev still crying over his shoulder.

As they ran toward the pickup truck, the propane tank exploded with a deafening boom, engulfing what was left of the fifth wheel in flames and flinging them all to the ground. Thick smoke, sepulchral black, billowed from the wreckage like a vengeful genie.

"Nothing is more alluring than the mystical forces of nature," said the strongman, gaping at the plumes rising from the twisted rubble.

Lev stared in a catatonic stupor, then started bawling again.

Dimitri was the first to recover his feet and set his partner upright. Lev looked up at him in awe. "I could've died back there. You saved my life, Dmitri," he said, his voice rising, as if to share it with the world.

"Don't mention it." For the first time, Dmitri looked down at the second-degree burns striping his arm. "You would've done the same."

"You mean I would've catapulted you through the air too?"

Dmitri tried to picture the image and shook his head. "I wouldn't recommend it. Not unless you want your little arm to go straight up my butt," he said with a satirical grin.

Lev grimaced.

Miles, the contortionist and driver ahead of Susan's rig, ran up, gasping for breath as he reached the pickup truck. His bald head gleamed in the light of the fire. "I radioed the lead driver," he said, his eyes flicking between them. "What the hell happened?"

Stroking her beard, Susan said, "I was making that turn there when the fifth wheel lurched and popped out from the hitch. It happened so fast!"

Miles walked to the truck's bed and inspected it. "Well, here's your problem," he said, puffing out his chest and pointing at the dangling safety pin. Lev scaled the twisted tailgate and hopped onto the bed as they all moved closer for a better look.

The strongman stared at the suspended safety pin with a befuddled expression. "That can't be," he said, raising a brow. "I rechecked the safety pin at the truck stop! Twenty minutes ago!"

"He's right," interjected Lev. "I saw him going through the protocol myself." He lifted his chin, daring anyone to discredit him. When no one did, he jumped off the bed and approached the contortionist. Scrutinizing Miles, he thrust his small finger out and said, "I wouldn't be surprised if this were sabotage!"

Everyone recoiled. Dmitri stepped back, tapping a thoughtful forefinger on his upper lip.

"And I have a damn good idea who it was," added Miles with a knowing nod.

Lev and Susan exchanged looks of knowing disbelief.

* * *

Kids teemed through Stevenson Park as parents shouted tips from the sidelines of a middle school baseball scrimmage. The coach cupped his hands around his mouth and yelled, "Play ball!"

The batter took his stance at home plate with fierce determination, muscles tensed, as the pitcher unleashed the ball. Then, with a resounding crack, the batter sent it sailing over the diamond. The ball arced high into the sky, losing momentum as it dropped toward the unprepared outfielder.

Mickey's glove was above his head, but with his attention fixed on the approaching vehicles down the road, the ball whizzed past him, landed in the scruffy grass, and rolled away. Cheers and boos from the crowd and frustrated shouts from his teammates erupted. Ignoring the noise, he dropped his glove and ran toward the mound. Mickey bounced on his toes and pointed at the road, crying, "A circus! The circus is coming! LOOK!"

Every head turned to see the fleet of semitrailers that stretched down East North 7th Street just outside the fence. A wave of kids swept to the sidewalk as they goggled at the kaleidoscopic panels advertising fearsome lions, towering elephants, and horses crowned with tossing plumes. The coach waved his arms and bellowed about teamwork in a futile attempt to regain control, but the allure of the circus was too strong. Even the parents were spellbound by the spectacle.

The trucks trundled into the vacant lot across from the park. Few locations in historic downtown Abilene offered a rare confluence of cultural amenities: the Spanish colonial Paramount Theatre, The Grace Museum, and most importantly, the public bathrooms at Stevenson Park.

"Stop right here," shouted Bill, his fist raised like an umpire calling strike three, his badass biker tattoo popping on his bicep. The truck's air brakes hissed as he zigzagged across the lot, directing the other drivers in their parking ballet. As the boss canvasman, he knew precisely where each tent needed to be in relation to the big top. Tightrope walkers huddled together, clowns clustered in a crowd, and acrobats stood in a ragged line, waiting for his word.

Bill brought his callused hand to his lips beneath a bristling mustache and whistled loudly. A snug white tank top accentuated his muscles, and his thick black beard, sprinkled with gray, was well-trimmed. "The king pole goes here," he said, raking the heel of his boot in an X in the dusty soil. "From this point, it will give us a radius of sixty feet, where the elephant trough rests. You know the floor plan, folks. Let's move!"

Knowing the routing, the performers scattered to their tasks. Meanwhile, the delighted towners watched as four majestic elephants sauntered gracefully down the ramps, lending an air of grandeur to the bustling scene without the price of a ticket. The red-and-white canvas rose smoothly even without Susan, Dmitri, and Lev at their usual posts; they were busy with Highway Patrol and a recovery truck. Sturdy stakes were pounded into the hard ground to secure the guy wires that held the big top in place.

Bill hammered away, the clinking sound echoing across the grounds. Bubbles, the mischievous young calf from the herd, stood beside him, ready to assist. "This is a metal stake," he said, holding it up so the calf could touch it. "When I ask for a stake, you grab one and give it to me." His gentle grip guided Bubbles's slender trunk through the motions.

"Hi, Bill."

He paused the demonstration to look over his shoulder. "Hi Mila, how's your father?" he asked, giving the stake a few final whacks to secure it. Taking advantage of the momentary distraction, Bubbles quenched his thirst from the nearby trough.

"I'm looking for Mr. Milagro."

"Well, he's not here right now." Bill shielded his eyes from the bright sun to look at the young equestrian. Her rich brown hair shimmered, making a halo around her face. "He's meeting with the Abilene City Council."

"I need someone to look at Mocha's off hind hoof. She's limping."

"No problem. I'll check it out as soon as I finish here," Bill reassured her.

"Thanks," she said, tilting her head with a smile. "I can help with the stakes if you like."

"That's all right. I already have a helper." He winked, a smile spreading across his tanned face. "Get this. I just trained Bubbles for this task. Watch." He whistled to the calf and held out his hand. "Bubbles, give me a stake."

Instead, Bubbles spouted a trunkful of water at him and scurried away. A wave of laughter rippled through the workers, Mila included.

By the time the sun nudged the western horizon, tents and rigging stood ready, awaiting the first show. Star performers and lowly clowns alike shared back slaps and congratulations. But the carpet clown, a short, bald man named Daniel Dewhurst, scowled at the merriment. His silence wasn't natural. It stemmed from the countless injustices that had plagued his life. His desolate eyes mirrored the look of listless vultures perched on branches of dead trees, waiting for the living to breathe their last.

Thirty-three workers struggled to keep the circus afloat, and Daniel was the unfortunate one assigned to dispose of all the animal waste, including elephant feces that towered over his wounded pride. He loathed the circus animals. Every last one of them. Especially Elsa, the largest of the four elephants, who had developed diarrhea in her old age, and Samson, the lion, who dumped the foulest steaming piles he had ever scooped.

Monday, August 23, 2004. 8:47 p.m.

One night, inside clown alley after a performance, Daniel removed his clown costume and dejectedly slipped into his old denim overalls. They were the softest, most comfortable overalls, but their frayed cuffs and rips in the knees were nightly reminders of his inadequacy and failures. Standing rigid in front of the mirror, he frowned at his receding hairline, a quiet monument to fading youth. His reflection filled him with shame and self-disgust. The mirror, a cruel accomplice, amplified his growing distaste for humanity. *Why? What did I ever do to be burdened with such a wretched existence?*

Over the years, his anger had twisted into envy toward the "normal," the young and conventionally attractive. *What a funny-looking man. And he never opens up to anyone,* they whispered, loud enough for him to hear. Their disdainful glances and unkind words only fueled his resentment. He yearned to teach them a lesson. To make them understand the pain he felt every time he peered into the mirror.

Daniel scooped up a sliver of soap from the grimy dish, working up the rich lather to strip off the clown makeup. It took several minutes to scrub away the unrealistically happy red grin. Streaks of crimson, black, and indigo intertwined in the washbasin, forming a swirl of despair—something straight out of an expressionist's nightmare. The haunting image whirlpooled into the drain with a screaming resonance.

"Look at you!" Daniel shouted, jabbing his plump finger at the reflection. His face contorted, teeth bared—grinding like a chisel against stone. "You're the Dung King of Texas!" He reached for a towel, and with a stare as vile as any rogue, he said, "What have you ever accomplished in your pathetic life?"

The mirror gave no answer, offered no comfort. "All you do is make half-witted children laugh and scoop up crap every night!" he snarled, his voice dripping with contempt and eyes blazing at his reflection's flaws. The damp cloth thudded against the mirror and crumpled into the sink as he stormed out.

Unbeknownst to Daniel, the trapeze artist, Hector Delgado, had been watching him through the tent's flap door. *This is one sick man*, he thought. *He's tormented. The poor guy doesn't realize every job is as vital as any other. Where would the world be without janitors?*

Hector shook his head and turned to leave, only to freeze when he found Daniel standing before him, glaring.

"Were you spying on me, *Mr. Delgado*?" Daniel's voice was a low, threatening growl, his eyes boring into Hector's with malevolent intent.

"No," the trapeze artist replied, offering no details.

Daniel narrowed his eyes as Hector disappeared behind the tent.

* * *

Tuesday, August 24, 2004. 1:35 p.m.

The early afternoon crowd buzzed with anticipation. Mocha trotted rhythmically into the ring, her coat rippling like milk chocolate cascading down a fondue fountain, her mane and tail a whipped chocolate and cream garnish. A vaulting surcingle secured a thick pad snugly against her back.

Sheila, the lunger, expertly guided Mocha around the ring with the lunge line and whip. Showing no sign of a limp, the horse trotted rhythmically within the 15-meter circle, her white-bandaged legs rowing through the golden sea of hay.

Mila emerged from the shadows with poise, galloping into the light with the effortless grandeur of a Lipizzaner. The crowd was enchanted, swept up in the majestic strains of Johann Strauss's *Radetzky March*. She paused beside Sheila, the swish of her dark brown ponytail stilling. They took a moment to connect with the horse and ensure everything was set for the performance. Standing tall in her blue unitard, Mila took a deep breath and lifted her chin resolutely. *All those years of dance and gymnastics weren't for you to flop now.*

As Mocha completed her solo trot, the young vaulter raised her arm, and the music changed to a lilting waltz. Timing her steps to the rhythm of Mocha's trot, she signaled, *Get ready. I'm going to mount.* Reaching for one of the surcingle's padded handles, Mila vaulted onto the horse's back with a swift motion, barely skimming an unusual bump in the thick pad. As the horse maintained a steady canter, she executed the mill with a series of leg swings, transitioning into other intricate poses that required immense core strength and control. Strips of fabric from her unitard whipped in the breeze as the 15-year-old extended her legs into a perfect split. With a gleam in her eyes, she swept down onto the pad, lifting her arms in triumph as the crowd erupted in cheers.

I got this!

Mila gripped the right surcingle handle and settled her left foot off-center along Mocha's spine, missing the raised spot in the pad. Facing forward, she stretched her right leg and left arm outward, executing the flag for four strides. More cheers cascaded through the big top as horse and rider soared around the ring like an arrow shot from an archer's bow. At the pinnacle of her performance, Mila sat back, her weight landing heavily on the horse for her final routine.

Mocha pinned her ears back with a snort, her eyes suddenly wide with panic. Her head dropped between her knees, and she bucked violently just as Mila's left foot swung down, catching in one of the leather loops. In an instant, the horse bolted forward, her mane a billowing banner as her powerful legs launched into a frantic gallop. In the chaos, the lunge line whipped through Sheila's fingers, searing red welts into her palms as she recoiled.

The sound of thundering hooves stunned the spectators into silence before gasps and murmurs rippled through the crowd. Sheila fought to stay calm, walking quickly across the ring to intercept the frightened horse.

"Ohhh!" the crowd screamed.

Numerous spectators cupped their hands over their mouths as they watched the helpless teenager being dragged by her snagged foot. Mila could feel the hay and dust kicked up by the horse's gallop, inches from her head. She thrashed her arms, trying to lift her shoulders and avoid the thrashing hooves.

Several performers ran into the ring and grabbed hold of Mocha's bridle, halting her movement. But it was Sheila's steady voice that calmed her, calling, "Easy, Mocha. Whoa, girl, easy now." She moved closer, offering gentle caresses and a carrot, easing the horse's agitation until her breathing slowed.

Meanwhile, Dmitri ran up and slid his strong arms under Mila's shoulders. Adrenaline quickened her breath. "My ankle!" she choked through gritted teeth. "I think it's broken."

Dmitri lifted her body slightly, allowing Lev to ease her foot out of the loop and gently place her leg on the ground. White-faced, she grimaced at the movement.

"You're okay, Mila. Lev is calling the paramedics now. You'll be riding on a merry-go-round in no time," he said jokingly.

Despite the pain, she managed a tight grin. "No way, Dmitri. I'm not going anywhere near a merry-go-round. They're much too dangerous."

* * *

Several minutes after the paramedics drove away with Mila, Sheila stormed into the room, roaring like a jungle king. She plopped the thick white back pad onto the folding table, where the other performers sat in Last Supper formation. Heads turned, eyes locked on her.

"Look at this, everyone!" she cried, her voice cut like a sour note. A stiff finger jabbed at the underside of the lining. "Someone wove a push pin under the pad. This wasn't an accident. It was an attack!"

Everyone gasped. Their horrified eyes fixed on the push pin protruding like an ice pick aimed at their morale.

Sheila's eyes burned with intensity. "For months, strange things have been happening, and no one seems to know who or what is causing them!"

As usual, Miles exuded calmness, sitting with his legs crossed behind his head. He gave a small shrug. "I have a pretty good idea who it was."

"Wait, are you suggesting it was the same person who caused the fifth wheel accident?" asked Susan. They locked eyes, the same thought passing between them. Then she pounded her fist on the table. "We need to report this to Mr. Milagro right away! Does anybody know where he is?"

"Joe went to the hospital with Mila to take care of the insurance paperwork," said Sheila, a muscle twitching in her jaw.

"Then it's time we took matters into our own hands!" Suddenly furious, Miles untangled his legs and stood up so fast his chair clattered over backward.

"Until we know for sure who is behind these accidents, we can't go lynching anyone," Dmitri warned, flexing his muscles to reinforce his authority. He raised his hand before his face, fingers splayed wide like a crocodile's gaping jaws. They snapped shut—once, twice—before opening again, mimicking the slow, deliberate bite of a predator. "We need to keep our eyes peeled, like a croc lurking in murky waters, ready to *snap!*" With a decisive clamp, his fingers snapped shut, sealing the point.

Heads nodded in agreement, except for Miles, who stepped defiantly toward Dmitri. "I'm telling you, it's the carpet clown!" he growled, his face red. "That guy has been suspect number one since his first of May! I'll wring his neck with my bare—"

"All right, all right. Don't get bent out of shape," Dmitri interjected with a glimmer in his eyes.

"What? Is that supposed to be some kind of joke?" Miles shot back, smirking.

* * *

Milagro Circus was not named after a miracle but rather for its financially troubled owner. Those who'd been around the longest jested that it was a miracle the circus had managed to keep operating. A tall and thin man, Joe Milagro appeared even taller with his black top hat perched atop his salt-and-pepper hair. Whenever he playfully wiggled his mouth, his long handlebar mustache went along for the ride, delighting children and occasionally exciting single women in the crowd. His pleasant eyes, as black as crude oil, crinkled with sincerity. For those fortunate enough to meet him, he often displayed a distinct mannerism—a cocked brow that signaled his genuine interest in their conversation.

To revive the failing circus, Joe had introduced a pig race: six pigs, six vibrant lanes, each color-coded to liven up the monotone seats and give every audience member a pig to root for. It was an expensive gamble, but one that quickly paid off.

It helped that each pig had a distinct personality. Chiquita was a tiny piglet, delicate as a seashell, adored although she never won any races. Cha-Cha was aptly named for her unique gait, which echoed the rhythmic flow of a Latin dance step. Marmalade earned her name after being found with her sizable snout stuck in a 5-ounce jar of orange marmalade, looking as embarrassed as someone walking into a glass door. Sassy, true to her name, was bold and lively. She was always the first to leap into the pool or challenge a bigger pig. Rosie's delicate pink skin rivaled rose petals, but her thorny demeanor made workers wary of her bite. Cleo earned her name from an Egyptian-style photo shoot, where she was fitted in a gold-trimmed skirt and poised on a red velvet Cleopatra sofa, legs crossed regally. Joe built a playpen for his six superstars on an old flatbed trailer, featuring a small vinyl pool with a wooden ramp and even a small slide.

Spectators lingered after each show to admire the animals, especially the fierce predators. This didn't sit well with Abilene city officials, already wary of granting a four-week permit near Stevenson Park. Had Joe not assured them everything would run smoothly, the circus might've ended up pitching tents in dusty Moreno Valley, west of Palm Springs and north of San Diego.

* * *

Thursday, August 26, 2004. 9:48 p.m.

No fearsome growling tonight. No ripping of flesh into chunks. The tigers were out cold, the horses snoozing comfortably. Crickets chirped in the distance as the man in the moon cast his watchful gaze over the sleeping Earth.

Daniel climbed the ladder to the pigpen and opened the gate, startling the gentle creatures from their slumber. If anything could trigger misophonia, the shrill cries of pigs were undoubtedly among the worst. His blood boiled as he gripped the shovel, raising it over his head.

"Shut up, you damn motherless swine!" he shouted, his eyes bulging with rage. Spittle spewed from his mouth, riding the air like venom on the wind.

Daniel lunged forward and immediately slipped on a pile of feces. His leg zigzagged like a novice ice skater, but he regained his footing, swearing. "I'll get the best of you, you damn critters!" he fumed, scraping his shoe against the truck bed. The shovel swung from side to side, each swing more violent than the last. Tension gripped his frame as the shovel clashed against the flatbed, sending sparks flying.

Squealing, Chiquita dashed up the ramp and jumped into the pool, as if *that* was any escape. Sassy was right behind her, followed by Marmalade, whose bulk splattered Daniel's legs. Cha-Cha grunted a warning and lunged at the intruder's leg, sending him stumbling back in surprise. Before she could scurry away, he struck her hind leg with a sharp crack of the shovel. Cha-Cha's squeal pierced his eardrums, snapping him back to his senses. The other pigs joined in a bizarre cacophony as Cha-Cha hobbled out of reach.

Joe was tabulating the day's receipts on his clunky keyboard calculator when cries filtered through the trailer's window screen. He shoved his top hat on at an angle and threw on his red coat. Stepping outside, he found the boss canvasman already in motion.

"What's going on?" Joe bellowed.

"I don't know. Something's upset the pigs," Bill said, his chest bare and a towel slung over his shoulder. He quickened his pace to keep up with the ringleader's whooping crane steps. Ahead of him, the lapels on Joe's coat flapped with every stride, then fell flat as he stopped short. Just beyond them, Daniel was already halfway up the truck's ladder, clutching Cha-Cha in his arms.

"Dan!" thundered Joe over the pigs' squeals. "What in tarnation is going on here?"

"Mr. Milagro," Daniel said, looking guilty.

Cha-Cha lifted her snout, curled her nose, and her eyes gleamed with joy at the sight of her valiant savior. She struggled to free herself from the clutches of the clown.

"I went in to clean the pigpen, but Cha-Cha ran out when I opened the gate. It wasn't my fault. She jumped off the truck and hurt herself when she hit the ground." Daniel's beady eyes darted between the two men, watching to see if they'd buy his story.

Joe nodded, disbelief plain on his face. "Bill, take the pig and have a look at her leg," he said, squinting at Daniel.

Bill cradled the pig gently in the crook of his elbow. Cha-Cha snorted softly, nuzzling his bicep for comfort. His fingers probed the injured leg, checking for bruising. She flinched when he touched a spot already turning black and blue. He traced the length of her leg, feeling for her pulse, assessing whether the break had damaged any blood vessels.

"It's the fibula, all right. It's broken," he said, shaking his head and shooting the ringleader an I-told-you-so stare. "Cha-Cha won't be racing anytime soon."

"It's not my fault, Mr. Milagro," Daniel insisted, jumping off the ladder and kicking up a cloud of dust around his shabby deck loafers. "I swear on my father's grave, it's not my fault!"

Joe turned to Bill. "Get someone to help with a splint and take Cha-Cha to the nearest vet."

Glad his partner had finally seen the obvious, Bill departed with the injured pig nestled close. Cha-Cha snuffled softly as if to thank the ringleader for his most judicial decision.

Daniel opened his mouth to protest his innocence, but the boss had had enough.

"Stop right there!" Joe's voice boomed, making Daniel flinch. "I will not tolerate any more accidents!" He pointed his double-jointed finger. "I don't know what you're up to, Dan, but every time something goes wrong, you're always right there with some lame excuse!"

The corners of Daniel's lips curled downward. "I had nothing to do with Cha-Cha's broken leg," he repeated, hiding behind indignation.

"Nevertheless," Joe scrutinized him. "This is your last chance. I'm holding you fully responsible for every animal's well-being. If anything else happens, and I mean *anything*, you are through!"

Daniel stood rigid while Joe tilted his head back. For a moment, the threat of physical violence hung thick between them. The carpet clown considered the drawback of a traveling circus. *I'm too far from home to lose my job over a pig. And who knows where we might end up? I'm sure as hell not trekking back to Hastings by myself!* Dropping his gaze, he was quick to acquiesce.

The ringmaster cocked a brow and watched Daniel slink off, like a sly coyote with a jackrabbit in its mouth, keeping a wary eye out for larger predators that might steal his kill. The clown shot a sideways glance back before vanishing behind a trailer. Joe exhaled hard and surveyed the skies, his black top hat leaning at an astonishing angle without falling off his brilliantine-slicked hair. He closed his eyes, recalling the night the canvasman had warned him about the clown.

Monday, June 17, 2002. 10:07 a.m.

"Explain why you think I shouldn't hire him," Joe had replied, throwing his soon-to-be-donated pickup truck into fourth gear. The rusted red truck rattled and squeaked over the rough terrain of southern Nebraska, shuddering like a small plane in a downpour.

Bill clutched the grab handle above his head. "There's just something about his eyes that doesn't sit right," he said, staring out the window, his body swaying with the truck. "He's evil, I tell ya. I've got this bad feeling about your plan to launch the circus, with him around."

Reluctant to assume the worst, Joe brushed his well-defined chin and turned his head, spitting out the window. "I feel it's only fair to give the guy a chance. I think I'll *recruit* him," he said, wiping the tobacco drip away. "Everyone deserves a chance. If I were in his shoes, I'd want an opportunity too."

"But you're not in his shoes," Bill retorted, crossing one leg over the other.

The truck hit a pothole, and Joe yanked the steering wheel, straightening the vehicle. "Let's give the guy a few months to prove himself."

* * *

Hector Delgado hungered for the adventure and excitement only a circus could provide, and the thrill of the catch ultimately drew him to the trapeze. One could glimpse unfathomable passion in the dark pools of his eyes. His father was the first to recognize this irrepressible yearning and encouraged his son to travel alone to Australia for trapeze training at seventeen. Hector pursued a once-in-a-lifetime opportunity after signing a release form. The talk around the community was that his father had planned to rid himself of his son after his wife's sudden death. But making that decision was the most meaningful thing he'd ever done for his son. Fortunately, only those dear to him grasped the good that sprang from his heart.

Upon returning to the States in 1971, Hector, ripped from vigorous training, pursued his passion with a local circus. There, he met Veronica Small, whose yardstick-straight posture and unnaturally clean hair—like it might squeak when rubbed—struck him as both elegant and surreal. He fell hard.

Their relationship quickly led to marriage and three daughters. Jessica, the first to bring him joy, had her mother's gentle eyes. Jill, built for distance like a giant Asian flying squirrel, dreamed of soaring like an eagle over orange and purple canyons on a languid winter's eve. Then came Cecily. She was born too soon, her lungs fragile, her survival uncertain. Hector spent five months at her side and vowed never to let harm near her again.

Saturday, August 28, 2004. 10:02 p.m.

After admiring the Texas sky, Hector and Cecily had fallen asleep on their folding chairs. A low growl—too close for comfort—jolted him awake. Blinking away the haze, Hector spotted Samson barely twenty-five feet away, the tufted tip of the lion's tail twitching as it sniffed the air. Without looking away, he gently nudged his daughter and clapped his hand over her mouth. Slowly, he raised a finger to his lips, then pointed at the escaped predator. When she saw the massive lion, Cecily's face stiffened with fear.

Then the beast roared, striking a chord in Hector's spine. *We've been spotted.* Both father and daughter immediately froze, barely breathing. Samson's large amber eyes were alert, and his tail jutted out with the tip curved upward. He growled and took a calculated step forward.

"Cecily," Hector said softly. "See that truck over there?"

She nodded, her body trembling with a raw fear.

"We're going to walk slowly toward it. When we get halfway, I want you to run to the truck, get inside, and close the window. Do you understand me?"

Cecily glanced at the truck. It seemed impossibly far away. She wasn't sure her legs would carry her that far. "I can't, Dad," she said, her voice quivering.

"Yes, you can, sweetheart." Hector rose and grabbed his chair, holding it like Rocco during a live performance, pointing its four legs forward to confuse the single-minded lion. *Crack! Pop!* Voicing the sounds with each snap, he lashed out with an imaginary whip. Samson growled, stepped back, then assumed a fierce stance. His eyes were glued on Hector and Cecily as they crept toward the truck. *Crack!* Hector cast the imaginary leather rope, and the lion responded by slashing the air with razor-sharp claws. The more Samson pressed, the harder Hector whipped the air.

"Now, Cecily!" he cried.

"Aaaagh!" She bolted.

Samson roared and charged, flinging dirt into the air.

Hector threw the chair to the ground and lunged forward, driving his legs and hips into a tackle against the lion's ribcage. Catching him in mid-leap, Samson hit the ground with a loud thump and rolled under the truck. With the wind knocked out of him, the lion struggled for breath, his chest rising in shallow bursts, his head lifting groggily.

Hector bolted to the front of the truck, shouting at his daughter to close the window.

"Dad!" she wailed, panic blooming behind her eyes.

"Roll up the window!" he ordered again.

Cecily crouched over and cranked hard. Suddenly, Samson's claw slashed through the opening, snaring a lock of her hair. A mighty roar boomed inside the cabin like thunder, and Cecily shrieked, her trembling hand fighting the crank. With her free hand, she repeatedly pounded out two short and one long blasts on the horn, the final note stretching longer each time.

Hector scrambled onto the truck's container. "Samson!" he bellowed, clapping his hands. For a moment, the predator's gaze locked onto him. They stared each other down, challenging the other to back down and show who had the biggest balls.

Hector gritted his teeth and shouted, "Come on, you son of a bitch. I know you want me as much as I want you." He roared without breaking eye contact, "Come on!"

Samson's mane shimmered in the moonlight as he shook his head. He roared fiercely and withdrew his large paw from the window, allowing it to close completely. He sprang onto the hood, contorting it, and it snapped back into shape when he leaped onto the container. Hector slowly backed away. The lion's growl was deep and slow—he knew the hunt was over. His strides were measured and deliberate, his menacing presence undeniable.

Hector had nowhere to go. Even if he jumped off the container, Samson would surely follow—his jaws aiming for his neck. He held out his left hand and cracked the imaginary whip with the other. The lion roared and slashed at the air, crouching on his powerful hind legs . . .

Samson lunged at his prey.

Hector thought he had heard a rifle discharge when he fell back, but he had no time to process it. The lion's full weight sprawled over him, pinning him against the container. As he shoved the massive body off, his eyes landed on the tranquilizer dart embedded in Samson's neck. Shaken and bruised, he staggered to the edge of the container.

Hector rubbed the back of his neck, trying to shake off the adrenaline. He huffed and said, "Do you always show up late for parties?"

"Depends who it's for," Joe replied, standing in front of several crew members who had convened behind him, their faces tense and dust-streaked.

Cecily clambered out of the truck and ran to her mother while Hector climbed down.

The ringleader snatched his top hat off the ground, shaking the dust from its brim. "Rocco, how did that lion get loose?" he asked, settling it firmly onto his head.

"No clue," responded Rocco, his eyes narrowing with suspicion. "I check the cages after each performance, without fail."

"Where do you keep the key?"

"It's on a hook by the door in my trailer," Rocco said, his voice clipped and impatient. "I told Emilio I'd dice up the onions for tomorrow's stew. I only stepped away for an hour."

A ripple of unease passed through the crew as they edged closer. Bill couldn't contain himself. "Someone could have grabbed the key and placed it back without your knowledge," he said.

"But why?" Rocco hesitated, his brow furrowing. "Why would anyone do such a thing?"

Joe swept his gaze across the crowd, calculating who was present . . . and who wasn't. He turned briskly to Rocco and said, "Take a couple of men and get Samson back in his cage."

"Yes, sir," Rocco replied, quickly gathering help.

"Are you thinking what I'm thinking?" Bill asked.

"Say no more."

Joe and Bill hurried toward Daniel's trailer, their footsteps crunching on the dry grass underfoot. Under the dim circus lights, the small, egg-shaped trailer sat with its peeling paint and crooked steps, looking comical in the gloom. Fueled by rage, the ringleader flung the door open without knocking. Inside, they found the carpet clown sprawled on his cot, a whiskey bottle slack in his grip. He had drunk himself into a stupor, the trailer thick with the stench of alcohol and other offensive odors.

"Daniel, wake up!" Joe barked.

Bill kicked at him with his steel-toed boot, but after several blows, Daniel didn't stir. The bottle hit the floor, spilling the last of its whiskey.

"Never mind, Bill," said Joe, tugging at his shoulder to stop further abuse. "He's wasted. Must've been in this state since finishing his rounds. It must not have been him." *We can stay up all night cutting up jackpots, but this will be the icing on the cake!* They left Daniel's trailer in disgust, flicking off the light before slamming the door.

As they hurried off, Daniel overheard Bill arguing that the clown was the one who set the lion free: "That lousy piece of shit does nothing but gripe all day. I'd bet my life it was him. Even if he's drunk out of his skull!"

Daniel lifted the blinds to peek through, a sly grin creeping across his face. Relishing his drunken act, he thought, *Good, I kept those two characters off my back.*

* * *

Sunday, August 29, 2004. 4:05 p.m.

Joe felt the pinch. Without the pig race, he'd been forced to cut wages by 30 percent across the board and halved his own pay. The circus crew accepted the drastic decision instead of dropping two employees.

"We must reduce our expenses by any means possible," Joe said, his hands fiddling nervously with the fringed sash. His eyes were bloodshot, with dark circles hinting at sleepless nights. "I'm open to ideas," he said, his voice laden with defeat.

"How about we reduce the animals' food rations?" Rocco asked jokingly.

"I'll personally feed you to Samson before we do that," said Bill, turning to Joe. "These animals are my family, and we're responsible for their welfare."

"W-why don't we bring back the p-p-pig race and put Gypsy in place of Cha-Cha? Is-is there a Texas law that says goats can't im-im-impersonate pigs?" asked Marty Lewis, better known as Jo-Jo the clown. "She can fill the missing color slot!"

Laughter rippled through the group. At first, it was a silly notion, but as Joe considered it, the idea began to sound plausible. Marty beamed, soaking up the accolades and thumbs-up he'd kicked into high gear. His thin face nodded repeatedly, his protruding chin exaggerating his grin. To keep the momentum going, he added, "W-we can . . . We can put a rubber pig nose over Gypsy's. You know . . . " Marty swallowed hard and took a deep breath. "J-j-just like the ones they sell at gag stores, the ones with the elastic bands. We could even get rubber pig ears!"

The more he spoke, the more energized they became, realizing they had a chance to turn the circus around. Marty's heart was beating fast. *Wow, I'm the first to present a great idea, not the usual loudmouth lion tamer!*

News of the reinstated pig race hit local radio stations the next morning, along with a front-page headline on the Abilene Foremost. See the mysterious sixth pig! read the flyers, posters, and banners. Much to the ringleader's delight, attendance at the day's performances skyrocketed.

* * *

Friday, September 3, 2004. 11:27 a.m.

There were no clouds in the sky to form cotton ball figures. Gone were the Chihuahuas, bears, and furry bunnies that drifted across the blue sky. Vanished were the dolphins, whales, and jellyfish that floated in the sea. The wind had erased them forever, as if a giant toy had been shaken, wiping the sky clean of every sketch and swirl.

Wearing denim overalls, Daniel stood before the washbasin and splashed cool water on his face and back. As it trickled down his skin, a smile crept across his face, a rare sight. Seeing a black swan in the Sahara might've been more likely. Grabbing a comb from his rear pocket, he brushed his thinning, wet hair to one side with a trembling hand, then dried his face. The mirror reflected a lonely man filled with insurmountable hate, a hallucinating mind, fashioning ideas only *he* could comprehend. A cold breeze swept through the room, causing the hair on the back of his neck to stand on end.

Two ghostly tentacles, their ethereal forms writhing, reached out from the mirror's depths, hovering over him like serpents poised to strike. Paralyzed, Daniel watched as they moved, wrapping around him with predatory swiftness. One slithered across his face and clamped over his mouth, stifling his scream, while the other coiled behind him, dragging him forward. The mirror rippled like a secluded forest pond, disturbed by droplets from a branch. A dark, swirling cloud seeped from its depths, twisting into an amorphous shape with eerie fluidity. Its presence spread like a creeping shadow, casting unearthly menace into every corner.

No longer struggling against the mysterious force, Daniel allowed the tentacles to sway his body, hypnotizing him. He stared into the mirror, mesmerized by the demonic entity that swirled in a whirling, ever-changing pattern. *A murmuration of starlings*, he thought. Tendrils of black fog wove together, their edges dissolving into the air only to reassemble into sinister new forms. Two black pits flickered into existence as eyes, burning with ancient wrath. A gaping maw yawned open, as if to swallow him whole. The creature released a low, guttural growl, its breath whipping Daniel's hair back like a tempest's warning.

A strange calm washed over Daniel as the creature loomed closer. Silence hung between them. The evil in its eyes burrowed into his frail mind like a dark seed taking root, spreading through his thoughts and weaving itself into his being. Drawn to the seductive pull of malevolence, he chose the easy path. *If it's chaos you want, then chaos you shall have . . . as long as I'm spared.*

Soon the tentacles released him, dissipating into the stale air. Daniel stood, aware of what had transpired. A strange connection lingered, as though their thoughts had begun to intertwine. And the message was loud and clear. Walking away in a trance, he felt the entity fade, his sinister grin lingering like an echo of what had taken root.

Daniel reached for the pail and shovel he despised, clanking them to alert the animals he was coming. With a sneer, the clown went to work as if nothing had happened.

* * *

Play, a healthy behavior, is a common language between the wind and pennant. The prevailing winds willingly engage with the eight triangular pennants high above the big top, teasing them, one by one, and gently nudging them for attention. In response to their reluctance, an intense gust quickly awakens them from their slumber. Soon, a playful dance ensues, like two pups meeting for the first time. The pennants flap their tails in unison, flirtatiously daring the wind to keep up. They master the art of whipping their tails without harming the wind and learn to communicate with other pennants. Their steady rolling and waiving, now in full swing, enhance the coordination that will carry them through the day.

* * *

11:55 a.m.

Elsa had been with Milagro Circus since its inception, dazzling audiences with her performances. She had mastered the fundamentals of raising the big top. At each new location, she eagerly handed metal stakes to the workers and used her immense power to hoist the towering supports that kept the tent fabric taut. It was a feat that had earned the elephant star status among the circus workers. But that was months ago.

Her ambition waned after she withdrew from the herd. Elsa had fallen ill, plagued by foul-smelling diarrhea. Knowing she was near death, Joe Milagro placed her, unrestrained, in a small private tent to ensure her comfort during her final days.

Throughout that sweltering day, she stood languidly in the middle of a brown, water moat while a swarm of flies teased her relentlessly. Tears trickled down Elsa's withered face, her long eyelashes clumping like wet pasta. There were no stars in her eyes, only sorrow and grief.

With no remedy for the arthritic elephant, it was only a question of time.

When Daniel opened the tent flap, the blood drained from his face, and his heart lurched at the overpowering stench. In an apoplectic fit, he threw down the pail and shovel with a thud and a clang.

"Holy shit!" he exclaimed, sprinting up and down Elsa's length. He cursed and blasphemed. His eyes bulged beneath furrowed brows, and his nostrils flared with fury. Grabbing the weather-beaten shovel, he yelled, "There's no way in hell I'm going to clean up this filth!"

One hundred billion outraged neurons ran amok. He swung the shovel like a baseball bat, striking the elephant's withered rump, the blade tearing through her thick skin. Elsa's eyes became crazed. She trumpeted fiercely and struck Daniel on the shoulder, sending him soaring across the tent. The pail spiraled away as his body struck it.

Daniel climbed shakily to his feet and brandished the shovel like a sword. "Stay away from me, you beast!" he shouted, ignoring the cut on his arm. The sounds of laughter and applause from the big top faded into a distant murmur, overshadowed by the low, rumbling growl of an enraged Elsa. Breathless and rattled, he thought only of saving the audience from the turmoil he had unwittingly unleashed. In one frantic motion, he flung the handle aside and bolted toward the exit.

Instead of steering the rampaging elephant away from the public, Daniel ran through the rear entrance of the big top with Elsa in close pursuit.

"Get out!" he shouted. "Everyone out! Elsa's gone mad!"

Under the big top, the Delgado family was halfway through their trapeze routine. Cecily arced gracefully through the air on her return, executed a 180-degree turnabout, and caught the approaching bar with unwavering precision. After completing the shooting star, she landed smoothly on the pedestal board beside her sisters. On the edge of their seats with bated breath, the audience cheered and applauded . . .

The deafening roar of the crowd drowned out Daniel's frantic cries. With their attention focused overhead, no one noticed him stumbling into the center ring, let alone heard a word.

Elsa rammed the red aluminum bleachers like a freight train, sending people flying; popcorn and soda cups showered the crowd.

"It's raining!" a small child cried. The boy's father looked up, startled, and tried to shield his son from falling bodies. Pandemonium spread across the tiered seating like fire. Frightened spectators scrambled to escape from the twisted wreckage . . .

"Lista!" shouted Hector.

Gripping the fly bar, Cecily launched off from the pedestal board, gaining momentum as she swung downward toward her father. As always, the cast out electrified her with the freeing sensation of flight, lighting her with joy. A tingle spread through her feet as she extended her toes to tickle the underside of the canvas. Her father swung up and above the pedestal board during her back beat, then she plunged for her trick . . .

Dazed and disoriented, Elsa wrapped her trunk around a man who sprawled at her feet and thrust him back into the audience. He landed awkwardly but safely on top of two women several rows up, bumping his peach-fuzz scalp. Spectators shrieked at the unscheduled show as the elephant trumpeted and hammered her ribbed trunk against the metal rail, inciting a general panic. Elsa continued thumping, demanding attention and respect. The crowd pushed and shoved one another, some trampling others like battered doormats.

Sweat glistening on his brow, a bull handler stepped forward with a bullhook to push Elsa back. He jabbed repeatedly at her face but she fought fiercely. She smacked him across the face with her trunk, knocking the bullhook and his baseball cap aside. *I've never seen Elsa behave like this!* Another strike on the shoulder sent him reeling to his knees. He held his arm over his head to blunt the next blow when Daniel appeared with another bullhook. Dodging Elsa's waving trunk, the carpet clown forced the elephant back with the tool, allowing the battered bull handler to get up. Working together, they pushed Elsa toward the center ring, clearing a path to the rear exit for the panicked people . . .

"Hup!" Oblivious to the mayhem below, Hector signaled for his daughter's release. Cecily's baby-blue leotard glittered as she flew through the spotlight. Hanging upside down from the catch bar, he reached out and clamped his hands on her wrists. During their back beat, her eyes glistened with delight. But as they swung forward, he saw a look of concern cross her face.

Something's wrong, she realized, as screams and angry trumpeting sounded below. When Hector released his daughter for the return, she broke the first rule of flying: Instead of locking her eyes on the approaching bar, she glanced down . . .

Daniel and the bull handler kept prodding Elsa away from the crowd. Confused by their shouting, she lost her footing and stumbled backward into the massive king pole, her colossal weight splintering it like a rotten twig . . .

Cecily's arms flailed, but it was too late. The trapeze bar swung toward her, but she wasn't in position to catch it. Three fingers grasped at the bar, straining to get a grip even as she knew it was futile. In slow motion, she watched the ring finger slip off, followed by the pointer, leaving a single finger holding her weight. The world seemed to rotate in slow motion. Her father's frantic shouts, the audience's screams, and the trumpeting below faded to silence. Only the thudding of her heartbeat remained. Gravity and the angle of the swing defeated her grip. She dropped feet first.

Cecily's toes hit the platform, her heels hanging in midair. Suspended for just a moment, she shrieked, arms flailing, as Jill, Jessica, and Veronica reached out and pulled her to safety.

Her mother gazed into her frightened eyes. "And where do you think you're going?" she asked, pulling her into a tight embrace . . .

Too weak to stand, Elsa pushed with her hind legs but fell back, further damaging the king pole. The strain snapped two main guy wires, their sudden failure sending the pole shifting violently, cracking like a giant nutcracker's grip. It growled as it leaned to a precarious 30-degree angle, working loose several metal stakes and forcing the tent to droop inward. Eight guy wires shuddered under the immense strain, barely keeping the pole from collapsing onto the crowd. The floodgates to pandemonium had been opened, and spectators scattered in every direction.

The bull handler barely had time to brace before Elsa's trunk slammed into him, flipping him onto his back in a cloud of dust. His heart beat frantically as he rolled onto all fours and peered at the bullhook just out of reach. A drop of blood fell from his split lip and darkened the ground between his hands. *This is not the Elsa I know.*

Amid the chaos, three figures burst into the center ring. Lev and Susan shouted to distract Elsa while Dmitri snatched up the bullhook. With Daniel staggering beside him, Dmitri helped drive the elephant back from the fallen handler. But Elsa spun, her eyes locking onto Susan; then she charged.

Screams echoed as Susan stumbled and slammed to the ground, hay tangling in her frizzed-out hair and mouth. Dmitri grappled with Elsa, moving to protect his fallen comrade. Despite his size, Lev rushed forward to help Susan, who could not stop coughing. Just then, Elsa struck Dmitri a fierce blow to the head, sending him reeling as his vision faded into a sea of stars.

Locking eyes with her aggressor, the elephant rushed Daniel. She blared her trumpet with a discordant, sour tone, striking the bullhook from his grasp and sending it soaring several feet. Her distressed black eyes took in the chaos. An unspeakable fear rippled through the big top—one she'd never seen before. Elsa swung her head from side to side, uncertain. She had not meant for this to happen. She played her trumpet to say *Don't be alarmed! I'm not going to hurt you!* Then her eyes found Daniel again, and grievance swelled. She resumed her trumpet playing, reaching higher notes that meant: *This is the man who started it all! He brought on my pain and suffering. He is the one to blame!* She couldn't have said it plainer, but no one was listening. No one cared about her cries of injustice, nor did they try to understand her pain or offer sympathy.

Scrambling to retreat, Daniel tripped and fell, knocking the wind out of his lungs. Elsa lumbered to him, her trumpet sounding with unprecedented intensity. Her left foreleg lifted, ready to smash Daniel's head into the ground.

Blood splattered Daniel like warm summer rain and streaked him with red paint after a mighty thunderclap. His pupils dilated as Elsa towered over him. While her raised foreleg hovered, her trunk unexpectedly went limp. Blood streamed down her rough, wrinkled face as she slowly tipped over like a giant sequoia. Purely on instinct, Daniel rolled to escape the elephant's bulk. The ground shook from the impact of Elsa's 8,000 pounds, sending up a cloud of hay and grit. When the dust settled, they were eye-to-eye, inches apart.

Daniel closed his eyes in relief.

Elsa closed her eyes in death.

The magnificent creature was dead, and Joe ached to know he would never hear her trumpet again. Smoke from the elephant rifle lingered in the air, permeating his clothes and skin. Though her death saddened him, he was relieved Elsa would no longer suffer the ravages of old age. *If only I could be so lucky.* In silent tribute, the circus owner removed his top hat and treasured red coat, laying them beside her massive, lifeless body.

A single tear streaked through the dust on Joe's face.

* * *

High above the circus top, where the severed king pole came to rest, the single black pennant hanging from its tip no longer danced in tandem with the playful wind. It lay limp and lifeless—for no fun is to be had when death takes center stage.

* * *

The next day, the headline from the Abilene Foremost read: Elephant Runs Amok, 4 Die In Disaster!

> In a tragic turn of events, a circus turned into a nightmare as Elsa, the nation's oldest performing elephant, went on a rampage. The chaos unfolded as the massive creature, once a beloved performer, broke free during the show, sending spectators into a frenzy of panic. Among the four dead, Mary Hennessey (12) was trampled by the mob escaping the collapsing tent and elephant. The incident has sparked a debate among animal rights activists and circus attendees: Should old elephants be allowed to perform in circus acts?

In a televised interview, Mary's father, Robert Hennessey, stood before the news crew, his lips quivering. "Elephants over a certain age should be retired from all circuses!" The wind ruffled his gray hair, and his eyes fought to hold back tears. "There must be laws to retire senior animals and prevent tragedies like this!" His gaze bored into the camera, releasing the floodgates.

* * *

Daniel Dewhurst retired from circus life in shame. He left without a proper sendoff, towing his egg camper north on US-277 toward Nebraska, knowing it would take roughly sixteen hours to get home. As the miles rolled by, he thought of Elsa, whose panic had turned the big top into a graveyard. He replayed the moment again and again; the snap of the tent pole, the screams, the stampede. The crew's faces haunted him. Their contemptuous stares made him question whether he truly belonged in their world. He drove in silence, the camper rattling behind him like a coffin on wheels.

During the journey, the first signs of throat complications reared their head. His voice grew hoarse, then raspy, then painful. Concerned, he scheduled a doctor's appointment as soon as he arrived home. In the weeks that followed, stabbing pains sent him through a maze of medical visits. Countless blood tests made him wonder if he had any left in his veins. Eventually, he was diagnosed with glottic carcinoma. Surgeons planned to remove his malignant tumor in his larynx and follow up with aggressive radiation treatments.

Though the surgery succeeded, radiation left his throat raw and ravaged. Insurance spared him financial ruin, but his body was only beginning to break. To further complicate matters, Daniel's health declined rapidly when he developed cirrhosis of the liver, a consequence of years of binge drinking. For the rest of his life, he would need to take synthetic sugar to control his ammonia levels. Day after day, Lactulose tethered him to the toilet, but at least his liver stayed happy.

The 4:05 train whistled to announce its arrival at the Hastings Burlington Station, echoing the town's origins as a late-1870s rail hub where locomotives once departed in five directions daily. Just south of the station, a call bell rang out, its sound drilling into Harriett Picoli's ears like an earwig burrowing into her brain. The way the clapper hit the bell, she swore it was the bong of Big Ben. She heaved her legs off the wicker coffee table, dislodging the stack of hardcover books that served as one leg.

The magazine she'd been avidly reading, featuring the best-dressed and worst-dressed celebrities, slammed onto the floor. She struggled to push up from the sagging, floral-print tuxedo sofa, cookie crumbs raining down. Assigned as caregiver to Daniel Dewhurst by Assuage Hospice Care (AHC), Gretchen stormed toward his room in her uneven, worn-down clogs. Her heavy steps imprinted on the carpet like bear prints in damp soil. She ricocheted down the hallway, her bouncy ringlets slapping her plump cheeks with each plodding step.

Lurching through the doorway, Gretchen barreled into the small, bland room, sending tremors through the walls. Daniel trembled. "Didn't I tell you not to ring the bell more than once? I heard you the first time!" she hollered, arching her left brow. "How do you expect me to clean the kitchen floor with you interrupting me every ten minutes?" Her eyes bored into his like hot pokers, branding him as her property. The flab under her arms jiggled when she planted her hands on her ample hips.

Daniel wished he could speak, but the larynx procedure left him with nothing but grunts and whimpers. *Better this than being dead.* Eyes pleading for mercy, he tried to make her realize he had rung the bell only once, but that was over twenty minutes ago! Daniel lay in bed with his legs crossed, holding his sizzling urine, as if keeping a shaken 2-liter soda bottle from exploding. Though he tried to resist, the urge was overpowering. He clenched his teeth, his face warping with strain. Suddenly, his eyes popped open.

And then it happened.

Gretchen's eyes grew wide. A questioning look. A look of disgust.

He let out a long sigh, and his eyes lost their focus. Everything about him softened, the grimace melting away like a ball of wax on a scorching day, replaced by a smile as relief flowed through him. The warm urine engulfed his senses like a macaque stumbling on a hot spring in the tundra, wiggling his rump deeper into the steam. But then the hot spring died, turning the warmth into bitter, chilling discomfort.

The moment hung in the air.

Gretchen knew precisely what had occurred. In an instant, the fearful look returned to his eyes—that I-did-something-wrong look. A look that knew a beating was in order. She understood the anatomy of the eyes. She was the eye whisperer. When people refused to speak, she relied on their portals to the soul to do the talking.

"Did you wet the bed again? Hmm?" Her voice carried that familiar dread.

Daniel flinched.

"I . . . told . . . you . . . not . . . to . . . wet . . . the . . . bed!" she yelled, her meaty hand slapping him upside the head with each word that spewed from her venomous mouth. Her face twisted with fury. Daniel whimpered and cringed against the barrage of blows, his eyes pleading for an end to the torment.

"Now I need to change the sheets again! Aren't you ashamed of yourself? You make me work *very* hard! I don't think that's fair, Daniel! Do *you* think that's fair?" she asked, her eyes bulging as if she were about to eat him whole. "Well . . . *do* you?"

Daniel looked confused. The deterioration of his memory had aligned with Gretchen's assignment as his aide. No matter how hard he tried to determine her motives for his harsh treatment, he failed to find any answers. Sometimes she overmedicated him, subjecting Daniel to relentless bouts of diarrhea. Other times, she skipped administering his medication because she was immersed in her tabloid magazines, crossword puzzles, and soap operas. On those days, which occurred with increasing frequency, the accumulated ammonia clouded his mind and dulled his motor skills. Even walking often seemed beyond his capacity. Collapsing to the floor only induced another round of beatings.

"Hello?! I can't wait a lifetime!" She grabbed his arm and pulled him up. With rough hands, she stripped off his soaked pajamas, plopped his feeble body on a metal folding chair, and left him trembling in his urine. The urine-drenched sheets were yanked off and flung into the hamper. A fresh sheet cracked as she snapped it in the air, parachuting over the bed. Gretchen never let up. She beat the bed into submission, aggressively tucking the ends of the sheet under the mattress.

* * *

Gretchen had always been bossy. She'd figured out it was easier to don a sizable magisterial crown and force others to do her bidding. But she was also crafty enough to fool people, including her supervisor, who found her delightful and competent in the interview. Her bright, cheerful attitude was a role she played only when necessary. Away from management's prying eyes, her true personality shone through. Gretchen's sneering and constant finger-pointing bred unease among her patients, more than any ulcer-causing bacterium gnawing at the stomach lining. Indeed, a more suitable name for her would have been Gretchen H. Pylori.

When a supervisor from AHC showed up unannounced for a routine check, his gaze lingered on the purple bruises mottling Daniel's skin. Lifting Daniel's arms, Jim traced the string of dark marks running down his shoulder and forearm.

"How on earth did this happen?" he asked.

"I was just as shocked as you are." Gretchen's lie flowed swiftly and naturally. "When I arrived yesterday morning, Mr. Dewhurst was struggling to get out of the bathtub. He tried to bathe without my assistance, even though I've repeatedly told him not to. But you know how much he loves to bathe."

Jim was clueless, but he nodded anyway.

"After I let myself in, I found Daniel slipping and sliding in the bathtub, so I rushed forward and grabbed his arm. I suppose my grip was a little too firm, but I only meant to keep him from drowning. A woman of my stature doesn't know her own strength. In fact, people often ask me if I've ever been a female wrestler." Gretchen grinned at her ingenuity. Her tale clicked into place, so neatly she almost believed it herself. She blinked, puckering her lips.

"Well, the answer is no, but I'm sure I could take down any woman twice my size." She thrust her hip toward him, and the supervisor grinned nervously. She approached Daniel, who lay stunned and helpless in his rumpled bed, and ran her fingers through his thinning hair.

"You should've seen him. He was slippery as a wet noodle! When I lost my grip, he fell and banged his arm against the bathtub. But don't worry. I'm well-trained in treating cuts and bruises. Once I got him out of the tub, I lectured him about the dangers of bathing without my assistance. That's my job. Isn't that right, Mr. Dewhurst?" Gretchen leaned in close and lifted her left eyebrow in warning.

Daniel's eyes focused on her sneering lips, and he recoiled from the hot breath that seared his face. He tried to make sense of the nonsense she'd spun, but it sounded like the mockingbird had stolen another song from a bird in flight. Nevertheless, he decided nodding was the prudent response.

"Great job, Gretchen," said Jim. "Our company needs more caregivers like you. I just need your signature to acknowledge my visit." He handed her his clipboard and a black felt-tip pen.

After signing the form with a smooth flourish, Gretchen showed the supervisor out and stormed back to the bedroom.

Daniel was a prisoner in his own home, unable to escape or call for help. He shuddered as her stomps echoed throughout the house. *This is hell. I've done everything this woman has asked, but nothing satisfies her.*

Gretchen towered over the bed and struck the side of his head, each blow snapping his neck to the side. He whimpered, his head bobbing, trying to avoid the blows.

"Next time I ask you a question, I expect you to answer right away!" she bellowed, her voice reverberating in his ears.

Daniel turned his head away, his gaze settling on the blank wall. At least he didn't have to look at her bulging eyes that popped from their sockets every time she exploded. When she'd first arrived, he had thought Gretchen was like living inside an active volcano, unpredictable and perilous. Now, he thought it was more like standing before a raging bull.

Gretchen stormed out of the bedroom, neglecting Daniel's medication for the third consecutive time. This oversight allowed more toxins to seep into his bloodstream, further deteriorating his fragile mental state. Sometimes, he lay in bed confused and dazed, wondering where he was and how he got there. Other times, she overmedicated him, forcing Daniel to struggle toward the bathroom, gripping his walker for support while his body trembled under the strain.

* * *

Just after dawn, once the battered milk truck had rattled through tis route, Daniel's intestines churned wildly from the previous night's double dose of lactulose, rumbling like a snow-capped mountain on the verge of an avalanche. He tried to hold his bowel movement until Gretchen arrived, but the minutes dragged on.

Please hurry. I can't hold on much longer!

His eyes widened with fear and loathing as sweat poured from his forehead, soaking the pillow beneath him. *Tick. Tick. Tick.* The cheap plastic clock hung askew on the wall, its seconds dragging by. It read 7:46; only a minute had passed since he last looked. The pressure in his colon intensified; his eyes crossed as he clenched his sphincter muscles.

Though doubtful of success, Daniel realized the situation was untenable. He stared at the walker, willing it closer. *If only I could call it to me, like that masked man who whistles for his trusty horse.* He forced himself to sit, legs sliding over the bed's edge. His hand trembled as he reached for the walker. The farther he stretched, the more his fingers shook.

A deep, guttural growl.

He froze, waiting for his stomach's protests to subside before trying again. His heart raced, and his body shivered like a spider's web quivering under the weight of morning dew. Sweat trickled down his neck, soaking his flannel shirt as waves of anxiety and nausea gnawed at him. The looming threat of Gretchen's reprimand lingered at the edge of his thoughts. His fingers found purchase on the walker, and he pulled it close.

I did it!

He let out a long sigh.

Sliding off the bed, he landed off balance and teetered as the walker tipped dangerously. He had no time to spare. His heart pounded wildly as he lurched across the floor, unsteady as a toddler taking his first steps. The aluminum walker rattled in his haste, each step less stable than the last.

Left foot. Right foot.

Left foot. Right foot.

In response to his prayers, Daniel reached the bathroom with no time left. But the cool linoleum floor couldn't hold back the weight of snow rushing down the mountain slope. The surge became an avalanche, cascading down his hairy legs like muddy waters after a torrential downpour. He struggled to yank his soiled pajamas down, his feet zigzagging through the watery excrement until he hit the floor with a painful thump. Slipping from his grasp, the walker clattered against the toilet, then lay on its side, mocking him.

Gretchen H. Picoli entered the kitchen wearing the grin of someone freshly promoted. Caring for Dewhurst was effortless, and she had ensured her position as his caregiver by influencing assignment decisions. Setting her purse on the dining table, she strutted to Daniel's bedroom, lifting each leg as though marching through six inches of snow. When she reached the bedroom, a wave of confusion washed over her at the sight of the unmade bed and missing walker. She scowled. *What the hell is he up to now*? Her ears perked at faint sounds filtering in from the bathroom. Tilting her head, she listened intently. *Aha! There it is again!* It was the scraping of hollow metal against the floor.

Her generous body swayed as she burst through the bathroom door. In an instant, her face contorted into a grotesque spectacle: her eyeballs bulged, and the pupillary sphincter dilated so wide that a blinding halo momentarily overtook her vision. Veins in her temples popped like fireworks. Her jaw dropped, the disc snapping out of place. She couldn't decide whether to scream or collapse. Either way, cardiac arrest seemed preferable to cleaning up this mess!

"You son of a bitch!" she screeched, her stinging tongue flapping like a tattered sail.

Daniel groveled in his excrement, trying to explain. What came out instead were dry, mule-like shrieks, raw with pain. A nurse's clog slammed into his ribcage with a sickening squelch, flipping him onto his side. Her foot jammed into his soiled buttocks before he crashed back down. Gretchen paused, pushed aside a ringlet of hair that blurred her vision, then smacked her lips and pulled up her sleeves. She resumed the assault. She kicked, and kicked, and kicked. The mule shrieked in pain with each blow.

The ex-clown thought she would never stop.

* * *

Friday, September 3, 2004. 8:25 p.m. Day of elephant incident. Evening show canceled.

The tent's interior was as dim as the dark side of the moon. When the man stepped inside, the temperature rose a few degrees, and the pale light over the washbasin illuminated the path to the oval mirror. His heavy footsteps kicked up dust, particles dancing in the light beams as he slowly approached. The mirror's frame curled with timeworn vines and dulled gold, whispering secrets only the past remembered.

He watched intently as his image faded, revealing a dark, luminous cloud that seemed to absorb all light around it. Shadows deepened, creeping closer, a darkness hungry for his soul. The demon's eyes were immense Tahitian pearls, shifting in place under crushing gravity, emitting an eerie, otherworldly glow. Only a twisted mockery of joy lived in those depths, as cold and sharp as a blade. It dwelled in a different dimension, trapped, waiting for the right moment to escape. Though its lips moved as it spoke, its words lagged several seconds, like a poorly dubbed line in a foreign film. The air thickened, suffused with impending doom, as though reality itself were fraying at the edges.

"Releasing the lion and unhitching the trailer went according to plan," the demon snickered, fogging up the mirror. "And hiding a pushpin in the saddle pad was a clever idea."

"Please forgive me for not keeping you better apprised, but there was very little time."

"You did well enough for a mortal. You serve the greater purpose." The creature's brows jumped in wonder, and its mouth gaped in a satisfied grin.

"You are the Doyen of Torture. The Grandmaster of Pain, oh Master," the man said, bowing. "Unfortunately, a young girl by the name of Mary Hennessey was trampled to death . . . "

"That's the easy way out!" the entity boomed, its face swelling tenfold, forcing newly formed jagged teeth against the glass.

The man jumped back as a sudden blast of anger erupted, kicking up dirt and swaying the tent walls like a fast-approaching storm.

"Death is quick and easy! I want slow, cruel torture that makes people cry out in mortal agony!"

The man shielded his face with his forearm before the sound wave could traverse the glass, eyes shut tight. His teeth clenched, lips tensed. The floor trembled beneath him as the mirror jolted and swung on the single nail. The gust blew back his hair, sending him staggering.

When it subsided, the man cast his gaze into the mirror. The reflection revealed the despotic beast to be as ancient as the forbidden fruit, ageless as time itself. "Yes, Master. It shan't happen again," he replied, bowing his head.

"A pot boils only that which it contains; outside of that, the flames are an easy way out." As the Grandmaster of Pain retreated, its face shrank to fit within the frame's confines. "There have been many great moments in history when tormenting people was a thrill, an exciting game employing many forms of torture, but none gave me more pleasure than the era you mortals call medieval times." A peal of wicked laughter. A hearty sigh. "I hunger for those times. You must *recruit* more people. I have more torment to dispense," it cackled, fluttering the man's hair with each evil huff of laughter.

"Yes, Emperor of Agony."

As the man turned to leave, the demon's vicious tittering faded into the dimension from which it came. He stopped by the entrance, lifting his hat. Shoving the flap open, he stepped into the night, where the warm air wrapped its fingers.

A boy pedaling through the circus grounds skidded to a stop. "Hey, Mister, did you feel that tremor?"

Joe Milagro's eyes, as black as pestilence, searched the boy's angelic face. His top hat stood tall, and he jutted his chin, dusting off his long red coat. Its tail slithered like that of a plague-infested rat. "'Fraid not, young man. Say . . . Ever think about joining the circus?"

The boy's hazel eyes flashed with a glimmer of excitement.

LA BRUJA MALDITA

Tuesday, May 10, 2005. 8:36 a.m.

A crow, its feathers black as the night, soared over the bustling district of Los Angeles. With its wings fanned like fingers grasping air, the bird jetted past MacArthur Park, a feeding ground overrun by pigeons. The wind murmuring in its face, its keen eyes observing, the dark silhouette glided over Koreatown. Ignoring the strip mall at West 6th Street and Alexandria Avenue, a spot habitually frequented for crumbs, the crow circled the towering pine trees Mrs. Willow planted twenty years ago and climbed higher. It swooped under the orange 76 ball at Western Avenue and 8th Street, then banked sharply west past Crenshaw Boulevard. Hovering like a seasoned sailor over a vast ocean of weather-beaten telephone poles, the majestic crow docked and anchored its gaze on a smashed window below. The bird bobbed to get a better view and celebrated the discovery of its favorite prey with a hearty shake of its tail feathers.

Diving like a daredevil off a towering cliff, the crow glided onto the bedroom windowsill, where broken glass lay in a mosaic beneath its claws. Its sharp, beady eyes scanned the room, landing on the plump bullfrog perched on the iron sleigh bed. The bullfrog licked its bulbous eyes and resumed its sit-and-wait hunting pose. A gnawing ache stirred in the crow's belly, and its beak clacked with anticipation like a Geiger counter near uranium. Yet the bullfrog remained still, ignoring the bird. Knowing the risk, the crow hesitated. Despite its strong desire to feast on the frog's succulent flesh, the crow reluctantly decided against the attempt.

Detective Andrew Baca and his partner, Greg Sanders, stood by the bed, scanning the frilly pink room. Baca tilted his head, eying the crow, his hands resting on his pudgy waist. His coat emphasized slumped shoulders and a round belly. Despite the extra weight, his strength and agility let him traverse even the most challenging terrain with surprising ease.

The pink drapes had been roughly pushed aside and hung outside the windowsill in disarray, evidence that someone had jumped out. The stench of feces and sulfur seeped into the plush carpet and deep into the bedspread threads. Several burnt spots marked the rug where the sulfur stench was strongest. Imitating the call of an angry bull, the frog blinked and belched its deep jug-o-rum call, overpowering the blaring television. Baca frowned. *That's interesting. Who ties a frog to a bed?*

The crow watched cautiously as Andrew directed his attention to the window. Large glass fragments splintered under his weight like stale pretzels, startling the bird. It hopped away, ruffling its feathers. Convinced the frog was out of reach, the crow gave one last series of Geiger counter clicks with its beak and took flight. Its keen eyes fixed on the city, the crow let out a scolding cry and climbed higher, vanishing into the sky.

"I've never heard a crow make that sound," said his tall, slender partner, scrunching his freckled face.

"The call of contentment," Andrew replied, examining the scattered glass across the carpet. "They feed on seeds, fruits, and vegetables but are also fond of lizards, snakes, and frogs. Even spotting a potential meal can be enough to stir excitement."

The leash around the frog's plump waist prevented it from leaping. Its back was covered with tiny bumps, and its protruding eyes shone like two shooters in a game of Ringer. Andrew snapped pictures of the frog, the shattered window, and the scorched carpet. Satisfied, he said, "There's nothing else to see here." On his way out, he extended a white-gloved hand to turn off the television, which had been blaring one of Southern California's most recognizable free mattress commercials.

The detectives entered the living room, where a female officer was interrogating a young blonde on the sofa, dazed. Someone had draped a blanket over her half-naked body, but she held it only loosely at her throat, leaving her brown-and-white striped bra and panties visible. They skirted the wooden coffee table, adorned with a bronze sculpture of a man and woman locked in a kiss.

Rising from her crouch, Officer Williams acknowledged Detective Baca with a nod. "She seemed okay at first, but the more I questioned her, the more frightened she got." They looked at the woman.

"No, no, no," she cried, rocking and shaking uncontrollably.

"Her name is Bridgette Witherspoon," the officer said, handing the woman's ID to the detective. Her soft brown eyes swept over him, slow and calculating, impressed by his analytical mind and calm demeanor. "She works at the Kearny Heights Country Club as a cocktail waitress. According to Miss Witherspoon, her boyfriend, Erin Carmichael, was turned into a frog last night. By a witch."

Andrew Baca maintained a stern, thoughtful expression. Like the back of his gray cashmere coat, the corners of his brown eyes were wrinkled, but they betrayed no surprise at the officer's comment. His calm demeanor stemmed from his passion for accuracy, even in the face of the bizarre. Known for his ability to sift through each case with a fine-tooth comb, he had solved complex cases that stumped other detectives. He even carried such a comb in his back pocket to gloat.

"Miss Witherspoon," he said, dropping to one knee and gazing into her tear-glossed blue eyes. Her face was pale and smeared with tears, yet most unsettling was the stench of feces as he leaned toward her. "Can you tell me what you saw? Who was dressed as a witch?"

Bridgette didn't respond. Her delicate upturned nose hinted at privilege and arrogance, but her soft blonde hair was in disarray, tangled like windblown silk. If not for his impartial stance, he'd have considered her the sort who would look down on others, living off Daddy's wealth without a twinge of guilt. A contusion along the left side of her face suggested she'd been struck with a blunt object. Her skin reeked as if she'd been plunged into the earth's bowels, steeped in suffocating decay. *I thought the fly-infested dairy farms in Ontario smelled terrible. This young lady unquestionably takes the cake!*

"Did someone douse you with a chemical?" Andrew patiently continued his grilling, but she didn't answer. He gently placed a finger under her chin, trying to align her gaze with his.

"Aside from the blow to the face, she has no other visible marks on her body," offered Officer Williams, hooking her thumbs into her belt.

The detectives exchanged a glance, both recognizing Bridgette had been silenced by trauma. They didn't expect her to speak; her body language spoke of horror too deep for words as she rocked back and forth. Deeply concerned for the victim, Andrew requested an ambulance. Just as he turned to step outside for some fresh air, the distraught woman broke her silence.

"She . . . breathed . . . on me," said Bridgette, her voice a childish whimper and the rocking picking up pace. Her stare remained chillingly vacant as if her spirit had been whisked away, lost in the void, never to return.

Andrew stopped, his breath hitching as he snapped his gaze back over his shoulder. Bridgette was surfacing from the cavern into which she had plunged. Ignoring the bullet wound lingering since the arrest of two bank robbers, he limped toward her before she could fall back into despair. His kneecap twinged as he knelt to face her again. Bridgette's eyes focused for the first time that morning. His kind face, with a diminutive mole on the right cheek and large crinkly earlobes, seemed to plead, *Tell me your troubles. I will carry you through hard times.*

Bridgette gave a strangled gasp. "She breathed . . . her stench on me . . . and she melted Erin's face . . . with her vomit. Then she turned him into a frog." Her shoulders jerked as sobs escaped her.

Andrew placed a hand on her shoulder. "Who did this?" he asked, peering into her wide cerulean eyes. "I'm here to help you, Bridgette. Can you tell me who did this to you?"

"The witch!" she wailed, her voice echoing.

* * *

Bridgette struggled to answer questions all morning. No one in their right mind would have believed that a witch had flown into her bedroom, turned her boyfriend into a frog, then leaped from the window onto a levitating broomstick and soared off into the night sky. Yet she had seen the hideous green creature—its grotesque form burned into her memory. No matter how hard she tried, she couldn't erase the gruesome images.

With their diverse ethnicities, Bridgette and her best friends, María Elena Montes, Daiyu Chu, and Shalonda Phillips, were known as the UN Squad in high school. They were the snobbiest of cliques, refusing to let anyone else in. Nevertheless, Bridgette was sure she had never done anything to merit such a wrathful assault from a witch . . . except . . . She blinked. Maybe in tenth grade: Julie Soto, the nerd with oversized buttocks. Their scorn was born of envy; Julie was undoubtedly the best gymnast in school. She'd been the only one to master every tricky gymnastic drill: the aerial cartwheel, the fly spring, the Arabian front, the complex press handstand, all in just days. She was agile, and even the UN Squad didn't measure up to her.

One afternoon at a meet, Julie was working on the uneven bars. She had just executed a flyaway half-turn, followed by a strong backswing to generate the momentum for a Gienger, when the UN Squad stepped up to ridicule her. Chanting in time with the rhythm of Julie's swinging maneuvers, the four girls lined up in a staggered cheerleading formation and recited their poetic injustice:

> Julie Soto has a big butt
> That sticks out like a boar's ass
> You don't want her walking by
> 'Cause she'll kill you when she passes gas

Resplendent in their blue and white gym clothes, the girls turned in unison, thrusting their shapely buttocks out before smacking their hands on their cheeks. A roar of delight went up in the gymnasium, electrifying the student body. Cheers surged through the crowd, boosting the UN Squad's clout as they jumped on the bandwagon of scorn. Several boys hooted and catcalled while the girls laughed hysterically at poor Julie.

Abandoning her routine, Julie made a clumsy dismount and bolted, tears of humiliation streaming down her face. Thomas de la Cruz was the only one who followed her to offer comfort.

Unlike her classmates, who exuded confidence and favored fashionable accessories and well-fitting clothing, Julie wore hideous sweaters and baggy pants that looked like hand-me-downs, often faded and frayed. No other girl in school would be caught dead in them, or even be seen with Julie and her dreadful frizzy hair. She stood drenched in an unforgiving storm of emotions. This inhumane treatment flooded her, and it would take more than forty days and forty nights of therapy to recover. *But what about the dove? Would I also have to send out a dove to see if my tears had receded from the ground?*

Julie's most prominent features were her buttocks, a beacon slicing through the night. Her shapely protrusion seemed buoyant. Students often joked that if she fell on her behind, she'd bounce right back up. No doubt, a joke meant to last a lifetime.

Despite being a remarkable scholar, she struggled with social engagement, often feeling isolated. She daydreamed about running away, imagining she lived in a cave with a family of friendly bears, sipping tea and singing cheerful songs. *Bears are friendly, furry creatures.* She would know, her room was full of plush ones.

In sixth grade, she experienced her first social humiliation. One morning, she had the brilliant idea to wear her mother's stockings instead of her usual socks to school. They gave her newfound confidence. She studied herself in the mirror and liked what she saw. *They'll all accept me now that I'm fashionable and chic. Why wouldn't they?* Julie was sure she was on the brink of social acceptance. She grabbed her red backpack and strode out the door, greeted by chirping birds and the sun's radiant warmth.

When she arrived at school, sniggers and snide comments greeted Julie. She stood immobile against the playground fence, acerbic words clinging to her like tungsten darts. Unlike most cold, indifferent stone statues, this one had a delicate heart, causing her porcelain, ivory eyes to well up. Unable to bear the ridicule, she fled across the school grounds, tears streaming. Her feet hammered the asphalt, carrying her straight into the principal's office, where she telephoned her mother for help. But the fresh pair of socks did little to spare her from further disgrace.

Julie suffered another embarrassing moment in the ninth grade when her choir instructor, Mr. Jeff Byrnes, called on her to sing in front of the class. The students were restless, and the teacher's repulsive armpit odor eclipsed the humid room like a thick quilt. Julie rose slowly, shuddering at the thought of singing before forty pairs of eyes. She'd hoped to finish the year without singing, but that would've been too easy. Her head hung low. Butterflies rippled in her stomach; her cheeks quivered.

"Mistuh Byrnes," Julie said through clenched teeth, her eyes riveted on his scuffed shoes. "I can't zing 'cause my cheeks are shaking." She lisped, wishing she could crawl beneath his desk, unseen.

"Why don't you sit down to stop your cheeks from shaking," he replied with a devilish grin.

A cacophony of laughter ensued. Thinking it was harmless, Mr. Byrnes retold the story in each of his other classes, until Julie became the laughingstock of the school.

A year later, she endured yet another humiliation. While walking down the hallway, a student rushing to class collided with her, sending her books skittering across the floor. When she bent to gather them, laughter erupted around her. The student body pointed with disdain at her round, firm buttocks, as if her body were a punchline.

"Hey, Julie. You've got daisies growing out of your ass!" one loud student yelled.

The laughter stretched on endlessly. Julie's head throbbed. Laughing mouths and pointing fingers met her gaze wherever she turned. Even Peggy, her long face reminiscent of a neighing horse, joined the mockery. She wanted to disappear, to hide forever. But there was no escaping the gut-wrenching ignominy. Only after arriving home did she notice the rip in her jeans. Her daisy-print underwear had been on display the entire time.

One day, Theresa Ríos was seething after falling off the beam in a gymnastics competition. Fueled by a toxic mix of jealousy and humiliation, she stormed toward Julie, brimming with malice. "I'm going to teach you a lesson after school," she spat, her voice shaking.

Secure in her victory, Julie met Theresa's fiery gaze with unwavering calm. Strength flickered in her eyes. "True skill isn't about winning," she said softly, raising her eyebrows in empathy. "It's about hard work and good sportsmanship."

With that, Julie turned and walked away, leaving Theresa seething.

As they exited the classroom at the end of the day, Theresa grabbed her opponent by the shoulder and shoved her aside. Julie's slender back slammed against the brick wall, sending pins and needles down her spine. Rage surged through her as her schoolbooks hit the ground with a hollow thud. Instinct took over. She clutched Theresa's hair and drove a fist into her tormentor's stunned face in a burst of angry blows. Julie towered over her cowering adversary, nostrils flaring like an enraged bull.

Damn, that felt good.

As she watched the blood trickling from Theresa's nose, a new sensation swelled inside her. This marked the birth of the new Julie Soto—the catalyst for a bold new persona. That day, she vowed never to endure abuse again. *Those UN Squad bitches better watch out*, she smirked, wiping her knuckles on Theresa's sweater.

* * *

Founded in 1959, Chronicle Motion Pictures emerged as a prominent Hollywood studio, overcoming challenges that left many competitors behind. Initially located in Albuquerque, New Mexico, the studio expanded rapidly with the success of its romantic movies. In 1971, it relocated to a 150-acre lot in Pasadena, solidifying its presence in Hollywood. The remarkable special effects in its films attracted Lucio Soto, who joined the booming company to combine his love for science and technology. He found his footing in the industry and dedicated his life to it.

When Lucio was a child, his parents moved to Hollywood, California, where he developed a passion for mechanics. After graduating from high school, he began his career as a special effects technician for the studio. In 1961, he met and married Elvira Reyes, who appreciated his quiet, reserved nature and droopy bloodhound expression. Their marriage was soon blessed with two daughters, Leticia and Julie. At the age of twenty, Leticia left her parents' modest home in Echo Park to pursue her dream of singing in a rock band. The following year, Julie surprised her mother by walking away from dentistry to chase her dream of culinary arts. While Elvira hoped Julie would establish her own dental practice, Lucio supported his daughters' freedom to fail and learn through trial.

* * *

Tuesday, May 10, 2005. 10:30 a.m.

The sun had burned away the last wisps of fog, revealing softly curving hills bursting with vibrant hues of green. Butterflies flitted among the wild blossoms edging the parking lot, their delicate wings catching the light as they danced in the shimmer of morning.

"To what do I owe this honor?" Lucio gave his daughter a smile that looked all the more fragile under his sagging eyes.

"Dad, I always count on you for my school projects," Julie said, pressing a tender kiss to his unshaven cheek. "My twenty-fifth reunion is coming up, and I want to make it the most memorable one ever."

"I'm still recovering from the last one," he said with a chuckle. "Remember when you blew up the volcano after adding too many chemicals?"

She chortled, her eyes crinkling under her elegantly arched brows. "How could I forget? It took me three days to get all the gunk out of my hair."

Lucio escorted his daughter to studio 3C, a short stroll past storage facilities housing props from *The Puzzle Syndicate*, *White Crow*, and *Funnel* were stored. Some of his creations had garnered recognition and awards, making him a sought-after designer in the industry.

Several months ago, his daughter had asked him to create a green witch mask for a cosplay event, one with bulging veins to conceal narrow tubing along the jawline and tiny ports at both corners of the mouth for squirting liquid. *Complex but feasible*, he thought.

Over four nights, working as methodically as a spider spinning its web, he crafted the mask to Julie's specifications. In his work with prosthetic faces, Lucio often cut half the eye off a sewing needle, creating a miniature oyster fork. Then he shortened one tine and bent the tip of the longer one into a U.

With this delicate instrument, he could isolate a single strand of hair and punch it through the mask in one swift motion. This halved the production time and created a far more realistic effect.

The sun's rays blazed through three skylights, casting fearsome silhouettes onto the floor. A soft hum suffused the vast space when Lucio flicked the light switch. He fumbled through his keychain, sifting through a tangle of metal until his fingers brushed against the security cage key. "Now, tell me again why you need a smoke screen?" he asked.

"I want to make a grand, colorful entrance," she said, her eyes lifting with a quiet plea. "I have some great ideas to transform the reunion into a memorable one."

"Well, in that case, I have just the right thing." The security cage door slid open, rattling against his shoe. He reached inside and pulled out a long metal cylinder with two prongs at one end and a label indicating the smoke color. "This cartridge produces a striking display of thick gold smoke that lasts forty-five seconds."

Julie studied it for a moment. "Can I take the red one too?" she asked, testing her luck.

Happy to oblige, Lucio handed his daughter the second cartridge and relocked the security cage. He spared her the pyro paperwork and hazmat fee. "I don't mind helping my little girl with her projects." His usually insensitive eyes lit up as he cracked a smile. There was plenty of love behind them, but it took Julie's presence to chisel through and let it show. Then, with a wary glance around, he added, "But there are some things I won't be able to borrow anymore. The studio is monitoring activities more closely because something was stolen a few weeks ago."

"Really?" She arched a brow. "What was it?"

Lucio, the sole caretaker of the storage facilities, was concerned about getting another write-up. "An expensive pulley," he said, guilt flickering across his face. "A device used in the *White Crow* films that hoists the vigilante into the air. The studio needs it because *White Crow: Challenge of the Ninja* is in preproduction."

"I'm sure it'll show up eventually," she said, kissing her father goodbye. "By the way, since I'm on the reunion committee, would it be okay if I stayed at your place until the event is over? It'd be much easier than commuting to Azusa every day."

"You don't need to ask," he said, shoving his hands in his pockets. In his eyes, Julie could do no wrong. Her footsteps echoed as she left, cylinders tucked under her arm. Before leaving the building, she turned to face him one last time. Lucio watched her, remembering the painful days of frizzy hair and name-calling. Now, she was an intelligent, striking woman, and he'd never been prouder.

* * *

Tuesday, May 10, 2005. 8:35 p.m.

Though the volume was low, the television's news report on the upcoming anniversary of John Lennon's death remained audible to Mr. and Mrs. Phillips. Their daughter, Shalonda, sat on the leather love seat with her legs crossed, talking on the phone with Daiyu Chu about the recent assault at Bridgette's home. As a focused young woman juggling college and part-time work, Shalonda lived with her parents to save on tuition.

Mrs. Phillips sat up after the segment ended. "Someone should make 'anniversary' into a negative aspect. You can't say that this is the twenty-fifth anniversary of John Lennon's death! What's so happy about that?"

A loud explosion startled them, rattling the large family portrait hanging over the bookcase and ripping the side door off its hinges. The door soared across the living room, splintering a wooden console table in the foyer.

"Ahhh!" Both women cried out.

Shalonda let the phone slip from her grasp, clamping a trembling hand over her mouth.

"What was that? Did something explode? Hello?" Daiyu's voice crackled from the tiny speaker.

Mr. Phillips sprang to his feet and spewed every known obscenity. But then, an unexpected shock wave crashed over him, freezing him in place. "What the hell?" His deep mahogany face contorted with fear, as though he'd seen the devil stroll through the shattered doorway.

Snickering, a witch planted her feet in his living room, bold as a garden gnome. Her eye sockets were as black as coal, and veins branched like ancient tree roots beneath her skin. Dead leaves and twigs clung to her brittle hair, stiff with decay. Her purple dress fanned out from her waist as she hobbled forward, never breaking her menacing gaze.

"The opposite of anniversary, dearie, is demise-versary!" the witch shrieked, her voice slicing through the air. She cackled a dreadful tune and, with the point of a finger, set off another explosion that hurled Mr. Phillips across the room and slammed his brawny body against the wall. Then she pointed at Mrs. Phillips, who followed her husband with a mighty blast detonated at her feet. Her slim physique struck the wall with a thump before collapsing onto the back of the love seat. Shalonda stared in disbelief, unable to turn away, her lips trembling. She glanced at her mother's limp body, and with a sudden adrenaline rush, she sprinted up the stairs.

Cackling, the witch lifted her velvet dress and dashed with long, graceful strides out the side exit to a waiting broom. Gripping the broom's handle, she rocketed skyward like a winged fury unbound, then plunged headfirst through Shalonda's bedroom window, spraying glass fragments across the carpet. The witch cartwheeled and backflipped, striking a perfect finishing pose with her back arched, legs together, and arms up by her ears. Her acrobatics completed, the witch eyed Shalonda's quivering body with a grin that curdled the air. She clutched the terrified girl by the hair and swung her against the sliding closet door, ripping it off its metal track.

"Aghh!" Shalonda bellowed.

The witch giggled and brought her hands to her chest, mimicking a mouse on its hind legs.

"Do you remember me, my dear?" she asked, glancing sideways and wetting her bottom lip with her slimy tongue.

Shalonda sobbed, her breathing quick and shallow. "I don't . . . know you," she croaked.

"Let me refresh your memory, sweet girl."

The witch brought her filthy green hand to her lips and snickered. Turning her back on Shalonda, she leaned forward, jutting her meaty buttocks outward, presenting them as though offering them on a silver platter. She paused, then recited the old taunt:

Shalonda Phillips has a big butt
That sticks out like a boar's ass
You don't want her walking by
'Cause she'll kill you when she passes gas

Shalonda, whose butt was shapely but not as round as the witch's, vaguely remembered the incident from tenth grade. Beads of sweat rolled down her face. "J-Julie," she said in a quivering voice. "Is that you?"

The witch opened her green mouth wide and vomited on her. Shalonda shrieked in agony, her eyes burning from the noxious fluid. Overwhelmed, she dropped to the floor, her long legs flailing like a fish out of water. Calmly, the witch reached into her pocket and took out a live bullfrog mottled with gray. Its impassive, boulder-like eyes stared into infinity. She tied a tether around its webbed hind feet and secured the other end to the bedpost, where the bullfrog sat, unmoving.

Shalonda lay on the floor, writhing in pain. She felt the witch looming over her, basking in her fear. Then, suddenly, the oppressive presence vanished, and an eerie silence followed. She stopped whimpering and held her breath. *Is she really gone? Vanished just as quickly as she appeared?*

Unable to see, Shalonda shifted her head side to side, listening for sound. She sat up slowly and recoiled as the huge, hairy wart on the witch's nose touched her own. As her lips parted in silent terror, the witch hissed and breathed a bowel stench on the girl. She slung Shalonda's unresisting body over her shoulder, hopped through the windowsill onto her broomstick, and zipped toward the thickest branch of a towering avocado tree.

The corner of the witch's upper lip curled with the loftiest of scorn as she steadied Shalonda on a tree limb. "That's a thirty-foot drop. Stay still. Unless, of course, you'd prefer to plummet to your death," she sneered.

Terrified, the girl whimpered, certain the witch could turn her into a frog with a mere flick of her finger. That's what the rumors claimed. The witch had supposedly attacked her best friend and transformed her sex-craved boyfriend, Erin Carmichael, into a bullfrog. While the story was fascinating, it might be flawed, considering it came from a woman who smoked a lot of pot. In an instant, the witch had encased Shalonda in a massive duct tape cocoon before vanishing.

Later that evening, Julie Soto removed her frizzy wig and green mask, breaking the spirit gum's hold on her face. As she looked in the mirror, she hardly recognized herself. Gone was the dull, lifeless mop everyone knew; now it was straight and full of luster. The nerdy girl with a large butt had transformed into a sexy, radiant woman, brimming with long-overdue confidence. Her black leotard hugged every curve of her body and shimmered in the soft light, showcasing the sleek muscle tone she had gained from years of rigorous gymnastics.

* * *

Wednesday, May 11, 2005. 5:10 p.m.

Julie grabbed the green mask and slipped it on. As she'd requested, her father had disguised tubing as veins along the jawline, leaving a 24-inch slack beyond the neckline. Already wearing her custom leotard with snap-in clips, she snapped the remaining tubing across her shoulders and down her arms, then inserted the ends into the wrist-mounted triggers.

After inserting an aerosol container of capsaicin spray into the right mechanism, she flexed her hand to test the metal trigger at the knuckles. A violent jet of lacrimatory agent blasted from one corner of her mouth, making her step back. On her other wrist, she slid in a similar container with the foulest stench of feces. She didn't test that one, not in her room. With it, she could finally seek revenge on her tormentors. Those cruel people who made vulgar comments about her butt were now going to reap the benefits of smelling like one.

She slipped into her witch dress, swaying her hips to admire the shimmer of the outer charmeuse. The ripstop nylon beneath, ideal for zero porosity, rustled softly as it settled into place. A lace front concealed the mask's flap, and the sleeves were long and wide. Two plastic handles were secured at her waist, each tethered by suspension lines that threaded through hidden channels and connected to the hem of her skirt. When pulled, the handles lifted the rear of the dress like rigging on a kite, catching the wind and snapping it into the curved arc of a paraglider. Ideal should the situation demand escape.

Three pockets held her tools of performance: smoke bombs, balls of C4, and a very irritable bullfrog. Standing tall in black lace-up boots, the dress projected power—cold, ruthless power that only Victorian Goth could provide. Julie flashed a wicked smile at her reflection before starting her reign of terror.

* * *

Wednesday, May 11, 2005. 7:28 p.m.

A waxing crescent moon softly illuminated the night sky, revealing a spray of stars. Crunching to a stop in the alley behind Daiyu Chu's house, the compact SUV with dark-tinted windows veered slightly left. *Damn it. That better not be a nail in my tire.* Dressed like she was heading to a Halloween masquerade, Julie stepped out of the car and was hit with the overwhelming stink of skunk. After placing a straw broom, the pulley from the *White Crow* set, and a 40-inch black aluminum rod on the cement block wall, she backed up to get a running start for a cartwheel leading into a backflip that landed her seated on the wall. She swung her legs over and silently dropped the five feet to the ground.

After retrieving the items from the wall, she slipped quietly to the house, looking up at the bedroom window, where Daiyu seemed to be watching a Chinese game show. Rock music blared from a neighbor's window. *That racket will provide some good cover, considering the damage I'm going to cause.* Her eyes narrowed into slits, glinting with determination as she aimed the spear directly overhead. The spring coil ejected the spearhead and lobbed it into a thick tree limb, where its four prongs burrowed in deep.

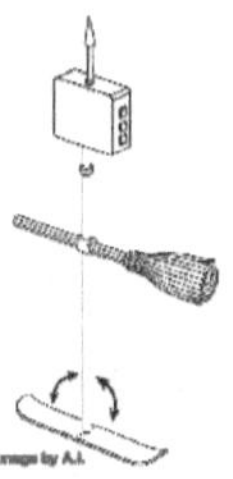
Image by A.I.

Julie fastened the metal rod to the pulley and affixed the broom horizontally to a clip, giving the illusion of a floating broom. She unfolded the ski-shaped platform at the base of the rod and balanced on one foot; from afar, the witch appeared to be sitting comfortably on a broomstick. She pressed the retrieve button, and the pulley lifted her until she was flush with the window. Pushing against the windowsill with her left leg, she swung out like a clock pendulum, somersaulted through the window on the downswing, and landed in a superhero crouch. Shards of glass sprayed across the wooden floor.

"Aaah!" Daiyu shrieked, sheer terror blazing in her eyes. Her body trembled uncontrollably, and her knees threatened to buckle under the weight of fear. She clutched her chest, trying to steady her frantic heartbeat. Her eyes darted around the room, searching for escape. Cowering, she couldn't help but glance into the witch's dark, unfathomable eyes. If the rumors were true, she didn't want to become the next victim. *I can't be a frog! Green is not my color.*

In a dramatic shuffle, the hag turned her back on Daiyu and ignited the lighter she had taped to her palm. She lit the fuse to an explosive and tossed it at her high school bully. The blast sent the girl soaring, slamming her against the dresser with brute force. Her sleek black hair blew back and then plunged forward before she collapsed on the floor.

With a sly grin stretching across her face, the wicked witch glided toward the door, her bony fingers twitching with anticipation. She paused after cracking it open, her gnarled hands resting against the frame as she listened to the confused din of voices racing up the stairs. Reaching into a pocket, her fingers closed around a smoke bomb. In one swift motion, she hurled it to the ground, where it erupted into a thick cloud of smoke.

Daiyu's parents could be heard asking if she was okay in their native Chinese tongue. "你沒事吧?" Without hesitation, Mr. Chu burst into his daughter's room, demanding an explanation. "告訴我發生了什

麼事?" His mouth was askew like grandma's sloping hat during Sunday service. He waved his hand to clear the smoke, his head oscillating like a lawn sprinkler.

"Hissss!" The witch emerged from the smoke screen, and Mr. Chu recoiled. His mouth opened in an O as round as his terrified eyes. Flexing her hand back against the trigger, the mace traveled up her right arm, over her shoulder, and into the mask, where it spewed from one aluminum tip. Daiyu's father emitted a piercing cry and clawed at his burning, watery eyes, now rendered utterly blind. Mrs. Chu staggered back, sure the witch had vomited on his face.

"Aah!" She turned to run.

"Not so fast, my precious." The witch grabbed another explosive, lit the fuse, and hurled it in Mrs. Chu's direction. Its detonation sent her airborne like a marionette with cut strings, arching through the air before hitting the wall and sliding, unconscious, to the floor.

Pleased with the mayhem, the witch returned to the bedroom and slammed the door shut to muffle Mr. Chu's screams. *Now for the finishing touch.* She withdrew a frog from a pocket, fastened a string around its leg, and tied it to the bedpost. *This should give them something to gossip about.*

Daiyu slumped sideways against the dresser, her face serene.

"Isn't that priceless?" The witch's squinting eyes leered at her. "I have the perfect retribution for you." She crept closer with a chuckle, careful not to rouse her. When her left hand flexed, the mechanism sent a burst of liquid stench up her arm, over her shoulder, and into the mask. It sprayed from the aluminum tip and coated Daiyu's face with filth.

After struggling to hoist Daiyu over her shoulder, the witch trudged to the window and laid the girl across the sill. She stepped onto the floating platform and adjusted the height, then hefted the unconscious body back over her shoulder with a grunt. With a flick of the control, the pulley kicked into reverse, hoisting the witch and her limp quarry skyward. To anyone watching from the side, it might have seemed a witch had leapt onto her broomstick and vanished into the night. Minutes later, Daiyu hung from a knotted oak limb, twenty-five feet off the ground, bound tight in a duct tape cocoon.

* * *

Wednesday, May 11, 2005. 9:05 p.m.

With velvet night enveloping the living room, the silence was broken only by the steady ticking of the clock on the wall and the intermittent clinking rhythm of ice cubes dropping into the freezer bin. Julie reached her parents' home exhausted and sweaty from her nocturnal adventure. She quietly closed the back door, hurried past the china cabinet, and entered her old room. Feeling relieved after finishing another task, she placed her purse beside her sunglasses on the dresser and tossed the duffel bag on the neatly made bed. In the distance, a siren wailed, likely a consequence of her recent exploits.

In less than a week, Julie had terrorized three girls from the UN Squad without getting caught. Though long overdue, sweet revenge put a wicked smile on her face. The excruciating pain and anger from high school had twisted her heart. Something had to be done, something nefarious to erase the memories from her mind. Her tormentors had no right to ridicule her. They hadn't cared that she was helpless, alone, and humiliated.

But now things had changed. She had vowed to hold the UN Squad accountable for their actions, even to the point of inflicting bodily harm. With her mission nearly complete, she was almost ready to put her past anguish behind her and move on with her life.

Eager to try on her newly arrived theatrical contact lenses, Julie tore open the package, fingers tingling. After thoroughly washing her hands, she inserted the scleral lenses into her eyes and stared at her reflection to marvel at the effect. Their large size encased the whites of her eyes with a vivid, blood-red hue, suggesting bleeding arteries. She appeared wickedly sinful, the true incarnation of evil. A mischievous grin played on her lips. *These are perfect for the reunion. Even better than the black ones.* She could hardly wait to see their expressions, but first, she had to take care of one more bully.

Julie had just started wiping the spirit gum from her face and neck when a sudden knock at the door startled her. "Just a moment!" she hollered, dropping the cotton ball in the sink and snatching up her sunglasses. She opened the door and gaped. Thomas de la Cruz! Several inches taller and much more filled out than she remembered, but definitely Thomas.

"I hope you don't mind me dropping by. I saw your mom at the grocery store this afternoon. She told me you're staying here this week for the reunion, so I thought I'd stop by to see how you're doing," Thomas said, his hands stuffed deep into the pockets of his faded jeans.

He'd been let in by her father, who'd disappeared down the hall without a word, leaving them standing alone at the threshold of her room.

Julie was speechless. She could see the same crooked smile tugging at the corners of his lips, yet he shuffled his feet with uncertainty.

"So, how are you?" he asked to fill the silence. *Ugh, why would I ask that? What a stupid question.* He could see she was fine. And by fine, he meant gorgeous. Her hair was beautiful now, like one of those models in a shampoo commercial that promised healthier, fuller, shinier locks. *And that figure!* It would knock any man's socks off, and maybe his shorts, if he were lucky. Even in the dim light, he could see the bulge of her pubic hair and her large nipples pressing against her leotard. Her enviable figure was as smooth as her lips, and when she turned sideways, her most salient feature, those firm buttocks, shone like a beacon. Thomas's face turned bright red. His heart fluttered.

"I'm fine, I guess!" she said with a shrug, then laughed.

Thomas laughed with her. *You got that right*! "What's with the sunglasses?"

"Oh, these?" she giggled. "I got soap in my eyes while showering, and now they sting like crazy. They're . . . super-sensitive to light and completely . . . red," she stammered, immediately regretting the comment.

"May I come in?"

"Where are my manners?" Julie laughed nervously. Her hand lingered on his bicep when she pulled him inside. During the years of abuse, Thomas had been the only person in school who showed her compassion, and she liked him for that. She'd fantasized about fervent encounters with him, their bodies locked together, discovering each other's passions. But he was too blind to see the pleading in her eyes.

"You have something gooey on your face," he said, the finger that brushed her cheek sending a shiver up her spine.

"It's acne medication," she said, dropping her gaze so he wouldn't see the rush of desire. "When it dries, the film peels away oil and dirt. Do you want to feel it?"

Thomas was caught with his hand in the cookie jar; he'd been gazing at her breasts. Julie guided his trembling hand to her cheek and laid it gently over the spirit gum, reveling in the warmth of his touch as it seeped into her skin like morning dew softening thirsty petals. Her eyes closed with the caress.

"I was worried about you," he said, finding it hard to swallow.

"Oh, why's that?" she whispered.

"Since you're back in town for the week, I've become increasingly concerned for your safety. A witch has targeted three of our own, and there's no telling who might be next."

Julie blinked, snapping out of her trance. "Wait, what?"

"Haven't you heard? It's all over the news! People are talking about a witch destroying property and turning people into frogs!"

"You're kidding, right?" A little chuckle. A raised eyebrow.

Thomas silently led her across the room, brushing up against the bed, and switched on the slow-to-tune television. A brunette woman in a white V-neck pullover looked seriously into the camera.

"I'm reporting live for Channel 10 from the one hundred block of Octavia Street in Koreatown, where a witch has once again terrorized community residents. The latest victims are the Chu family. Behind me, you can see the ambulance pulling away with Míngzé and Xiang Chu, who have received second-degree burns during this brazen attack.

The home shows severe damage caused by multiple explosions." The camera panned to show the two-story house as the reporter continued. "Authorities speculate that the witch gained entry through their daughter's bedroom window. Daiyu, a graduate of Westlake Meadows Academy, is currently missing. Several witnesses claim to have seen a witch with green skin. Stranger still are the accounts from three other families, who claim the witch transformed their daughters, and a young man, into frogs."

As the camera again focused on the reporter, she turned to an elderly woman at her side. "Good evening, ma'am. What is your name?" The camera zoomed in on the woman, who stepped forward gingerly.

"Evelyn Sinclair," she said, her voice quivering. Her eyes, shadowed with fear, suggested unspoken burdens and a dark secret that loomed heavy in her mind. Only the top button of her white embroidered cardigan was fastened; oddly, the other three buttons were missing.

"Rumors about a witch terrorizing the city of Los Angeles have been spreading like wildfire. Your home is next door to the Chu's. Did you hear or see anything unusual from this latest attack?" the reporter leaned in with the microphone.

"Why, I can't say that I have, my dear. I haven't seen anything unusual since . . . " Evelyn gazed vacantly into the distance, and an anguished expression crossed her face. The reporter shifted uncomfortably, unsure how to proceed. After a prolonged silence, the elderly woman fixed her watery eyes back on the reporter, gave a small nod, and said, "Since that day I kissed a frog."

The field reporter chuckled, the woman's comment giving her an unexpected opening for the live interview. "And you didn't find your prince with that smooch?"

"No, I can't say I did," the woman said vaguely. "Just a few warts." With that, Evelyn turned and wandered away as if on eggshells, leaving the reporter and the audience with more questions than answers.

"There you have it, girls," said the reporter, trying to keep from laughing. "Stay clear of those frogs. You never know what might happen. Back to you, Steve."

Julie shook her head. "That is the most peculiar story I've ever heard!"

Thomas switched off the television. "The three victims are Daiyu, Shalonda, and Bridgette. Three of the girls from the UN Squad—the ones who humiliated you in high school!"

She didn't answer, knowing any response would give her away.

"You recognize the pattern here, right?" he continued, his voice swelling with pride. "That leaves just one more girl."

Julie and Thomas locked eyes and cried simultaneously, "María Elena Montes!"

Julie's mind raced. Thomas had made the connection, which meant she'd have to act fast before anyone else figured it out or before he took his suspicions to the police. For now, all she could do was keep a straight face, even as her pulse spiked beneath the surface.

He stood in the doorway, pondering his dilemma. If María Elena was the next victim, that could only mean one thing, and he didn't want to admit the possibility. But he had to ask.

"Julie," he said diffidently. "Are you . . . the witch?"

Staring at him from the refuge of her dark shades, she felt him searching her soul. He would never understand the choices she'd made, not after those people had made her life a living hell. This was personal. Despite the attraction that sparked between them, she wasn't about to let him ruin her revenge.

Julie walked up to him and kissed his cheek. "I'm not the witch."

He lingered for a breath, unsure, then gave a stiff nod. "I'll let myself out."

The door clicked shut behind him.

Suffused with guilt, Julie removed her sunglasses before the mirror. Crimson eyes flared back at her, bright with truth and consequence.

* * *

After the disastrous interview with the television reporter, Evelyn Sinclair closed the door with her foot. Taking a deep, unsteady breath, she slid the deadbolt into place, the solid click reassuring her safety. *I almost spilled the beans during that interview.* She leaned against the door, hand to her lips, the weight of her secret pressing on her chest, bringing sleepless nights. *No one must ever know the truth about my son. What would happen if the world discovered I was to blame for the tragedy in Miami?* A tear slipped down her cheek, tracing the creases etched into her skin.

A vintage lamp in the corner flickered to life, casting a soft glow that created a haven against the encroaching shadows. The pungent scent of pain relief ointment hung in the air. Tightly drawn shades shielded her from the outside world, keeping prying eyes at bay. The floor creaked beneath her feet as she shuffled across the room, each sound thick in the hush. Evelyn opened the closet door, its familiar rasp a comforting sound. Stepping back into the shadows, she tapped her thigh. Once. Twice. A third time.

Silence.

Then—

Two dolls emerged from the darkness, their tiny feet pitter-pattering across the floorboards, moving on their own. Her heart lifted.

They always knew what she needed, even before she said a word.

Clad in stiff brown frocks with striped Peter Pan collars, the 12-inch dolls looked up at her with acrylic eyes that blinked out of fashion rather than necessity. They were more than just dolls; they were her lifeline, her reason for living.

They reached out and gently patted her vein-riddled legs. Working together, the dolls grabbed the hem of her dress and began to climb, grasping the fabric between their tiny fingers. One placed a rubber foot onto the lip of her patch pocket for leverage. When they reached her bosom, Evelyn cradled them to her chest, her embrace tender and full of longing. They stared blankly, like porcelain keepers of her sorrow, their little hands softly patting her wrinkled face.

When she was young, Evelyn could pick them up effortlessly, but arthritis had stiffened her joints and twisted her fingers. She could no longer tie her sneakers or bend over to pick up items from the floor. She had grown to rely on them to climb into her arms for warmth and attention.

Evelyn had grown used to their constant wandering. Sometimes, she would find them walking around in the middle of the night. One doll recently lost a shoe while exploring its new home in California.

"Mama," they cried. She could hear the air releasing from the crying mechanism in their chests.

"Hush, my babies," she said, humming a lullaby. "Don't fear, little ones. No one will ever hurt you."

* * *

Thursday, May 12, 2005. 9:38 a.m.

Detective Andrew Baca was on the phone with Mr. Chu, who had called to offer additional information on the *Bruja Maldita* case, Spanish for "wicked witch." The detective uncovered vital details on the UN Squad. *At last, something real.*

"They found Erin!" Greg Sanders shouted as he rolled back from his desk, stretching the endless telephone cord that could double as a jump rope.

Andrew immediately put Mr. Chu on hold. "They found what?!"

"Erin Carmichael!"

* * *

Thirty-five minutes later, an unmarked police car squealed to a halt in front of the Witherspoon's residence at the corner of Saturn and Vineyard Avenue, just a few blocks from Venice Boulevard. Baca and Sanders removed their shades as they approached the on-site officer.

"A neighbor heard muffled screams coming from the Witherspoon's yard," Officer Clark said as he led the detectives around the side of the house to a cedar gazebo nestled on a wooden deck. It was surrounded by well-manicured shrubs, with perfectly spaced red rose bushes guarding the rear block wall. In the center of the yard stood a massive oak that shaded the east side of the house from the rising sun. Officer Clark pointed into the branches at a bulky gray cocoon strapped to the tree limb. "Up there. That's Erin Carmichael."

"I knew there had to be some explanation!" Greg tilted his head upward, staring at the cocoon.

Playing on a hunch, Andrew reached for his handheld radio and requested that additional units investigate trees at the Phillips and Chu residences. *This could be the breakthrough we've been waiting for. If we're lucky, soon three fewer people will be missing.*

Greg chuckled softly. "First the frogs, now this? What kind of message is that supposed to be?"

"It's her calling card," Andrew responded. He had to admire the witch's ingenuity and flair for the dramatic. *She's either one clever woman or one sick puppy . . . or maybe both*!

"What are we going to do with the frogs now?" Greg asked.

A muffled voice drifted down from above: "Screw the frogs! How about getting me down from here?!"

* * *

Thursday, May 12, 2005. 7:39 p.m.

Julie parked her blue SUV in the alley and scaled the privacy wall into the Montes' yard. She fired the spearhead into the roof overhang, rode up on the platform, and pushed away from the windowsill with her leg. Once again, the witch burst through the window in a shower of glass. Completing her somersault, she was surprised to see two uniformed officers instead of María Elena Montes with her perfect white picket fence teeth.

Officer Merbach's thick mustache curled over his upper lip as he gasped, his skin turning several shades of gray. Officer Dolter stood frozen, mouth agape, eyes bugging out with fear. They were face-to-face with a literal evil witch tormenting the City of Angels. *The stories are true! The witch doesn't have eyes!* Deep hollow sockets as black as coal sank into nothingness. Her face was pale green with roping veins, and her chin, that godforsaken masculine chin with a hairy wart, jutted hideously outward like a bicycle pedal.

Before the officers could process it, her unsightly hand plunged into a pocket and flung several smoke bombs. The clay balls struck the floor, and a thick gray cloud saturated the room. As the smoke enveloped the space, she vanished, leaving behind an unnatural silence. So unnatural, the officers drew their guns simultaneously.

Merbach cautiously stepped forward, his heart pounding with dread. The smoke thickened like London fog, wrapping him in a cloak of shadows. *Am I next?* The question reverberated, amplifying his fear. He strained to hear any hint of the witch's presence. A cold sweat trickled down his back as he cast a worried glance at his partner, now just a silhouette fading into the gray backdrop.

Shrouded in thick smoke, the witch stood motionless, listening. A wooden floorboard creaked, subtle, but enough to betray Merbach's approach. As he emerged from the haze, she unleashed a bloodcurdling hiss. His face contorted in horror, and her lips curled into a slow, venomous smile. She relished the fear blooming in his eyes. Then she vomited a peppery fluid directly into them. His gun clattered to the floor as he screamed, stumbling backward. Merbach clawed at his eyes, writhing in pain. She snapped a kick to his chin, sending him crumpling onto María's bed, unconscious.

In sheer panic, Officer Dolter swung his gun around. Hearing something land on the bed, he fired two shots blindly into the smoke.

The bed stopped squeaking.

I got her!

The witch retrieved the spear embedded in the eave and aimed it at the telephone pole in the alley.

BOING!

The spear jetted, embedding its prongs in the weathered wooden crossbar. She hooked herself up, hopped onto the miniature ski, and shot forward as the pulley mechanism reeled in the line. The platform skimmed across the patchy lawn, bucking and lurching like a jet ski tearing through whitecaps. She held on as she zipped away from the house. *Come on! Come on! Pop open!* A sudden gust of wind billowed her dress out like a parachute. The pulley lifted her through the air. She realized, too late, she wouldn't clear the wall . . .

Merbach lay unconscious, his face contorted with pain and blood trickling from his nose.

"You fuckin' bitch!" Dolter hollered, horrified to realize he had shot his partner in the shoulder. Fuming, he radioed for an ambulance and ran to the window in time to see the witch glide away on her broomstick under a star-filled sky. Gripping his gun, the officer fired his last four rounds. Three bullets missed, but he thought one tore through the purple dress.

The witch flinched as the platform clipped the wall. It detached from the rod and hit the ground with a hollow metallic clunk. Surprised by the jolt, the witch held onto the pulley for dear life and hit the release button. The spearhead popped free and retracted into the pulley. She plummeted to the ground, bruising herself, but the pulley remained undamaged. Ignoring the pain, she quickly gathered the dismantled gadget (pulley, rod, and broom) and hopped into her SUV, leaving skid marks and a lingering puff of smoke. As Julie's vehicle sped away, Thomas jumped out from behind a bush and watched it pull a hard left onto the street.

* * *

Friday, May 13, 2005. 7:16 a.m.

Working in her Azusa garage, Julie set up a worktable to craft a new broom; the straws on the old one were insufficient to hide the red and gold smoke cartridges. Despite the pain in her side, she stayed focused on the job and her imminent deadline. Attaching the long cartridges turned out to be easier than she thought.

Soon, the wooden handle resembled a rocket with boosters on each side. Julie fastened a long, steel wire to an embedded nail at the end of the handle and grabbed several rows of damp straw to conceal the containers. Using a leather belt, she secured the straw to prevent it from becoming unruly. With precision, she tightly wrapped the steel wire around the straw, binding it firmly to the handle. Satisfied with the binding, she attached electrical wires to the cartridges and stapled them along the broom handle, routing everything to a switch at the top. Once engaged, the switch would ignite the cartridges, unleashing a breathtaking display of colors. With a satisfied smile, Julie hung the broom to dry. She stepped back, admiring her handiwork with a glint in her eye. "I'm definitely my father's daughter," she said aloud, excitement bubbling. "I can't wait to make my grand entrance."

* * *

Friday, May 13, 2005. 3:05 p.m.

It took several hours for the committee to decorate the gymnasium and set fifty banquet tables. No one was more eager to finish than Julie, who fretted at the delay when the chairperson couldn't find the gymnasium key. Once inside, her mind wasn't on decorating but on her spectacular entrance, including the well-deserved reprisal of Mr. Jeff Byrnes. *Why don't you sit down to stop your cheeks from shaking*?

His callous words echoed in her mind again, reopening the scars that had never healed. Later that afternoon, the other committee members went home to dress for the reunion, except Julie, who deliberately stayed back.

Standing midway between the stage and the bleachers, she withdrew the pulley from her backpack, pointed the spearhead directly over her head, and fired. The spearhead spiraled twenty-five feet and penetrated the arched wooden beam, where four prongs expanded for a firm grip; one prong remained exposed due to the slant and deceleration of the ascent. Her heart racing, Julie hopped onto the stage. She found the perfect anchor point, drew a miniature fork-shaped spear from the pulley's compartment, reset the spring, and snapped it into place. Though the line was already deployed, she looped it around one prong and shot the fork directly overhead. It skyrocketed into the air and embedded into the wooden beam, leaving the line dangling along the wall. Julie left the pulley, rod, and broom behind the drapes.

* * *

Friday, May 13, 2005. 8:15 p.m.

Andrew Baca had a hunch the witch would show up uninvited at the Westlake Meadows Academy class reunion. Based on the recent alumni assaults, he was sure she would target the event. *This woman's got such a foul taste in her mouth, she'll stop at nothing to inflict pain.*

Andrew sipped his coffee, sliding his free hand into his pocket while the end of his coat draped around his large wrist. A dark stain on his tie caught the eye of several people milling around the gym, but he didn't care.

"Seems like the media had the same idea," Greg said, nodding toward the Channel 10 news reporter interviewing a few guests.

Andrew followed his gaze and saw the camera light shining on a group of alumni near the stage. "Just great," he said, shaking his head.

"This could turn into a circus if the witch does decide to show her ugly-ass face."

Earbuds looped around his neck like forgotten vines, the cameraman focused on a former cheerleader performing an old routine. His sneakers echoed against the wooden floor as he stepped back. Reporter Ann Marie Johnson, poised in a tailored pantsuit, kept the crowd engaged with stories of the supernatural, her dark brown beehive hairstyle stiff from heavy hairspray.

The crew had just flown in from Indianapolis International Airport, with a stop in Denver, Colorado. Ann Marie, the late-night anchor for WPND-TV, had been covering a segment on a haunted grandfather clock when the network incorporated the witch story. With the assistance of the police department, the crew had managed to find the next probable witch sighting.

After the principal of Westlake Meadows made his opening address, he handed the microphone to Mr. Byrnes, the longest-serving teacher at the school. His rugged face was severe, giving the impression of someone not to be messed with. He approached the microphone, acknowledged several returning students, and tapped the mic. "Is this thing working?" Jeff winced and stepped back to kill the feedback. "Ladies and gentlemen, I am delighted to extend my warmest greetings to all. Welcome to this year's Westlake Meadows class reunion!"

A wave of applause and cheers splattered over the room, fizzling into soft, effervescent murmurs. Jeff leaned into the microphone again, beaming and nodding appreciatively.

"Twenty-five years ago, I had the honor of teaching many of you in my choir. Yes, it was a total waste of time for some of you," he said with a chuckle. "However, I am delighted that so many alumni have achieved success, and in the process, inspired countless others to pursue a career in the entertainment field. Your achievements have made Westlake Meadows Academy very proud!"

Another wave of excitement splashed across the room, washing away the last traces of fear. Beaming for the first time that evening, Jeff hushed the cheers. "I understand we have a celebrity in the entertainment industry among us . . ."

Her purple dress undulating around her knees, Julie rose from her crouch and crept along the wooden beam as easily as she had on the balance beam. She stopped directly above Mr. Byrnes, who was praising Elisa Escarra for her huge success as a pop performer. Listening to him drone on was enough to make her sick. Julie cocked her head and muttered sarcastically, "Some great singer." In a flash, she pulled five smoke bombs from her pocket and dropped them one by one along the front of the stage. Each exploded in a fury of thick smoke, severing Byrnes from the crowd.

The room fell silent in shock. With the recent publicity about the wicked witch, everyone looked around, their eyes radiating fear and their hearts pounding. For several long, tense moments, the crowd stood wide-eyed, watching the hissing waves of black fumes billow like erupting volcanoes. Then another explosion lifted Jeff off the ground and flung him back several feet. Everyone flinched, and a few women screamed, digging their manicured fingernails into their escorts' arms.

As easily as a marine in boot camp, the witch dropped the loose end of a rope she'd tied around the wooden beam and descended hand over hand to the stage floor. Jeff stood just in time to receive a blow to the face with a metal rod. The impact turned him about-face and sent him wobbling away. Taking advantage of his stance, the wicked witch swung the rod again and struck him solidly on the buttocks, sending a spasm of pain up his spine. His face stretched into a throbbing mask of despair, his screams filtered through the smoke screen, and the gymnasium exploded in hysteria.

"My butt! My butt!" he cried, gripping his butt cheeks to stop them from quivering.

La bruja maldita sneered at the choir teacher. Her high-pitched voice taunted, "Why don't you sit down to stop your cheeks from shaking?"

Jeff turned to face his assailant, gaping in disbelief. "Julie, is that you?" he asked. The witch's eyes glowed like red-hot pokers, and the sneer on her face spread as wide as a crescent moon.

Flexing her hand back against the trigger, the witch hissed to shower pepper spray into his face. His eyes ignited with pain, tears streaming as he stumbled back, coughing and clawing at the air. Howling like a banshee, Jeff scrambled blindly through the smoke, shrieking for help.

Detectives Baca and Sanders sprang into action. "Help the teacher!" Andrew shouted as he ran toward the stage.

The gymnasium lights went dead.

Screams pierced the dark, followed by the sobs of women and the shuffle of panicked feet. Total blackness consumed them, save for the moon's reflection casting pale streaks across bewildered faces.

The cameraman kept filming, his viewfinder shaking as he captured faces twisted in fear, eyes darting from shadow to shadow in search of the hidden enemy.

Then the auxiliary lights flickered on.

Harsh and blinding.

Another wave of screams broke loose, sharper this time, but brief. Relief followed, shaky and half-formed, as the crowd blinked against the glare and tried to make sense of what remained.

Feeling overconfident, the witch sprinted from the control panel to the pulley. She grabbed the contraption behind the theater curtain and pulled on the dangling line. The miniature fork landed beside her feet with a single bounce, leaving the line free. Working expeditiously, she assembled the apparatus and hopped onto the platform before the smoke dissipated. As the pulley mechanism reeled in the line, the witch slid across the stage floor, picking up momentum as if being pulled by a motorboat.

Andrew climbed onto the stage. *I have got to cut back on chocolate chip cookies*. Just as he pulled himself upright, he witnessed the most spectacular sight in his fifty-two years. His mouth dropped open as he rubbed his eyes in disbelief.

A hideous witch jetted out of the smoke on a levitating broom!

"She's a real fuckin' witch," he squawked. Every eye gaped at the apparition. Her hair and dress fluttering gracefully, the witch soared silently over the startled crowd. The off-center departure launched the witch into an elliptical orbit—an elegant arc she maintained by reeling in more slack. She grinned impishly, delighting in the pandemonium that raged anew below. This was her pinnacle, the moment she had dreamed of. All her hard work had paid off. When she pressed the button on the broom handle, red and gold smoke spiraled behind her, as vivid as a tequila sunrise.

After reaching the periapsis of the swing, the witch discharged several explosives that illuminated the room with vivid, sparkling lights and cast shadows of despair on the walls. The powerful blasts blew people off their feet, overturned tables, and shattered plates. Terrified alumni and teachers stampeded toward the exits.

Paralyzed, Detective Baca stood mesmerized as he watched the witch soar overhead and begin her return arc, oblivious to his partner's shouting.

"Shoot her! Shoot the fuckin' witch!"

Instead, Andrew broke through the dissipating smoke and waited for her approach.

The line's breaking strength was three hundred pounds, but the poorly lodged spear in the beam undermined the support. Releasing more slack during the apoapsis of the swing, the witch careened toward the stage like a spider in the wind. Suddenly, the spearhead broke free from its grip as the witch entered the stage. The fall detached the metal rod from the pulley and tossed her flat on her back with a loud thump. Realizing her predicament, she rose immediately, only to find herself face-to-face with Detective Baca.

"Trick or treat?" he asked, balling his hands into fists and swinging wildly.

The witch dodged his first punch, but his next blow clipped her chin, loosening the mask's facial bond and knocking her flat on her back. Before Baca could blink, she propelled herself into a kip-up and was in his face.

"I'll settle for a trick," she hissed, with one-third of her left cheek torn off. Simultaneous blasts of fecal stench and pepper spray hit the detective full in the face.

Andrew doubled over, his screams pulsing through the gymnasium, sending fresh waves of terror through the milling alumni. Ecstatic over the fear she'd been able to inflict, the wicked witch mimicked his agony by screaming and flailing her arms.

"The pain! The pain! I can't stand the pain!" she shrieked.

Taking tiny mouse steps, she picked up the metal rod and struck his head. The detective's legs went limp, and he collapsed unconscious. Not exactly what she had planned; nevertheless, she was ecstatic with the results. The witch picked up the pulley, minus the bent pedestal, and dashed out the rear exit.

After calling the paramedics, Greg ran to assist his injured partner. Andrew's head throbbed, blood trickling from a nasty cut near his temple.

"Andrew, are you all right?"

Detective Baca rolled to his side, head pulsing and eyes throbbing from the stings of hundreds of bees. "Tell me you got the license plate off that broomstick."

Greg produced a handkerchief from his rear pocket and applied pressure to Andrew's wound. "Not only do you look like crap, but you smell like it, too," he said. "I have an ambulance on the way. Did the witch say anything to you?"

Andrew rolled back flat to minimize the room's dizzying spin. "I don't remember what she said, but she must have been talking through her ass because that's what her breath smelled like!" He heard his partner's swift footsteps and the rear door slam. "Get the bitch," he called after him, though he meant to say "witch."

* * *

Under the cover of darkness, Greg raced along the gym's perimeter, his gun in hand and the edges of his coat swaying with each stride. Several traumatized alumni pointed silently after the witch. As he rounded the corner, he caught a glimpse of a blue SUV screeching away, swerving to avoid two people in formal attire.

"Stop!" Greg shouted, aiming his gun at the car without firing. Given the light traffic that evening, the driver skidded down the driveway erratically, leaving behind puffs of smoke and the lingering scent of burnt tires.

Greg reached for the handheld radio strapped to his belt. "This is Detective Greg Sanders. We need an APB on a blue SUV, California plate two, Grant, Adam, Taylor, one, two, three. Repeat: two, Grant, Adam, Taylor, one, two, three. Driver is armed and dangerous. Requesting air support."

"Male or female?" asked the dispatcher, followed by a roger beep.

Greg lifted an eyebrow. "She's the witch we've been after!" he shouted.

The dispatcher was heard broadcasting the APB in the background, " . . . enraged female driver in a witch costume considered armed and dangerous."

Greg clipped the radio back onto his belt and waved at the approaching ambulance. Two paramedics with a gurney followed him inside the building, where amazingly, only two people had been injured. Panic-ridden faces demanded answers, but he couldn't comfort the crying women or assist the stupefied men. Instead, he led the paramedics through the confused crowd. Several women clutched their phones, hysterically recounting the witch's incredible power and colorful aerial display, their mascara staining their faces like dark rivers flowing down their cheeks.

If they hadn't seen it with their own eyes, they never would've believed it. The sorceress's tremendous power and dazzling flight convinced everyone she was indisputably real. The gates of hell had opened, and the first wrath unleashed on humanity was a witch.

Greg cleared the path for the gurney. "Please remain calm," he said, his commanding voice catching the interest of the news crew.

Ann Marie forged through the crowd and grabbed Greg's shoulder, leaving the paramedics to their own devices. "I presume you're the officer in charge?" she asked, her eyes boring into his.

"Detective Baca is my superior," he said. "But right now, he needs medical attention. I am Detective Greg Sanders."

Ann Marie looked into the camera with the microphone in hand. "We are live at the Westlake Meadows Academy reunion, where the authorities have arrived," she said, taking one step closer to the increasingly perturbed detective. "Detective Sanders, everyone here tonight saw a levitating witch with their own eyes. We caught the incident on tape. How can you explain this incredible sighting?"

"Believe me, I'm as baffled as everyone else. My guess? This gym was rigged like a movie set. But people don't usually get hurt on movie sets."

"Are you saying this . . . creature, for lack of a better word, was a *real* witch?"

Greg gave an exasperated laugh and rubbed his hand against his dimpled chin. "I'm not sure what's real anymore." His anxious eyes gazed into the camera. Then came the memory—something that would quell the ridiculous rumors flooding the town. He pointed his finger at the camera and said with a sardonic smile, "I'll tell you this much. She is *not* a real witch. She is a normal human being. A real witch doesn't fly away in an SUV." He looked over at the paramedics. "Excuse me, I have some injured men to tend to."

Ann Marie Johnson stood dumbfounded. *Why didn't the witch fly away on her broom? She had the power to do so.*

* * *

The SUV screeched to a stop behind the Metro Media Plaza at Oxford and Wilshire, not far from the famous Wiltern Theater. The witch blinked her scarlet eyes. She had a bump on her head from her rough landing on the stage, and pain bloomed across her bruised cheek from the detective's dexterous blow. Looking into the rearview mirror, she examined the mask and affixed it to her face anew.

"If your head were a baseball, I'd have knocked you out of the park," Julie said with a grin that quickly faded at the blare of police sirens in the distance. She jumped out of her SUV with the pulley in hand. Hiking the purple skirt above her knees, she bolted toward the north end of the building, allowing the warm spring breeze to rush up her dress. Her feet hammered the pavement, an unpleasant reminder of how she used to run from her problems at school.

Her breath coming in gasps, the witch rounded the building and paused momentarily in front of an upscale beauty salon, flanked by a law firm and a chiropractor's office. Her red eyes swept across the lawn, noting the six towering oak trees and a large decorative rock next to some shrubs. She hauled the heavy rock from its resting place, leaving insects scrambling for cover, and heaved it through the beauty salon's front window. It shattered the thick glass and landed on the ceramic tile with a resounding crunch.

As the alarm ripped the night apart, the witch hastily detached the vial of fecal stench from her wrist. She dribbled a small amount on the sidewalk before flinging the vial through the broken window, spewing its stench into the salon.

* * *

"That's the vehicle," the officer confirmed as he reached for the two-way radio. "Dispatch, we've spotted the suspect's vehicle behind the Metro Media Plaza."

The paramedics were still administering an eye wash to the two injured men when Greg's radio crackled with the news of the SUV's discovery. He keyed the switch on his radio. "This is Detective Sanders, requesting additional backup and a canine unit to the suspect's location. How much longer until we have air support?"

"Five minutes. They're already in proximity."

That was what Thomas had been waiting for. He'd been hovering near the detective, unnoticed, before slipping quietly out the door. *If anyone can end this terror, it's me. She's got to listen to reason.*

Greg itched to resume the chase, but he stayed in the gym until he was sure his partner would be okay. When the eyewash finally started to ease the stinging of capsaicin, he left his partner and the choir teacher in the hands of paramedics.

The gym doors thudded shut behind him as he climbed into the unmarked car. It roared to life, its red emergency light beacon spinning and its siren wailing. The tires screeched as he set off on the four-minute journey.

* * *

The wicked witch hustled toward the oak trees. For the first time since launching her campaign of revenge, her eyes shone with fear. Julie's heart quickened as she looked up into the nearest tree. She shot the spearhead into a thick branch, where it embedded into the limb. A press of the button yanked her upward through the branches where crenate leaves hid her from view.

Julie's spectacular flight across the gymnasium should have been the pinnacle of her revenge. She hadn't expected her reprisal to end this way. Now it had landed her in a delicate predicament with the law. Worse, it left her trapped in a tree, completely alone. Sweat coursed down her body, soaking the leotard.

It's their fault! They made me like this. Those girls failed to understand that everyone is created equal. It doesn't matter whether you're fat or thin, attractive or not, if you have a big butt or a flat one. There's someone for everyone! We are all equal in spirit. Our souls yearn to be kind to each other. Why is that so hard for the world to understand?

* * *

A raft of police cars and a K-9 unit surrounded the abandoned SUV, lights flashing. Greg was the last to arrive on the scene. "Start the canine on the vehicle interior. We're dealing with a deranged person with access to explosives and other potentially harmful chemicals," he shouted, his tie flapping in the breeze. After sniffing the vehicle's interior, the German shepherd led the contingent to the north end of the building.

As the main artery in Koreatown, Wilshire Boulevard bustled with life even under the thudding pulse of the police helicopter overhead. Its 30-million-candlepower beam swept across twin white buildings, filtered through oak trees, and lit up the police dog and officers rounding the building. All six stood with weapons drawn before the shattered glass, the shepherd barking furiously, ears pricked and teeth bared in a snarl. At the handler's command, the leash snapped free, and the dog lunged into the salon, its nose locked on the trail of stench. One by one, the officers followed, boots grinding glass into tile.

A crow made a few low passes before extending its claws to land on a nearby light post. Drawn by the faint but unmistakable scent of bullfrog, it was determined to locate the succulent meal. Hopping to the edge of the metal casing, it fluttered its glossy wings. The clever scavenger peered at the oak tree, its beady eyes locking on a shadowy figure stirring within. Bobbing silently, the crow moved in a ritualistic dance, then decided against venturing into the tree. Instead, it rattled: *Click, click, click!*

Greg entered last, then froze, glancing over his shoulder at the familiar sound. He could see the crow hopping with delight on the light post. The crow resumed its dry rattle, piquing his curiosity. Driven by a sudden hunch, the detective broke from the group and sprinted toward the oak trees at the north end of the property, the crow's Geiger counter clicks still echoing in his mind. As the helicopter circled overhead, the spotlight followed him at every step, forming migrating shadows across the lawn. With his gun drawn, he moved cautiously beneath the trees, losing visual contact with the officers in the sky.

Using a thick branch for leverage, the witch stood briefly to shift her weight, then released slack from the pulley. Her legs swept upward, coiling over her head like a scorpion's tail. As gravity inverted her, she pressed against the pulley's housing and shifted into a handstand, one leg looping firmly around the line to anchor her. Her skirt fell over her torso, revealing taut, leotard-clad legs like blades drawn in silence. *I don't want any problems, mister. Just go away!* Her vermilion eyes blazed with warning, and her breath steamed in shallow bursts as she steadied herself against the pulley. Through a break in the leaves, she spotted a plainclothes officer approaching, brandishing a gun.

Her breathing thickened.

Her pupils dilated.

With the detective below her, she relented and let go of the line. Down she slid, gravity pulling her like a spider on silk. The rustling leaves caught Greg off guard, and he glanced upward with a gasp. His jaw slackened, eyes bulging with raw terror. Hissing like an enraged mother raccoon, the witch sprayed capsaicin into his vulnerable eyes with a flick of her wrist. His screams fractured the night as she shot back up into the tree, triumphant.

Greg fought the urge to rub his eyes. He had been sprayed with capsaicin during the riots in 1992 and knew his only defense was his firearm. Burying his face in the crook of his arm, the detective pointed his gun into the tree and fired six shots in quick succession, shredding leaves and striking the witch in the back with the final shell.

"Aaargh!" she wailed.

The witch plummeted to the ground, her shoulder slamming into his temple, knocking Greg unconscious. Oblivious to the pepper spray, he lay peacefully on the grass with the witch crumpled next to him, unbidden tears washing the capsaicin from his burning eyes.

* * *

"Wake up." Mrs. Sanders shook her son gently by the shoulder, her bloodshot eyes sunk deep into her angular face. "Wake up, Greg."

Little Greg stirred in his hospital bed as the cold air pricked his skin, raising goosebumps on his arms. "Moms?" He thought his eyes were open. He was sure of it. He could feel them blinking, but his brain didn't register any images. "Moms!" he yelled out in distress. "I can't see you!"

"I'm here, Gregory." She ran her thin fingers through his unwashed hair. The frightened look on his gaunt face brought tears to her eyes, but seeing him awake filled her with quiet relief. "You had a nasty fall off the balcony, and now you're at the hospital," she reassured him. "The doctor said you're going to be fine. The concussion has temporarily affected your sight, but it will return in a few days."

She lied. The doctor had no idea whether he would ever regain his sight.

"Moms, I don't want to be blind," he cried. His frightened eyes searched blindly, probing for a glimmer of hope. Restless, Gregory turned his bandaged head. Not even the gentle stroke of her hand could calm him. "I need to see!" he pleaded, tears wetting his hospital gown. "I can't be a good cop if I'm blind!"

* * *

"Noooo!" Thomas roared as he raced around the building.

He watched as the witch plummeted from the oak tree. For a moment, he stood frozen, grief flooding his eyes behind his black-rimmed glasses. Snapping out of it, he ran to her, his knees scuffing the lush green grass as he knelt beside her immobile body.

For the first time, Thomas faced the evil witch. Her menacing features sent shivers down his spine, but knowing it was Julie softened the shock. He tugged at the green prosthetic face until the spirit gum could no longer hold it. With a bullet lodged in her spine, she couldn't move, yet she managed a smile at the sight of his tear-ridden face.

Her hand was cold in his, her breathing uneven. Sweat glistened on her face as the spotlight swept overhead. Despite the fiendishly red eyes, Julie was still as lovely as ever. Her lips moved, aching for the sweet press of his. But he knew they'd never share that passion again.

"I love you, Julie," he said, his voice breaking as he watched her struggle for air.

"I love you, too," she whispered. That breath was her last. Her lifeless red eyes stared blankly into the night.

Drawn by the gunfire, the police officers crowded under the tree. On the ground next to Detective Sanders, a young man lay sobbing uncontrollably over the witch's body. One officer approached cautiously to feel for a pulse, shivering at the sight of the cold red eyes gaping at nothing. Her tousled hair covered half of her pretty face. She was nothing like the terrifying witch they'd been led to believe. There was no sign of a flying broomstick, no magic spells, or even the flick of her wrist to change them into frogs. The German shepherd snarled and whined, pacing in place.

"Can you confirm if the suspect has been apprehended?" the dispatcher asked, followed by a roger beep.

"I'm not sure, but there's activity on the ground next to the tree," the helicopter pilot said, the radio crackling softly.

The officer who had been checking her pulse shook his head and gently placed her hand across the blades of grass. He keyed his radio for the dispatcher. "The witch's reign of terror is over."

Another roger beep followed, and then the guns went down.

The nomadic crow, its wings a blue-black patina, flew away carefree, like a proud hawk. It soared and circled back, allowing the wind and its wings to do the work. Free flight required no effort, just imagination. It dove again and swept over the scene, its head tilting, its eyes blinking, and uttered two sharp cries: *Caw! Caw!*

HOUSE OF BROKEN BONES

(A Pre-Utopian Story)

Southwest Raleigh, North Carolina. Tuesday, May 21, 1974. 3:27 p.m., after the butterfly is set free.

The last thing Lawrence Devonshire remembered was diving into the cool waters of Lake Johnson, his head colliding with a jagged object. A searing jolt of pain shot through his skull and down his spine. His thin brown arms flailed as he struggled to get his head above the surface. His perfectly round afro, now plastered to his head, shimmered in the slanting sun. Warm blood streamed down the side of his face like a crimson river breaching its banks. Out of the corner of his eyes, he caught a glimpse of spring trees stretching to the skyline before everything went black.

* * *

3:12 p.m.

The school bus door sprang open, and Raymond Kane stepped onto the dusty ground to line up his eighth-grade students in single file. His weathered face, creased by daily struggles, was framed by a steadily receding hairline. Students sniggered behind his back at his plaid pants and a V-neck argyle sweater studded with tiny pills that begged for a lint roller. He could think of countless ways he'd rather spend the day than dealing with the chaos of the classroom, like camping in Baxter State Park or rafting the rugged Penobscot River.

"I don't like their lingo," Raymond had confided to his wife one night. "Half the time, I don't understand what they are saying! In your face, phooey, dude, how's it hangin', outta sight. How will the world understand each other with such idiotic phrases?"

Constance chuckled softly, her blouse rustling as she snuggled closer. She noticed the annoyance building on his face, his eyes hardening with anger, his pores fuming like active volcanoes. Her hand stroked his, and her eyes, glowing with the warmth of a smoldering ember, softened the fury rising in his. "The world is changing, dear," she said gently. "You just have to learn to blend in."

"Yeah?" Raymond responded sharply. "Well, it's changing too fast if you ask me! These young rascals will never hold the country's reins, mark my words."

Overhead, soft cumulus clouds glowed faintly in the afternoon sun. Guarding the peaceful landscape, the trees barely moved in the warm, gentle breeze as the school bus roared to life behind him and groups of students straggled into sight. Raymond glanced at his watch. "You're late!" His eyes flared with annoyance.

Two chaperones—class mothers, he thought sourly—escorted the students toward the bus. One of them looked as bashful as a first-time lover, uncertain where to rest her hands or her heart. The other's dark, curly hair sprang out in unruly spirals—likely styled by the forest's fingers—and her eyes were as black as onyx. "Sorry, we didn't mean to be late, Mr. Kane," she said in a British accent. "We lost track of time. Trying to identify all those insects, you know."

Raymond gave a puff of disgust and shook his head as a student came forward, cupping something in his hand.

"Look what I found, Mr. Kane," Jaide Basir said, lifting an insect so his teacher could see.

Raymond recoiled, the corners of his mouth tightening into a grimace. "Great, a moth," he said, rolling his eyes.

"Not just a moth! It's an American copper, part of the Lycaena phlaeas butterfly family." Jaide's gentle brown eyes scrutinized the tiny winged creature with delight. He held one wing gently between finger and thumb, allowing his teacher to glimpse its golden wings before releasing it into the wind. Shielding his eyes from the sun, he watched the butterfly flit effortlessly away.

"Now, why did you do that?" Raymond asked, arms thrown akimbo in mock outrage. "You could've had it for dinner!"

"Don't be silly, Mr. Kane," said Jaide, giggling. He squinted as the butterfly zigzagged into a tree. "I like setting things free."

Raymond herded the unruly group into a ragged line and started his head count. Halfway through, someone interrupted his numbering with a loud, "Who cut the cheese?" Everyone laughed except for the teacher, who paused to shake his head and scowl. Then someone farted, and the laughter erupted in earnest.

Placing his freckled hands on his hips, Raymond shouted over the uproar. "Listen up, everyone! I counted thirty-seven people when there should be thirty-eight. Look around and figure out who's missing." He scratched where scraggly hair met smooth scalp. *I've never seen so many confused faces at once.* He pulled his clipboard out of the bus for roll call when a boy with tousled hair shouted, "Lawrence!"

The beleaguered adult tugged at his sagging polyester plaid and said, "Who remembers seeing Lawrence?"

"I saw him by the lake," Jaide cried, brushing a lock of hair from his face. Thoughts of rescue, praise, and admiration took hold. He couldn't bear the thought of Lawrence being lost or in danger. Without waiting for permission, he bolted. "I'll get him!" he shouted over his shoulder.

Before Raymond could speak, Jaide had already sprinted across Avent Ferry Road to the hiking trail leading to the lake's southern section, where trees stood like ancient pillars.

Raymond clapped a hand to his sun-beaten head. “Great!” he exclaimed. “Now I have *two* missing students!” His voice dripped with annoyance, and his demeanor rippled like restless hues on a chameleon’s rugged back.

Jaide disappeared into the woods, raising one arm to shield his face from the sting of the prickly branches. Several white-tailed deer darted through the underbrush, startled by his sudden presence. Ahead, the lake sparkled in the sun. As he reached the clearing, a pair of spotted turtles floating along the lake’s edge caught his eye, their heads bobbing in and out of their shells. Scanning the surface, he saw a body floating face down in the water.

“Oh no!” Jaide’s eyes widened, deepening the lines on his forehead. Instead of following the trail, he plunged down the steep hill in a split-second decision to save time. Adrenaline coursed through his veins as his heart pounded. Slippery with pine needles, the slope sent him skittering until his right foot jammed in a treacherous mat of roots.

“Let go!” A hard kick at the roots with his left foot freed his sneaker from the tangled grip, and he ran for the lake’s edge. Panting from the effort, Jaide shouted, “Lawrence!” He pulled his T-shirt over his head and kicked his shoes off.

One deep breath, and Jaide dove into the lake. His slim body zipped through the still water and surfaced next to the unconscious boy. Breathing heavily, he shook his head, spraying water droplets like a summer shower. Turning Lawrence over, he towed him to the edge and dragged him out of the water onto dry ground. He ran through the CPR steps he’d learned as a scout: *Think ABC: airway, breathing, and circulation. Keep the oxygen flowing to the heart and brain to prevent tissue death.* He swept a finger through Lawrence’s mouth to check for obstructions, positioned his hands over his heart, and counted the chest compressions. With a firm hand under the neck, Jaide tilted the unconscious boy’s head back, pinching the nose closed before breathing oxygen into waterlogged lungs. When Lawrence didn't react, he repeated the chest compressions while remaining remarkably composed.

A perturbed Raymond hurried down the path after Jaide, his feet stomping and his body leaning forward, as if that might get him there faster. But when he saw Jaide administering CPR to a motionless boy, he gasped and bolted toward them.

On the third set of compressions, Lawrence convulsed, spewing a heavy stream of water out of his lungs. Both Raymond and Jaide exhaled in relief.

"Turn him on his side!" ordered Raymond, his brows lifting.

Lawrence continued to cough and wheeze, water trickling from his nose and mouth.

"I saw him lying face down in the lake, Mr. Kane, and I jumped in to save him," Jaide said proudly.

Raymond noticed blood oozing from a cut on Lawrence's head. "Hand me your shirt," he said. Snatching it from Jaide's grasp, he wrapped it around the injured boy's head to slow the bleeding. He lifted Lawrence's limp body and carried him back to the school bus, where the driver called for paramedics on his two-way radio.

Thirty minutes later, Lawrence was in an ambulance heading to a hospital in Wake County. Everyone watched it speed away, siren blaring. When the news of Jaide's daring feat rippled through the crowd, applause and cheers erupted. His face crimsoned with embarrassment. He stood proud, hands on his waist like a superhero after pulling someone from the jaws of death. His eyes glimmered. If he could, he would save the world.

Raymond wrapped his arm around Jaide's shoulder as tears pricked his eyes. Something shifted in Mr. Kane. The narrow-minded teacher embraced the idea of blending in with the younger generation. *Maybe Constance was right. Maybe I can have a real connection with these kids.*

"You know, son," he said, his posture shifting subtly. "I just want to say that everyone, especially Lawrence, appreciates your heroic efforts today." Raymond swallowed hard, the words heavy in his throat. "What you did at the lake was so bitchin' . . . to the max . . . outta sight," he said, giving Jaide a thumbs-up.

* * *

Inflation hit the nation hard after the Watergate scandal and the Vietnam War. Gasoline prices skyrocketed. Unused due to circumstances, large metallic beasts lined the streets as men in wooden chairs spoke softly of the land of milk and honey, a place they once touched but now only remembered.

A police cruiser sped down the town's main street, siren wailing its distorted Doppler shift. Children kicked a ball in a side street like foosball figures, scattering whenever a car eased past. A worn softball ripped through the air and slapped into a leather glove with a loud whack. Albert, lacking both mask and chin guard, lifted his leg for a dramatic throw back to his younger brother but hesitated in mid-kick.

"Hey, Jaide!" he shouted. "Wanna play some catch with us?"

"No time." Jaide shrugged, flopping the collar of his paisley-print shirt. The small flares of his brown corduroy bell-bottoms flapped with each step. "I'm here to see Lawrence."

The two brothers ran up to him. "Bummer," said Albert, leaning against the porch's peeling white balustrade. "I heard he almost died!"

"I know. I'm the one who saved his life."

Albert slammed the ball into his mitt again, his jaw slackening with disbelief. "No fuckin' way!"

"Yup." Jaide grinned, running his fingers through his hair. "I dove into the lake and pulled him out."

"You're like a real-life action hero!"

"Nah," Russell said, stealing the ball back. "He's like one of those superheroes in the comics."

Jaide could hear them arguing about comics versus movies as they wandered back to the middle of the street, thinking it felt great to be compared to a superhero. He marched up the steps, his leather platform shoes scuffing against the concrete. When he entered Lawrence's room, an episode of *Good Times* was playing on the television. *Enter the Dragon* posters plastered the bedroom walls, while sports memorabilia, an elastic wrestler toy, and a fighting robots game filled the bookshelf. The sound of children playing drifted through an open window, taunting his friend's restlessness.

"Feeling better?" Jaide asked.

Lawrence gave his friend a feeble smile and sat up gingerly as blood pulsed through his bandaged head. "It only hurts when I laugh," he said, biting his lip to keep from laughing. "They shaved my hair around the cut and ruined my afro."

"Maybe you should shave the rest of it then." Jaide grinned at the idea. "You could be the next movie detective."

"Don't knock it. I can play a badass cat."

They laughed, and Lawrence held his throbbing head. In the background, the TV audience roared with laughter. Jaide kept him company until the episode ended, then stood up and bid his friend farewell.

"Jaide, I owe you my life," Lawrence said, ignoring the television. "I want you to know I appreciate what you did for me. Whenever you need help, no matter what, I'll be there for you."

"Don't mention it." Jaide quickly waved off the thanks.

"No, I really mean it." Lawrence's eyes were intense. "Anything you need, no matter what."

"Be careful what you wish for," said Jaide, giving him a thumbs-up.

* * *

Akron, Ohio. Sunday, September 12, 2004. 3:22:17 p.m. EST

Engrossed in her search for the peanut butter low in sugar, the woman ignored the clatter of the shopping cart. Her long, chestnut hair was pulled back in a loose bun, several strands feathering her face. She assumed her eight-year-old son was just his usual restless self. But as the rattling persisted, it began to grate on her nerves.

"Jimmy, stop shaking the cart!" she snapped, her patience wearing thin.

"I'm not shaking it, Mommy," he said. "It's that man in the cart. Look!" He pointed, his eyes as wide as his mouth.

The woman huffed. "What have I told you about telling stories?" When she turned to look, she let out an ear-splitting scream. The two specialty glass jars of peanut butter she had been holding shattered at her feet. A pale, sickly man in a rumpled suit lay spread-eagled in her shopping cart, his eyes rolled back, his body jerking in violent spasms. Then, to her shock, he vanished, leaving behind soiled groceries and a chill crawling up her spine.

* * *

Wichita, Kansas. Sunday, September 12, 2004. 2:22:37 p.m. CST, (3:22:37 p.m. EST – for continuity with other timestamps)

The sun's rays filtered through the vertical blinds, striping his rugged face. Deep lines and a strong jaw revealed a life spent in outdoor pursuits. Graying at the temples, his brown hair slipped across his broad, bare shoulders as the bed quivered. He groaned, assuming his golden retriever had jumped onto the mattress. *Ugh, it's not time to get up yet.* He still had several hours before dragging himself out of bed to start another evening shift at the power plant.

Clad only in his pajama bottoms, he lay on his side, eyes shut, hoping his dog would let him return to his slumber. When he couldn't take it anymore, he groaned, "Buddy, get off the bed!"

In response, he heard a frightened whimper and felt the cold nose nudge his dangling hand. A jolt of fear hit him—Buddy wasn't the source of the disturbance. The man opened his eyes to see his golden retriever standing in front of him, staring fearfully at something behind his master.

The night shift operator kicked off the sheets and jerked to his feet, heart thudding. A man in a wrinkled black suit shook uncontrollably. His face was ghastly pale, his blue eyes sunken, his black hair disheveled. Then, without a sound, he vanished, leaving a filthy residue on the sheets. The golden retriever sniffed, tilted his head, and gave a questioning whine.

* * *

Athens, Georgia. Sunday, September 12, 2004. 3:22:52 p.m. EST

New wave music about a lobster played in the arcade, where three girls peered anxiously into a claw machine. Their tiny hands pressed against the glass, watching as the crane opened its metal claws and dropped on cue over the coveted pink teddy bear. The whirling of the motor competed with the music as the girls held their breath, each hoping to snag the prize.

Disrupting their mission, a man in a wrinkled black suit materialized inside the glass enclosure, his body squashing the plush animals beneath him. Dark, sunken eyes rolled back in his head, and his mouth gaped open as if in a silent scream. Jumping back, the girls cried out as the soiled man shook violently, their uvulas vibrating in unison. As quickly as it had appeared, the ghoulish body disappeared, leaving saliva dripping down the glass and grimy stuffed animals.

* * *

Millers Creek, North Carolina. Sunday, September 12, 2004. 3:23:02 p.m. EST

He was beautifully balanced, as he was biased.

Driving down US Route 421, Jaide eased off the accelerator when something by the side of the road caught his eye. *Was that . . . a man's body?* He wasn't sure. *Maybe a dead animal?* But the way it lay outstretched, with one limb doubled over, made him think twice. He slowed and pulled the car off the road. After checking for traffic, he made a U-turn and headed back. From a distance, he could see the body sprawled on the ground. But as he maneuvered closer, it became chillingly clear it was human.

The car's tires crushed the grass, and the uneven ground jolted the vehicle with each bump. In the distance, rolling green hills stretched toward a line of trees that guarded the forest's secrets. Killing the engine, he tossed his sunglasses on the dashboard and got out. He stood frozen, overwhelmed as his worst fear became reality. It was a man all right, but his contorted face made it impossible to guess his age. His dark hair was matted and unkempt, his lips dry and cracked, and his eyes sunken in. From the stench, Jaide surmised the man had soiled himself before dying.

He was about to report the corpse to the local police department when the man jerked abruptly. *Holy shit*, he thought with a start. Horror swept across his face as the man convulsed in a cascade of violent spasms, each more brutal than the last. The corpse's lips twisted in a silent scream for help.

Reaching for his phone, he punched in numbers.

"Jaide?" answered a soft voice.

"How soon can you get to my house with your medical supplies to start an IV?" he asked, alarm choking his voice.

"I'm on vacation this week. I can be there in ten minutes." Hannah switched the phone to her other ear. "Jaide, are you all right?"

"I found an unconscious man on the side of the road!"

"What's his condition?" she asked calmly, taking control of the situation.

"He's deathly pale and convulsing, likely due to dehydration. His eyes are rolled back, and his respiration is rapid," he said, assessing the man's face. "I'm guessing he's about forty-five."

"Sounds like he's already in shock. I'll bring supplies to stabilize him. Just be careful when you move him. He may have fractured bones."

"I will," he answered, relieved that Hannah was home. For a moment, he considered driving the hour into Statesville to the nearest hospital. But the seconds kept ticking, and he knew Hannah was the better choice, for now. Back at his car, he pulled the emergency blanket from the trunk and got to work.

Jaide's chest tightened as he glanced in the rearview mirror at his incapacitated passenger. On the drive home, he was reminded of the same pull he'd felt as a teenager, diving into the lake to save a drowning classmate. That moment had etched itself into his psyche, not as trauma, but as a calling. He didn't just help people. He believed he was meant to.

I hope this works. Poor guy! He desperately needs help.

Minutes later, he turned onto a dirt road leading to his property, the rear tires hurling pebbles like cannonballs. The road bucked beneath them, forcing him to ease off the gas. Every jolt felt like time slipping away. Jaide's ranch-style house was nestled between lush green trees on a half-acre lot. Its brick veneer siding gave it character, while the roof bore a dozen broken shingles, which were evidence of the high winds that often tore through his neck of the woods.

"I got here as fast as I could," Hannah said, running to meet him.

Jaide stepped out quickly. "I should warn you, it's not a pretty sight. He's soiled himself." As he opened the rear door, the stench hit them. "I had to drive with the windows down."

Holding the blanket at each end, they carried the mystery man into the guest room and placed him on the bed. Jaide went to the well-stocked supply room and returned with an oxygen tank. He looped the cannula around the man's head, connected the other end to the tank, and exhaled with relief as the low, constant hiss of air began to flow.

Hannah scrubbed her hands thoroughly, then asked, "Did he have any identification?"

"All I found was a wallet with a big wad of cash and a locker key in his pocket. No ID whatsoever."

Snapping on her exam gloves, she bent down to insert an IV needle. Her blonde hair slipped over her shoulder as she leaned in.

Jaide's heart fluttered.

"He's so dehydrated I can't get a vein," she said after several attempts.

"How about trying his foot?"

"Wait, I got it." With a steady hand, she inserted the needle and threaded the catheter into a vein, securing it with anchor tape. The hairs on her arm stood on end when she unintentionally brushed up against Jaide. Ignoring her physical reaction, she attached the connecting hub to a 14-gauge trauma line. "Where did you find this guy?" she asked, sounding composed.

"Off Highway 421, before Westgate Drive. I thought he was dead until he started convulsing," he said, watching her hands work with quiet respect.

Hannah shone a penlight into the sick man's eyes and noted his unresponsive pupils. Hearing the lung crackles, she shook her head, afraid that his accelerated heart rate and inadequate blood supply could lead to dysrhythmia and ischemia. "His heart rate is 140. If he were conscious, he'd be complaining about chest pains."

She slung the stethoscope around her neck and wrapped a manual blood pressure cuff around his arm. "His systolic is 79. Without IV fluids and antibiotics, his organs will suffer from hypoperfusion."

"What do you think his chances are?" asked Jaide.

"That depends on the degree of organ decompensation and the patient's general health before the shock," she said without looking up.

In her haste to grab two intravenous bags, her thumbnail caught the soft plastic of one. A sudden tear opened near the port, and fluid began to leak. "Oh my gosh!" she cried, watching it cascade down the end table onto the carpet. "That was my last bag."

Jaide blinked, then stepped back, offering a towel. "What was it?"

"Cimetidine."

"I think I have a case in storage." Panic surged through him as he sprinted away.

Inside the makeshift storage room, Jaide faced stacks of hospital supplies that reminded him of his calling to help the poor and disadvantaged. This led to his career with a medical supply company, selling supplies and servicing hospitals across North Carolina to stay close to his mission. *Well, I said I wanted to help the needy. No better time to put those degrees in anatomy and human services to use*, he thought with resolve.

While he searched for a replacement bag, Hannah hooked up a 6% hetastarch-dextran solution to restore intravascular volume and support cardiovascular function.

Jaide returned, his heart beating fast. "You're in luck, I found one."

"You mean John is in luck."

"John?"

"John Doe," she said, amused. "Based on his condition, I'm using esomeprazole to prevent gastrointestinal bleeding. I'd say he's gone through three or four days of trauma."

"That's impossible," Jaide exclaimed. "Someone would've noticed his body before I did!"

"Unless his body was dumped just before you drove by." She grabbed a pair of scissors and began to cut off the soiled clothes.

"I don't see any physical trauma or injuries," she murmured, sweeping over the body. "He may have been locked up for days and then left for dead. But look here. There's hair underneath his fingernails, the same color as his."

Jaide's brows went up. "A sign of desperation."

"Uh-huh," she replied, running a finger across John Doe's limp hand. "There's some bruising around the knuckles."

Jaide leaned in closer. "Looks like he was pounding his way out of his confinement. What a terrible way to die." They locked eyes for a moment. "Being trapped without food or water for several days brings on madness, until lethargy escalates and the victim loses consciousness."

While cleaning John Doe with warm soapy water and washcloths, Jaide gently rolled him onto his side so Hannah could reach the lower back and hips. With the cleansing complete, they eased him into a fresh pair of pajama bottoms. This was the first time Jaide had seen Hannah in action. He admired her natural intelligence and confident nursing skills, especially how she took control of the situation, right down to the fecal occult blood test for gastrointestinal ischemia, which can release toxins into the bloodstream.

One of Hannah's few joys was mentoring novice students as they developed into professional nurses, but in the process, she neglected her own well-being. Her green eyes brimmed with despair. Her somber mood often drew comments from coworkers at the hospital: "You're a beautiful woman. Stop looking so glum. Go out and have some fun," they'd say. She'd just smile and reply, "I'm a single parent with two teenagers. Who has time for relationships?"

After several hours of monitoring John's condition, she hooked her purse over her shoulder and trudged to the door. "He's in much better shape than when we started. Just make sure he gets the hospital follow-up."

Jaide nodded. "Must you go?"

"The kids will be home soon after spending the whole day with their father, and I have to start preparing dinner," she said, rubbing her arm.

"I guess a mother's work is never done," he said, opening the door as she stepped out.

"I'll drop by again tomorrow to check on him. If there's any drastic change, call me." She forced a smile.

Instead of reaching for her, Jaide slipped his hands into his pockets. "What if I call you for dinner?"

Hannah looked at his gentle face, her eyes unsurprised yet quietly dejected. "If you think you can cope with my busy schedule and unruly teenagers, then you're more foolish than I think you are," she said, shifting her feet. "Jaide, you have a kind heart. I like that about you. But truthfully, I think my kids will mow right over you."

"That remains to be seen," he said, lifting his chin defiantly. When she said nothing else, Jaide kissed her cheek. Their eyes met momentarily, but she softly pushed him away. Halfway down the walkway, she turned and gave him a long assessing look.

Late that night, Jaide stood over the man he'd rescued, still grappling with the mystery behind his battered appearance. John's sunken eyes remained rolled back, but his face had regained some color, and his breathing had stabilized. The IV fluids had eased the convulsions, save for occasional flinches in his atrophied legs. As the sun dipped below the horizon, Jaide sighed, wearied by the day's emotional toll.

Cold, inhuman fingers clamped around his arm. He gasped and stumbled back, but the grip only tightened. For a heartbeat too long, he couldn't breathe. Fingers, like ice, dug into his skin. John's blue eyes locked onto his, chilling in their unnatural clarity. The man said nothing, but his eyes did all the talking: *Help me. Don't leave.*

Then the man slumped back.

Jaide lingered, the plea seared through his mind. Would his care suffice? Here, he wasn't just a patient, a number, or a case to process. He was human, and that mattered. It had always mattered. Healing is a duty owed freely, not some transaction.

Against the grain of reason, conviction guided Jaide's choice.

* * *

The next day, John Doe remained comatose, but the convulsions had ceased. During her visit, Hannah checked his vitals. She noted the sluggish but reactive dilation, replaced the empty IV bags, and adjusted the flow rate.

Jaide fitted an adult diaper with quiet focus. Together, they moved the man's limbs to stimulate circulation.

Hannah dropped her penlight into her purse, her movements clipped and tight. "What is this man still doing here?" she asked. "He should be in a hospital."

Jaide turned toward her, eyes lit with belief rather than defiance. "Something happened last night," he said, swallowing hard. "He reached out to me. He wanted my help."

Her brows lifted, voice tight with disbelief. "He spoke to you?"

Jaide paced, searching for words. "Not exactly," he admitted. "He pleaded . . . with his eyes."

"Wait, what?"

"I know it sounds crazy," he said. "But when he looked at me, I knew." He paused. "There was a connection, something deeper than words."

Hannah crossed her arms, choosing her words carefully. "Jaide, I think you're too entrenched in your own perspective to see past your personal bias. What if he dies under your care?"

Jaide's voice rose. "If I hadn't driven by that highway, he'd already be dead."

Hannah let her arms fall, her stance softening. *John Doe is improving. His vitals are stable. There's a chance, however slim, that he might wake soon. But is that enough to justify keeping him here?*

She glanced at her watch. "I have to go, or I'll be late for work." She stepped closer, her voice low. "I hope, for his sake, you're making the right decision."

The following day, Jaide fell asleep while reading a dystopian novel about machines wiping out humankind, only to discover they needed humanity to find purpose. The book lay face down, its pages caressing his leg. Had he been awake, he would have noticed that his guest was registering rapid eye movement, a sign of returning brain activity. A sequence of images flashed through John Doe's mind:

Following a knock at the bathroom door, a playful voice said, "Come out, come out, wherever you are." A teenage John Doe remained still as he crouched on the toilet seat. Another person shouted, "That's enough with the fuckin' horseplay. Let me show you how it's done!" He heard the door slam against the wall. The metal face plate tore off the wooden frame and slid across the floor. It glided past the stall door and collided with the toilet beneath him. The boy shuddered.

He stared at her with astringent eyes. "That's ridiculous! Everyone and their mother will try to dig up Kathryn's grave! Look what happened to King Tut!"

Trapped inside a freezer, a young John Doe could hear his father screaming, "Out of the way!" Then he heard the thud of a metal object striking the padlock. Every time his father swung the axe, everyone, including John Doe, cringed at the sickening sound.

"Stop!" The security guard drew his gun from his holster and shouted at John Doe, who ran past in a black ski mask. He made it safely out of the bank, but when he darted across the street, he put himself in harm's way before a speeding fuel tanker. Its tires skidded on the rain-beaten asphalt. John Doe gasped.

The pastor gazed upon John Doe and said, "While we live in a world where money is king, evil will always exist. The least we can do is look after those less fortunate than ourselves."

Beads of sweat rolled down his neck. John Doe trembled as he removed the flashlight cover and, with a jerk, exposed the battery compartment, only to find it empty. He breathed deeply and cried out, "Let me out of here!"

Rapid dreams came and went, lasting from a few seconds to a minute. The stranger's leg twitched, and behind the lids his eyes shifted as quickly as a seismograph needle recording a tremor. Neural activity showed strong conductivity along the nerves. Despite minimal myelin loss, signals remained intact.

Jaide slumped in his cushioned chair, breathing slowly and evenly in his sleep, oblivious to John's progress.

* * *

When Jaide woke the next morning, John Doe's eyes were open, focused on the ceiling. Though physically awake, he was still lost in a disoriented haze. Jaide stood at his side, rubbing his chin thoughtfully. *Who could've done such a horrible thing to another human being? What could anyone do to deserve such cruel punishment?* He sat gingerly on the edge, careful not to disturb the man. Given his guest's improving condition, he considered whether to take him to the hospital for evaluation.

"You must be the one . . . who saved my life." John Doe's voice croaked, as if speaking from the grave.

Standing quickly, Jaide looked down at the young man. "I found you unconscious on the roadside. Any kindhearted man would have done the same."

The patient studied his surroundings. Country music played softly from an old-fashioned radio on a wooden table beside him. Across the room stood a sturdy oak dresser, its surface cluttered with perfume bottles, old letters tied with ribbon, and a framed mirror. The dresser bore the faint scratches of time, revealing its age and character. *A woman's room.* His gaze landed on an open three-tier jewelry box filled with costume jewelry. *An older woman's room.*

Something deeper flickered beneath John's surface: regret etched into the furrow of his brow, and gratitude softened the corners of his mouth. Blinking slowly, he shifted his arms, each movement aching. Though sunlight spilled through the window, he had no sense of time or what day it was. He turned toward his savior, whose soft brown eyes held a quiet kindness. "Where am I?" he asked, his voice frail.

"You're in my house in Millers Creek, North Carolina," Jaide said, reaching for a water bottle. He unscrewed the plastic cap. "Today is Wednesday, September 15, 2004. It's nine forty-five in the morning, and my name is Jaide." He held the bottle so the man could take a sip, enough to wet his throat and soothe his chapped lips. "What's your name?"

The mysterious man ran his fingers through his oily hair, thinking. He had no memory of ever being in North Carolina, no idea how he ended up there. "Alex," he said finally, his eyes unfocused. "Alexander Blackwell."

* * *

The tempting aroma awakened his senses, but after just a few sips of chicken broth, Alex vomited into a trash can beside the bed, his body shivering. "I-I can't," he said, breathing heavily, his heart shuddering, each beat like distant thunder.

Jaide helped him roll back under the light blanket. "One step at a time," he said, offering a wet wipe, his voice a soothing balm to the man's frayed nerves and aching body.

Alex closed his eyes and allowed the bed to consume him. Every muscle throbbed with the dull persistence of a fever that never broke. After regaining his composure, he tried the soup again but ended up dry heaving, his hope flickering like a dying flame. He'd thought he could keep it down.

Later that afternoon, Alex managed to eat a little without puking, and by nightfall, he had no trouble keeping down some applesauce. He even felt strong enough to begin light physical therapy. That evening, he met Jaide's lady friend, though her name escaped him. Everything was happening too fast to track. She was pretty, but not like his Stacey. Clearly trained as a nurse, she worked quietly and efficiently, removing the IV line and applying a pressure dressing. Her visit was brief, just long enough to check his vitals before heading to work. Alex could tell Jaide had feelings for her, but he sensed she wasn't ready to commit. Still, something told him it was only a matter of time before she warmed up to him.

Alex owed his savior everything. If not for Jaide, he'd be rotting in a field, filling the stomachs of wild critters and worms. The least he could do was explain how he ended up there. He cleared his throat, propped himself against the pillow, and told the most unusual story Jaide had ever heard. As a child, he discovered he could teleport by clearing his mind and focusing on where he wanted to reappear. This incredible feat prompted his father to demand secrecy.

He started innocently enough, clearing into his brother's room and pilfering small objects as a joke. One day, Bart spent hours searching for his wallet while Alex stayed hidden in his room, reeling with laughter. The best part was returning it to make his brother look foolish. Accompanied by his father, Alex stormed into Bart's room to say, *Is this the wallet you accused me of stealing? All this time, it was sitting on your dresser, you blind bat!*

Before long, Alex began plundering his neighbors' purses and wallets. As the years progressed, so did his rapacious nature. He became a skilled burglar who baffled police by clearing into high-security targets: department stores, banks, jewelry stores. His biggest caper was lifting two sacks of cut diamonds from an international gem distributor and selling the lot to a famous retail chain. Operating between New York and Long Island, Alex amassed a fortune worth over $3 million without raising suspicion.

Jaide wondered whether saving his life was such a good idea. He had allowed a professional thief into his home, a corrupt man whose actions flouted everything he believed about money. With his hands in his pockets, he asked, "Could you demonstrate this clearing ability?"

Silence filled the space between them. Eyes locked, both wondered who would back down first.

Still weak, Alex swung his trembling legs over the edge of the bed and licked his dry lips. He shut his eyes and cleared his mind. *All right*, he thought. *This will be easy*. Taking a deep breath, he concentrated on the doorway. But when he opened his eyes, Alex was stunned. He couldn't clear. There was no separation of molecules, no cold shiver coursing through his spine, no tingle in his stomach. Dumbfounded, he glanced at Jaide, embarrassed, and knew precisely what his host was thinking. Rubbing his eyes, Alex closed them again and breathed deeply. He imagined himself standing by the door, but when he opened his eyes, he found himself sitting on the edge of the bed as before.

"You must think I'm crazy," he said with a mortified look.

"If your story is true, Mr. Blackwell, it's possible that your near-death experience altered the way your neurons fire and process information, much like a flickering lightbulb nearing burnout." Jaide sat on a chair and crossed his legs. "That last burst of energy is what probably got you here. Perhaps you're a normal man now," he added, rubbing his chin.

Alex couldn't say it out loud but nodded. Once he longed for normalcy, but now the reality was different from what he'd hoped. "I truly appreciate what you've done for me," he whispered, slipping back into bed. "I should be strong enough to leave tonight. I insist on compensating you for your time and expenses."

"That's not necessary," Jaide replied, dismissing the notion with a wave of his hand. "Besides, it contradicts my principles."

Alex's eyes lit up with a spark of interest. "Religious principles?" He could sense Jaide's apprehension; this hint of secrecy only piqued his curiosity. "I'm intrigued. Perhaps I can help you."

Jaide took a deep breath before voicing his mission. "I'm on a quest to bring peace and happiness to the world," he said, his voice steady and resolute. Gesturing emphatically, he shared his vision for solving humanity's miseries, emphasizing virtue and equality. It stemmed from a profound belief: humanity must free itself from the grip of money to end the systemic injustices plaguing it for millennia. At the heart of his speech was a single conviction: that humanity could ultimately unite. While he acknowledged the challenges of transitioning to such a system, he believed it was possible through collective effort and a shift in mindset. "If the world is going to rethink its relationship with money," he said, "I've got to get the word out."

His drive for worldly goodness enthralled Alex. He had never met anyone with such bold aspirations and determination for change. Jaide's ideas were simple yet effective. *All nations could coexist for humankind's benefit, regardless of ethnicity or religion, if only money weren't in the way. There must be a path I can take to help him. Humanity would benefit greatly from a currency-free society.*

A pang of regret for ignoring his girlfriend, Stacey, struck him. He could have been the kind of savior Jaide wanted to become. She had urged him to use his remarkable talent for the benefit of humanity. The words she had yelled at him from across the room rang in his ears: *This God-given power should be used for the good of the people! You should be saving lives and helping the police apprehend criminals!* Instead, he chose greed and corruption.

"Excuse me for asking," said Alex, sitting up. "What led you to this perspective?"

Jaide shrugged as his eyes drifted away into an unpleasant past. "When I was nineteen, my father was laid off from work and lost our home. The hardship was too much, and my parents packed their bags and returned to India. Watching them go was the most painful moment of my life. I stayed and managed to support myself, but I vowed to bring them back so we could be together again."

"That explains why you want justice and to fight for the disenfranchised."

"With a passion."

"You'll need all the help you can get, my friend. I can hardly wait to live in your fraternal world, but you know it will take years to happen. How do you plan to bring it about?"

"I have several plans," Jaide said, glancing at his watch. It was late, and he was tired from the twenty-four-hour care. Rising to his feet, he retrieved the novel from the floor. "If plan A doesn't work, I can always fall back on plan B."

* * *

The next morning, Alex borrowed some clothes and left, promising to return in several days. After a long taxi ride to Statesville, he flew to New York. There, he retrieved his driver's license and personal items from a bus depot locker and made several transactions in a laundering account.

Alex spent the next three days with his parents in Massapequa, Long Island. He chopped vegetables and stirred the pots while his aging mother sat at the kitchen table and shared family stories. Outside, he helped his father tackle long overdue yard work, pruning the overgrown hedges and mending the broken fence. Weakened, he found the work exhausting, but the satisfaction of seeing the tidy garden made it worthwhile.

Before leaving, Alex called his parents to the living room. He handed them a large wad of cash, along with fat envelopes for Elizabeth, Walter, and his eldest brother, Bartholomew. His father's eyes welled up with gratitude, and his mother hugged him as if she'd never let him go.

On Monday morning, he flew back to Statesville, just as promised.

"Please wait. This won't take long," Alex told the cab driver. He carried no luggage, only his dignity, as he walked toward the all-too-familiar house with its sun-faded shutters. After his near-death experience and reflecting on his corrupt ways, he was plagued with guilt. *I've got to set things right or I'll wrestle with my demons for the rest of my life.* Spending time with his parents helped him face the decisions he'd long avoided.

"I told you I'd be back," he said when Jaide opened the door. "I can't stay. There's a taxi waiting." Alex thrust a thumb over his shoulder. "I've been thinking about your social reform and the joy and peace it will bring to the world. A mission like this will take time, effort, and a great deal of money. I would love to see this new world where people look after one another and monetary crime is eliminated. Your kindness opened my eyes to the life I'd fallen into, something my girlfriend couldn't accomplish." He reached into his coat pocket and withdrew an envelope. "Which is why I'd like you to use this gift to finance your efforts to change the world."

Jaide took the envelope. Inside was a cashier's check for $1 million. He gasped, his heart racing. A shudder ran through him. "I can't possibly take this," he said, his gaze locked in stunned silence.

"The money isn't for you. It's for the cause, to help bring about your ideal world."

"Nevertheless, it's stolen money."

Alex gave him a frank look, tinged with disappointment.

"Some people believe things happen for a reason, that some things are meant to be. Jaide, this is your calling. Perhaps finding me on the side of the road will be the catalyst for a new age for humanity. Use the money for your cause and make the world a better place. You're just one man; don't carry the world's weight on your shoulders. You need others to help you."

Jaide knew he'd need help, lots of it. His concept was monumental, requiring thousands of supporters. With that in mind, he accepted with a humble nod. "Where will you go now?"

"I have a few things I need to take care of." The reformed jewel thief smiled feebly. "It's ironic, isn't it?"

Jaide squinted. "What is?"

"That it takes money to eliminate money."

* * *

Baby blue.

The sky was filled with it.

There was a time when the color filled his childhood days, when soft baby blankets cocooned him in innocence. What was once associated with simpler times now reminded him of icy, forbidding thoughts that left his spirit hollow. In times gone by, baby blue had made him yearn for life. But now, at the precipice of truth, he finally understands that his life wasn't what it seemed. The sky, once a symbol of purity, now taunts him, mocking his past and the criminal path he chose. And when he looks across the vastness of the baby-blue, he feels a pang of truth, for he knows this serene hue will be the last color of freedom he shall ever behold.

* * *

The taxi stopped near the hospital employee entrance, where Alex had waited for Stacey Foster before their many lunch dates. He woke from his daydreams of her just long enough to tell the driver, "Just wait here." He sank back, out of view, his stomach tightening as his foot wagged with nervous energy. *Come on, it's almost noon.*

A few minutes later, Stacey exited the old brick building. *Just like clockwork.* She wore a rose-colored scrub set, her hair pulled back into a ponytail. Her lips curved with familiar warmth, but her eyes held a remote coldness. She appeared thinner and no longer had that swivel in her walk he had always adored. What remained was a power walk.

Though her stride was purposeful, even unfaltering, she glanced over her shoulder more than once, wary of being followed.

Alex closed his eyes momentarily, allowing his memories to engulf him. Her laughter echoed in his mind as a wry smile twisted his lips. *I wonder if she had anything to do with my near-death experience?*

Questions crowded in, but he had no intention of confronting her. He wasn't sure if he could handle the truth. Alex preferred to hold on to the fond memories. He smiled. *Funny how life works. It seems like only yesterday she was shyly covering her small breasts with her hands the first night we made love.* He sighed, remembering how she'd roll her eyes whenever she was upset with him. And that happened a lot. A sly smile crept across his face at the thought of their hard-fought chess games. Smart and beautiful. Those were her trademarks, as unmistakable as a handwritten page in a diary.

"You may go to the next stop, driver," he said, his voice low. The taxi pulled away, and Alex didn't look back.

Moments later, the cab stopped in front of an old brick building with a cement archway over the entrance and a bust of the town's founder perched on top. Alex stepped out, gave the driver a generous tip, and paused before the police department. His gaze lingered on the bust's achromatic gloom, stark against the baby-blue sky. Bracing himself, he took a deep breath and squared his shoulders.

Inside, the officer at the front desk replaced the phone receiver and focused on the man walking into the lobby. The civilian wore a navy blue suit and a lizard-skin belt, its shiny, unscratched buckle glinting like it had just come out of the box. The officer gazed curiously into the man's troubled eyes. "May I help you?" he asked.

Alex leaned forward and placed his hands on the desk. His handsome face twitched briefly, but his blue eyes remained calm and steady. "My name is Alexander Blackwell, and I want to turn myself in."

* * *

Washington, D.C., Tuesday, May 24, 2005.

The sleek silver sedan drove down Pennsylvania Avenue NW and slid smoothly into a vacant spot. Lawrence Devonshire removed his black gloves with an air of sophistication—the result of strict parents and high expectations.

Sitting in the passenger seat, shielding his eyes from the blaring sun, Jaide Basir stared stoically out the window at the restaurant. "Expensive venue?"

"Reputation second to none," replied the senator, shutting off the engine.

Their eyes locked.

"No offense, but would you mind if I pick the place? I'm craving a greasy pastrami sandwich."

Lawrence shrugged. "Fine by me," he said, firing up the car again.

"It's not too far from here," said Jaide, reaching into his pocket for a piece of paper. "Checked out a few places online before I landed. This one had the best reviews for pastrami."

Lawrence grabbed the note from his hand. After reading it, he pulled into traffic. "Isn't this a bad part of town?"

"It might be."

The senator laughed and shook his head. "All right," he said, turning right on 15th Street. "This establishment better be as good as you say it is."

They had been friends for many years, but their phone conversations dwindled as they grew older. Lawrence had less time after becoming an outspoken proponent of equal rights for all Americans. As a senator, he had committed to making justice the cornerstone of his professional life.

Jaide had persistently tried to arrange the meeting, making several attempts with Lawrence's secretary to unveil his peerless social reform. After carefully weighing his options, he determined that

Lawrence, backed by his love for the US Constitution, was the right man to transform the nation, and he hoped, the world. He believed it with conviction. Lawrence had charisma, a look that captured attention, and the influence Jaide would need to pull off the most significant social and political overhaul in the history of humankind.

Jaide rested his ankle on the opposite knee, avoiding the dashboard. His eyes creased with concern. "How is your mother?"

"Not great," Lawrence said with a faint smile. "The doctors have discovered a brain tumor that's causing her blackouts. They can extract the tumor through her nose, but the surgery isn't until next month."

Jaide winced. "Why so long?"

"I've heard the hospital has budget problems. My guess is the surgeon picks his cases based on insurance plans."

"Preferential treatment should be against the law," Jaide said, shaking his head.

"So, what's on your mind?" Lawrence asked, wondering whether his friend was finally ready to call in his debt. Jaide had saved his life, after all.

"This may come as a shock, but I want to discuss a plan to eliminate currency. Worldwide," Jaide said, lowering his leg.

The senator jerked, twitching the wheel so the car swung over the line before he corrected. "I don't think I heard you right. Did you say 'eliminate money'?"

"Yes." Jaide chuckled at the predictable reaction.

Lawrence scratched his neck, trying to clear his confusion. The lines on his forehead grew thicker as he faced him. "And how do you expect people to acquire goods?"

"Societies will function without currency. In other words, everything will have no external value; nothing, that is, except humanity itself," said Jaide, drumming his fingers against the window frame.

Lawrence exploded into genial laughter, slapping the steering wheel several times. "Jaide, I'm the one who bashed his head on a rock."

"Eliminating money, my friend, will solve our global problems . . . including medical preferential treatment." He turned to Lawrence, whose laughter ended abruptly. "We are all born with a divine right to be happy. But somewhere along the line, as adults, we lose sight of the true meaning of existence. Too often, money becomes our main motivation."

"But money makes everybody happy," Lawrence said, turning into the parking lot of a rundown pastrami shop. The building needed repairs and a fresh coat of paint to cover several years' worth of graffiti. Eying the knot of homeless people and young punks passing around a brown paper bag, he clicked his key fob and wondered if this was a good idea after all. A few steps later, Lawrence pressed the button again. The car beeped twice, as if the repetition might somehow offer some imagined extra layer of protection.

They stopped just outside the door to glance at the colorful chalkboard displaying the day's specials: chicken club sandwich, curly fries, and a drink. As Lawrence skimmed the board, Jaide waved several people ahead of them.

"I'm talking about true happiness. The kind that lives in our hearts and minds," he explained confidently. "The same happiness that lives in every innocent child."

From the corner of his eye, he saw a woman walking toward them, carrying a bag of groceries. Her son followed, jumping over cracks in the cement and singing. "This is what I mean," he said, reaching a hand to stop the woman and assuring her she wasn't in danger.

He turned back to the senator. "This child is innocent, untainted by money or greed. All men have this intrinsic capability."

Jaide leaned down and gave the boy a big smile. Giggling, the boy smiled back shyly. Turning to the woman, the visionary traced a smile over his mouth with his finger. "Laughter," he said, peering into her dark eyes. "Do you understand me?" Jaide traced another smile and repeated, "Laughter."

"Si," she nodded. Waving a hand expressively, she added, "Las carcajadas de un hombre son la miel del mundo." Realizing they didn't understand, she repeated, "Las carcajadas de un hombre son la miel del mundo."

"What did she say?" asked Lawrence.

"Not sure, maybe something about laughter being the window to our soul." Jaide nodded and clapped his hands. "You are so right, sweet woman."

Sunlight streamed through the large windows, casting a warm glow over the worn tables and chairs. At the far end, a well-stocked bar beckoned with an array of liquor bottles and glasses, twinkling like stars in the afternoon light. The walls and shelves overflowed with Old West memorabilia, each piece whispering its tale of a bygone era. Country music hummed in the background, weaving a tapestry of nostalgia and authenticity. The restaurant's décor wasn't just seen; it was felt, wrapping visitors in a welcoming embrace of history and warmth.

A waitress sporting a nostalgic peach-and-white checkered dress and a neatly coiffed style tucked under a hairnet led Jaide and Lawrence to a booth. They each ordered iced tea and a pastrami sandwich, slathered with mustard and pickles. Lawrence added grilled onions with a side of coleslaw, just like he used to back in grad school in the Bronx.

"Jaide, the world isn't flawless," Lawrence said, straightening his tie before tucking it into his immaculate white dress shirt. "Not by a long shot. We just have to make the best of it."

"You're right," replied Jaide, leaning forward. "*We* are going to make the best of it."

Lawrence stared at him, eyes narrowed. "Besides, what will you do with the people who don't want to work for the benefit of humankind?"

Jaide smiled, clasping his hands. "Every society has rule-breakers. It's important to let the democratic process address these problems as they arise. However, with the right system of incentives and recognition, we can encourage everyone to actively contribute to society's well-being. This could include public recognition, opportunities for personal and professional growth, and access to additional resources. In a system where everyone contributes based on their abilities and skills, everyone feels valued. The main focus is to eliminate 70 to 90 percent of society's problems to promote peace and harmony. By ensuring that basic needs, such as housing, food, clothing, and healthcare are met for all individuals, we can create an environment where people are motivated to work for society's benefit rather than out of necessity."

Lawrence leaned forward, giving him a disapproving look. "How is that possible? We can't even feed the homeless in our own country, much less the rest of the world."

"Says the man who gave up on humanity!" Jaide slammed his palm on the tabletop, attracting several glances from people nearby.

Annoyance crept over Lawrence's face.

"You know very well there's enough food in the world to feed everyone," continued Jaide. "The biggest problems are food waste and cold storage. Nobody wants to pay the cost, which is why things haven't changed." He tapped the table twice for emphasis. "Globally, we slaughter seventy-five *billion* animals for food every year. Of that amount, an estimated eighteen billion end up in landfills."[1]

---

[1] Kenny Torrella, "We raise 18 billion animals a year to die — and then we don't even eat them," *Vox*, December 12, 2023, https://www.vox.com/future-perfect/22890292/food-waste-meat-dairy-eggs-milk-animal-welfare.

"That's terrible," said Lawrence with alarm.

"Damn right!" Jaide straightened in his seat. "Across the board, waste is estimated at between 30 and 40 percent of *all* food.[2] Retail stores exacerbate the problem with overstocking and poor inventory management."

"Much of it has to do with unsold products past their expiration dates, and damaged or bruised fruits and vegetables that are no longer aesthetically pleasing," Lawrence added, nodding in agreement.

Jaide gave him the thumbs-up. "Food frequently spoils during transportation and storage, resulting in more waste."

Amid the flurry of activity, a waitress rushed past their booth carrying dirty dishes. Lawrence could see the head chef surveying the chaos with a critical eye. Blinking away the distraction, he turned his attention back to Jaide.

"At the consumer level, food waste is frequently due to impulse buying and super-sized meals at restaurants," Jaide continued. "And let's not forget the buffet line, where restraint goes to die."

Lawrence raised his right hand. "Guilty as charged."

"We've all been there, haven't we?" Their laughter echoed a shared experience. "It's an environmental issue when you consider the water and energy needed to harvest, grow, package, and transport food. And the ultimate result? More methane in our landfills from rotting food."

Lawrence chuckled, still thinking about his sly remark.

Taking a sip of tea, Jaide closed his eyes, savoring the refreshing taste. "After some research, I discovered that most waste comes from a lack of infrastructure in developing countries. On the other hand, in developed countries, the low cost of food encourages more waste as the portion size increases. Higher-income families waste more than

---

[2] "Food Waste FAQs," USDA, accessed August 2, 2024, https://www.usda.gov/foodwaste/faqs.

lower-income ones. According to the USDA, the percentage of waste is greater at the consumer level than at the retail. However . . ." He paused, his eyes flaring with anger. "I was disturbed to discover that large retailers hold annual competitions to see who can pump out the most rotisserie chicken. Those that go unsold nationwide are thrown away. All of that, for what? A trophy?"

"That *is* alarming." The lines of the senator's mouth tightened, distress flaring in his eyes.

"We should produce only what we consume. We need to stop slaughtering animals for the sake of profit."

"So, how do you propose solving these issues?"

"In America alone, much of the fruit that falls from trees decays before it can be collected. Millions of pounds of produce rot in fields every year. Frankly, our food distribution system sucks!

"Let's create a global logistics system that coordinates distribution centers and mobilizes transportation: trucks, trains, planes, and ships to deliver fruits and vegetables worldwide while they're still edible.

"What the?" With a bewildered look on his face, Lawrence slapped his forehead.

"In India, 30 to 40 percent of produce is lost because they lack cold storage. I say supply the workforce and build all the cold storage they need. And let's not stop there! Let's supply cold storage to underdeveloped countries around the globe!" Jaide beamed. He drove his message home, nearly rising from his seat.

Lawrence was shaking his head in disbelief. "Wait just a darn minute," he said, holding up both hands. "That's insane. No one in their right mind would even suggest that, Jaide. The cost would be astronomical!"

Jaide leaned forward and whispered, "So why not eliminate the cost?"

The senator froze, his mouth slightly agape. He blinked and looked into Jaide's eyes. For a moment, he seemed to consider the idea, but then . . . "No! It can't be done!" he cried, shaking his head.

"Tell me, Senator," Jaide said, thrusting a finger in the air and sweeping his hand across the table. "Could we accomplish all these things if there weren't any costs?"

Lawrence knew the answer was obvious. His heart beat faster; he wanted to lie, but it was impossible. "Maybe." His shoulders rose as he sighed, defeated. "Yes, we could."

"Here we are, gentlemen. Two pastrami sandwiches," the waitress chirped. Her sudden appearance let the ambient clatter of dishes settle around them.

"Ah, saved by the bell." Lawrence winked at his partner, a smile creeping into view.

The waitress set the red plastic baskets on the table and refilled their tea glasses. Grateful for the break, Lawrence took a hearty bite of his sandwich. He gave Jaide a thumbs-up to continue.

The sandwich was far from Jaide's mind. Eager to maintain his momentum, he leaned back and raked a hand through his hair. "Lawrence," he said. "The world has relied on money for thousands of years. It has hurled humanity into a senseless rat race and degraded our ethical compass. This is why global problems persist and worsen each year. And it only gets worse every year. But there is hope for us. We can change this. We must change this."

Jaide nodded, his gaze softening with compassion. "We can make this world a better place by bringing joy to the lives of every single person. All this begins with one simple shift: We must strive not to become men of success but rather men of value, as Albert Einstein once advised.[3] Wouldn't you love to live in a world without theft, lies,

---

[3]As quoted by William Miller, "Death of a Genius," *LIFE Magazine*, May 2, 1955, 64.

and murder? A world where people look out for one another in harmony?" he asked, placing a hand over his heart for emphasis.

"Who wouldn't?" Lawrence said through his half-chewed bite. He swallowed and added, "But that's an impracticable task, if not impossible."

"If we eliminate money, we remove the evil that it generates: envy, anger, hate, crime, and other social and financial problems," Jaide continued, his voice steady. "A well-mannered community filled with affection and empathy is the ideal way to live. We can recognize our place in this world and ask ourselves four simple questions: Where are we today? What have we done to create this mess? What can we do to rectify this? What do we want to accomplish? These are simple questions that require no complex answers. You don't need to be a genius to tackle them." He shook his head. "The path to happiness has been ignored for thousands of years, but now it is time to bring it to light. I want to begin by giving you a sense of what a world without currency would be like."

As a visionary and idealist, Jaide's passion burned brightly. "Let's give humanity a chance to advance," he said, eyes drifting upward as if listening to a higher power. "Working for the benefit of humankind will propel us forward. We must stay committed to helping those in need. Imagine a life free from the shackles of inflation, deflation, recession, or unemployment. Without money, society will elevate us by uniting us in a shared humanity where every contribution and resource holds intrinsic value.

"It's a dog-eat-dog world. Money brings out the worst in humanity. By eliminating currency, we eliminate all kinds of evil. Take, for instance, banks pushing deceptive subprime loans into foreclosure and bankruptcy. Hedge fund managers who charge hefty fees for bogus investments. Mortgage brokers who swindle homeowners in equity-skimming schemes."

Lawrence jumped in. "How about developers who flip properties at a nominal cost to create the illusion they're worth more than their actual value? Or predatory lenders who target the lower class and senior citizens with deceptive practices?"

Jaide blinked. He hadn't considered those. "And that's just the tip of the iceberg."

The senator scratched his neck. He understood where Jaide was headed, and truthfully, he had become disgusted by the sheer number of ways humankind had taken advantage of one another. His expressive eyes grew troubled, and his fingers tapped lightly against the cushioned seat.

"The sooner we eliminate money," Jaide went on, "the sooner we stop medical and dental professionals from jeopardizing patients' health for profit by billing insurance companies through upcoding, performing unnecessary procedures like C-sections, hysterectomies, and coronary bypasses to inflate claims, prescribing drugs for kickbacks, and drilling into perfectly healthy teeth."

Jaide paused to take a bite. The sour taste sent his salivary glands into overdrive, a tingling spreading through his jaw as he savored it. With a flicker of resolve, he stared out the window, taking in the degradation of the nation's capital. *The people have lost their pride, and the problems keep piling up.*

After washing down his food, he turned back to Lawrence and said, "We recently saw a massive corporate scandal."

"Right," agreed Lawrence, suppressing a shudder. "Enron perpetrated the biggest accounting fraud in history, bilking investors out of billions."

"And you know what's just as bad?"

"Ponzi schemes that rob investors blind, and so-called traders pumping up stock prices, then dumping them for profit."

Jaide nodded, thrilled that the senator was getting into the spirit of his plan. "Precisely," he said with an approving wink. "Imagine a world without misappropriation of funds, no deception in the entertainment industry, no unscrupulous contractors taking deposits for jobs they never finish, and no dishonest chiropractors exploiting fake car accident claims, or collusion between companies to inflate prices."

As Jaide became more enthusiastic, his hand gestures broadened, threatening their drinks. "Consider a world where no state or city officials inflate their salaries, accept bribes, and/or pocket secret kickbacks."

A chill settled over the senator. The lines on his face deepened as he thought about the injustices and struggles so many people endured. On at least two occasions, his elderly mother had been conned out of significant savings.

Leaning in closer, Jaide tapped the table again. "Picture a world without kidnapping for ransom, depression and suicide caused by financial strain, murder for insurance money, bank and store robberies, vandalism of ATMs and vending machines. And what would the world be like without illegal organ harvesting?"

"A much safer place for our poor and weak," admitted Lawrence, lowering his sandwich mid-bite. "That's been going on since the '80s. 'Transplant tourism,' they called it. I'd love to see a stop to that, not to mention the illegal drug trade and cartel violence."

"Wouldn't we all?" Jaide said, his voice rising with excitement. "I don't know about you, but I'd take a world without identity theft, income tax violations, illegal dog fighting, and hacking into bank accounts . . ."

Lawrence tipped his head slightly, challenging his friend in a verbal game of criminal checkers, and said, "Drug smuggling."

"Digital piracy," said Jaide, locking eyes with the senator.

"Modern high-seas piracy."

"Workers' compensation fraud."

"Charity scams," Lawrence said smugly.

"Nigerian letter scams," Jaide shot back.

Stopping to think, the senator said, "Increased juvenile delinquency."

His opponent blocked his move. "Forest fires started by out-of-work firefighters!"

Jaide laughed, enjoying the senator's surprise. In a calm voice, he said, "We live in a tangled web of money and crime. Don't we, Senator?"

Lawrence stared at him, appalled by the crimes humanity indulged in.

Jaide pressed his hands together in prayer. "And yet, we expect God to bail us. We are so entrenched in money that we don't realize the Lord is waiting for us—to wake up!"

At a loss for words, the senator closed his eyes. His lips thinned and his jaw tensed.

"Einstein once said, 'Without ethical culture, there is no salvation for humanity.'[4]" Jaide rubbed his hand across his face. "If you're poor, life on Earth is miserable," he said, his voice somber. "In contrast, how many of the wealthy few, the elite, haven't manipulated the system, lied, stolen, even killed for their material goods?"

Lawrence didn't take offense. He knew Jaide was referring to career criminals.

"Just like a story has a beginning, middle, and end, we should strive to give humanity a happy ending."

"Who doesn't love a happy ending?" Lawrence nodded in agreement.

"Now I ask you, Senator. What would *you* do in a society without our corrupt ways?"

"Rejoice!" Lawrence said. A smile creased his eyes and

[4] Albert Einstein, "The Need for an Ethical Culture," a speech given at the Ethical Culture Society, New York, NY, January 5, 1951.

glimmered with hope that cut through the doom and gloom shrouding his face.

Jaide leaned back and asked, "So what are we waiting for?" He chuckled. A clear 'I told you so' written across his face. "Let me tell you what *we* are missing in our lives . . ."

Having laid out the negativity, his face lit up like a beacon of hope.

"Humankind deserves the best in life. We are not born to worry whether we have enough to make ends meet. We are born to be happy, not to struggle. We are born to cherish our *entire* lives, not to retire during our last frail ten or fifteen years when we can least enjoy ourselves. I say, master a profession that brings you joy, give it your all for twenty-five years, and retire at forty-five when you're still young enough to embrace your family and the world."

Lawrence did a double take. "You want us to retire at forty-five?" His eyebrows raised with the slightest hint of sarcasm.

Jaide nodded, grinning.

"Tell me, what can you do at age sixty-two? Can you run a marathon, swim the English Channel? Can you summit mountains with arthritis and other diseases? And guess what? The retirement age keeps getting pushed back out of fear that the country will deplete its social security funds. Is this going forward or backward? I don't understand this new math."

The murmur of conversations enveloped them, punctuated by bursts of laughter. Jaide took another bite, letting Lawrence reflect. He searched the senator's eyes for understanding.

"Look at it this way," he continued. "Money—or rather, the lack of it—has held us back. It prevents us from building additional schools and universities we desperately need, especially in less-developed countries. It keeps us from hiring more teachers, reducing overcrowding, and publishing updated textbooks."

"Now there's something we can agree on," Lawrence said, folding his arms on the table.

"Can you imagine the suffering we could alleviate with more hospitals, all with the latest medical technology?"

The image of his ailing mother was front and center in the senator's mind.

"Medical research centers lack the funds to discover cures for cancer, bipolar disorder, Down syndrome, AIDS, autism, Alzheimer's, cerebral palsy, and Parkinson's, to name just a few. Shame on *us* for allowing money to determine whether we can perform medical research!" Jaide admonished, his hands clenching the table. He paused pointedly. "Money stops us from changing our gas cars for clean, efficient solar-powered vehicles. We can't fix our roads or install enough light posts, much less contend with homelessness and poverty. Greed prevents us from eradicating slums and transforming rundown communities into places of pride."

I know of several cities in California that would welcome your plan, thought Lawrence.

"By now, we should already have a base on the moon and several space stations between Earth and Mars. Funding shortfalls have kept this global dream out of reach."

"I won't argue with that," said Lawrence, wiping the corners of his mouth. "Many great programs have suffered due to a lack of funds."

Jaide glanced at the artificial hanging plant, its cobweb vibrating softly under the air conditioner's gentle stream. "Enough with the negative issues we have created in this house. Now comes the fun part." This was his favorite part of the spiel: the promise of fulfilling our deepest desires, of honoring our reason for being. "Allow me to explain what humanity can accomplish without money."

"I'm all ears." Lawrence popped another fry into his mouth.

"Everyone will have enough food and clothing." Jaide smacked his fist against the table, punctuating the end of world hunger. "Every family living in this house of broken bones will have their own private home."

"That's quite a noble gesture," said Lawrence, glancing at the waitress making her coffee rounds.

"In the early days of civilization, humans started on the wrong foot by creating currency. Ever since then, we have lived with restrictions, hatred, envy, murder, lies, and crime. There are plenty of broken bones, no doubt. And now . . .

It is time to mend these broken bones."

"Nice analogy," Lawrence interrupted, taking another bite.

Jaide's hand went up, closing the gap between his thumb and forefinger. "Take ants, for example. They are creatures no bigger than a grain of rice that live in harmony as a unified entity. They work together to support the colony by tapping into nearby resources and modifying their habitat. They build roadways, supply food and water to all, and repair their colonies, without the need for money. For crying out loud! They even have graveyards!

"It's time for the world's governments to do what they're supposed to: provide safety and public order, hope, food, education, homes, clothing, good health, happiness. Only then can people discover their purpose and help advance all of humankind."

Jaide leaned forward, ready to unleash his grand finale.

"For those who prefer resort-style living, I envision Las Vegas as the model for every community. Instead of cramped, roach-infested apartments, picture casino-style resorts that offer luxurious suite-style living, transforming every block, every city, every nation. Each resort would feature first-floor amenities: a supermarket, a pharmacy, a fitness center to promote healthy living, and entertainment options like nightclubs, arcades, theaters, and five-star restaurants. These mega-resorts would be built to the strictest fire and earthquake safety standards. Each property would span 100 acres, roughly the size of 300 typical homes. By building upward, with thirty-story high-rises, they could comfortably house 1,500 families in spacious, comfortable suites. Building skyward is the clear solution to housing shortages.

"And for those who prefer single-family homes, we'll offer upgrades that reflect cultural richness and personal pride with Spanish courtyards, Japanese gardens, homes adorned with Moroccan tiles, or minimalist Nordic design. Inside, families can personalize their spaces with hardwood or marble flooring, fine artwork, designer furnishings, and extraordinary kitchens. Every home will reflect beauty and self-expression."

Lawrence's jaw dropped. All he could see were dollar signs. Lots of them, enough to fill a stadium. "Jaide, every time you open your mouth, the price tag explodes. You're well into the zillions by now," said Lawrence, shaking his head.

"All I ask is to take money out of the equation. Imagine what can be accomplished." Jaide pulled out his phone, pretended to tap a few numbers on the calculator app, and held it up. "According to my calculations, this is the cost of my plan."

0, read the screen.

Lawrence rolled his eyes. "I should've seen that coming."

"Now let's talk about transportation. Our highways are more congested every year. Instead, clean, efficient monorails can transport people from resort to resort, city to city. Cars and trucks will run on electric and solar power to eliminate pollution and restore our beautiful blue sky."

Guests chatted animatedly at their tables as an emergency vehicle wailed by outside. Lawrence listened with a furrowed brow, trying to consider objectively what his friend suggested.

"Car companies can build smart vehicles that keep drunk people from driving, enable night vision for nighttime driving, follow speed limits to curb reckless driving, detect motorcyclists within a twenty-five-foot radius, and communicate with traffic signals to anticipate red lights and prevent intersection collisions."

"A detection system for motorcyclists is a clever concept," Lawrence said, leaning back. "I like that!"

"So do I," said Jaide, nodding triumphantly. "But it's not just about clever tech or safer roads. If we want to change the world, we have to start with the mind . . .

"We'll build universities to spark curiosity and quench the thirst for knowledge. Everyone will have the same opportunities to become doctors, dentists, nurses, teachers, and chefs trained in global cuisines, including French pastry and Thai street food. Musicians will master every genre, and technicians will modernize traditional knowledge. We'll need more people in these fields to serve the needs of the many. And to shape the world they'll inhabit, a new generation of engineers and drafters will dream up the cities of tomorrow . . .

"If everyone has an education, everyone becomes equal. The old will be respected. The young will be raised to become great thinkers. In our new society, teachers will be revered for the first time in the United States."

"That is long overdue," Lawrence said, nodding.

"And this will hit home for you," Jaide continued, lowering his voice. "We'll build more hospitals where no one worries about how to pay or waits months for treatment . . .

"Providing individuals with the finer things in life will foster their growth. Offer them large parks with exotic trees, waterfalls, a brook to wade in, hiking trails, shade structures, rock climbing walls, and play systems with the latest mind-stimulating activities for kids. Amusement parks will go high-tech and plentiful, reducing wait times to fifteen minutes or less . . .

"There'll be scores of salons and barbershops. When people feel dapper and confident, they treat their communities with respect. Why vandalize what you're proud of?"

Jaide paused, gazing hopefully at some kids a few tables over. In the momentary silence, the senator considered the possibilities and nodded with approval.

"With everyone working for the benefit of humankind, our societies will have what they need to thrive. To avoid waste, factories will produce only what is needed. Currently, the US government and the Federal Reserve track GDP and tweak interest rates to manage unemployment. Instead, governments could spend their energy monitoring production."

"That would require a complete overhaul of our entire system," Lawrence said, the weight of it finally settling in.

"But it will be for the best, Senator." Jaide paused. "Our new society will foster a culture of love, trust, hope, and giving. When everyone works for the good of humanity, neighbors of every background, belief, and language will build each other's homes, trade stories over lunch, and shake hands at the end of the day with one simple phrase: 'Thank you, brother.' For you see, only a life lived for others is worth living, as the brilliant Einstein once eloquently put it.[5] We will respect one another. We'll learn to tip our hats to strangers, to say 'good morning,' and mean it."

"But Jaide," said the senator, raising a hand. The hiss and sizzle from the open kitchen grew louder. "If everyone works for the benefit of humankind, that would mean full employment. How do we determine who is worth more? What about workers with less desirable jobs, like janitors and garbage collectors?"

"Don't look at it that way," Jaide waved away the objection with a smirk.

"There is no other way to look at it!" Lawrence said, his voice throbbing with conviction.

---

[5] Quoted in "Einstein Is Terse in Rule for Success," (Short title) *New York Times*, June 20, 1932.

"*Everyone* will work to advance humanity. Janitors and trash collectors are just as important as workers in any other field. Wouldn't you like to enter a spotless public restroom anywhere?"

"Who wouldn't?"

"Wouldn't you like to see clean city streets?"

"I expect clean streets in every community."

"They are essential workers, just like any other. Janitors, trash collectors, hospital orderlies, restaurant workers—" Jaide swung his arm to encompass everyone in the diner. "They deserve full respect—no less than doctors and nurses. Some may choose not to attend universities but to enter a field that provides care for others. These individuals also have the drive and heart to serve their communities."

Lawrence clapped a hand over his mouth to stifle his true thoughts. "Look," he said, pushing his basket aside. "Everything you have articulated is true. However, hurling a monkey wrench into our system is absurd!"

"You think it's absurd only because it's never been tried. People are always afraid of the unknown. But think about this. Imagine it the other way around, where humanity has been manufacturing goods at no cost and working without pay for thousands of years, all goods and services free to everyone in a glorious, crime-free lifestyle. Here's the big question in reverse: Senator, why don't we abolish our free society and develop a system where people work eight hours a day, forty hours a week, every day until we reach the age of sixty-six? Furthermore, let's exchange paper and iron to pay for our clothes, food, and a thirty-year mortgage, costing hundreds of thousands of dollars. And give up a world without crime? Would you say I'm crazy, or that my idea is brilliant? You tell me which one is absurd?"

Lawrence gritted his teeth, a nervous tic pulsing on his jawline. Silence stood between them. He took a deep breath and sat back. "I have no response to that." A moment later, he added, "Jaide, your ideas are monumental. I'll give you that. What are you going to do? Publish them?"

"I have a better solution." Jaide sat back without breaking his stare, a smirk forming at the corner of his mouth. "I have you."

Lawrence never saw it coming. His hands went up in a defensive gesture, an invisible shield against Jaide's subversive ideas. He fired off a barrage of emphatic no's. "I did say I'd do anything for you, no matter how difficult it was. But this is completely unrealistic, not to mention impossible! How would I even begin to accomplish such a massive undertaking?"

"That's easy," said Jaide, leaning forward, ready for the kill. "You know how Abraham Lincoln abolished slavery?"

Lawrence rolled his eyes. "Who doesn't?"

"I want *you* to abolish money," said Jaide. "Let's begin with our nation and reach out to others if all goes well."

It felt like being hit by a ton of bricks. Lawrence's fingers burrowed into his short hair as he shook his head in disbelief. "That would cause utter chaos! People would run amok, pillaging stores right and left!" He stared, unblinking.

"I admit that's a possibility at first, but things will settle down. Our choices dramatically impact our lives. You have the power to choose a new reality, one that sets your life on the right path."

Jaide let the words hang, settling over the senator like dust in sunlight. He let the silence do its work—let the meaning take root.

Then he said, "Reset the world, Senator."

Lawrence dropped the last piece of his sandwich into the basket. "It's impossible," he said, his face flushed, voice tight. "The world runs on money. It's built on it. I can't change that!" He tugged at his collar, breath tight. *I wish I'd never agreed to lunch today!* His brows furrowed. In a few swift moves, he dropped a large bill from his wallet on the table, slung his coat over his shoulder, and was on his feet. Glowering, he drew a sharp breath. "I can't take this anymore! This conversation isn't going anywhere for me. You—" Lawrence pointed an accusatory finger. "Go find yourself another sucker." He turned and headed toward the door.

"Where is the undying equality and justice you claimed to protect?" Jaide sat back, resolute. "Where does that leave the little people?"

The senator stopped dead in his tracks, glanced up, and let out a disturbed sigh. *Oh, no. You're not going there!* He spun around and loomed over Jaide, "Listen, you son of a bitch. I worked my ass off to get where I am today. How dare you tell me I'm only looking out for myself!"

"Hey! Hey!" The cry came from the table next to them. "This is a family restaurant. My wife and little girl can hear you."

Glancing over, Lawrence saw the man's pleading eyes. His wife wore a concerned look; the little girl stared at him, fear emerging in her gaze. Conversation stilled as diners craned to watch.

"My apologies," he said, shaking his head in humiliation. "There was no need for profanity." Slapping his thigh in defeat, he added, "Please enjoy your lunch on me." He reached for his wallet and pulled out another large bill. After placing it on the man's table, the tension eased.

Sitting down across from Jaide again, Lawrence's shoulders sagged. The comfortable hum of conversation resumed. He stared at his friend. "Look, I'm sorry about the SOB remark."

"All good."

"I can't stress this enough. The world runs on money. Nothing else," he reiterated, picking up where he left off.

"Yes, that's true. But you must admit that the world can also run on dignity and respect. It may be shocking to hear that the world can live without currency and look out for one another. But it can be done because we are made of heart and spirit. You can make it happen. You're charismatic.

You have a great presence.

People will listen and follow.

And most importantly, I want the poor and the weak to say: Now I am strong."

It was Lawrence's turn to sit back. Realizing that his friend wouldn't back down, he shook his head and chuckled. "You're going to turn the world upside down with your enigmatic ideas."

"No," Jaide said confidently. "*You* are going to turn the world *right side up*. By creating currency, humankind started on the wrong path. Today, I ask you, Senator. Which side of the bed would you like to rise from? The right side or the wrong side?"

The senator chuckled. "The right side, of course."

"It can happen." Jaide chewed absently on a cold French fry.

A waitress glided between tables, topping off iced tea. The gentle clinking of ice cubes made Lawrence think of a tropical paradise.

"If you eliminate money, all you have left is your heart," added the visionary.

The senator shook his head, still unsure. "I suppose. But it will never happen, I tell you."

"Look." Jaide leaned in closer. "I admit, this proposal is an extreme solution to our global problems. I'm not saying it's perfect. For that reason, let the Senate tweak it to make it practicable, then set it in motion. Let's make it happen," he said matter-of-factly.

Lawrence narrowed his eyes in wary contemplation.

Sensing the silence stretch, Jaide pressed on, his voice softening. "Have you ever stepped out in the early morning when the black sky turns a faint blue? Stars twinkle above, and you say, 'Wow, this is going to be a glorious day!' There are 6.6 billion people in this world, Senator. Isn't it time for the 5.8 billion people who struggle to make ends meet to experience that kind of joy? Simply because we are all citizens of heaven, and of one shared humanity."

Jaide glanced over his shoulder and signaled to the waitress. "Would you be kind enough to put the rest of my sandwich in a bag? I wasn't as hungry as I thought."

"I'm sorry about that." The waitress gave him a generous smile, her hand reaching into her apron pocket for the tab. "Would you like a slice of apple pie with it?"

"Throw in another tea as well, please."

Lawrence held the door as they walked out into the glorious May afternoon. Jaide's long hair fanned in the breeze. A mourning cloak butterfly zigzagged onto the senator's shoulder, fanned its wings, and fluttered away.

At that moment, a gaunt and grimy man stumbled toward them, interrupting their laughter. Tattered clothing, unwashed hair, and a scraggly beard spoke volumes about the challenges and setbacks of his life. "I don't mean you any harm," he said politely, his tongue licking at the corner of his cracked lips and running over several decayed teeth. "But I've had nothing to eat all day."

Their eyes locked, and without a thought, Jaide handed the man his bag of leftovers, along with a $20 bill. The homeless man accepted the gifts without a word and shuffled back to his resting spot. Once there, he ripped the bag open and attacked the sandwich, barely pausing for breath between bites.

Lawrence sniffed indignantly. "You brought me here on purpose, didn't you?"

"Yes, to have lunch."

"You know what I mean."

"Lawrence, picture that man in a suit with a crisp white shirt, well-shaven and clean after a hot shower. He is no different from you. His troubled circumstance results from the manipulation of money."

The senator scrutinized the homeless man one last time before they walked off. "So, where do you want me to drop you off?"

"Actually, I'll catch the bus at the corner. I have the rest of my day planned. You know, the tourist thing: monuments, museums," he said, leading him toward the bus stop.

"Jaide, I can't promise you anything. I'll consider your proposal, even though I already know it can't be done. Changing three hundred million lives overnight is implausible."

"I know it will be an arduous journey, but at least I have taken the first step."

Lawrence sighed and stepped forward. "I'm curious," he said, raising his voice over the roar of a passing truck. "How do you expect me to handle this massive challenge?"

"Listen to the hearts of your constituents. When you've heard enough, deliver with conviction. Have faith in yourself. You, my friend, must be the candle that refuses to blow out in the wind," said Jaide. "Light it first in the Senate, then get every nation together and spread the word."

"I'll be ridiculed," he said discontentedly.

"Simply because no one has dared to make such a bold statement. You, however, can take it with a grain of salt. Let them laugh without it affecting you. This is the resolve I see in your eyes. Consider yourself as formidable as the ocean. What would the Senate do then? Talk back at the ocean? Your message will come back in waves to wash over them."

Lawrence was impressed by his friend's persistence. In a final attempt to convince him of the impossibility, he said, "Jaide, I'll need significant resources. A project like this won't be cheap. How do you propose that I pay for this massive undertaking?"

With a sly grin, his friend reached into his coat pocket and handed him a brown envelope. Inside lay a certified check for $1 million.

Lawrence's jaw dropped. *That son of a bitch*!

"Now, isn't *that* ironic?" said Jaide. "You *need* money to eliminate money."

The senator knew what he meant. Lawrence stuffed the check back into the envelope. "Where did you get this?"

"Let's just say it's a donation for the cause." Jaide slapped his friend on the shoulder. "Use it wisely. Please take a few days to think about our freedom and happiness. Embrace all living creatures and the beauty of nature. In the end, if you decide not to take on this project, give the check back. I promise we'll still be friends," he said with a shrug.

"Don't be surprised if I return it," said Lawrence, waving the envelope.

Jaide could hear the rumbling engine and the hiss of air brakes as the bus approached. Raising his arms, he jumped in the air, crying, "I can see it. I can see it! Today is the day we are finally free!" Jaide kept cheering like a marathon runner finishing first. He pointed at Lawrence and said, "You want proof that it can be done? Just listen to your heart. It has a lot to say."

The bus hissed to a stop, and the door opened.

Before Jaide could climb aboard, the senator shouted, "How are we expected to live according to your perfect world?"

Jaide turned toward Lawrence. "It's easy." He placed one foot on the first step. "Live for one another." The door closed behind him, and the bus pulled away from the curb. The roar of the engine dwindled into the distance.

* * *

Tuesday, May 31, 2005. 6:37 p.m.

They could have gone to Wilkesboro, but Jaide elected to take Hannah and her teenage children to a popular restaurant in Statesville. She was right. Charlie and Nikki's behavior wasn't just discourteous. It revealed deep-seated anger, likely the result of their parents' long, bitter divorce. When she first introduced Jaide, they blew him off. Hannah apologized on their behalf, which didn't help much. Over time, she'd lost control of them. And the harder she tried to fix it, the deeper she dug herself in.

A glance in the rearview mirror showed Charlie with earbuds in, immersed in his favorite tunes. Their eyes met briefly before the teen turned sullenly away to stare out the window. Nikki mirrored him.

"How do you kids feel about playing mini golf after dinner tonight?" asked Jaide, glancing over his shoulder.

No response. Their barrier was as high as the Berlin Wall.

Hannah glared over her shoulder, her eyes darting between the two. "Kids, Jaide asked you a question. Please answer!" she said, raising her voice.

Still no response.

"Nikki! Charlie!" she barked.

"What do you want?" her daughter drawled, dragging out every syllable as she stomped her foot. "Can't you see I'm listening to music?" She rolled her eyes and readjusted the earbuds.

Hannah let out a long sigh and shook her head. "I'm sorry, Jaide. You can't say I didn't warn you."

"Don't worry about it," he said, patting her hand. "Life is a work in progress."

He slipped his fingers through hers, and she didn't pull away. Hannah wondered whether accepting the dinner invitation was a mistake.

The restaurant was crowded, even on a weeknight. Though the room was well-lit, the candles offered a touch of intimacy. A delectable aroma hung in the air, making their mouths water. When they sat down, the kids immediately buried themselves in their phones. Jaide saw the strain in Hannah's face and knew she'd need backup. He set his jaw. With Nikki busy texting and Charlie drumming on the table, he stood, walked around to their side, and snatched their devices, shoving them into his coat pocket.

"What the hell do you think you're doing?" Charlie shouted. Heads turned to gawk.

"I'm respecting you."

"That's stupid," Nikki said indignantly, snapping her chewing gum. "It doesn't make any sense!" The two teens laughed at his comment.

"I'm giving you what you want—my respect and undivided attention," he said, suppressing a smile. Sulky teenagers didn't intimidate him.

"We didn't ask you for anything," Nikki retorted.

Jaide kept his eyes focused on the boy. Of the two, he had the most bilious nature, all bark and no bite. "Charlie, have you ever saved anyone's life?"

"What do you care?" he said, slumping lower into his seat to avoid the stares.

"I saved a drummer's life." Jaide knew he had their attention when Charlie's eyes came up to meet his, suddenly interested. *Everyone loves a drummer. They're cool people.* "He was probably one of the best drummers I've ever heard. After practicing for three years, a pretty well-known heavy metal band invited him to play some gigs with them." He kept the momentum going, embellishing the story. "I'll never forget the night when he got up during one performance and mooned the audience." He laughed and pretended to wipe a tear from his eye. Engrossed in his story, they laughed along with him.

"No fuckin' way."

"Yes fuckin' way."

Twenty minutes later, the teens were snarfing their mozzarella sticks while he and Hannah attacked a shrimp Caesar salad. Jaide kept up a running patter, asking questions that encouraged them to share stories about their activities. Starting to warm up to him, Nikki gathered her courage for a question of her own.

"Um, you seem to know about a lot of stuff. Could you help me with my essay on Black Tuesday and the Great Depression? I couldn't get anything useful out of the people I interviewed."

Jaide ran his fingers through his hair and grinned. "So, what question do you have to tackle?" he asked, his eyes landing momentarily on the Blue Jays-Athletics game on one of the big-screen television sets.

Nikki's eyes searched the ceiling, as if to locate her question in some heavenly rotating file device. "If I were president, how would I solve the Depression after the stock market crash in 1929? I'm supposed to come up with a plan to fix all the unemployment and poverty."

"That's it?" He sat back while Nikki shrugged and laughed, embarrassed. "Is that the best you can give me? It's elementary. And I promise you will have fun writing this essay, so pay close attention." Jaide shook his head and pretended to scroll through his overhead filing system. "I don't know how many people worked or what they earned before the Great Depression, but I know it was much less than now. Therefore, to explain my solution for the Great Depression, I'll present it in today's terms.

"As president, the biggest mistake you can make is pumping billions of dollars into financial institutions. Hundreds of thousands of people across the country will lose their homes when they lose their jobs, and banks, mortgage lenders, and insurance companies will be hit hard."

Nikki studied him. "So why shouldn't I put money into those institutions? Isn't that the only way to turn the economy around?" she asked, her nose wrinkling.

"Sadly, when money is involved, you can't trust people. Crooked executives will pocket a large portion of it. The economy will recover on its own, but it will take years. People will credit a failed stimulus package."

"So, is there a different method?" She hesitated.

"Yes," he said, leaning forward as if sharing classified details and glancing over to make sure Charlie was listening too. "You give every person who filed a tax return the previous year $10,000 to splurge."

"What?" Their eyes lit up.

"Jaide, please don't mislead her," Hannah said. "This is her homework we're talking about."

He winked at her. "Right or wrong, Nikki will turn in a well-crafted report."

"Got it," she replied with a wry smile. "She'll be graded on effort."

Jaide gave her a thumbs-up and turned back to Nikki and Charlie. "What would you do if you both got a check for $10,000?"

"I'd buy everything!" exclaimed the boy.

Their eyes shone with delight as they imagined all the things such a fortune could buy.

"Many people would buy new appliances: refrigerators, ovens, dishwashers, even pool tables and flat-screen TVs. Others would splurge on cars, boats, or RVs. And some," he added with a grin, "might go for a little self-improvement: tummy tucks, nose jobs, maybe even a new chin. Still others would use the money to chase bigger dreams: a house, a business, a long-overdue vacation."

"Slow down, I can't write that fast!" Nikki was scribbling in her spiral notebook, her thoughts fizzing and popping like a shaken soda can. Jaide kept going, grinning at her comical reaction. Like her daughter, Hannah's smile lit up her face. Her hands clapped with delight as he listed all the ways they could spend their money.

He waited for Nikki to catch up. "With that kind of cash flowing into the economy, stores and businesses would rebound. For crying out loud, don't let the stores go out of business! Put the money right into the hands of the American people! In response, Wall Street would see a jump in all sectors. But the greatest thing about this stimulus package is that you, Madam President," Jaide said, pointing at Nikki, "would be credited for turning the economy around in less than thirty days, guaranteed!"

Hannah was riding the crest of his excitement, her eyes sparkling with delight with each new idea. A lot of what he said made sense, but uncertainty flickered across her face. "But wouldn't the cost be astronomical?"

Jaide grabbed his cell phone and tapped in some numbers. "It would cost roughly $1.5 trillion. Well worth it for a stimulus that would take thirty days, instead of a slow, decade-long recovery that benefits only the powerful."

"Mom, can we go home now?" Nikki asked eagerly. "I want to start writing!"

Smiling, Hannah turned to Jaide. "I've never seen her so excited about her homework."

They arrived home at half past nine. Nikki and Charlie ran inside.

"I want both of you to take a shower!" Hannah shouted.

"Not now, Mom." Nikki turned her ashen face toward her mother. "I want to type my essay while it's fresh in my head."

Hannah shook her head. "You made an impression on them. I'm amazed," cocking her head with a smile. "But I'm afraid things will go back to normal after you leave. The disrespect will resume."

Jaide stared into her forlorn face. "They need love."

"I'm their mother!" she exclaimed. "I give them everything they need!"

"Being a mother doesn't make you loving," Jaide said softly. He reached for her hands and held them. "You see these tender hands of yours?" He lifted one and brushed it against his cheek. "Use them to stroke your daughter's hair." Then he guided her other hand around his waist. "Hold your son like this—and kiss his forehead."

As their eyes locked, she couldn't look away from his gaze. In those soft brown eyes, she felt the warmth of smooth brandy. She leaned in, her lips ready for his, but he surprised her with a gentle kiss on the forehead. Although sweet, it crushed her heart.

It's only a matter of time, he thought. His hair flowed gracefully over his shoulders as he walked away.

A smile lit Hannah's face. Ravished by his charm, she leaned on the doorframe, her face against the cool cedar. *He is the most cordial and decorous man I have ever met*. She listened until his footsteps had faded away.

* * *

Washington, D.C., Friday, June 3, 2005. 8:38 a.m.

The closure of Burleith Community Hospital came as no surprise to anyone. After barely surviving the first round of historic federal budget cuts, it seemed impossible for the hospital to stay open when the next round took effect in late May. BCH implemented across-the-board cuts of $10 million, eliminating 110 full-time positions. After ninety-five years of service to an ethnically mixed community, the hospital could no longer afford to treat patients.

When Lawrence heard the news, he rushed to the hospital's administrative office to ask about his mother's surgery. The parking lot teemed with confusion, and he struggled to find a spot. In desperation, he left his car in a red zone alongside several other frantic drivers. He hurried toward the entrance, passing the drop-off zone where emergency vehicles, taxis, and private cars were all jostling to transfer patients to already overwhelmed hospitals.

Inside, the chaos continued. Hundreds of patients and residents pleaded and argued over the disruption to services. The senator maneuvered through the crowd and took a number from the red dispenser on the wall. He stood for a long time, glancing at his number periodically and clutching it like a lifeline. After a restless three-hour wait, he was called into one of several office cubicles.

Lawrence sat on the edge of his seat, his upper body leaning forward, looking both determined and desperate. The clerk's jaded expression and slouched posture said it all as she tapped his mother's information into the computer. When she pulled up the file, he asked, "Is there any way the doctor could do the surgery tonight, before the hospital closes?"

"Sir," the administrator said impassively, "even if that were possible, there are at least fifteen other people ahead of your mother."

"Ma'am, transferring my mother to another hospital would likely add three to four months to her wait. That's unacceptable, especially when she's already scheduled for surgery here in just seven days!"

The clerk's dull eyes met his. "I'm sorry, there's absolutely nothing I can do. This hospital is closing tomorrow night. I feel your pain, Mr. Devonshire. I, too, have nowhere to go. And I've got children to feed. If you complete this form, we'll forward your mother's file to the hospital of your choice. That's the best I can do."

Lawrence's heart sank. Squeezing blood out of a turnip would have been simpler. He grabbed the transfer form and left in a panic. He must now compete with hundreds of patients seeking to be placed on the surgeons' waiting list at other hospitals.

He spent the next several hours calling surgical centers across Virginia, Maryland, Delaware, and Pennsylvania. Every call ended the same way. No availability. No guarantees. No hope. Disillusioned, he accepted a protracted appointment at Winter Hills Hospital, weeks later than her original date, though it secured her place in line.

Lawrence had sold his mother's house in North Carolina and moved her into his home in Burleith, a quaint two-story house shaded by lush green trees. He had hired a hospice nurse for daily care, and at night he took over, often sacrificing sleep. That night, he arrived home exhausted. The shades were drawn, and the lights were set low.

"Mr. Devonshire, you need to know about your mother's condition," the caregiver said, her voice low. "She hasn't been eating well and has had trouble keeping food down. The only thing she can tolerate now is the chocolate protein drinks." She slipped on her coat and said softly, "I think the end is near."

He nodded without meeting her eyes and showed her out.

At his mother's bedside, Lawrence felt a deep, aching sorrow. She lay in a neatly made bed, surrounded by soft, muted colors. Her frail form lay beneath a light blanket, rising and falling with her shallow breaths. Her arms were thin and translucent, delicate veins visible beneath the skin. The cruel grip of glioma had ravaged her, leaving her weary, like a flower wilting under an unrelenting sun.

Leaning down, he kissed her gently on the head, causing her to flinch. As she gradually opened her eyes, a faint smile emerged when she recognized him. Her lips parted, trembling.

"Son, what did the doctor say?" she asked, her voice barely above a whisper.

He set his jaw and sighed, determined not to let her see his anguish. "The hospital is closing because of budget cuts, Mother," he said, his voice thick with despair. He fought to hold back the tears. "I spent the whole day trying to get you into another hospital."

Not fully understanding, his mother gathered her strength to ask, "Will the new doctor operate as scheduled?"

Lawrence couldn't hold back the tears any longer. They flowed down his cheeks as he rested his head against her frail shoulder, whimpering like a child. His anger and remorse soaked into her pink cupid-print gown as she reached out and patted his head lightly. "Don't worry, Son. I can hold on," she reassured him, emphasizing their unbreakable bond.

* * *

Monday, June 6, 2005.

It had been raining for three straight days. On the night Lawrence's mother died, a torrential downpour drenched the District of Columbia. After the ambulance left just before midnight, he stood in the driveway and let the rain wash over him.

The senator dropped to his knees, slapping the rain-slicked cement with the palm of his hand as water from the downspout rushed around him. “You could have been saved!” he wailed, clenching his fists and squinting through the deluge. “And I couldn’t do anything about it!” Lawrence whimpered, rocking back and forth. “I couldn’t do anything about it!” The rain saturated his black trench coat and needled his body with unrelenting vengeance, pounding his back as if whipped for his abysmal performance.

“Mother!” he howled in anguish, but no one felt his pain or heard his mournful cry through the storm’s din.

Lawrence tilted his head toward the night sky, his eyelids flickering. “Mother,” he whispered, shivering. “Forgive me.”

It had become abundantly clear that his mother died because of money.

Lawrence shut his eyes and allowed the pitter-patter of rain on his back to lull him to sleep, while his trench coat, as capacious as a camel’s hump, continued to soak up water.

Not so far away, hidden under thick foliage for shelter, a mourning cloak butterfly pinned its wings closer to its body for warmth.

* * *

Hart Senate Office Building. Tuesday, June 7, 2005. 7:46 a.m.

“Yes, Mr. Banks,” Connie Freeman said, scribbling in shorthand. Her platinum hair, brushed back in soft waves, caught the overhead light as she glanced at a photo of her eight-year-old daughter in a butterfly costume from a school play. She nodded, nearly dislodging the phone from her shoulder. “I’ll remind him of the ten o’clock meeting. I’m sure he’s stuck in traffic and will be arriving momentarily.”

Just as she set the receiver down, the office door burst open, startling her. Connie gasped as Lawrence Devonshire stumbled through the doorway, his expression lost and confused. Her dark brown eyes behind reading glasses swiftly took in his drenched trench coat and unshaven face. Water bled from his coat and pooled around his shoes. His eyes were bloodshot, with dark circles signifying a long, sleepless night.

"Senator Devonshire." She stood up in shock, concern flooding her eyes as she took in his shaking, frail body.

The senator lifted his chin and asked in a slow, husky tone—one she'd never heard before, "About how many . . . recognized countries are there . . . in the world today?"

"Around two hundred and thirty, Senator, give or take a few," she said slowly, unsure of both the reasoning for his question and his current mental state. She watched a bead of water slide down his nose and plummet to the floor.

"How fast . . . can you type two hundred and thirty letters? Give or take a few."

Lowering them just above the bridge of her nose, Connie peered at her distraught senator over the rim of her glasses.

* * *

The Senate Chamber, United States Capitol. Friday, July 15, 2005. 9:37 a.m.

In the absence of the Vice President and the president pro tempore, Senator Mark H. Wittiger of Arkansas, designated earlier by written order, called the Senate to order.

Senator Wittiger read through the daily schedule and asked, "Before we begin today's agenda, do we have a guest chaplain this morning?"

The presiding officer said, "Reverend Barry Clemens, from Metzger Baptist Church in Portland, Oregon, will offer today's opening prayer."

The guest chaplain approached the podium. "Let us pray," he said in a raspy voice, his gaze quickly sweeping the Senate. "We take this moment and ask, dear Lord, that you give us the wisdom to make the right decisions in our troubled times. Grant our lawmakers the grace to do what is best for our nation, our communities, our families, and our brothers and sisters, regardless of skin color. Grant them the humility and agility to reach swift agreement, that they may help those experiencing poverty and hardship. We pray in Your loving name. Amen."

The Honorable Mark H. Wittiger led the Pledge of Allegiance after the guest chaplain ended the morning prayer. Taking his seat, he scanned the chamber, then nodded to the Assistant Majority Leader.

Assistant Majority Leader: "Mr. President, following leader remarks, the Senate will hear from Senator Devonshire of North Carolina, who has been allotted thirty minutes to present his proposal for social reform. Immediately after the senator's speech, there will be a period of morning business. At that time, senators will be allowed to speak for up to ten minutes each concerning the Foreign Operations Appropriations Bill. There will be a recess from eleven thirty until one p.m., followed by a vote on the bill's passage by five thirty."

Presiding Officer: "Without objection, it is so ordered."

Acting President Pro Tempore: "Are there any opening remarks from the leader?"

Majority Leader: "No, Mr. President."

Acting President Pro Tempore: "Senator Devonshire, you have the floor."

Debonair in a navy pin-striped suit, Senator Devonshire made his way toward the podium with confident strides. He stood as calm as the sea on a moonless night, his posture and gaze reflecting unshakable determination and a vision.

Taking stock of the leaders before him, he said, "Mr. President, I rise today to give hope not only to the citizens of these great United States, but to the citizens of *all* nations around the world. I hope this speech will be remembered as the dawn of our country's most bountiful age. I invite you to listen with an open mind. And with a belief in possibilities.

"Mr. President and distinguished colleagues." His voice boomed around the room. "I ask that you put your prejudice and preconceived notions aside and let me finish my presentation before making any judgments." His stern gaze swept the room, commanding attention.

"We are all born with a divine right to be happy. But somewhere along the way, as adults, we lose sight of the true meaning of existence when money becomes our primary survival drive. We have seen greed and its corruption span generations, both in our nation and around the globe, with no end in sight. And quite frankly, I am sick of it."

Most senators nodded, their expressions tight, some exchanging looks of wonder as they leaned forward, intent on his words.

Senator Devonshire's presentation, later known as the Currency-Free Speech, closely mirrored Jaide Basir's earlier speech, with only slight modifications to reflect the erudite tastes of the Senate. For fifteen minutes, he laid out the moral and systemic rot that underpins the world. His speech cut deep: from corporate greed and political lobbying to healthcare inequities, environmental exploitation, and the commodification of basic human needs. He wanted to ignite the Senate just as he was at the pastrami shop. His words weren't just a catalog of corruption; they were a dare to imagine something radically different. What began as a long list of moral decay had evolved into a shared hunger for change.

They all wanted it.

They all hungered to hear the solution. One by one, the senators began to see the rot for what it was.

"Today, I stand before you to offer a solution to our global dilemma. One that can eliminate 75 to 90 percent of our problems." The senator paused, gauging their reactions. "I want to address the concept of eliminating money, once and for all."

The moment he said "eliminate money," the chamber erupted in boisterous laughter. Only the acting president pro tempore smiled quietly, his expression tinged with surprise and disbelief. Devonshire waited, unshaken, until the laughter faded, recognizing it as a necessary release of tension.

And then it happened. The pushback he had anticipated.

Although he had asked for no interruptions, Senator Lafayette Bell, from Georgia, stood to request recognition, his ears twitching slightly, as if attuned to the tension.

Acting President Pro Tempore: "The senator from Georgia is recognized."

Senator Bell: "Thank you, Mr. President. Everyone in their right mind understands that money is a fundamental medium of exchange. We've relied on it for thousands of years—and we'll continue to rely on it. Have you completely lost your mind?"

A commotion broke out until Senator Wittiger banged his gavel to restore order. He gave Mr. Bell a stern look.

Acting President Pro Tempore: "I'd like to remind the Chamber to refrain from using disparaging remarks."

Senator Bell: "My apologies, Mr. President."

Acting President Pro Tempore: "Senator Devonshire, are you willing to yield for questions?"

Lawrence stepped back, hands on the podium, and lifted his chin.

Senator Devonshire: "It would be an honor to take some questions, Mr. President. But first, I would like to respond to Senator Bell directly."

Mr. Bell faced him with a smirk. *Come on, you dirtbag. Give it your best shot!*

Senator Devonshire: "While it's true that currency has long underpinned global economic systems, it's time to consider its massive negative impacts. A currency-free society could be the answer to those problems. To help our society thrive, we must explore bold alternatives, chief among them, a resource-based economy. This system would encourage communities to collaborate on equitable resource distribution, ensuring everyone's needs are met. Built on trust and driven by technology, this system could revolutionize transactions, making traditional currency obsolete."

Senator Bell: "Fine words, Senator Devonshire, but I'm sure you don't understand what you're saying. You seem to be throwing buzzwords around. Do you even know how resource-based economies function? No one here has seen such a system function in practice. It's completely theoretical, an unproven system. How exactly would a resource-based economy even work?"

Senator Devonshire: "In a resource-based economy, the focus is on the strategic management of resources. Governing bodies work to meet the needs of individuals and communities while controlling waste and reducing ecological impact."

Lawrence held his head high, keeping his eyes focused on his detractor.

Senator Bell: "This is preposterous!" He stomped his right foot. His face flushed with anger. "You're proposing a fantasy, Senator Devonshire. A dangerous fantasy that will lead to ruin!" He huffed and stormed back to his seat, leaving a tense silence in his wake.

Acting President Pro Tempore: "The Chair recognizes the senator from Pennsylvania."

With deep-brown eyes that perfectly matched his smooth skin, Senator Elroy Manson stood with both broad hands planted on his waist. Beads of sweat glistened on his bald head.

Senator Manson: "Thank you, Mr. President. Let's not waste any more time, Mr. Devonshire. We should be working on important matters instead of playing meaningless what-if games. The notion of a currency-free society is nothing more than a theoretical exercise, and it is a potential path to chaos and uncertainty. Such a shift would undermine our current internationally accepted medium of exchange, creating a false sense of value influenced by opinions, feelings, and tastes! This proposal would make establishing value on goods and services extraordinarily difficult."

Elroy removed his glasses, rubbed the lenses with his tie, and settled them back on his nose.

Lawrence smiled. *This is easier than I thought it would be.*

Senator Devonshire: "I see. So, when you purchased your new car last month—a beautiful car, by the way—did your opinions, feelings, and tastes have nothing to do with it?"

Elroy shifted his feet, adjusting his tie.

Senator Manson: "Well, yes, but . . ."

A chuckle rippled through the chamber.

Senator Devonshire: "Senator, I've thought deeply about this, and my answer hasn't changed. A personalized value assessment approach that aligns with individual needs and desires could foster a richer, more inclusive understanding of value. Moving away from a standardized system empowers people to assign value based on quality, not just a monetary scale. This more diverse understanding of value could incorporate environmental, social, and personal well-being alongside economic considerations."

Conversations flared up, the chamber's din rising fast. The acting president struck the gavel to call for order.

Acting President Pro Tempore: "The Chair recognizes the senator from California."

Though just 4 feet 10, Senator Patricia Moore's eyebrows conveyed a feisty, unshakable presence. She smiled, then cast a disapproving gaze at Lawrence.

Senator Moore: "Shame on you, Senator Devonshire! Shame on you for proposing this outrageous plan. Are you happy now with your fifteen minutes of fame? Have you considered that this proposal could dramatically increase the potential for bartering, making global negotiations and economic mobility more difficult? Instead of moving us forward into a sustainable future, your deranged ideas will take us back to the Stone Age."

Senator Devonshire: "I agree. While bartering might occur at first, the long-term benefits of a life without crime and inequality would far outweigh the challenges of bartering. Our work as senators, and as visionaries, is to refine this proposal until it is bullet-proof: to anticipate and defend against the unforeseen."

Lawrence leaned forward to meet her gaze.

Senator Devonshire: "With your help, Senator Moore, we will implement regulations to facilitate universal negotiation and economic mobility in a currency-free society."

Acting President Pro Tempore: "Let's take one more question before the closing argument. The Chair recognizes the senator from Nevada."

The tall, charming senator walked with a limp to the podium. A prominent aquiline nose gave him a distinctive profile.

Senator Paul Doyle: "Unlike my colleagues, I am not here to castigate you, Senator Devonshire. If we were to eliminate money, could this proposal increase the risk of crime and corruption in a world without financial regulations? And what transition plan do you have in place?"

Senator Devonshire: "The impulse for crime would be drastically reduced. To ensure minimal disruption, new laws must be enacted to prevent emerging forms of crime and corruption and to establish strong oversight mechanisms. However, the success of these measures will also hinge on extensive public education and awareness campaigns. Every citizen must understand the principles of the new system and how the transition will proceed. Another element is the creation of comprehensive social safety nets to meet everyone's basic needs during the transition."

A small round of applause spouted from one corner of the room, and pockets of murmuring emerged anew. The acting president brought the Chamber to order for the third time.

Acting President Pro Tempore: "You have five minutes left, Mr. Devonshire."

Senator Devonshire: "Thank you, Mr. President. My esteemed colleagues, it is widely accepted that politicians and money go hand in hand. I would not be surprised to discover that many in this Chamber today are as much concerned about how this proposal could impact their lifestyles and status as they are about the wider ramifications. Politicians undeniably benefit from the current economic system and have a vested interest in maintaining the status quo.

"You may believe my proposal is too idealistic and not suitable in practice. Many of you may use your political and financial leverage to influence other lawmakers, spread misinformation in the media, and attempt to sway public opinion against a currency-free society. You may consolidate support from powerful industry groups who have a vested interest in maintaining the status quo.

"Colleagues, I implore you to look deep into your hearts and ask yourselves: Am I doing all I can for humanity?"

Lawrence's gaze swept the chamber, noting the steely expressions etched across many faces, unwilling to face the truth. Challenging their complacency, he asked, "Ladies and gentlemen, why do we continue to allow paper and iron to inhibit our societies and govern our lives?

"In the United States alone, over one hundred million people rely on antidepressants. Nearly half do so because of financial hardship. They struggle to pay bills, see a doctor, care for their children, put food on the table, and make mortgage or rent payments."

He stepped forward, his words lashing out like tongues of fire. "Can you imagine the millions whose spirits would be lifted if financial stress were removed? What have we become? And why can't we mend our ways?"

The murmuring grew louder, punctuated by occasional chuckles.

"Let us restore simplicity and dignity. Specifically, let us regain respect for one another. We should be considerate and thoughtful of each other as we were in the early days. Perhaps most vividly during the 1920s, when optimism, community, and a shared sense of purpose briefly outshone materialism."

Swimming in his ocean of jubilation, Senator Devonshire stood silent and allowed his colleagues to soak in his love and compassion for the world. He stared with optimistic flames, instilling reason and truth into their hungry hearts with words that flowed with practiced ease.

In closing, he said, "From the beginning, our society evolved around a flawed concept. We have allowed *this* concept to guide our lives and make us into what we have become today: greedy, corrupt, and foolishly dependent on money. The world has seen its share of corruption. We must mend our ways, and we must do so now.

"I propose to you a society of brotherly and sisterly love, a love in which we all embrace one another and live for the benefit of humankind.

"I propose a society built on strength and courage stemming not from the pocketbook, but from the heart. Our hearts define us and have greater significance than any evil created in this house." He paused for effect, his gaze exploring the room lit by the faint glow of possibility. "Human intelligence sets us apart, a trait unique to us. Let us embrace our role in this ever-changing universe and leave a lasting impact on humankind."

More heads nodded in agreement, while others leaned forward in their seats, hanging onto every word. Dropping his voice for effect, he finished, "This house we live in has many broken bones. We must mend these broken bones—it is time."

A dramatic hush followed his closing words. No one dared break the silence or debunk him. Their gazes met, each wanting to clap but afraid of ridicule, even though the proposal was breathtaking. Tired of the endless cycle of suffering and inequality, Senator Bill Mason from Arizona stood with a bone-chilling expression and clapped three times, loud and slow, mockingly. He buttoned his suit jacket and faced the acting president pro tempore rather than addressing the senator from North Carolina. “Mr. President . . . When can we start drafting the proposal for a currency-free society?”

* * *

It would take months for the United States Senate to draft the Currency-Free Act of 2005. Fueled by conviction, Senator Lawrence Devonshire was determined to secure overwhelming bipartisan support. For a free society to run efficiently, it would have to gain mutual interest from other nations willing to take bold, crucial steps to abolish currency and embrace human-centered principles.

Unwilling to wait for the machinery of government to catch up, Devonshire moved swiftly to rally global momentum. In the ensuing months, the senator managed to secure the floor at the United Nations to herald his social reform.

* * *

The UN General Assembly Hall. Monday, September 5, 2005. 9:00 a.m.

Senator Devonshire stood confidently before two hundred and thirty state members, including the five standing and ten non-standing members of the Security Council. Delegates whispered into earpieces, translators murmured in soundproof booths, and a few representatives scrolled through tablets to learn about the speaker. Everyone in the grand hall eagerly awaited what this energetic young Black senator from North Carolina had to say. *What could justify inviting small sovereignties and unincorporated territories, many of which aren't even recognized as members?*

He stepped forward and placed his hands on the podium, his laser-sharp eyes scanning the crowd. With upright posture and quiet confidence, he began his speech, reiterating the ideas Jaide had once shared in a shadowed corner of DC. Today, he was proud to take his friend's colossal undertaking to the next level.

For twenty-five minutes, he spoke—not with fire, but with precision. He dissected the global economy like a surgeon: exposing the arteries of oppression, the tumors of deceit, and the fractures in healthcare, housing, and education. He cited statistics, but also stories. A child in Somalia who died for lack of insulin. A farmer in India crushed by loan sharks. A mother in San Francisco choosing between high rent and chemotherapy.

Lawrence packed it in tight. He wanted to get their hearts ablaze with anger just as his heart had seared when his mother died. What began as a never-ending list of corruption became a mass of escalating rage coursing through the hall for a quick fix.

They craved it.

They demanded decisive action.

One by one, the delegates began to recognize the decay that had strangled humanity for too long.

"Today, I stand before you to offer a solution to our global problems. One that can eliminate 75 to 90 percent of our corruption." The senator paused, a smirk forming. "I want to address the concept of eliminating money, once and for all.

But then it happened again.

Their reactions shifted unfavorably the moment he said "eliminate money." In the United Nations, they also laughed at him mockingly. They laughed in Spanish. They laughed in Japanese. They laughed in Chinese. They also laughed in Russian and Korean. But no matter which language they laughed in, it all sounded the same to him.

Lawrence didn't flinch, nor did the tide of derision bother him. Instead, he waited patiently until the crowd recovered from their ridicule, just as Jaide had recommended. In his mind, he was stronger and wiser than they. His panther-like stare cut through the laughter, demanding attention.

In a final offering of hope to the assembled nations, he said, "In every country, the wealthy prosper while the poor decline. We turn a blind eye to the hungry, naked, sick, and forgotten. These are not innate human behaviors, but negative traits forged by money. We can reverse this by abolishing currency in our societies. When currency no longer governs our choices, humanity can finally turn its attention to what truly matters:

"Instead of sending soldiers to other countries to fight, we will send men and women to impoverished nations to build homes, schools, and hospitals. We will eradicate illiteracy. Every child will receive the education they deserve. Every adult will have the opportunity to become an esteemed professional in their chosen field. The people of the world will work together to lift one another from despair . . . "

A glimmer of hope flickered in the chamber. It was subtle, but unmistakable.

Lawrence continued, "Nothing brings more joy than helping others. It's a natural high. It is the same elation people feel when they come together after a natural disaster to clear the rubble away from the dead and the living.

"Without monetary restrictions, your nations could build all the concrete plants needed to construct buildings, bridges, and parking garages in densely populated areas. To reduce environmental impact, we will use processed fly ash in concrete applications as part of our strategy to reduce greenhouse gas emissions.

"Your nations can expand their iron and steel industries to build magnificent skyscrapers, warehouses, and machines. Keep in mind that recycling plays a vital role in reducing the need for raw materials. Steel scrap retains its strength through reprocessing, making it a sustainable alternative to refining iron ore.

"Why mine the earth, when yesterday's machines can build tomorrow's cities? Remarkably, a metal frame for a standard two-thousand-square-foot home is equivalent to six recycled automobiles. What is that I hear? You want a three-thousand-square-foot home? Fine by me. Just bring me nine clunkers."

A ripple of laughter spread through the chamber, some amused, some surprised, some unsure whether they were allowed to laugh at all. Lawrence chuckled with them, letting the moment breathe.

Then, with a grin, he added, "That's far more efficient than cutting down forty to fifty living trees for a wooden frame.[6]

"Without monetary restrictions, roads can be paved, even in remote locations. However, the transportation sector remains the largest consumer of oil, accounting for 68 percent in the United States and 55 percent worldwide. To mitigate the effects of peak oil, we must consider solar-powered and electric hybrid vehicles as viable alternatives. Moreover, if we abolish currency, we can avoid global economic collapse due to peak oil, as Mr. M. King Hubbert theorized in 1956.[7]

"Your nations can establish modern waste management systems, recycling centers, and sewage treatment facilities to reduce health and environmental risks. New standards will eliminate excessive packaging. Planting an abundance of trees will prevent environmental degradation and deforestation to keep our planet green and beautiful.

"Right now, over twelve thousand pieces of space junk orbit our planet: dead satellites, broken parts, and forgotten fragments, racing around Earth at thousands of miles per hour. It's a cosmic junkyard, and it's growing by the day.

"But what if we could clean it up and replace the clutter with something better?

"I propose we build twelve large space stations. Each would serve as a hub for internet, weather, and global communications. These stations would do the job of thousands of satellites, but with far less

---

[6] "About Our Scrap Metals," ABC Recycling Scrap Metal Recyclers, accessed August 2, 2024, abcrecyclingga.com/about-metals.

[7] Kenneth S. Deffeyes, *Hubbert's Peak: The Impending World Oil Shortage* (Princeton University Press, 2001), 1.

chaos. And from each one, we can launch small vehicles to retrieve the debris we've left behind."

He paused, letting the idea settle.

"Twelve stations instead of a sky full of trash. That sounds like progress to me."

The chamber fell silent. Not out of confusion, but in awe. Delegates glanced at one another. Then, from the back of the hall, a single pair of hands began to clap. Within seconds, the room erupted in applause. Tentative at first, then thunderous.

"In this new ethical world, there will be no so-called 'developed' or 'developing nations,' no marginalized communities, no walls of inequality. Instead, there will be one global community, bound together in unity and peace. Eliminate poverty, and you erase the injustice of economic inequality that has been the norm in this world for thousands of years. Give everyone love, and they will love you in return. So why not let your country flourish? Let it become an advanced society with modern technologies."

The hall remained eerily silent. Senator Devonshire stared into the assembly, his jaw set. "A free society also reasserts the belief that all men and women are created equal," he said. "Everyone should know their rights, how to defend them, and how to respect others' rights. Our currency-free societies will not abolish your religions, your traditions, or your culture. However, all nations *must* recognize the belief that marriage does not give anyone the right to abuse or enslave another.

"The time for respect is now. The time for love has arrived. As one, our world can work toward simplifying life to ensure everyone is treated equally and given comfort and safety. We will respect you, as you will respect your neighbors on every side. Friends, it's time to stop living in fear and start looking out for one another. And it can be done, because we are made of heart.

"Our goal will no longer be profit. Instead, we will work toward the benefit and advancement of humankind. We will draft a worldwide doctrine, the Constitution of the World, to which every man and woman who reaches the age of eighteen must pledge to become a full-fledged member of our new society. And it will sound something like this."

Amid a taut silence, Lawrence paused to take a sip of water.

"I, Lawrence Devonshire, recognize that I am now a full-fledged member of our global currency-free society. I promise to uphold all city, state, and federal laws that protect our safety and help every family live with the dignity and happiness they deserve. I solemnly swear to follow the doctrines of good sense, honesty, decency, politeness, and trust. I attest that all of humanity is created equal and deserves respect. I promise to be considerate and help others during my twenty-five years of professional service and throughout my retirement, so help me God."

The senator gazed around the room, his passion for humankind pouring out. He made eye contact with each person in turn to ensure everyone felt seen and included.

"Do *you* understand me, Nicaragua?"

The room remained eerily silent, but then the delegate from Nicaragua, after hearing the translation, rose to voice his answer: "Sí, entiendo."

"Do *you* understand me, Japan?"

"Hai, wakarimasu."

"Do *you* understand me, the Philippines? France?"

"Naiintindihan ko."

"Je comprends."

"Do *you* understand me, Germany? Italy?"

"Ich verstehen."

"Capisco."

"Do *you* understand me, Poland? Portugal?"

"Rozumiem."

"Eu entendo."

"Do *you* understand me, Turkey? Greece?"

"Anliyoram."

"Katalavaíno."

Relishing his accomplishment, the senator smiled broadly. "Now, I'd like to introduce a few friends I've made along the way to the United Nations." Lawrence stepped back from the podium and gestured toward a side door, where a group of people had been waiting for his cue.

Born and raised near the idyllic alpine Lake Königssee, a German citizen entered the hall wearing black embroidered lederhosen and a green Miesbacher jacket. His upper lip, hidden behind a caterpillar mustache and a bit of foam from a refreshing mug of beer, appeared on two large screens flanking the UN emblem. Waving at the assembly, he led the procession across the center stage, down the steps in the first aisle, and up the incline before stopping beneath the east mural, its surface awash in blue, gold, and beige.

The assembly broke into applause, growing louder as more joined the celebration. The ovation continued as representatives from every nation, dressed in traditional attire, made their way across the stage and into the aisles, thirty-three per group. Lawrence's chest swelled. This wasn't just a speech anymore. It was a vision made visible.

Behind the German came a swirl of color and culture: a Thai dancer in golden silk, a Sudanese elder in flowing white robes, a Brazilian in carnival feathers, a Canadian in Métis beadwork. The names blurred, but the message was unmistakable—the world had shown up.

From one of the world's oldest civilizations and the source of four great inventions—paper, printing, gunpowder, and the compass—a woman from China entered next, her brocade dress as silky as the flag she waved. Behind her came a kaleidoscope of humanity from Sri Lanka, Iceland, Ghana, Bosnia and Herzegovina, Brunei Darussalam, and dozens more. Lawrence caught his breath. Two hundred and thirty nations. Two hundred and thirty stories. And for a moment, they all walked the same floor.

Liechtenstein's representative led the third group with a stride that suggested alpine confidence. His loden jacket and breeches framed legs of steel, honed, no doubt, by years of hiking and skiing. Behind him came a blur of faces and fabrics from Indonesia, Mexico, Saudi Arabia, Australia, Nigeria, Russia, and more. Some waved flags. Others clasped hands. One woman tossed candy into the crowd.

A citizen from Armenia entered the fourth aisle, clad in a silk shirt and traditional *arkhaluk*, humming a patriotic tune that debuted in 2002 to celebrate Armenian Independence Day. He was followed by citizens from Fiji, Haiti, Ireland, Bhutan, Ukraine, Greenland, Kosovo, and dozens more. The chamber pulsed with applause, camera flashes, and the rustle of cloth.

In the fifth aisle, a man from Albania held his flag high, his cone-shaped *qeleshe* perched proudly atop his head. His red and black sash caught the light as he led a jubilant line followed by Morocco, Zimbabwe, Syria, Vietnam, and more. Lawrence noticed a woman from Saint Lucia blowing kisses to the crowd. Another from Lebanon danced a few steps before taking her place.

Then came the Americans and Chileans—cowboy and huaso—side by side in boots and ponchos. The Chilean's spurs jingled as he walked, and his short jacket exposed a wide sash around his waist. Behind them came a tide of flags and faces: Guatemala, Lithuania, Bangladesh, Greece, Israel, Dominican Republic, and dozens more. Lawrence smiled. *This was diplomacy without a single word spoken.*

Finally, Spain's representative surprised everyone when he stepped onto the stage in a tight green-and-gold matador suit called *traje de luces*. His black montera in one hand, his flag in the other. He waved with theatrical flair before leading the final group: Nicaragua, Portugal, South Korea, Colombia, Nepal, American Samoa, and

Nauru. The last representative stopped beneath the west mural, an abstract composition in shades of brown, orange, and beige.

For this once-in-a-lifetime event, 230 people were provided room and board for three days and two nights, round-trip airfare, and $1,000 in US currency, totaling $971,500 of Jaide's mystery money. The massive project was skillfully orchestrated and implemented by his secretary, Connie Freeman, who typed, mailed, and followed up on 230 letters, give or take a few.

Lawrence stepped back up to the microphone, his gaze sweeping the sea of happy faces, and said with a flourish, "Ladies and Gentlemen of the world, I present to you . . . the human race."

Excitement swelled as delegates exchanged knowing glances, envisioning how these ideas could come to life. The hall had never felt so alive. Beaming, Lawrence scanned the cheering crowd with hopeful eyes as a single warm tear trailed down his cheek.

Standing in the aisles, the guests reveled in a surge of hope. This was their day to shine and to be seen. Each member of the United Nations was delighted to be part of this historic moment. The applause reverberated, and more than a few of the participants broke out in tears.

Sitting off-center in the first row, Jaide and Hannah stood, their arms around each other. Trembling, she clamped a hand over her mouth and smiled through rolling tears.

"Come on," Jaide said, pulling her toward the stage.

Hannah slung her purse over her shoulder and hurried to keep up.

Jaide and Lawrence stood face-to-face, smiles softening into quiet understanding. Amid the noise, their hands found each other. Not just in celebration, but in recognition of all they'd overcome.

"Come here, you son of a bitch," said Lawrence, drawing him in for a jubilant hug. "Just for the record, I don't owe you anything anymore."

"Ah, what about the million dollars I gave you?" Jaide asked, holding out his hand.

"According to your doctrine, that money no longer exists." Lawrence laughed and pulled him in for another hug.

Unbeknownst to everyone in the building, a monarch butterfly had wandered in through the side entrance. It bobbed and swooped, gliding effortlessly across the crowd.

Overjoyed, Hannah fished her phone out of her pocket and said, "Smile for the camera, gentlemen."

Her flash came first, but not the last. Reporters surged forward, jockeying for the best angle. The photo that would grace headlines around the world captured Jaide, eyes closed and hands lifted in quiet triumph, beside Lawrence with an unexpected butterfly perched on his shoulder, its wings spread wide like a silent witness to history.

Senator Devonshire's gaze swept across the sea of cameras. *How fortunate I am to be part of the human race!*

A VICIOUS CYCLE

In the tumult of the Napoleonic Wars in 1807.

The high sun casts a warm glow over the vast Atlantic Ocean, where France and Great Britain's conflict comes to a head. The British and Danish navies navigate the Danish-Norwegian waters, exchanging battering cannon fire. Tension hangs in the air as crashing waves hammer the ship's hull. Amid the chaos, the British sailors, their faces set in grim determination, load and fire the cannons relentlessly. But their efforts fail to stem the brutal barrage. Danish iron balls shatter rudders and masts, sending inexperienced hands scrambling.

A cannonball strikes the British mast at midpoint with an explosive crack! The sound reverberates as the ship lurches to port and deckhands scatter in terror. The mast, now splintered and groaning, hurtles down with ferocious force, narrowly missing the captain as it crashes to the deck.

His eyes bulge as he grinds his teeth. "Where do you think you're going? You yellow-bellied bilge rat!" he yells at the fleeing seamen, his blood seething. His wavy hair, soaked from ocean spray, clings to the pockmarked skin beneath. "Man your posts and fire at the gunboats!"

One sailor tries to dodge him, but the captain catches his shoulder and shoves him back to his station.

Boom!

A whistling shriek cuts through the tumult. The iron ball rips his head off his shoulders, his body eerily upright before collapsing, lifeless, on the deck.

Cannonballs thud and splash into the ocean, indifferent to the sailors' screams and the groans of twisting wood. Their echoes mingle with cries and crackling flames as thick smoke billows skyward. Frigid water floods the shattered British hulls, engulfing sailors as the deck vanishes beneath them.

Denmark's small gunboats deliver a significant blow to the British navy, forcing the newly established United Kingdom to look to the hillsides of Scandinavia for timber to build additional ships. But the French blockade of the Baltic Sea in 1807 bars the timber supply. In response, Great Britain turns to the forests of its North American colonies, relying specifically on the Dankworth Lumber Industry, managed by Dolores Dankworth, its widowed heir. She writes to Hezekiah Coopers, a deputy of the king's court, to report illegal timber cutting that affects all major lumber companies in the region.

In early 1810, Hezekiah sails to Saint John, New Brunswick, with well-trained men to confront Ellis Amspoker and his rogue cutters. In the shadowed forest, a massacre unfolds. Amspoker's men, unarmed and outnumbered, use stockpiled timber for cover, but the militia cuts them down swiftly. Blood from seventeen ill-prepared men disgorges onto the white pine, seeping into its grain and tainting its essence. Families splinter, leaving behind fatherless children and widowed women in the wake of senseless slaughter.

Soon after, teams of six mules haul the timber to the Dankworth Lumber Yard, where an indifferent worker labels the bloodstained pine with number 7734 before crossing the Atlantic. British ships built with the cursed timber sink within weeks during the wars; the entire crew of the HMS *Narghile* vanishes when the vessel goes down in the Kattegat between the kingdoms of Denmark and Sweden.

Merritt Gastrell, an English clockmaker famed for his elaborate designs, buys scrap from batch 7734. He crafts exquisite long case clocks exclusively for nobles and royals. Not until 1875 does a popular song bring the term "grandfather clock" into common usage in England and America.

Months after purchasing the cursed pine, he begins work on a new long case, using a mahogany finish to hide the blood stains. His intricate design features a bonnet with two reeded columns attached to the door. At the top, a swan's neck pediment is adorned with two side finials, a centered planton, and two brass globes depicting the Western and Eastern Hemispheres. The hood gleams with églomisé glass panels, and the lunar dial rotates once every 29 ½ days in sync with the moon's cycle.

Not long after the clock is finished and stored in the warehouse, a fierce lightning bolt pierces the ominous black sky and strikes the building, setting it ablaze. The fire devours Gastrell's workshop in an inferno, billowing thick smoke and embers into the sky. Amid the destruction, the clock is the only wooden object that emerges unscathed.

An auction is held for the lone survivor, but the public's interest is piqued when they learn that the clock is crafted from cursed pine, the same stockpile used to build the ill-fated HMS *Narghile*.

Unaware of the curse, an outspoken businessman with a bushy white beard and a threadbare ulster coat buys the clock and arranges delivery to his magnificent Georgian-style home. Upon opening the crate, he clutches his chest and collapses mid-sentence from apoplexy.

The clock is left untouched; no one winds it. Dust settles across its bonnet, and furniture is rearranged to avoid its presence. Yet in the stillness of midnight, a faint ticking seems to echo from the long case. Impossible, as the clock remains unwound. It stands idle for nearly twenty years until Nicholas Zytca, an immigrant from Warsaw, Poland, drawn to its strangely intricate design, buys it for twenty-seven pounds in 1897.

At age nineteen, he journeys to America with his apprehensive young wife, Asusana, in search of a better life. Upon arriving, Nicholas changes their family name to Zitcaby. A few years later, they welcome their daughter, June. After the death of both parents, June inherits the *timeless* long case and marries late, only to be immediately abandoned while pregnant by her drunken husband. On August 2, 1939, June Zitcaby gives birth to a son and names him Fazal.

Graduating from Thistleton High School in Kentucky at eighteen, Fazal Zitcaby learns the clock repair trade and rebuilds the works of the long case. He marries his high school sweetheart and moves to Richmond, Indiana, where they let their roots intertwine like ancient oak trees. They welcome a baby girl into their lives, but she tragically passes away at ten due to complications from pneumonia.

To escape his grief, Fazal dives into clock repair work, setting up his tools in a cluttered garage. His hands stay busy. Tweezers slide over gears. Polishing cloths glide across brass and glass. Days blur into years. Meanwhile, he forgets to wind the grandfather clock. It stands silent and patient, pushed into a shadowy corner where sunlight never fully reaches.

Customers arrive, admiring the silent clock as they wait for their heirlooms. Fingers brush the mahogany case. Pets sniff it. Birds perch on it. A neighbor collapses in his garden. One by one, they die. Even though the clock remains unwound, it mysteriously chimes once to announce a new death. The occasional chimes baffle Fazal, but he blames the striking train, believing it holds a sliver of old tension. At times, he suspects vibration from a passing truck, the slam of a back door, or shifting humidity. Whatever the cause, he never makes the connection.

Most peculiar is the single chime heard from their bedroom on the anniversary of his daughter's passing, untouched, unwound, suggesting it remembers.

Fazal opens a dry cleaning shop in February 2000, where the long case is displayed in a well-lit corner. For several years, his business thrives, but he begins to lose revenue due to his inability to meet deadlines, leading to poor customer service. To attract new customers, he arranges an interview with a central news station to broadcast a story about the Ellis Amspoker curse and the clock's eerie legacy.

* * *

Friday, May 13, 2005. 7:48 a.m.

The WPND-TV news van from Columbus, Ohio, arrived at Fazal's Dry Cleaning to report on the intriguing tale of an ostensibly haunted grandfather clock. Ann Marie Johnson and Vincent, the cameraman, were working on a segment about American phenomena. With a flight time of under three hours, they rushed to complete the segment. Their next destination was Los Angeles, California, where they were slated to investigate reports of a wicked witch terrorizing residents near the Koreatown District.

As Vincent set up the camera, Ann Marie, wearing a chic three-button pantsuit, snapped directions. "Fazal, you stand right here," she said, pointing her manicured finger to the right of the floor clock, cursing her ankle-strap high heels. She coughed delicately into her hand to cover a snicker at his cheap, ill-fitting suit. "Have you ever been on television before?"

Fazal let out a soft, childlike chuckle. "Never," he said, shifting his weight uncomfortably. "But my wife tells me I'm quite dramatic."

"Great," Ann Marie responded dryly, her eyes frowning at the coarse strands poking out from his bushy eyebrows. "When the red light comes on, that means the camera is rolling. Just look into the lens and be yourself. And for goodness' sake, take off those dreadful sunglasses!"

Fazal recoiled. "My eyes are sensitive to light," he said, his eyebrows bobbing.

"Sensitive or not, sunglasses on camera are *not* a good look." Ann Marie snatched the shades off his face, leaving him gawking as the countdown ticked down.

Three . . . Two . . . One . . . Cue.

"Ann Marie Johnson here. Today, I'm standing beside what might be the most amazing grandfather clock ever built. This floor clock, as it was known in the early 1800s, is at the center of a fascinating history. Joining us is the owner of this *timeless* piece, Fazal Hickaby."

"Zitcaby," the proprietor corrected meekly, his graying hair dangling like straw from a sun-worn hat.

"Mr. Zitcaby, enlighten us about this wonderful mechanism, now on display at Fazal's Dry Cleaning on Ardmore Street in Richmond, Indiana." She caught his startled expression.

The camera pulled back to include Fazal, whose unkempt beard and plump face gave him the look of a slightly befuddled grandfather, one with many wonderful tales to tell. "Well, the story, as told by my maternal grandfather, begins in New Brunswick at the start of the nineteenth century. Seventeen men died at the hands of a deputy of the king's court for illegally cutting down trees. They were brutally murdered simply for trying to support their families!"

Fazal, known for stretching the truth, was just getting started. He held out one hand as if gripping the barrel of a gun and curled his finger around the imaginary trigger with the other. "Hezekiah and his militia surrounded the illegal loggers and let them have it! Rat-tat-tat-tat-tat!" he said, narrowing his eyes and sweeping the imaginary weapon across the room.

"Sounds like they were using machine guns," said Ann Marie, her forehead creasing. *I'm pretty sure machine guns weren't invented until the late nineteenth century.*

"Yup." Fazal nodded, running a finger along his too-tight collar. "Thompson submachine guns, to be exact."

The two crew members exchanged incredulous looks but suppressed their laughter.

Seeming more at ease, Fazal leaned forward and peered into the camera, his left eye looming large in the frame. "Legend has it," he said, lowering his voice as if the clock might overhear, "a group of *fifty* men were massacred on a stockpile of timber." He lifted his hands into monster claws to spook the viewers. "Blood and guts splattered across the freshly cut timber like a lawn sprinkler."

With a reverent nod, he ran a tender hand down the side of the clock. Ann Marie kept her distance. *No telling what this weirdo might do, let alone a killer grandfather clock.*

"Death and destruction have followed the wood like an evil omen throughout history. British ships built from its timbers sank, and the warehouse where this clock was made burned to the ground. This gem, crafted from the cursed timber, was the only piece to survive the fire."

"She's certainly bewitching," Ann Marie said, stepping closer to admire the intricate woodwork. Vincent zoomed in as Fazal explained the detailing.

"I wouldn't get too close," the dry cleaner warned, throwing his arm out to shield the clock. "The poor fool who bought this clock died the day it was delivered."

A visible tremor ran down Ann Marie's spine at Fazal's unsettling expression.

"You wouldn't want to be the next unfortunate fool, would you?" he asked, leering at her.

The reporter and cameraman both shook their heads.

"How did you end up with the clock?" Ann Marie asked. "And why haven't you died?"

"My grandfather bought it after the death of the . . . unfortunate fool, when it was no longer running. He hoped to repair it someday, but he never got around to it. It wasn't until I came along that this masterpiece came to life again."

"You mean, it just started working on its own?" asked Vincent, lifting his head above the viewfinder.

A flabbergasted look crossed the dry cleaner's face. "You see these two hands?" he asked, wiggling his fingers in front of the lens.

The camera zoomed in and out to focus on the stubby fingers and deeply creased palms.

"I fixed it!" said Fazal, his voice rising. "*I* brought it back to life with my own two hands. You know, many people believe this old clock is still haunted." Fazal's eyes stretched as wide as his tall tale.

For some reason, Ann Marie was expecting a sinister laugh. "That is indeed a spellbinding story." She smiled at the camera, signaling Vincent to end the segment.

It didn't take long for Ann Marie to end the interview. She'd been in the business long enough to recognize a dead end when she saw one. Clearly, Fazal was just out for publicity, angling for his fifteen minutes of fame at the station's expense—and giving it to him would be as unprofessional as his ridiculous sunglasses.

"Well, there you have it, folks. The clock is ticking on your chance to see this incredible timepiece at Fazal's Dry Cleaning in Richmond, Indiana. Next up: Is there a wicked witch flying around Los Angeles? Stay tuned! This is Ann Marie Johnson, reporting live for WPND-TV, Columbus."

"That's a wrap!" the cameraman said, reeling in his microphone cord. "If we hurry, we can still make our flight."

Ann Marie checked her watch. "Let's do it!" With a playful smile, she reached into her blazer pocket and shouted, "Fazal, catch!" The sunglasses sailed in a high arc, and Fazal sprang forward to catch them before they struck the floor.

The two reporters rushed out to the busy one-way street where the news van had been illegally parked with hazard lights on. As honking cars filled the air, Vincent swiftly positioned the equipment in the van's rear and shut the door behind him. Inside, Ann Marie was already buckled in, her focused expression locked on the road ahead. Vincent glanced at her and slid into the driver's seat, ready to chase the next twist in the story.

"Can you believe that guy?" she asked, shaking her head. "No one will believe that ludicrous story about the old decrepit clock!"

Vincent brushed a lock of fudge-brown hair out of his face and jammed the key into the ignition. "Oh, I don't know," he said. "People eat up that crap like there's no tomorrow." He fired up the engine. "Besides, it's no more incredible than a witch raising hell in Koreatown."

The van's rear tires left behind skid marks as it sped south on Ardmore Street.

Fazal stood confounded, blinking at their abrupt departure. "Must've been something I said," he mumbled as he stowed his sunglasses. "I just don't understand people."

Several minutes later, the spring-action shop bell heralded the arrival of Eli Mayeda, a tall, middle-aged go-getter with a rugged face and Boykin Spaniel hair trimmed close to the ears. A long-time customer, he now dreaded visiting the shop. On several occasions, his suits hadn't been ready as promised, requiring repeat trips that wasted time and gas. *Damn it, I'm sick of this dumbass and his excuses.* Eli strode up with a scowl that said, *Just screw me one more time.* The ring on his thick finger hit the counter with a metallic clunk that echoed in the quiet little shop.

"Just one moment," said Fazal, his fingers flying over the keys of an adding machine, creating the sound of distant rain on a tin roof.

"I don't have a moment." Eli shot the proprietor a stern look that could split him. In a tone as bitter as bile, he said, "I have a meeting in one hour, and I need my suit."

"Just two seconds," Fazal said without looking at him, hitting the total button. His expression collapsed into disbelief at the number.

More bothered by the total than the reprimand, Fazal grabbed the ticket from Eli's hand and deftly flipped through the metal tiles of the card file. When he found Eli's receipt, his heart sank. There was no assigned slot for the suit. Remorsefully, he looked over his shoulder and shook his head.

Eli's eyes bulged and his teeth clenched. His brows lowered perilously over his eyes, creating deep ripples across his forehead. "What do you mean, my suit isn't ready?" he wailed, slamming his fist against the counter. He wanted to leap over the service desk and batter Zitcaby's dim-witted face to a pulp, leave him lying in a pool of blood. "Yesterday, you promised me you'd have it by ten this morning!"

"I'm sorry, Mr. Mayeda." Fazal squinted. "With the missus being sick, I'm trying to do the work of both of us." This was a lie, of course. He knew Eli would completely lose it if he learned she was horseback riding with some glee club friends.

Eli pointed a contemptuous finger at Fazal as he stomped backward toward the door. "You've screwed me for the last time, Zitcaby!" he hissed. "Mark my words, Fazal. I'm going to make your life hell! I will make sure your shop closes once and for all!" He spun around brashly and stormed out, slamming the door with such force the shop bell vibrated like a garter snake's tongue flickering in the temperate grasslands of Nebraska.

Fazal stood with his mouth agape and eyebrows raised. "Have a nice day," he said, amused. His smile faded. "He's right. I've been losing clients due to my laziness! If I want to keep my business, I need to get down to business." Deep in thought, he wandered around the counter and stood before the old grandfather clock. "Everything would be fine if I had more time to get things done!"

Placing a finger to his thick lips, Fazal marveled at the notion of having extra time to accomplish his repetitive work. He pulled a barrel key out of his suit pocket and studied it. "I can turn the clock back, and that will solve everything!" Though he knew the idea was impractical, if not preposterous, he unlocked the clock door, indulging a curious impulse, and gently pulled the handle. The hinges creaked softly.

"All I need is just ten minutes here, ten minutes there. What more can I ask for?" He nudged the minute hand back ten minutes to amuse himself. If nothing else, the change cracked a foolish smile. "There, you see. That wasn't so hard. A few extra minutes, and all my problems will be solved." Fazal flicked his wrist with a mission-accomplished gesture, and his nostrils flared in triumph as he returned to the calculator to scrape the bottom of the barrel.

Moments later, the shop bell tinkled. Eli swaggered into the establishment with a look that screamed, "Just screw me one more time, Mr. Dry Cleaner, and you'll regret the day you were born!" Teeth clenched in anger, he slammed the claim ticket down with a sharp, metallic clunk that echoed around the shop.

Fazal's face froze in surprise. *Was the meeting canceled? Or has he returned to make my life difficult as promised?*

"How did you . . .?" Fazal immediately reached into his coat pockets for Mr. Mayeda's claim ticket.

"I'm here for my suit. Can you please make it quick?" Eli said with a scowl, pushing the ticket closer.

Fazal blinked, eyes wavering between the stub and the irritated man. "How did you get the claim ticket out of my pocket?"

"Listen, Mr. Zitcaby, I don't want to play any more of your games. Give me my suit, and I'll get out of your face for good."

Fazal was bewildered. *Maybe he didn't understand.* "I told you . . . your suit isn't ready."

Eli reached over the counter and clutched Fazal by the lapel of his wrinkled coat. "Listen, you dirtbag! I have had enough of your lame excuses!" His black, humorless eyes bulged, veins rising along his temples like a raging river. Fazal's wide eyes were naked with fear. Deciding it wasn't worth it, Eli shoved the proprietor away and stalked toward the door.

"You screwed me for the last time, Zitcaby!" He pointed a condemning finger. "I promise you, Fāzel. I'm going to make your life difficult!" Eli stormed out of the shop—and even his shadow seemed offended. The door slammed behind him with such force the shop bell burst into action like a red-naped woodpecker jabbing at a tree for larvae.

Fazal remained motionless with his mouth ajar, his eyes blinking, and his bladder aching for release. The only sound was the mocking ticktock-ticktock of the grandfather clock, summoning him for another round of jest. "Did the clock have something to do with this?" Fazal mumbled. "I moved the dial back ten minutes, and Mr. Mayeda reappeared. But that's impossible! Or is it?" He lifted a finger to his lips and cautiously approached the grandfather clock, fixing his stare on its intricate face. He withdrew the barrel key from his pocket, unlocked the casing, and slid the minute hand back ten minutes. "This is crazy," he said, chuckling to himself.

His mind racing, Fazal rushed toward the door and looked out, his breath fogging the glass. No one was in sight. "There must be some explanation," he babbled, hysteria rising in his chest. As Fazal approached the call area, he heard the creak of the door and the familiar chime of the shop bell. His stomach lurched with dread. Fazal whisked around, eyes widening like he'd seen a ghost. His heart raced. His jaw dropped. Standing in the doorway, wearing those same evil, glazed eyes, was Eli Mayeda.

Fear got the better of him. Fazal ran up, grabbed Eli by the shoulders, and pushed him out the door. "There's been a death in the family, and the shop is temporarily closed!" he said, flipping the sign to CLOSED.

"You bastard! I have a meeting this morning, and I need my suit! I'm going to ruin you, Zitcaby!" Eli's venomous words boomed through the glass and stung like a swarm of angry bees.

Terrified, Fazal slithered down the doorframe. After a tense silence, dread clarified into purpose. He knew what must be averted. Burdened by knee effusion from osteoarthritis, he stood like a toddler, arms outstretched.

Keys jangled in his trembling hand as he opened the tall case door. Between pudgy fingers, the clock's long dial felt fragile as time itself. He dragged the minute hand back thirty minutes. *That should be enough time . . . I think.* Taking a deep breath, Fazal shuffled, unsure of where to start. *The clock is ticking!* He darted toward one pile of clothing, then spun back to another. His fingers clawed through fabric until, at last, Eli's suit emerged.

Fazal had never worked so expeditiously in his life. His heart thumped as he checked for stains and tears needing attention. After placing the suit in a dry cleaning machine, he pressed it to remove the wrinkles and restore its shape. A bead of sweat rolled down his neck as he pulled the plastic bag over the suit.

The proprietor let out a long sigh, his heart still pumping and his eyes clouded with uncertainty.

The door swung open and the bell played its familiar chime.

Eli Mayeda entered the shop, his claim ticket already extended.

"Mr. Mayeda," Fazal said, looking up at him. A smile broadened his lips as he relished the deepest sense of accomplishment he'd felt since the day his shop first opened. "How wonderful it is to see you again. I have your suit ready, as promised." Fazal handed the suit over with a flourish, collected the fee, and gave Eli his change. "Please come again, Mr. Mayeda. We appreciate your business," he said, flashing his best smile.

Eli was caught off guard. His head jolted back, ruffling his wash-and-wear hair.

"Much . . . obliged," he said, disconcerted, slender lips curling into genuine appreciation. Feeling content, he handed the proprietor a five-dollar tip and hurried out the door for his meeting.

Fazal knew he was the luckiest man in the world. Granted prodigious capabilities that other men could only dream of, he reveled in his newfound power. And who wouldn't love to rewind time to mend his mistakes? Living flawlessly felt nothing short of ethereal. From now on, he could reach his ambition without a ladder. All it took was his faithful grandfather clock.

As sure as the sun rises, Fazal found himself manipulating the grandfather clock for silly reasons: enjoying an extra cup of Neapolitan ice cream by beating his wife to the near-empty container, outdoing her at crossword puzzles by looking up the answer in advance, even closing the shop earlier to dodge the ever-nitpicking Emma Jenkins and her tireless twin boys. The boys inevitably left smears of chocolate on everything they touched, including the counter's hard-to-reach corners. If only he had the nerve to make Emma Jenkins clean their messes herself!

Soon, Fazal became his community's most helpful and admired member. He was always in the right place at the right time. In less than two months, he had manipulated the grandfather clock at least fifty times, never considering how his frivolity affected the world. And he loved it!

* * *

July 17, 2005

Dear George,

I hate putting you through such anguish, so I'll keep it short. After two months of indecision and procrastination, I've reached the point where I can no longer feign this relationship. I've decided to continue my life with Xavier. Please don't be upset with me. It just happened. I never meant to hurt you. Living with a chained heart isn't living. You once told me that everyone should live to their heart's content so their spirit can be free. And you were right, George. I feel free now. Since you introduced me to Xavier nearly six months ago, my heart has yearned for this freedom.

George, it's better to end this sooner rather than later. I feel we aren't suited for each other. Please don't consider our breakup anyone's fault, especially not your own. Neither of us is to blame. You are the sweetest man I've ever met, and I wish you only the best. Please find it in your heart to forgive us.

Sincerely,

Clémence

* * *

Despite the sun pouring through the bay window, George LeDoux's world dulled in despair. For the past two days, he had done little more than stare at the letter, its scrawled truth festering in his mind like slow acid. Each night, after trudging home from the graveyard shift, he found the folded sheet of paper still waiting on the kitchen counter. Life was hard enough without this blow. It was a slap in the face he never saw coming.

George believed he had finally found the right woman to build a modest nest with, like two sparrows assembling leaves of hope and twigs of optimism. So much so, he gave the last of his hard-earned savings to bring Clémence from his homeland, Bordeaux, France, to a new life in Lafayette, Indiana.

His mother, Eva, was against the match from the start. "No need to make a rash decision. Women come and go," she told him over her second cup of coffee, leaning over the stove to sniff her beef stew. She turned the flame down so the red wine sauce was barely simmering, wiped her plump and sun-aged hands on her apron, and squeezed his cheek. "When they find a man with enough money to keep them financially secure, they'll stick around. But if someone else shows up with more, POOF!—they're gone like a puff of smoke in the wind."

Eva dipped the wooden spoon into the stew, stirred it clockwise three times, and slurped a taste. She offered him a sympathetic smile. "You're better off accepting a woman who pursues you. Not chasing a woman you lust after, but a woman who falls in love with you. Such a woman will do anything for you. I pursued your father because I loved him as much as I do today. Your father was smart. He wanted to live in peace and harmony, so he accepted me into his heart even though I'm not beautiful. Forget your friends. Listen to your mother. An ugly woman knows how to tame a man's primitive side, in spirit, in heart, and yes, in body too."

Dismissing his mother's advice as the ravings of an older woman, George foolishly pursued a girl with captivating olive-green eyes, a smile that shimmered like the northern lights, and short sandy hair that fluttered in the breeze. His narrow quest for this elusive ideal overshadowed any chance at true connection. Yet Clémence came close to fulfilling his every wish.

In his futile efforts to win her favor, George had gone deep into debt for a powerful white muscle car. She reveled in the sensation while he drove along Highway 52—the wind whipping through her short sandy hair, almost reaching a silent orgasmic rush. But like everything else, the allure faded away, much like the sunset and the fading smile on his face.

He was left to toil night after night alongside the very man who had seduced her away. With a tight grip and fury, George snatched the car keys from the kitchen counter and stormed out of the apartment.

* * *

Monday, July 18, 2005. 7:35 p.m.

The door swung open and Fazal stepped cautiously into his home, his eyes darting to make sure the coast was clear. Clutched in his hands was a painting he had purchased from a local gallery. He crept upstairs and slipped into his bedroom, the thrill of the purchase already tangled with guilt.

Despite his valiant effort to keep his mounting addiction hidden, Agnes, his wife of thirty-six years, stood calmly inside the walk-in closet, arms folded.

"Where do you think you're going with that?" she asked, her tone unmistakably chastising.

Caught off guard, Fazal flushed and nearly dropped the precious artwork. He forced a laugh and offered a casual smile. "I thought we could use a painting that personifies fervent love," he said, leaning the frame against the wooden four-poster bed.

In the painting, two wisteria trees rose from a bed of crimson earth, their trunks reaching delicately into a sky ablaze with gold and amber. Their canopies brushed gently, leaning into one another for warmth. Its vibrant colors breathed life into the room, as if the artist had captured the sun's warmth and fervor on canvas.

"Hmm, trees. How extraordinary," she said, followed by a gagging sound.

"These aren't your ordinary trees," he replied, smiling as he caressed her shoulder. He raised his arm to point out the painting's hidden features. "These are trees in love."

Agnes stared intently at the print. "I don't get it. Where do you see love?"

Fazal could hardly contain his delight. "Crimson is the color of love. This red African soil holds deep, untamed fire. Look how the roots interlock in the burning passion, tangled like two naked bodies bound together in the heat of desire."

Agnes fanned her blouse, a shiver racing across her skin. "Yes, I see what you mean." She swallowed hard.

They made love next to the painting he had hung. He showered her with kisses until every inch of her flesh quivered. Somehow, Fazal had managed to get his way yet again—just as he had once convinced her to stop shaving her legs to enhance the friction in their lovemaking. He tickled her plump legs with his beard until she writhed beneath him.

"Stop that!" she squealed, bursting into peals of laughter and shoving his excited body away.

"I was wondering when you would stop me," he said, gasping for air. "Your hairy legs were beginning to tickle *me*!"

* * *

Monday, July 18, 2005. 11:17 p.m.

Agnes lay asleep on her side, her long hair spilling across her shoulder with her right ear rising like a mountain peak above rolling clouds. Her eyes twitched beneath closed lids:

In my dream . . .

I am overwhelmed by the sheer pleasure that permeates my senses.

Amid the celestial glow, I see my daughter, forever young at ten.

Visions of forgotten memories dance before my eyes like the notes of a piano that linger in the recesses of my mind. You, my daughter, are the melody, a tuneful chime, a delicate ring, and the gentle pinging of raindrops. Nature itself becomes a poignant reminder of your presence; every creature carries a unique note, from the haunting cry of an owl down to the melodious chirping of birds.

You elate me with just your glance.

The moment of contact is divine, like love's first kiss or the first spring rain, never-ending, never fading, brimming with warmth and affection. In dreams, there is no sense of time, quantity, or quality, only presence and absence coexisting in the same space. The wind's embrace reveals your spirit's grace. How lovely your whisper travels.

"Come with me, Mother. Your time has come. I yearn for your presence to fill this void and unite our souls. Here, there is no pain, only undying love."

Often, I have pondered the divergent path our lives might have taken, envisioning you as a grown woman.

Regret fills my heart that our shared dreams never materialized.

I see a man alone at night, confused and worried. If I leave him now, the moon and the sun shall dance backward repeatedly, night after night, day after day, year after year. I feel my presence is needed here on earth, where the senses are distorted, and the flesh is weak. If I go, what will become of him?

"Don't worry about Papa. In time, a little girl will set the moon and the sun on the right path."

I had a dream, perhaps a dream within a dream, where the path is vast and the destination is unknown. When I saw you, I realized my journey was over.

And so, with tearful eyes and a heart brimming with longing, I surrender to the embrace of eternity, knowing our reunion in heaven shall be an everlasting symphony of love.

In dreams, I close my eyes and think of you.

If only sleep were eternal.

* * *

Tuesday morning, July 19, 2005.

The gold velvet drape on the four-poster bed muted the morning sunlight. Alone in bed, Agnes stirred as her satin pajamas whispered against the sheets. She heard the water gushing in the shower, where her husband was lathering himself with the last of her favorite body wash. The thought of dust collecting on the carpet nagged at her. Agnes yawned, pushed herself up, and pulled the vacuum cleaner from the closet. She bent to plug it in when the bathroom door creaked open.

Fazal emerged wearing only a towel wrapped snugly around his waist, droplets of water glistening on his skin. "Whoa, wait," he said, raising his hand to halt her. "You're not vacuuming right now. I'll take care of that."

Agnes turned to him, surprised but grateful. "But I—"

"Shh," he interrupted with a gentle smile. "You can start on breakfast. I promise I'll make it quick."

"Fine, but please make sure you get the corners, or I'll grab you by your wrinkly ear and make you do it again," she giggled, sliding her hand down the front of his chest.

Fazal kissed her cheek and nudged her along. Minutes later, the vacuum roared down the hall, ignoring the lint clinging stubbornly to the baseboard. Its high-pitched hum drowned out Agnes's melodic voice and the percolator's rhythmic gurgling. His mouth watered as the scent of *queso seco* and sweet, ripe plantains sizzling in the pan wafted up the stairs.

When Fazal finished vacuuming the landing, he turned off the machine just in time to hear Agnes calling him for breakfast. *Perfect timing, I'm famished.* The thought of her tantalizing meal made his stomach growl in anticipation. He set the vacuum against the white panel, beneath two art pieces hung with symmetrical precision. It stood rigid, without ambition, expressionless as a London sentry. Its cord hung limply down its side, winding like a mountain road.

"I hope you realize you made me miss my plasticware party this morning," Agnes scolded, cringing as he scraped the chair against the tile.

"I can't help that you're so alluring," he said, scraping the tile again as he scooted up to the table.

Agnes let out a frustrated sigh. *How many times do I have to remind him about the finish?* As she leaned over to fill his mug, her foot caught the edge of the area rug under the table. Coffee poured down her front and onto the rug. "Oh my goodness," she said, setting the pot on the table and pulling the coffee-stained robe aside.

"Honey, are you okay?" Fazal jumped to his feet, concerned.

"I'm just a total klutz."

"Well, I won't argue with you there."

He grabbed a cloth and blotted at the coffee stain on the rug. "You go change your clothes. I'll take care of this mess."

"Well, all right," she winked. "But don't touch my eggs, or else."

Fazal's eyes had already drifted toward the plate. Two eggs glistened beneath a glaze of crystallized brown sugar and melted butter, Agnes's signature indulgence. His hand crept forward, drawn by temptation, but she slapped it away.

"You know whole eggs are bad for you. Those are mine," she said, nudging his egg substitute forward with mock sympathy.

In retaliation, he pinched her ample behind as she turned to walk away. Agnes jumped and spun around, arms crossed, foot tapping, her glare daring him to deny it,

He suppressed a grin. "What'd I do now?" he asked, feigning innocence.

"You know exactly what you did."

"I have no idea what you're talking about," he said, resuming his chore.

Agnes sighed heavily. "Why do I bother?" she asked, hurrying to the bedroom.

Once she was out of sight, Fazal thrust a forkful of her crystallized eggs into his mouth, closing his eyes to savor the taste. He deliberately scraped the fork against the plate for the second bite, snickering.

"I heard that," she hollered.

Fazal chuckled to himself, unfazed. After carefully sipping his coffee, he turned his attention to the morning paper, its pages rustling softly, filling the quiet room. Suddenly, Agnes screamed. The sound of her tumbling down the wooden steps shattered the silence, ending in the sharp crack of a spindle.

"Agnes!" he shouted, rising so abruptly his chair clattered to the floor.

Fazal gasped, spotting Agnes crumpled at the foot of the staircase. A piece of the Victorian fluted spindle lay beside her, and the vacuum's power cord dangled above the fourth step, its metal prongs bent by strain. *The cord snared her ankle!* Two broken spindles marked the spot where her head had lodged. In that instant, he knew she was already gone.

Grief-stricken, Fazal dropped to his knees beside her, gently caressing her face with his rough, calloused fingers. *It's my fault. My carelessness killed her.* Tears streamed down his face as he cradled her body, apologizing for leaving the power cord in her path. Memories of their cherished moments flooded his mind as he sobbed uncontrollably.

Through the anguish, somewhere in the shadowed corners of his splintered mind, a spark flickered. *I wonder . . . maybe . . . just maybe . . . there's still hope.* He knew precisely what he must do. "Don't worry, my love," he said, nervously wiping away his tears and bringing his lips up to her ear. "For you, I shall travel to the farthest reaches of the world. And since the world is round, my love for you shall have no end."

Fazal kissed her tenderly on the cheek before storming out of the house.

Tires squealed to a halt in front of the shop under a blanket of fog. Fazal flung the door wide and rushed inside, his heart pounding. He snapped the light switch, and the fluorescent bulb flickered several times before stabilizing. His breath stalled in his throat as his glassy eyes begged for salvation. *Is the magic still working?*

Thump thump, thump thump.

Taking a deep breath, he began his mystical journey toward the clock. In an instant, a spinning tunnel of rushing air and sound enveloped him, clawing at his stride. The faster he tried to move, the harder progress became; with every step, the grandfather clock loomed farther away, as if time itself resisted him. By the *time* he reached the clock, Fazal was gasping for air, his chest painfully tight and heaving like a well-played accordion. The keys rattled as he swung the door wide open. Grabbing the minute dial with a bloodied hand, he rotated it backward until the hour hand rested at five o'clock.

* * *

Tuesday morning, July 19, 2005.

The thrum of hydraulics lifting the 96-gallon garbage container woke Fazal. He lay still, aware of the time shift and the impending tragedy. *This time, things will be different,* he vowed silently. He would send his wife to the plasticware party, and she would never know the difference.

Agnes lay by his side, her oily hair draped over her face and her left ear poking through like a shark's fin slicing through the ocean's surface. *Incredible, she's alive!* The rise and fall of the bedsheet enchanted him, and seeing her angelic face brought tears to his eyes. When Agnes awoke, he allowed her to prepare for the party. He even offered to iron her blouse, but she refused, remembering how he had melted her stockings once. It had taken her two hours to scrape the burnt nylon off the iron's coated surface.

"Why don't you vacuum the hallway instead?" she suggested, getting up to shower. She allowed the terry robe to slip from her shoulders and pool on the floor. Behind the glass door, the stream of warm water grew uneven, thrashing heavy pulses against the pane with each shift of her body. "Don't forget, we have guests arriving tonight," she called out, eyes closed as shampoo streamed through her hair.

Fazal didn't have to think twice. He dove back into bed, curled up like a wounded animal, and pressed a hand to his temple. Humming softly and wrapped in a towel, Agnes emerged from the bathroom to find him moaning with theatrical flair.

"What happened?" she asked, her face riddled with surprise.

"I have a massive headache," he groaned, head gyrating side to side.

His act was so convincing that, after dressing, Agnes returned with a glass of water and ibuprofen. And like a chastised child, he meekly swallowed the pills in her presence. *At least I didn't have to use the vacuum!*

Shortly thereafter, Agnes left the house with her plasticware catalog in hand, the door clicking into place behind her.

Fazal sprang from bed to embrace a stellar day, twirling and shouting in ecstasy. He'd defeated the odds. Their morning ritual unfolded without Agnes falling down the stairs. There was no thumping or banging like sneakers in a rotating dryer.

The sun hung over the horizon, its presence increasingly palpable as minutes unfurled. The only measure of time came from the elongating shadows of trees stretching across the grass—silent sundials beneath a sailing sky.

Heading south on 10th Street, Agnes stopped at a residence with golden roof tiles and a dried-out lawn. She shifted into reverse and backed into a tight spot between two cars, stopping two feet from the curb. Swinging the door open, she stepped out, unaware of the fast-approaching garbage truck. The driver slammed the air brakes, but the front bumper ripped the door clean off its hinges. As the truck's side-view mirror clipped her face, it snapped her neck like a twig.

She never felt the asphalt.

Fazal was about to leave for his shop when the phone rang. The voice on the other end sliced through his morning with unthinkable news: Agnes was dead. *I can't believe it. Everything was going so smoothly!* His legs gave out, and he collapsed onto the floor with a soft thump. Kneeling, he slammed his fist against the tile, spittle spraying as he roared in anguish. The cordless phone soared across the room, shattering the dresser mirror into bright splinters.

Rising slowly, he dug a hand into his pocket and let the car key dangle. His eyes narrowed into slits, glinting with a desperate resolve. There was still hope; another chance for a new beginning.

Minutes later, he stood before the tall case, his face as anxious as a sailor facing a storm-tossed sea.

* * *

Tuesday morning, July 19, 2005.

Fluorescent lights illuminated the aisles of the convenience store as the aroma of freshly brewed coffee lingered in the air. A door chime echoed through the store like a haunting melody and faded into silence. Behind the counter, the cashier glanced up just in time to see a man in black sunglasses and a hoodie burst through the open doorway, heading straight for the cash register. His mind racing, he instinctively pressed the silent alarm button beneath the register.

"How can I help you?" he asked, his voice quavering with tension.

"You can help by putting your hands in the air," the robber commanded, leveling a pistol at the clerk's chest. His voice was low and menacing. He tossed a pouch on the counter and said with a smirk, "Fill it up with premium."

The clerk fumbled with the bag, praying the alarm had tripped. His eyes caught sight of the man's gold upper teeth, glinting through his grin. The register tray popped open with a faint ring, and he began to fill the pouch with bills. "This register doesn't have much money since it's early in the morning," he said, hoping the thief would move on in search of better stakes.

"Shut up! Get the money from under the tray too." The thief nudged the register with the tip of his gun.

The clerk's hands shook as he lifted the tray, his heart pounding against his ribs. Another handful of bills went into the pouch. Outside, a horn blared, sharp and frantic.

"Cops!" the driver shouted.

Snatching the bag, the thief bolted out the door and dove into the getaway car. It lurched forward as the driver careened through the lot, narrowly missing a pedestrian. The car scraped against the asphalt as it shot out of the driveway, sparking a high-speed chase down the boulevard.

* * *

Sheer curtains swayed in the spring breeze wafting through the kitchen bay window. Outside, hummingbirds flitted around the flower bushes, their iridescent wings whirring softly as they dipped their beaks into trumpet-shaped blooms.

Rooting through the cabinet for a French toast pan, Agnes asked over her shoulder, “Would you like ham or sausage for breakfast?”

“Neither,” said Fazal, his eyes lighting up. “I’m craving Chinese noodles with mushrooms and veggies.” He smiled and winked at her, knowing the dish was one of her favorites.

“I can make that happen if you don’t mind waiting an hour, but I’ll miss my plasticware party.” Agnes flashed a smile. Though she didn’t mind, a leisurely drive across town to the Chinese specialty market would be spiritually soothing. She untied her apron, hooked it on a wooden rack, and searched for her keys in the drawer.

The distant honking of horns and the hum of city life filled the air. Pedestrians scurried across a road lined with a vibrant mix of storefronts and cafés. Driving below the speed limit, Agnes turned onto a side street that crossed the downtown artery.

Meanwhile, Richmond police were in pursuit of two robbers in a battered blue sedan. As the getaway car cut a hard left, the driver clipped the curb and ripped a hubcap loose. It sliced through the air like a circular saw, hitting a parked car with a loud clatter before coming to rest. In the distance, the police siren wailed like a trumpet with sand vibrating in its crevices.

The driver wove through downtown Richmond at high speed, blowing through intersections and narrowly avoiding several collisions. Tires shrieked, hurling the car into a skid across the asphalt, its body swaying violently. A blast of burnt rubber filled the air. Then came the slam, metal on metal. Glass exploded like shrapnel, peppering the sidewalk.

Scrambling out of the wreckage, the two hooded men opened fire on the approaching police. In return, an officer’s bullet zipped through a car window and struck an innocent driver in the neck.

Agnes died at the scene.

When Fazal received the devastating call from the police department, his knees buckled beneath him. A searing pain shot through his chest as he crumpled to the floor. The phone slipped from his grasp while the chief inspector was still speaking. His face contorted with misery. Tears streamed down his cheeks, his anguished cries echoing off the walls. In that moment, he blamed the grandfather clock—for standing tall yet doing nothing, for marking time as if it still mattered. It had betrayed him, leaving him in a world where time offered no comfort, no promise, no solace.

When he regained his composure, Fazal stood before the tall case. This time, instead of pleading for his wife's life, he demanded a better outcome, as if the clock owed him for the very breath of its ticking. *I know you hold the secret to sparing my wife from the grip of death!* His crafty mind was set on discovering the correct formula, and nothing would stop him. It was just a matter of time. Lacking any guilt, Fazal reached for the hour hand and pushed it back.

Agnes died nine more atrocious deaths; each death as shocking as the last. But every time Fazal turned the dial back, his eyes shimmered with new hope. First, she died in a boating accident at the southernmost tip of Lake Michigan—mangled and swollen like a balloon. Fazal attempted to rescue his wife when she fell overboard, but the boat's propeller had already severed her neck before her body reappeared five feet from the stern. Then she plunged down a cliff and fractured her neck on a jagged rock during a horseback riding expedition. He even recreated the scrape of the kitchen tile floor with the wooden chair, right down to the playful snicker he gave after eating her crystallized eggs. This time, he made sure to reel in the vacuum power cord. But Agnes didn't need a tripping hazard to meet her end. She fell down the staircase on her own, thumbing through the latest plasticware catalog.

* * *

Tuesday morning, July 19, 2005.

On the thirteenth attempt to save her, Fazal and Agnes boarded the Primary America Falcon Train 71, departing Connersville, Indiana, at 5:15 a.m. and arriving in Chicago, Illinois, at 12:35 p.m. Agnes didn't understand her husband's desire to spend the afternoon in Chicago. She was glad to go along if it made him happy, although his anxiety puzzled her.

"The gardens are great this time of year," he said, settling into his cushioned seat.

"This is a wonderful surprise," she replied, placing the tabloid magazine beside her. "But frankly, I'm worried about you. You look frightened." She inspected him, noting the shadows under his eyes and the way his hands trembled slightly. "Is there anything you need to tell me?"

"No." It wasn't like him to tell white lies, but he had no choice. Fazal fought back tears and delved into his poetic mode to cover his anxiety. "Actually, I do have something to say," he added, taking her hand. "My emotions dwell in various colors." He forced a smile. "My spirit lives in deep red and burgundy. My passion for you," he paused to trace her plump cheek with one finger, "is no different, for it is my blood."

Agnes's face grew radiant as she caught the compassion in his eyes. It was a gentler side she'd known since they first met. Their love had always held a tinge of humor that evolved into gags and one-upmanship. She smiled faintly, remembering the night she'd finally outwitted him:

Fazal had passed out drunk, snoring across the bed like a bloated sea lion. Using glow-in-the-dark paint, Agnes adorned him from head to toe with a full-size skeleton. In the middle of the night, Fazal awoke with a full bladder. He floundered into the bathroom, only to see a skeleton staggering toward him in the mirror. A blood-curdling scream escaped him as he leapt three feet into the air and stumbled backward.

Agnes was in bed, howling with laughter. He'd never sobered up faster.

As the train hummed along the Indiana tracks, Agnes held his hand a little tighter as she leaned back and closed her eyes.

* * *

Lafayette, Indiana. Tuesday, July 19, 2005. 8:35 a.m.

George first encountered Xavier Odell at Time and a Half Tavern, with its battered tables and lingering scent of spilled ale. Wearing a distinctive gold ring on his pinky, Odell's voice boomed like the clarion call of a trumpet. His habit of chuckling and clapping people on the back carried an unspoken air of superiority. George had counted nearly a dozen that evening, including the one that nearly sent his drink over the rim. Despite this, his good nature earned him a graveyard shift at the local food distributor, working directly under Odell's supervision. "We're going to be great friends," Xavier had declared, arm resting on the counter. To George, he looked every bit the king of the tavern.

Xavier had first noticed Clémence at one of their impromptu gatherings. His laughter and feather-light touches were as persistent and unyielding as the wind, each one a calculated move to draw her attention and affection. Days later, he began openly courting her while George slept, unaware of the betrayal brewing beside him. He wouldn't learn of their nearly six-month affair until Nancy left him that heart-wrenching 'Dear John' letter.

George LeDoux's white muscle car roared east on Schuyler Avenue, the engine growling like a caged beast. He paused near the Time And A Half Tavern, his face a mask of anguish, mouth drawn into a tight line. Fury overtook him, and he floored the accelerator, leaving behind a pair of skid marks and the scent of burnt rubber. Wide-eyed pedestrians blurred past as he swung left on North 18th Street.

Speeding past Brady Lane, George gripped the wheel, his knuckles white with tension. He turned off the engine just before the railroad crossing. The silence hit him, striking sharply against the storm inside his head. His large watch, weighing down his wrist like a shackle, read 8:47. In just minutes, he knew, the Falcon 71 would roar across the flatlands like a rampaging gray rhino.

At the sudden clang of the bell, a mourning dove burst off the crossing sign in a whir of wings. George heard the horn growing louder. He fired up the engine and shifted into drive, nudging the car forward as the front tires bumped over the tracks. Halfway across, George killed the engine and hurled the keys out the window, his resolve unshaken. A trickle of sweat slid down his cheek.

Echoing the Pied Piper of Hamelin, the iron wheels, with piercing highs and resonant lows, seemed to sing a siren song, lulling the weary into a trance. For George LeDoux, feeling like a wretched rat ensnared by the haunting tune, the temptation of ending it all seemed like his only reprieve.

* * *

The Falcon 71 sped down parallel steel bars, crossing over the murky green waters of South Fork Wildcat Creek. As the commuter train rounded the bend at County Highway South, Tom Choi's eyes locked on the looming threat ahead. He sprang from the comfort of his cushioned seat in a panic, the hairs on his arms bristling.

"Son of a bitch!" he shouted, his heavily blemished face draining of color. The toothpick clamped between his teeth dropped to the floor as he blasted the horn repeatedly. He'd already crossed the safety threshold; time had run out. "Get out of my way!"

He slammed the brakes, and the sudden deceleration sent his gray, long-layered bangs flinging forward.

Passengers snapped like dominoes. Fazal's scalding coffee rocketed from his cup, arching over the forward-facing seat and splashing across the shoulders of the row ahead. A chorus of screams rose as bodies slammed into obstacles like flies meeting the stinging blow of a giant swatter. Agnes's plump arms flew out in a desperate attempt to slow her momentum, but they were too weak to stop her. The seat before her snapped her neck upon impact. Her frail body slumped into a fetal position . . .

George knew, too late, he'd made a catastrophic mistake. His trembling fingers fumbled for the door handle, though he dared not look at the fast-approaching train. Agonizing seconds ticked by before the handle clicked. He lunged out, the door flung wide behind him as he sprinted past the crossing gate into a dirt field. The rumble of the diesel engine sent dread rippling through him.

With a deafening roar, the train imploded the sports car into unrecognizable metallic art. The impact ripped the driver's door off its hinges and hurled it into his path. George thought he had eluded the accident, but when he turned to look at the metal mesh, he stumbled backward. His panic-stricken eyes grew wider as he noticed the door spiraling toward him like a meteor plunging from the sky.

"Mon Dieu!" he exclaimed, rolling over to dodge the impact. The twisted door burrowed into the ground with such force that it landed upright like a wooden splinter in a sore thumb. A coughing fit seized George, and when it finally let go, he wiped his face and blinked through the haze. His hair and eyebrows took on a lighter shade, giving him the dust-laden look of a miner after a cave-in. He lay facing the mangled door, three inches from his powdered face.

When the train screeched to a grinding halt, screams and moans of the injured rippled through the cabin. Passengers lay scattered. Some were thrown from their seats, others disoriented and writhing in pain within the misshapen coaches. Fazal knelt beside his wife, who was doubled over in her seat like a wilted flower. A wave of dread washed over him, fearing the worst. He clenched his eyes shut as a gut-wrenching scream tore from his throat and echoed through the wreckage. Holding her tight, he rocked back and forth, ululating with grief.

Brian was one of the lucky ones. He was hurled to the floor without hitting any deadly obstacles. As an ex-firefighter, he knew the first thing to do was to help the injured. Gripping his torn sleeve, he ripped the fabric off. "Here, hold this on your forehead," he said, handing the shred to a sobbing twelve-year-old girl. He kept his focus on the shaken girl, his unwavering gaze imparting calm. The gash across her brow showed beneath her bangs, a wound that would likely leave a scar. Her father, who had hit his head on the seat in front of him, looked on with a dazed expression.

"Do you know how to stop being afraid?" he asked, gently tilting her chin. She shook her head and stopped crying to look at the blood on the torn sleeve. Her eyes grew wide. "Think about others instead of yourself. Look around and tell me who needs help."

Her eyes swept the interior and landed on a pregnant woman embracing a crying toddler. With a burst of enthusiasm, she said, "That woman looks like she could use some help."

Brian followed her gaze. "Great," he said, nodding. "Who else?"

"That old man over there!" she said, pointing, her pain forgotten in the rush to help.

Brian pulled the girl into a quick hug. "See how easy it is? Always concentrate on others, and your soul will be pleased. How about you help that woman by distracting her child? I'll take care of the old man."

She smiled and clambered through the jumble of seats.

"Thank you for your thoughtfulness," the girl's father said, extending his right arm.

"It's our duty as human beings," said Brian, clasping his hand.

He walked toward the older man, leaned between the seats, and said, "Can I help you, mister?"

Fazal turned to face the man standing over him. His green eyes, much like a deep, verdant forest, held a quiet intensity. “It’s my wife,” he groaned, tears trailing down his face. “I think she’s dying.”

Brian laid his fingers against her neck, finding only a faint pulse. He had seen the dead and those on the brink of death in his field of work. This woman had seen her last. “She’s leaving us,” he said softly. “But she can still hear you. Hearing is the last sense to linger. Tell her how you feel.” He knelt beside him, one hand around Fazal’s shoulder. “Let her know how much you love her and cherish the years you shared. There must be something that connects you and your wife as one.”

Fazal nodded like a child.

Yes, there is something!

He leaned over her limp body, clutched her hand, and whispered into her ear, “We are trees.”

Agnes gripped her husband’s calloused hand and smiled knowingly. Then, without warning, she faded.

* * *

2:05 p.m.

Fazal spent the first half of the day at the wreck and the second half at Jefferson Ridge General Hospital, where sixty-seven patients were taken for injuries ranging from minor cuts and bruises to broken bones. Others were transferred to Blossom Morn Community for more serious medical issues and trauma evaluation. Sitting in the emergency room, Fazal’s mental state underwent a gradual but detrimental transformation. The spirit that once pulsed with life faded, leaving his soul feeling like a carcass on the roadside. Thinning hair lay disheveled around him, his clothes embarrassingly wrinkled. His thoughts were as far away as Mars, or Jupiter, to be exact. Now, his only wish was to step inside the dry cleaning shop one last time, to stare down the grandfather clock with vengeful, vehement eyes, and make it beg for mercy.

7:08 p.m.

Fazal was released after imaging ruled out internal bleeding beneath the bruise he sustained on his arm. He sat listlessly on the cushioned lobby seat, feet flat on the floor, shoulders heavy with grief. His cavernous eyes stared forward without seeing. Like sperm whales diving into deep waters, Fazal's mind faded for prolonged periods. Only the most patient observer could read the tranquil blue, watching for the rare, unpredictable moment his consciousness broke the surface.

Am I dead? I want to be lost, away from people and life. For what good is laughter when one does not have a heart? Maybe misery isn't so bad; it wraps around my soul better than joy. It keeps me company and understands my grief. Without my dear Agnes, it would surely be a senseless life. Oh, let me pass on so I may finally be free. Take me deeper where despair awaits.

9:47 p.m.

Fazal's scratched sunglasses concealed his tears as his body melted into the cushion like warm butter. A little girl in a white Mexican dress, embroidered with blood-red roses and spruce-green leaves, stared at him. Her jet-black hair was parted down the middle, falling over a face untouched by the varicella virus. She blinked at his sickly appearance and the way he slumped in his seat like a drunk on a park bench. Tugging at her mother's bell sleeve, she whispered into her mother's ear in Spanish. The woman turned her gaze on the man and recoiled. "Déjalo, mija. Es un borracho cochino." She grabbed her daughter by the arm and hurried out the door.

11:39 p.m.

Though it had preened itself, the fly cleaned its eyes with its forelegs, dusted them by rubbing them together, and took off. It flew in a few quick circles, twisted into a figure eight, and landed on Fazal's head again, repeating the sequence several times.

Fazal's body sank deeper into the seat. His eyes drooped into his skull from exhaustion, bags as murky as the Dead Sea's depths: no life, no oxygen. Depression knew no limits. It fed on the slow deterioration of his mind, growing stronger and harder to defeat . . . unless met with anger.

Agnes, return to me.

Fazal flinched.

Wednesday, July 20, 2005. 2:02 a.m.

The janitor angled the vacuum closer, hoping to rouse the man, but Fazal never stirred. He sat in a trance, unmoored from reality. The vacuum whined around his feet, then faded as the janitor retreated to the far end of the room. For seven hours, Fazal muttered nonsense and remained oblivious to the shifting bodies. As time dragged on, his blood simmered into rage. His muscles tensed, shoulders twitching under invisible strain.

The rabid dog finally snapped.

5:25 a.m.

The taxi driver's eyes flicked repeatedly to the rear-view mirror, nervous about his passenger during the drive back to Richmond. Fazal sat rigidly in the back seat, his unshaven face frozen in a grimace, his occasional mutter piercing the night's dull ear. Not once did he notice the driver stealing glances at his sunken eyes that were as dark as a moonless Transylvania night. After a long two-hour journey, the driver finally exhaled as they reached their destination.

"Wait here. I need to grab something," Fazal said as he slid off the taxi seat. The door slammed shut.

A fogbank drifted slowly into town, curling around lampposts and swallowing parked cars in its path. The driver watched Fazal make his way up the porch one jet-lagged step at a time. When he disappeared into his home, an eerie silence fell over the neighborhood, not even a chirp broke it.

An uneasy feeling settled in the pit of his stomach. He couldn't help but cast nervous glances at the decrepit houses. Nervously, he moistened his lips. *Is it safe here?* Every passing second felt like an eternity as he anxiously awaited the client's return.

Moments later, Fazal reappeared from his home with a sinister look on his sleep-deprived face. Noticing the giant sledgehammer in his hand, the driver recoiled.

"I don't want any problems, mister!" he said, his fear escalating. Before he could drive away, Fazal had yanked open the rear door and climbed in.

"Take me to Ardmore and Becker Street," Fazal barked. The driver hunched over the wheel, expecting to feel the sledgehammer in the back of his head.

When the cab stopped before the dry cleaning shop, Fazal got out and pulled out two large bills from his wallet. But before he could pay his fare, the driver sped away, leaving only tire marks and a gust of smoke. Fazal stood with his sledgehammer balanced at his side.

Under the glow of a streetlamp, the fog enveloped him like cigar smoke in a seedy bar. Fazal unlocked the glass door and swung it open, causing it to bang against the doorstop. A wicked grin spread across his face in the doorway. Headlights from a passing car cast his shadow, hammer in hand, into a grotesque ballet across the shop's walls. His face was a mask of malice, and his eyes showed no mercy as they fixed on the floor clock.

Fazal stepped forward, dragging the sledgehammer. He set it on the counter, planted his feet, and kicked the grandfather clock in the midsection. Its chimes clanged in protest.

"What do you want from me!?" he howled.

The wooden boards creaked as he paced, working himself into a frenzy. "I brought you back to life with my own hands, and this is how you repay me?"

Fazal pressed his face against the dial door, his breath fogging the pane. "Do you think that's fair?" he shouted, taking three steps back. Receiving no response, he resumed his lunatic ravings. "You took away the only woman I ever loved. And now she is gone forever!" His sobs subsided to a whimper, and when he had no more tears to shed, his grief raged into fury. "No one takes away what belongs to me! No one!"

Grabbing the sledgehammer, Fazal swung it with all his strength into the side of the case. With a crunch and a jangle of brass, the pine splintered, rattling the weights. Black liquid oozed out of the split wood in a malignant stream. Thick with history and fury, the ancient blood seethed down the wood. The tall case stood defenseless as Fazal cocked the sledgehammer back for the next hit, this time striking above the waist molding. The clock rocked, sending the delicate works clanging again. But it stayed upright, defiant, as the gouge oozed revolting fluid.

Riding high on his revenge, Fazal laughed shrewdly, squinting his eyes and bobbing his head in delight. He stood before the clock, tightening his grip on the hammer. The clock struck 8:15 as the sledgehammer glided through the air. With a swoosh, it smashed the side of the grandfather clock one last time, causing severe damage to the case and expelling more black sludge down its side.

The final blow dislodged the clock's anchor, and something inexplicable—perhaps spiritual, perhaps quantum—compelled the pendulum to accelerate. The escapement gear jolted free, vaulting over two cogwheels in the gear train, and reversed the mechanism's rotation. The force drove the weight to skip a cog entirely, triggering a new ratio: one full cycle every 124,800 hours. The clock, now anomalously self-sustaining, would not require winding for the next two centuries.

At precisely 8:15 a.m., the minute hand embarked on a counter-clockwise journey. It progressed slowly, circling the dial with hesitant resolve. Then it quickened, gaining velocity with each revolution. Within minutes, the hands blurred into invisibility, spinning with such speed that only the pulsing tick remained. The only evidence of time was the sun moving in reverse, its accelerated orbit around the Earth serving as proof of the temporal disruption. Night became day instead of day becoming night. The seasons raced across the skies as the months inversely roared by. Then the years flew by in the same fashion:

.rekopsmA sillE yb demrof srettuc doow lagelli neetneves fo puorg eht fo seidob eht otni dna enip etihw eht fo tuo spees doolB .ydob sih otni kcab sniard efil eht elihw srepooC haikezeH ta stniop dna noitisop sselefil a morf stfil dnah siH .noitanmad fo sdrow era rebmit delipkcots eht no efil ot gninruter retfa syas rekopsmA sillE taht sdrow tsrif ehT .swas gniriaper htiw dnuorg eht otni kcab detnalp si hcihw ,rebmit neht dna ,plup a neht ,repap knalb semoceb retsbeW haoN yb *egaugnaL hsilgnE eht fo yranoitciD naciremA nA* fo gnitnirp tsal ehT .ocixeM fo tnedneped semoceb saxeT .sdne ainrofilaC otni kcab dlog tup ot hsur ehT .reverof sraeppasid *semiT kroY weN ehT* dna ,enihcam gniwes sih seltnamsid regniS caasI .ydob sih stixe tellub a retfa efil ot kcab semoc nlocniL maharbA .enohpelet eht rof aedi sih sehctid lleB maharG rednaxelA .ogacihC ni deltnamsid si seirots net fo reparcsyks tsal ehT .rac leehw-ruof sih seltnamsid zneB lraK ,retal sraey owt dna ,rozar ytefas eht rof aedi sih sparcs ettelliG .C gniK .drawkcab enalpria derewop a ylf yllufsseccus thgirW rubliW dna ellivrO ,retal raey a dna ,sdne lanaC amanaP eht fo gniltnamsid ehT .sdne raw eht ,retal sraey eerht dna ,I raW dlroW stixe SU ehT .seivom tnelis ot yaw sevig *,regniS zzaJ ehT* ,mlif gniklat tsal ehT .drawkcab citnaltA eht ssorca olos ylf ot namow tsal eht si trahraE ailemA .srood yab bmob s'yaG alonE otni staolf dna dnuorg eht morf stceje bmob cimota eht nehw sdnoces fo rettam a ni elbbur eht morf sesir amihsoriH .natshkazaK ni sdnal hcihw ,tekcor 7-R na htiw kintupS seveirter noinU teivoS ehT

.noom eht no stnirptoof evael ot ton nosrep tsal eht si gnortsmrA lieN .augaraciN ni satsinidnaS eht sworhtrevo azomoS .dnuorg eht no gniyl tnemec fo seceip nekorb htiw detcere si llaW nilreB eht elihw ageiroN seerf dna amanaP stixe SU ehT .tiawuK fo tuo drawkcab nur spoort iqarI .yks eht otni senalpria owt lepxe dna sdnoces fo rettam a ni elbbur fo tuo tcere srewoT niwT ehT

It required several days for the universe to stop its regression sometime in 1807 before it began rotating forward at a normal pace:

The battle saga continues its polarization
Britain and France are at each other's throats
But to the victor shall be the nation
Who possesses the most valiant boats

Fires are blazing, and cannonballs are crushing
The stern has broken, and the Baltic Sea is rushing
Down are the ships that devastate the British navy
The *Hemsworth*, the *Notable*, the *Militant*, and the *Lady*

Soon, the British ships are exhaustingly depleted
Leaving commanders and sailors emotionally heated
Do not look to Scandinavia, as the French blockade will hinder
There's plenty o' ships to be made with North American timber

A noble, respectable constituent of the king's woods
Hezekiah responds to one of his North American administrators
Tell me, Dolores Dankworth, who is taking the illegal goods?
Amspoker and his band of men are the timber perpetrators

Pine trees reared their spiny heads against a cloudless sky, their crowns commanding a majestic view over the river that snaked in from

Musquash Harbour. A carpet of prickly needles covered the ground, helping the soil retain moisture. Only the occasional neighing and snorting of horses broke the silence. Hezekiah Coopers and his men knew they wouldn't be seen while traveling through the forest's cover. His face was stern and refined, and he wore a long two-button wool frock coat over a collarless tuxedo shirt and pinstripe trousers—an ensemble befitting a man of panache. His men also wore the obligatory vests of Victorian fashion, but with their sleeves rolled above the elbow for a relaxed look.

The twelve men rode swiftly to the edge of what would one day be called the Loch Alva Wilderness. In 1807, it was known simply as Big Lake—untamed and nestled where the bay channels into the river. Standing in the clearing, two men in faded denim overalls and dirty cotton shirts labored over felled pine, their bare feet pressed into the loamy soil.

"I reckon you two are working here for Ellis Amspoker?" he said. His horse anxiously stepped back and forth.

"Yes, sir," responded the outspoken man, a friendly smile on his sweaty face. "You aiming to winter here?"

"No," said the man on the horse. Gazing at the bright sun, he shaded his delicate eyes with the tilt of his hat. "We are looking for the proprietor. We are considering working for a few weeks before continuing our journey to New Hampshire."

"Plenty o' work here, mister," he said, slipping a straw between his lips.

"The name is Hezekiah Coopers."

"My name is Jacob, Mr. Coopers," he said, stepping forward. "This here is my little brother, Martin. He be a fine worker." Martin nodded, holding his weather-beaten straw hat between his hands. Turning back at Hezekiah, he continued, "Stick together. Ain't wise to move through these woods without knowing who walks 'em. Mi'kmaq folk been here long before us."

"We can handle ourselves. The Mi'kmaq won't be our concern." Hezekiah waved the warning aside, not out of disrespect, but with the confidence of a man accustomed to charting his fate. In a slow and exasperated tone, he turned toward Jacob again and said, "Now, where can we find this Ellis Amspoker?"

* * *

It was a three-mile trek along the Musquash River before reaching Ellis Amspoker's post. Using his two-draw field telescope, Coopers spotted hundreds of leveled pine trees on the sandy shore. He counted sixteen men, all receiving orders from a man sporting an elegant mustache and long sideburns. *That must be Ellis Amspoker, cutting our trees.* After shoving his telescope in the pocket of his frock coat, Coopers directed his men to fan out in a semicircle before approaching the crew. The element of surprise was key to preventing them from scattering into the woods like frightened deer.

Amid the cool forest air, tall trees reached for the sky, their broad trunks standing stately. Streaks of sunlight filtered through the forest canopy, casting patterns of light and shadow. The air was rich with the earthy scent of pine and the crisp fragrance of fallen leaves. They rustled underfoot, mixing with the distant calls of woodland creatures. A deer grazing on freshly grown grass froze, its ears twitching at the sound of men pressing forward through the landscape. Then it darted away.

Gunfire erupted from the encroaching men, Hezekiah Coopers's war cry marking him the clear leader. Shots echoed through the forest, sending birds and animals scuttling and bounding away. While some bullets zipped through the air and plunged into tree trunks, others struck fleeing men.

Ellis Amspoker and his band of illegal timber cutters hid behind the stockpiled pine; most of his men died within minutes. Blood soaked into the grain like a crimson river, winding through its natural markings. Ellis, last to fall, took bullets to the rib cage and shoulder, collapsing across a summit of logs. He raised his head, his eyelids fluttering, watching Coopers's confident stride carve through the open land. He could hear the stranger's boots scraping against the pine as he began his ascent. Amspoker's beige trail duster concealed the bullet wound in his shoulder, but he felt warm blood trickle down his arm—a clandestine trail of death.

Hezekiah loomed over the slumped man as the wind played with the tail of his long coat. There was no sympathy in his cold, wicked eyes, nor in the twisted mask of malice.

"I'll tell you this." Amspoker feebly lifted his arm and pointed at Hezekiah. "I curse you and anyone who comes in contact with our pine." His arm fell limp, and a thick red droplet formed on his fingertip. His blood, a pomegranate seed, shimmered in the sun's glow. The bead expanded until it splattered onto the pine, soaking into the grain, a permanent fixture of the cursed wood.

A few days later, Hezekiah Coopers's militia hauled the bloodstained white pine by teams of six mules to the Dankworth Lumber Yard. The timber was then loaded onto a ship bound for England, where it would be used to build navy vessels and a grandfather clock.

The universe progressed through two hundred years of historical events and culminated in the destruction of the grandfather clock. This ill-fated demolition prevented the earth and life from advancing; instead, the universe regressed as though time itself swung like a pendulum, never settling, never advancing. The regression automatically looped at the Loch Alva Wilderness massacre, where the dreaded Ellis Amspoker curse occurred.

It took several minutes for the universe to halt its regression before moving forward. All the universe's glory progressed through two hundred years of historical events and culminated in the destruction of the grandfather clock. This ill-fated demolition prevented the earth and life from advancing; instead, the universe regressed as though time itself swung like a pendulum, never settling, never advancing. The regression automatically looped at the Loch Alva Wilderness massacre, where the dreaded Ellis Amspoker curse occurred.

It took several minutes for the universe to halt its regression before moving forward. All the universe's glory progressed through two hundred years of historical events and culminated in the destruction of the grandfather clock. This ill-fated demolition prevented the earth and life from advancing; instead, the universe regressed as though time itself swung like a pendulum, never settling, never advancing. The regression automatically looped at the Loch Alva Wilderness massacre, where the dreaded Ellis Amspoker curse occurred.

It took several minutes for the universe to halt its regression before moving forward. All the universe's glory progressed through two hundred years of historical events and culminated in the destruction of the grandfather clock. This ill-fated demolition prevented the earth and life from advancing; instead, the universe regressed as though time itself swung like a pendulum, never settling, never advancing. The regression automatically looped at the Loch Alva Wilderness massacre, where the dreaded Ellis Amspoker curse occurred . . .

LIFEGIVER

In the cold vastness of space, there is a star-forming region in the Perseus spiral arm of the Milky Way galaxy known as W30H. There, red giants and yellow dwarfs celebrate the birth of a new star. Within the swirling clouds of gas and dust, hydrogen nuclei are crammed together. Collisions among atoms heat the cloud until hydrogen fuses into helium, unleashing energy as light, marking the star's awakening. Star systems are bound together by gravity, and the distance between them ensures a birth without complications.

The fledgling star was born too close to a red giant, triggering turbulence. The intense gravity between them created a Roche lobe through which material from the red giant flowed into the evolving star. Highly concentrated hydrogen, along with carbon, nitrogen, and aluminum, ignited a violent nova in the ill-fated star, dispersing star stuff into space. Debris raced through interstellar space over millions of light-years, where the gravitational pull of neighboring stars captured most of these fragments. One such fragment was cast into the path of a white dwarf star.

The boulder hurtled through a spherical assemblage of comets known as the Oort Cloud. It sailed into a solar system, passing through an asteroid belt toward the third planet. The chunk of rock streaked across the sky at thirty miles per second, breaking up in the Earth's atmosphere over the Atlantic Ocean. By the time it sliced through the mesosphere, it had dwindled to little more than flakes of dust, a fraction of a micron, wafting like dandelion seeds. Gentle winds nudged one flake westerly over the shores of Miami, altering its course southwest over a shorefront park ringed by skyscrapers.

* * *

Wednesday, July 13, 1966.

Kevin knew he was carrying too much but kept going. When he reached the pushcart, the stack of books leaned like the Tower of Pisa before it toppled to the floor with a resounding thud and a flutter of pages. Everyone in the cozy bookstore looked up, momentarily distracted. He stepped back and crossed his arms, glaring at the wayward books. *Crap!* Before he could pick them up, he heard the distinctive CLACK-CLACK-CLACK-CLACK of chunky heels announcing the arrival of the preorder woman.

Leaving the jumble of books, he fished through the HOLD drawer. In the brown paper wrapper was the fourth, or maybe the fifth, title the woman had ordered by the same author. "Evelyn," he said, "I have your book right here." A warm, genuine smile complemented his friendly personality. Peering at her narrow glasses, he wondered how this single working mother could support herself and her newborn baby.

"Thank you for holding it for me," Evelyn said, one hand clutching the frayed lapel of her white cardigan. "I don't know what I'd do without romance books! They're my escape, my passion, my solace."

Kevin stared at her, his brown eyes blinking with curiosity through several seconds of silence. *Maybe you could find somebody to have a real relationship with,* he thought as he handed her the book.

As if she read his thought, a hint of a smile played on her lips before she turned to leave. He and other covert eyes watched as she clumped back toward the door.

* * *

Evelyn was too engrossed in her novel to notice the shouts and laughter of children playing around her. She liked to sit at the park's entrance across the beachfront high-rises on Flagler Street. Even as downtown fortunes declined, it still reminded her of when Bayfront Park was known for political gatherings and free musical performances by local bands.

After a particularly steamy scene, Evelyn took a break from her book and leaned over to plant a kiss on her son's forehead. The steady hum of traffic had lulled Herman to sleep, his face serene and delicate, like the cherubic babies on baby food jars. She always loved opening those jars, just to hear the pop of the lid. Herman rustled beneath the blanket, knocking his white chicken cap with its clever red felt wattle askew. Passersby often stopped and exclaimed over how unusual and adorable the hat was. Herman opened his mouth to cry, but sleep claimed him first. A yawn bloomed wide as a meteorite flake tumbled from the sky and vanished down his throat.

Infancy and early childhood are crucial stages in developing a healthy body. Cells divide and multiply rapidly, allowing a child to develop a complex brain that will enable survival. But when the celestial dust speck drifted into Herman's protein-rich saliva, it disrupted this delicate process. Possessing wound-healing and antibacterial properties, the protein histatin caused the nucleus of hydrogen and helium to dissociate and collapse. Raw proton matter entered the child's body, fusing with his DNA. The new parent cells multiplied rapidly, spreading into the farthest capillaries of his toes and fingers with the usual genetic instructions that normal human DNA would bear. However, the cells' new primary directive was to flourish and give abundant life, just as stars spring from dust and gases in the billions. In the chaos of transformation, Herman's DNA interpreted the unknown element as polyethylene, a synthetic echo of something it could not name.

* * *

Friday, October 28, 1966.

That was strange. Evelyn could have sworn she heard a word—an actual word—spoken from Herman's room. She rose from the couch and left her book on the armrest, marking her spot. She cracked the door to his room and peered inside. Herman had pushed up into a sphinx pose, head high and back arched, his knit ladybug cap made him irresistibly adorable.

"There you are, my little dumpling," Evelyn said. She picked him up and dandled him above her head. "Are you trying to speak?" Herman kicked his feet and giggled when Evelyn blew raspberries on his pudgy tummy. "Say it again. Come on," she cooed between raspberries. "Say, Mama."

Herman didn't answer except to lift one of his delicate eyebrows. His hand reached for her nose and patted her cheek. Evelyn laid him back in the crib and tucked the blanket around him. After kissing him gently on the forehead, she turned to leave when, unexpectedly, she heard the sound again.

"Maa-maa."

Evelyn looked over her shoulder, startled.

Funny, the voice seems to have come from that rubber doll.

Herman only smiled and squirmed. There was nothing unusual about the crib. Everything looked perfectly normal. Several stuffed animals sat with their backs against the vertical wooden slats. Among them, a vintage doll held both arms extended as if asking to be picked up.

Intrepidly, Evelyn picked up the doll and turned it over. The mechanical "Maa-maa" wheezed out as air moved through the weighted crier. "Most peculiar," she said, setting the doll back in its spot and telling herself it had simply shifted. "Now you sit there and go to sleep," she scolded.

Evelyn kissed her son and wiped the lipstick from his forehead. "And you go to sleep as well." She shook an admonishing finger at him. Herman wriggled playfully, licking his bottom lip as a trail of saliva glistened down his chin. When Evelyn turned to leave, she heard the sound again.

"Mama."

A cold tingle ran down her spine. Her heart skipped a beat as she threw an uneasy glance over her shoulder. Her throat was dry, each breath scraping like sandpaper. Living alone was unraveling her nerves; a simple creak of a door or shutter crash was all it took.

Pull yourself together, Evelyn.

As she inched toward the crib, the wooden floor creaked beneath her. The doll sat innocently with its back against the bars. It had not fallen over, which would have explained the mechanical crier blurting out the word. A rush of adrenaline coursed through her. *Why couldn't you have fallen?* Her eyes probed the doll, its arms outstretched, face blank, staring into nothing.

Then it turned its head toward her.

"Mama. Mama. Mama."

Evelyn shrieked and clapped a quivering hand to her mouth. Each contraction of her heart shot ice through her veins. Breath caught in her throat as if the air had been sucked out of the room. Still as ever, the doll sat with both arms eerily motionless, its unblinking eyes fixed on her as if anticipating her next move. It seemed to yearn for affection, but only silence greeted its silent plea. Then, to her shock, it rolled over, pushed onto all fours, and stood erect.

"Oh my gosh!" Evelyn's mouth hung open in disbelief. She felt faint but stood her ground, legs quaking and one hand wrapped around the crib rail for support.

The doll balanced on the mattress and took its first baby steps, its tiny feet making soft indentations on the bed.

"Stay away from us!" Evelyn cried out. She scooped her son up and stumbled across the room. Trembling, she tried to grasp the doorknob, but her fingers refused to respond. *Open the door, Evelyn!* Her thoughts screamed. *Think of your son's safety!*

Finally, her fingers gripped, twisted, and the door swung wide.

Daring a glance behind her, Evelyn saw the doll had already climbed the liftgate, one leg hooked over the top. She shrieked, slammed the door behind her, and bolted across the living room. Blindly, she retreated until her back struck the entrance. Her legs gave out, and she slid to the floor, weeping. As silence pressed in, she stared up at Herman's bedroom door, bracing for what lay beyond. But it stayed shut—its stillness somehow more terrifying than movement. *Will it climb up and twist the doorknob*? Her fingers trembled against Herman's back, clutching him tighter than she meant to. Whatever that thing was in her son's room, it couldn't get out. At least, she hoped.

Lulled by her fearful whimpers and gentle rocking, Herman slept. Before long, she nodded off, exhausted by the emotional trauma.

Several minutes later, Evelyn felt the soft patting of Herman's hand against her mascara-smeared cheek. The touch prickled her skin, but it wasn't enough to wake her from her nightmare. Images of rubber dolls twirled, their twisted smiles and razor-sharp teeth mocking her with unblinking eyes. They circled weightlessly, slapping her face with clammy hands, leaving scratches that bloomed across her skin. Each sting made her body twitch, fighting to awaken. A scream echoed in her mind.

Jolting awake, Evelyn cried out, confused and unsettled. It took her a moment to realize the patting on her face was her son, cooing contentedly and learning how to spit bubbles. His eyes momentarily comforted her, but her fears of walking dolls immediately resurfaced. She struggled to her feet and placed him on the sofa, where he nestled among a doll and a few plush animals she'd arranged like a soft barricade. Normally, she'd indulge in nonsense baby talk, but her thoughts remained tethered to the thing pacing his bedroom.

She crept toward Herman's room, pausing between steps to keep the floor from creaking and attracting the doll's attention. The anxiety came in waves. Heart beating, she held her breath and pressed her ear against the door. Complete silence. Evelyn reached out, her skin prickling as she turned the doorknob. When the hinge squeaked, her heart skipped a beat. But Evelyn, unfazed, poked her head in and peered through the crack.

The doll stood in the middle of the room, like a faithful dog waiting for its owner to come home. Extending both arms, it cried, "Mama, Mama, Mama."

Evelyn gasped and slammed the door shut, shaking the walls. She clutched her hair and cried, "Why is this happening?" Cupping her lips with a quivering hand, she turned back to her baby on the sofa. Herman was on his stomach, attempting to grab the doll that had fallen forward. He kicked his plump legs, inching closer. While he sucked on his fist, a chilling thought flashed through her mind.

"Herman, don't," she whispered.

His tiny hand reached for the doll, and a faint electrical spark pierced its rubber shoulder. For the first time, she witnessed her son give life to an inanimate object. Its vacant expression unchanged, the doll turned its head, moving left to right and then back again as if getting rid of any kinks. Evelyn froze and dared not breathe.

The doll opened its eyes and sat up, then looked at Herman and said, "Mama." Miraculously, it stood, holding its arms out for balance.

Seconds crawled by as Evelyn clutched the lapel of her cardigan, her eyes blinking in astonishment. The doll stroked Herman's smooth face, feeling his nose, warm skin, and fluttering lips as he burbled. It stared without expressing any emotion, blinking out of instinct rather than necessity. Herman kicked his curled toes in delight each time the doll spoke. It meant no harm. Evelyn's fear slowly unraveled, and a shaky giggle broke through her disbelief. She stepped forward, cautious and captivated, watching the two side by side on the sofa; one made of flesh and blood and the other of rubber.

Kneeling beside Herman, Evelyn studied the doll closely. Twelve inches tall, it wore a blank expression, no smile, no warmth, just wide blue eyes, faded rosy cheeks, and glossy pink lips. Soft brown eyebrows arched beneath wisps of synthetic blond hair. A striped collar lent charm to its short-sleeved yellow dress, and its pumpkin-colored socks, snug and fuzzy like a woolly bear caterpillar, peeked out from beneath fringed moccasins.

The doll approached Evelyn and touched her face. "Mama," it said, the voice mechanism sliding back into place with a soft metallic clink. Evelyn smiled excitedly. Questions swarmed her mind, and the lack of answers terrified her. With a simple touch of his tiny fingers, Herman had transformed an inanimate toy into a living creature, defying logic. Then concern twisted her stomach. If her son's ability were exposed, the Department of Homeland Security or another shadowy government agency would surely take him away. A swarm of strangers in white hazmat suits would poke and prod him in the name of scientific research. She shuddered. *There's no way in hell I'll let anyone take my son away. I'll fight them to the death if I have to!*

Anxious to face the first doll, Evelyn approached her son's bedroom with trepidation. With a click, she unlatched the door and pushed it open. The doll was still standing patiently in the center. It looked up at her and blinked its eyes using the weighted eyelid lever. Its facial expression showed no emotion. "Mama," it cried, air sipping out of the mechanism. It stepped forward, then awkwardly ran toward her, managing to keep its balance. Evelyn's eyebrows shot up in astonishment, and a smile broke across her face. Stopping at her feet, the doll tilted its head upward and patted her shin. "Mama," it repeated. Evelyn marveled at the feel of its tiny rubber hand.

Ding dong!

The doorbell chime startled her.

Evelyn turned quickly, knocking the doll over. *Not a good time for Girl Scout cookies!* The doll was already rising when she grabbed it by the waist. She hurried to the sofa, where the other doll was playfully patting Herman's nose, and snatched it by the arm, making it squeak in protest.

The doorbell chimed again.

"Coming," Evelyn hollered, clutching the two dolls to her chest. She opened the closet door and flung the dolls inside, leaving the door ajar. Evelyn breathed a sigh of relief. After taking a moment to regain her composure, she answered the door.

"Ms. Sinclair?" The woman's nasal voice made Evelyn's skin crawl.

"Yes?"

"Are you okay?"

Evelyn stared at her blankly for a moment, then said, "Of course. Why do you ask?"

"I thought I heard someone crying, and I was worried something had happened," the neighbor said. She craned her neck to see inside, concern and curiosity competing in her eyes, but Evelyn sidestepped to block her view. "You have a cute baby, Ms. Sinclair. But you shouldn't leave him unattended. He might fall off the couch and hurt himself."

"Thank you. That's very kind of you, Ms. . . . ?" Evelyn asked through gritted teeth.

"Olivia Sanders," she said, sniffing with interest. Her palpable eagerness gave Evelyn the creeps—curious people were likely to gossip and spread rumors. "My husband, Taylor, and I live in apartment ten, right next door. If you need anything, don't hesitate to call us."

Evelyn flashed a dismissive smile. "Thank you, Mrs. Sanders. I appreciate your concern, but I assure you, everything is fine here." A doll walked across the living room floor.

As the neighbor walked away, Evelyn noticed the empty drinking glass in her hand. *She must have been propping it against the wall to eavesdrop.* She closed the door and clicked the deadbolt into place. "That was close," she said, leaning against the door and clutching the lapel of her cardigan. Keeping the dolls a secret wouldn't be easy—not with a snoopy neighbor like Mrs. Sanders.

* * *

Tuesday, May 14, 1968.

Herman's lack of interest in speech and his refusal to make eye contact worried Evelyn. He had begun banging his head softly against the wall for reasons she couldn't explain. Every daycare turned them away after a single visit. It was the start of his isolation and a string of doctor's visits Evelyn hadn't expected.

"Those are cute bunny ears," the medical assistant said after taking Herman's temperature and making a note on the chart. Lily wrinkled her freckled nose and teased, "Let me see you hop like a bunny."

Herman clenched his fists and hopped across the room, not letting up. The soft chenille ears flopped vigorously.

"He has plenty of caps at home," Evelyn said, nodding. She took his hand and guided him onto the chair. Herman squirmed, slid off his chair, and continued bouncing, a smile back on his face. "I guess it's my fault."

Lily tilted her head, her pixie cut sharp and clean, drawing focus to her eyes and cheekbones. "What do you mean?"

"He's worn caps since he was a baby. I guess he got used to the feeling, and now he won't go without one."

"I see," she said, watching the child's antics. "And what happens when you take it off?"

"He throws a tantrum," said Evelyn with an embarrassed shrug.

"Well, we don't need a tantrum here, so please make sure those ears stay put," Lily said, winking as she closed the door behind her.

Several minutes later, there was a soft rap on the door. Dr. Lloyd entered the room, holding Herman's chart in one hand and closing the door with the other. His lab coat hung open, revealing a blue shirt and a gold tie with a diamond pattern. "Hello, Herman," he said, his perfectly straight teeth gleaming in a broad smile. "Where's your red crabby hat with the claws that you wore last week?" Evelyn thought his laugh sounded forced. "I was afraid you were going to try and pinch me again today!"

Herman didn't answer. His happy hopping twisted into an agitated thrash, his eyes darting everywhere except at Dr. Lloyd, who gave a slight nod, as if confirming what he already knew. "I'm curious, Ms. Sinclair, why is he wearing mittens?"

"My son scratches his face a lot," she said, surprised by how easily the lie slipped out. In truth, she didn't want her son to handle any toys in public, let alone give life to them. Securely tied shoelaces around the base of his mittens ensured that would never happen.

"Let's get you up on the exam table," Dr. Lloyd said, getting a hand under each arm. As soon as Herman's feet left the ground, his anger flared. He kicked and twisted, trying to get out of the doctor's firm grip. Even with the mittens, his hands latched onto the doctor's arm.

"Easy there, Herman," Dr. Lloyd said, his voice soothing. But Herman snapped, lunging at the doctor's arm with bared teeth. Dr. Lloyd winced but didn't loosen his grip. "It's okay, Herman," he said softly, stroking the boy's hair with his free hand. "I understand. We're going to help you feel better."

Herman's grip loosened, his anger fading into exhaustion. Taking this opportune moment, Dr. Lloyd put his large hands on the child's face for a quick look at his eyes. There were no epicanthic skin folds on the inner corners of his eyes, no white Brushfield spots on the iris, and no evidence of a flat nasal bridge. An inspection of his hands and feet failed to reveal a single transverse palmar crease or unusual spacing between the large and second toe.

"Open your mouth and stick your tongue out, like this," Dr. Lloyd said, demonstrating with a quick flick of his own tongue. Herman mimicked him, watching the wooden stick until his eyes crossed. No protruding or enlarged tongue evident, no ear problems noted, no heart, lung, or gastroesophageal concerns indicated.

His physical examination complete, Dr. Lloyd placed Herman on his mother's lap and leaned back in his rolling chair. "I've spoken with numerous other specialists since your last visit, and as a group, we failed to determine any concrete answer. However, Herman's blood tests have raised some disturbing questions.

"Ms. Sinclair," he said, scratching his head, his short, sandy hair springing back into place. "Is your son's crib made of metal?"

"No," she said, giving him a baffled look.

"Has he ever drunk any cleaning solution or detergent, anything stored under the kitchen sink?"

"Of course not!" *Just get to the point!*

Dr. Lloyd inclined his head, his expression composed. "Has he ever swallowed any coins?"

"Doctor, what is wrong with my son?" she asked flatly, her eyes pleading. The suspense was killing her. She fidgeted.

"I forwarded your son's blood sample to a specialty laboratory because my lab found traces of helium and hydrogen compounds. The presence of aluminum-26 and manganese-53 leads us to believe he swallowed a metallic object at some point." Dr. Lloyd shook his head. "I know it sounds incredible, but the composition of his blood is suggestive of meteorites."

Unable to comprehend the medical jargon, Evelyn bit her lower lip to keep it from quivering. She hesitated before asking, "Are you telling me my son has Down syndrome?"

"No," he said, closing the chart and tossing it on his desk. "I just examined him for traits of the condition, and he is physically fine. Down syndrome is a cell division disorder resulting in an extra chromosome 21, or trisomy 21, and prior tests have given no evidence of a chromosomal disorder. Your standard prenatal screening didn't reveal any indicators of the condition."

She nodded, still confused. "What about autism?"

His eyes narrowed, lost in thought. "Does he stack things obsessively, or consistently put his toys in a straight line?"

She shook her head.

"We do know the presence of abnormal compounds in cells can inhibit the body's absorption of iodine and other essential minerals, which are crucial for synthesizing hormones like thyroxine and triiodothyronine," he said, though he knew the words meant nothing to her. "Iodine deficiency results in the deceleration of physical and mental development. In your son's case, a significant deficiency appears to be impacting his mood, behavior, and overall growth."

"What will happen to him?" she asked, holding Herman closer.

Dr. Lloyd wished he could answer her question, but he didn't have a clue. Despite years of medical training, he had never encountered, let alone heard of, a case like Herman's. He and his associates had spent hours debating and theorizing only to reach an impasse and conclude that this child should not be alive.

"This disease is new to the medical field," Dr. Lloyd said without averting his gaze. "But it's already been labeled as Hydrolium syndrome, HHe syndrome, or 1-2 syndrome, for the atomic numbers of hydrogen and helium." He leaned forward, his eyes compassionate.

"Without those minerals, his moods may be volatile. He may appear timid one moment and experience bouts of rage the next, posing a risk to himself and others," he said, shrugging. "Herman's social skills may be limited and destructive."

Dr. Lloyd reached for his chrome-plated pen and scribbled on a notepad. "With your permission, we would like to conduct more tests. I'm giving you a referral to Dr. . . ."

"No," Evelyn said, her voice firm despite the tremor underneath. She slipped on her sunglasses, shielding her puffy eyes, then swept her child into the crook of her arm and left the room.

"Ms. Sinclair?" The doctor stared after her, perplexed.

Evelyn broke down in tears as she stepped out of the medical building. She squeezed her son as she wept silently, ignoring the strange stares from people as they walked around her.

Herman put his arms around her neck and patted her back.

* * *

Friday, July 3, 1970.

At four years old, Herman's favorite activity was spending the day at Bayfront Park. Already dressed in his play clothes, he sat patiently while his mother retrieved his sneakers from the balcony, where they'd been left out to dry. Everywhere she went, the dolls followed her like puppies starved for affection. They often collided with her legs, rising only to extend their little arms and say, "Mama." While her son demanded most of her time and attention, Evelyn also had to constantly keep track of the dolls. They were almost as difficult to manage as Herman. She grabbed her romance novel from the kitchen counter and slipped it into the tote bag. After one final sweep of the apartment, she strapped Herman in his stroller and bustled out the door, hoping the sun wouldn't be too hot this early.

As soon as she left, the two dolls roamed freely, banging into furniture and occasionally knocking things over. One noticed that the balcony glass door was slightly ajar and pushed it open . . .

On the other side of the wall, Gregory sat on his bed listening to what sounded like the faint pattering of footsteps next door. *They sound . . . mechanical?* If he listened carefully, he could pick up a word or two. He flung the comic book aside, jumped out of bed, and placed his ear against the cool surface of the wall. His mother, Olivia, had told him that a real detective uses all five senses. "Look and listen to the faintest detail, and you shall become as good as they are," she had encouraged, knowing her son had set his heart on becoming a detective, which was evident by his passion for cop shows.

No one was home at Ms. Sinclair's apartment, that much he felt sure of. He had seen her striding past the window with her son in the stroller. This was his first clue that something wasn't right.

Gregory grabbed his plastic gun and shoved it into his back pocket. He slid the balcony door open and crept along the outside wall. The pulsing theme song to the Hawaiian cop show played in his head as he pulled the gun out and held it close to his shoulder. Standing barefoot, Gregory inched his way toward the edge of the balcony. He could hear faint patting sounds coming from the other side. *A burglar! Now it's up to me to catch the thief red-handed.* He peered around the wall and quickly pulled back to consider his next move. The element of surprise was crucial in apprehending suspects. Quietly, he clambered onto the wrought iron railing, balancing precariously with his free hand on the wall. This was it. The moment he'd trained for in his living room for years. He closed his eyes, counted to three, and leaned around the corner with his gun aimed.

"Stop, or I'll shoot!"

Gregory wavered in shock.

Two dolls were bent over, patting a cat figurine next to a flowerpot, their nylon hair waving in the soft breeze. Then they saw him—or at least, their eyes seemed to track him, though he was certain they couldn't see. They stood, arms raised. "Mama," they cried in unison as they stepped forward, their lips eerily still. A tremor shot through Gregory, knocking loose his grip on the wall. His fingers scraped past the railing—then he was falling. His last mental image was the balcony shrinking above him before he hit the floor.

* * *

Tuesday, July 21, 1970. 11:20 a.m.

Gregory thought he was awake. He swore his eyes were open and moving, but nothing registered, just darkness. "Moms," he said in alarm, his bandaged head shaking side to side. "Where are you?"

"I'm right here, Son," Olivia said, holding his hand, though she knew it offered little comfort.

"I can't see you!" Gregory thrashed in the narrow bed.

"Try to stay calm," she told him soothingly as she held him down. "You had a nasty fall, and now you're in the hospital. The doctor said you're going to be fine. You have a concussion that has temporarily affected your sight, but it will return in a few days." A lie. After three weeks at his side, shedding endless tears over his coma, Olivia was thrilled to see her son awake. The doctor had warned her that with such severe head trauma, Gregory might never regain his sight. It depended on whether the swelling around the cerebral cortex subsided quickly enough to avoid permanent damage.

"Moms, I don't want to be blind," Gregory cried, clutching the sheets as his heart raced. "I can't be a good cop if I'm blind."

"When you grow up, you will be a great detective," she said, kissing him gently.

Gregory stopped flailing, his breath ragged. He saw himself falling as the railing slipped farther away. And then there were the dolls. Blank-eyed, heads tilted in curiosity. Reaching with stiff, deliberate arms and calling to him in their mechanical voices. "Moms, I saw two dolls walking around on Ms. Sinclair's balcony! They're alive! They talked to me!"

"Gregory," she said with a slight frown. "You hit your head hard. Let's concentrate on healing so you can regain your eyesight."

"Moms, I'm telling you the truth! I *did* see two walking dolls. Ms. Sinclair is keeping a secret in her apartment. If you don't believe me, go over and see for yourself!"

Believing every word he said, Olivia held his hand in hers. She remembered her encounter with Evelyn as if it had happened yesterday. Since then, she'd heard strange noises and wondered about the odd, secretive woman next door. *Whatever she's hiding, I'll expose her. She'll pay for what she's done to Gregory, no matter how long it takes!*

After a long week, Gregory regained his sight and was released from the hospital.

* * *

Monday, September 8, 1980. 6:17 p.m.

Now fourteen, Herman bounced arrhythmically, snapping his fingers to the fast robotic beat of his favorite new-wave song. Perched atop his head, the cow hat spun as he whipped and stomped. For a moment, the cow seemed alive, grinning wide, tongue lolling, its tiny bell jingling like it too was partying hard.

Evelyn clutched her sides, gasping for breath between fits of laughter. Every time she saw the ridiculous cap, the giggles spilled out. And though she'd never admit it, the contagious tune had wormed its way into her heart too.

Herman stopped dancing momentarily and crossed his eyes to focus on the bell above his forehead. He shook his head. *Ting-a-ling-a-ling!* Laughing, he repeated the action several more times. If the record hadn't ended, he might have kept at it all day.

"What do you want to hear now, Mr. Cow?" Evelyn asked, still laughing as she picked up the vinyl.

He didn't have to think twice. "You Must Snap It!"

"But we just played it a thousand times. Are you sure you want to hear it again?"

Herman's smile faded.

"You Must Snap It!" he screamed, slapping her face.

Evelyn staggered back, her cheek stinging from the unexpected slap. Her eyes watered as she fought the wave of hurt.

* * *

Miami-Sunset Area. Wednesday, January 15, 1964.

Visiting Nautical South Mall was always a treat for Evelyn. Over the years, she watched the mall transform into a unique shopping experience. With a vision to make Nautical South a water wonderland, the developer installed a series of aquariums along every pathway, each meticulously designed to showcase different marine life. Shoppers marveled at the enchanting atmosphere of colorful fish and intricate coral reefs as they strolled from store to store.

Nautical South was where Evelyn had met Berto García-Famosa, a recent Cuban emigrant. She fell hard and quick. His laughter curled around her like a warm blanket, and when he leaned in, eyes glinting over his sexy low voice, her pulse stuttered. Even the language barrier felt like flirtation. Weeks later, at his home, Evelyn discovered he despised the English version of his name. He would playfully slam his fist on the kitchen counter and say, "Mi nombre es Berto, not Bert!" She would ruffle his curly hair to further annoy him and softly whisper, "Bert."

Several months later, against her parents' wishes, they were married. The months that followed were marked by quiet joy, anticipation, and a growing sense of family. Then, everything unraveled. In March 1966, just months before the birth of their baby, Berto was an innocent bystander shot in a drug-related shoot-out and lost his life. Evelyn's world was shattered. At just twenty-nine, she struggled to navigate the overwhelming emotional challenges of being a grieving widow. For years, she couldn't bear to hear her husband's name spoken aloud, let alone carry it as her own. Quietly, Evelyn reverted to her birth name. Despite her adversities, she managed to sustain herself and her baby with her husband's life insurance policy, which she later invested in Miami's booming economy.

* * *

Nautical South Mall. Tuesday, September 16, 1980.

Evelyn browsed through the blouses, hangers scraping against the metal rack. She could never resist a 15 percent discount at her favorite store, despite the risks of taking Herman out. *A little bit of sun and fresh air will do him good*, she convinced herself. Herman—sporting a jester's cap made of purple, gold, and green felt, adorned with bells—stood by her side. The gold bells tinkled whenever he shifted his head vigorously.

Evelyn tapped her son on the shoulder. "Honey, Mommy is going to try on these two blouses," she said, lifting his chin and forcing him to look into her eyes. "Promise me you'll stay right here and not get into trouble."

"I promise," he said, wiggling and nodding so the bells chimed.

With Evelyn out of sight, Herman began jumping to make the bells jingle louder, giggling and flailing his arms. Shoppers turned and stared, snickering as his movements grew more manic. "I'm a joker," he said, slapping the bell with his covered hand. He hopped into the next aisle like a giant bunny, making the bells ring in unison. "I'm a joker," he sang.

"You mean a jester," a girl with long auburn hair and green eyes corrected him. She gazed at his tricolored hat with scorn. "Why are you wearing that stupid hat?"

"My jester hat is beautiful," he said, a frown creasing his forehead.

"Well, I guess the colors are pretty, but I wouldn't be caught dead in it," she said haughtily. She slapped the nearest bell. Forgetting his annoyance, Herman reached up and hit the same bell, but the chime sounded muffled.

"No, not like that," the girl exclaimed, rolling her eyes. "It'll ring better if you remove the stupid gloves." She grabbed his hand and tugged at the knot. The first one came off so easily, she attacked the second one and threw them both on the floor as if they were dirty socks.

"Now you can hit it better," she said triumphantly, folding her arms across her chest and stepping back.

Herman batted at the tiny bell with his bare hand; the sound rang out clearly. He jumped in a circle, laughing and singing, celebrating his accomplishment. Turning back to give the girl another chance, he realized she had vanished.

Evelyn returned the fitting room tags to the clerk and hurried back to where she'd left her son.

Her stomach dropped. He was gone.

The blouses slipped from her trembling hands and tumbled to the floor.

"Herman!" she cried, her voice slicing through the store.

The overhead lights buzzed dimly as she wove through the aisles, mind spiraling with worst-case scenarios. Tears blurred her vision. Her heart thudded like a warning drum.

What if he left the store?

She froze. Her breath caught at the final thought.

I must find him before something horrible happens!

Panting, she darted down the main aisle, scanning each corridor. "Herman!" she shouted, oblivious to the stares. She veered sharply, nearly knocking a woman aside. "I'm sorry," she sobbed, barely slowing.

Fighting back tears, Evelyn worked her way toward the exit, where a woman stood examining the price tag of a sequined evening dress. Seizing the woman's arm, she asked, "Did you see a teenage boy in a jester cap go out?"

"I can't say that I have." The woman shook her head and patted Evelyn's shoulder. "If I see him, I'll tell him you're looking for him."

Evelyn offered a quick nod, eyes glossy with panic. "Thank you," she whispered, already half turned. She ran toward the men's department. *Maybe he followed someone over there!* Turning the corner, she caught sight of a clerk assisting a man wearing a short-brimmed hat, his right foot squeezing into a tasseled loafer.

"Pardon me," said Evelyn, her chest heaving. Her swollen eyes—twin bruises of anguish—met theirs. "Did you see a teenage boy wearing a silly cap?" She clung to hope.

The clerk, seemingly indifferent to Evelyn's plight, shook his head and returned his attention to the man wearing the hat.

Suddenly, a familiar voice chimed from the men's suit department.

"Beautiful people."

"Herman?" Her heart skipped.

Without thinking, Evelyn bolted, her heart overflowing with joy. Her fondest memory of Herman was his contagious, heartfelt laughter. It was therapeutic. Good for the mind and soul. But most importantly, it was genuine. She couldn't imagine sitting at the kitchen table over coffee without it.

The unmistakable jester's hat popped into view, and Evelyn's heart surged. Blood pounded in her ears as she pushed forward, desperate to reach her son before anything could go wrong. But then she saw it, her worst fear unfolding. Her jaw dropped, eyes wide and brimming with panic.

"Don't touch it!" she cried, reaching out.

Herman stood inches from a suited mannequin, his finger slowly extending toward its plastic hand. A flicker passed from fingertip to fingertip, a life-giving spark.

Time fractured.

The mannequin turned its head toward Herman, joints unfolding like a bear waking from a long winter's nap. Unlike the rubber dolls at home, this figure underwent a refined transformation. Its fiberglass shell served as a perfect conduit for a neurological link with Herman. The eerie figure tried to move but faltered, restrained by metal brackets clamped around its legs. It tilted its head, vacant eyes fixed on the bind.

Radiation from the foreign elements coursing through its frame softened the fiberglass until the leg oozed through the clamp. Then, stepping from the riser, it collapsed with a resounding clatter, limbs splayed in a most unnatural sprawl.

The floor manager ran to the scene, where she noticed the mannequin lying face down on the floor as if it had been clobbered with a blunt object. A teenage boy stood beside it, his eyes sparkling with delight. She had caught him red-handed. *These young punks will do anything for attention these days*, she thought.

Annoyance etched across her face, the manager threw Evelyn a look. “Lady, is *he* with you?”

Evelyn remained in shock, her vacant eyes drifting toward the mannequin on the floor.

With a stern expression, the manager turned to Herman and took a firm hold of his elbow. “This is not funny, young man. I want you to—”

A tapping sound interrupted her tirade. She looked down and blinked in disbelief as the mannequin’s white hand slapped at the floor several times, as though searching for something. She gasped and released the boy. The thing put both hands on the floor and pushed, lifting its upper torso. Then it lifted its gaze like a predator, taking in its surroundings and calculating its next move.

Holding the lapel of her cardigan and shaking her head, Evelyn stared as though witnessing the resurrection of Lazarus. Herman was dancing and grunting, elated by his creation. Meanwhile, the manager stood frozen, unable to scream. Even if she could, no one would be foolish enough to help. Her mouth opened, but no words flowed. Only shallow, panicked gasps escaped.

As the mannequin lifted itself from the floor, the manager’s eyes filled with panic. Her head jerked. *This can’t be happening*, she thought, grabbing at her heart before she collapsed. Evelyn wanted to help, but she was too frightened to react.

Then it stood.

On its own.

And took a single step.

On its own.

Unless the shoppers were paying close attention, none could detect the low frequency emitted by the polyethylene figure. The sound encased episodic impressions—contextual details like time of day, spatial context, and the mannequin's presence—in a fragile bubble before they could settle into long-term memory. Every human who witnessed the figure was affected, as if by a disease. Only Evelyn and her son remained immune, bound by the shared DNA that linked them to the creature.

"Come here," Evelyn cried out. Unsure of the mannequin's capabilities, she insisted, "Come *here,* Herman!"

Content with his new friend, the boy hopped about excitedly, but he failed to understand that friends are made of flesh and blood.

The mannequin flaunted a navy pin-striped suit with a white button-down and a bold tie, exuding the image of a top business professional at a prestigious firm. Black leather shoes set off the patterned pima cotton socks. A handsome fellow with a square chin and robust lips, CEO turned its milky-white head, its face unchanging. It didn't smile. It didn't breathe. It didn't even blink its glassy, unseeing eyes. They were fixed in an eternal stare that betrayed no soul, only the illusion of presence. CEO took slow, awkward steps that mimicked the walking dead. Unlike the rotting corpses on the silver screen, the eerie creature became skilled at walking with each careful movement.

The spark that brought the mannequin to life triggered a chain reaction in the fiberglass body. Daughter cells divided into trillions through mitosis, each nucleus encoded with DNA instructions that urged the host to search for and give life to others. It yearned to multiply and preserve its species as any life on earth.

As its sense of purpose solidified, the creature sprinted down the aisles with unwavering resolve, its vacant gaze sweeping through the store and its footsteps hammering the ceramic tiles.

The man in the brimmed hat was next to encounter the mannequin's chilling movements. His eyes bulged and his mouth dropped open. "Holy mackerel!" he said as dread wrapped him like a cloak. Without thinking, he flung the bag with his new shoes at the anomaly before bolting.

As rumors of the possessed mannequin spread, panic broke out. The looks of wonder were unlike any other in Miami's history, and it spread like the black plague. CEO created an uncanny valley[8], a dip in human response triggering revulsion. Shoppers recoiled in disgust as the business professional ran by in designer shoes. Children sought shelter behind their petrified parents, while others sought refuge among the endless clothing racks. Evelyn watched the dummy as it headed toward the boy's department.

Betraying no emotions, the unearthly figure stopped beside a rugged-looking mannequin in plaid flannel, jeans, and boots. Satisfied with its first find, CEO reached out and touched the mannequin's hand, sparking life into the figure just like Herman.

Evelyn flinched. Her eyes widened like a full moon rising. As she wove between the home décor displays, the sweet fragrance of lavender-scented candles clashed with the chaos unfolding before her. "Oh my," she murmured, stepping back in disbelief. Her hair clung to her face, damp and disheveled from running. *This is unbelievable! Only Herman can give life!*

This was precisely what she had always feared. To protect the world from calamity, Evelyn had spent fourteen years cloistered, veiling Herman's hands on their rare, necessary excursions. But deep

---

[8] Masahiro Mori (1927-2025), "The Uncanny Valley," Energy 7, no. 4 (1970): 33-35.

in her heart, she'd always known this day would eventually arrive.

Suddenly, Woody, the lumberjack, moved its head.

On its own.

And like its predecessor, the burly figure emitted a low frequency that penetrated the minds of everyone who saw its creation. With uncanny focus, it carefully assessed the situation before acting. Heat from the elements softened the tissue around its fiberglass legs, allowing the dummy to detach from the metal stand with ease. Woody paused, aware that its purpose was to give life to others. It followed its genetic code flawlessly.

"What the hell is happening? Now there are two of them! Run!" a voice shouted.

Parents, pastors, police, and community leaders from every corner could hardly believe their eyes. The gap in the uncanny valley widened to Grand Canyon proportions. Shoppers backed away, unable to tear their eyes from it.

After witnessing the two mannequins sprint across the store, a woman dropped to her knees, clasped her hands together, and recited the Rosary in Spanish. Woody veered down the aisle toward the praying woman, its rugged boots clomping against the tile floor, its molded face stern, hawklike brow unflinching.

Someone screamed, "Look out! It's coming this way!" The crowd scattered in sudden panic, and waves of screams splashed through the store as the sprinter clipped the praying woman, knocking her flat on her back.

Despite the turmoil, the duo continued to spark life in others, leading each creation to awaken and release a subtle frequency. Before terrified onlookers, Woody animated a mannequin that pulsed with a strange, magnetic coolness. The black-and-white checkered cap and scarf were nods to its nostalgic tastes. Its layered T-shirt and stonewashed jeans spoke of its laid-back, creative personality, hinting at sketching in a cozy café or exploring urban landscapes with a camera.

Like the others, Pixel sprang to life—its fixed eyes chilling, its limbs flailing with eerie urgency. It sprinted off, price tags snapping like panicked flags. Off balance, it collided with an older man, sending him hurtling into a belt rack with bone-jarring force. Metal clattered and leather tangled as the rack toppled, slicing open a deep gash above the man's left eyebrow.

Not one word of apology.

Pixel didn't even slow down.

A clearance sticker peeled off its elbow mid-run and landed on the man's chest like a ceremonial stamp.

Within minutes, life flourished like a weed patch after a heavy downpour. The seeds of life had been sown, and soon, the mannequins multiplied: two, then four, then eight, then sixteen. Some jogged and others ran, and though they all advanced independently, they somehow seemed to move as one. Hordes of shoppers dashed for the exits, screaming dire warnings as they scattered. Some fled before witnessing the terror.

Pixel stopped before a headless figure that gave the impression of a young marketing executive with a sharp eye for detail and color. Its fashion suggested a taste for art gallery openings and hidden city gems. The striped sweater added a touch of sophistication, while the sleek black suede jacket lent an edge of modernity. The clothes hummed with energy as Michelangelo animated, withdrawing its hands from the jacket's pockets and striding forward.

The headless figure stepped into the limelight like a solitary lantern in the woods, seeking the flickering spirits of forgotten mannequins, intent on igniting their stillness with the warmth of its spark. It shot across the floor and easily navigated the escalator's moving grates, the metallic hum mingling with the chatter of shocked shoppers. Disregarding the safety rail, Michelangelo swayed slightly during the descent. The scent of perfume wafted through the air, mixing with the faint aroma of freshly brewed coffee from a nearby café. Upon reaching the lower level, the creature was captivated by the mannequins in the women's department, each in a stylized pose and adorned in the latest fashion under bright, inviting lights.

Shopping for a suit to impress her boss, Grace heard the clatter of heavy shoes on the escalator, but was engrossed in the mauve two-piece suit to notice the headless dummy. She held the suit up to see how it looked in the mirror, admiring how it draped the contours of her body and trying to decide if it was in her color set. Her gaze traveled along the neatly pressed slacks. Then, out of the corner of her eye, she caught sight of the brown shoes and black trousers of someone behind her. The stranger stood uncomfortably close, practically breathing down her neck without the decency of an "Excuse me." Uneasy, she turned sharply and said in a sarcastic tone, "May I help y—"

Her knees buckled, and her head snapped back, way back. A jumble of shock and fear left her paralyzed, and then she let out an ear-piercing scream, her uvula visibly vibrating at the back of her throat. Grace was sure the devil himself had come to drag her into the bowels of hell, punishment for the years she'd spent quietly embezzling from the firm. She dropped the suit and swung her tiger-print tote bag at the dummy as if swatting an elusive fly.

Michelangelo jerked painlessly at each blow, but it was learning quickly and formulating its next move. A deft thrust of its hand yanked the purse from her grasp, and in the same movement raked it at her head, leaving a row of crimson welts across her forehead. Still screaming, Grace shielded her head with her delicate hands. One final blow struck her hard across the jaw with a wicked uppercut that snapped her head back and sent her sprawling, unconscious, onto the now-rumpled suit. Her flailing fingers caught the purse strap, pulling Michelangelo down on top of her.

Terrified women stood frozen, their eyes locked on the nightmarish scene. They watched from a safe distance, too petrified to intervene. Someone in the crowd mistook it for a sci-fi film shoot. But when he realized there were no cameras and no famous movie stars, his face was a portrait of fear.

One woman decided she'd seen enough. Determined, she launched herself at the mannequin as it struggled with the purse. She landed a flurry of blows on its shoulders, her floral dress fluttering. The crowd watched in stunned silence. Two other women, thinking there was safety in numbers, joined the assault. They kicked and beat the effigy, their faces contorting with fierce pleasure.

Then, as the creature rose, the blows ceased.

A dreadful silence fell over the aisle as the women quailed at the sight. Their impulse to assist the unconscious woman now seemed ill-advised. Paralyzed by fear, they cowered in the face of such an inexorable force. Not a single word escaped their trembling lips. Michelangelo twisted and slung the tiger-print tote. Its momentum carved a brutal path across the women's faces, dropping the first like a broken doll. The other two abandoned the fight before the mannequin could unleash additional blows.

Now free to offer life, Michelangelo turned stiffly, trampling Grace underfoot as it resumed its mission.

At the far end of the aisle, a striking display featured five female mannequins in sequined evening gowns, each posed with stylized grace. Their presence demanded attention. Though their faces lacked human detail, they shimmered beneath the floodlights, their glossy surfaces frozen in ceremonial stillness like polished stone.

Elevated on a platform above the others, Crimson Elegance dominated the scene, cloaked in a floor-length scarlet gown with a plunging neckline. With arms outstretched in a fluid arc, it gave the illusion of motion, suspended mid-dance.

Michelangelo yearned to touch them. Raising its arm, the creature leaned forward and gently brushed its cold fingers over each one. As its fingertip brushed the fiberglass, a faint spark of energy flashed between them. Then, drawn by an unspoken call, the female mannequins tilted their polished heads in eerie unison, surveying the aisle with blank intention. They flexed their arms and legs to loosen the stiffness of their dormant state. Heat from the elements allowed their legs to ooze through the metal stands. Once free, they moved cautiously, their steps as tentative as a newborn fawn's until they mastered the fundamentals of balance and propulsion.

Pandemonium overtook the store. Patrons scattered, yelping in fright as dread thickened behind the mannequins' procession. Led by Crimson Elegance, the newly awakened surged forward, searching for others like them, yearning to give life. Once every mannequin had stirred, they spilled into the mall and city streets, chaos trailing in their wake.

* * *

Cynthia's bushy eyebrows accentuated the warmth of her chestnut eyes, which her husband often admired. Her voluminous hair and double hoop earrings swayed as she turned to watch the fleeing crowd.

"What is happening? Why is everybody running?" she asked.

With concern etched across his face, Michael grabbed his pregnant wife by the elbow and pulled her back. "I don't know what's going on, but we'd better leave just the same."

Cynthia's pink lips parted in shock when she saw the first wave of animated mannequins. "Oh my," she said, her hand flying to her mouth. A drove of expressionless mannequins in a range of skin tones was streaming out of a large department store: some with heads, some without, and in a startling array of fashions, all running autonomously. She blinked at a sight that defied all reason.

"Let's go, Cynthia." Michael grabbed her arm, alarm tightening his voice.

"I can't run in my condition, Michael," she said, cradling her belly.

Michael scanned the area. Spotting a Japanese gift shop, he said, "Come on. We'll be safe here." Without hesitation, he pulled her inside and closed the glass door behind them.

The store was empty, except for the manager, Steven, and his assistant, Christian. Wearing a blue vest emblazoned with the store's logo, Steven hollered from behind the counter, "What do you think you're doing?"

"I'm saving our asses!" Michael said over his shoulder, not taking his weight off the door.

"Dude, you better leave before I call mall security." Steven clenched his fists as he confronted the young man, who refused to back down.

"Hey, guys! Check out the commotion out there!" All eyes turned toward Christian, whose rugged features and muscular build gave him the air of a seasoned boxer. "Like, that's totally freaky, man," he said.

Steven approached the glass door and stared as chaos flooded the mall corridor. Grim-faced, he reached into his pant pocket, withdrew a key, and locked the door with a decisive click.

"What the hell is going on?" he murmured. He flinched as a woman fell forward, spilling the contents of her purse. She rose quickly, slightly dazed from the fall, and continued running without retrieving her belongings.

The store manager grabbed Michael's shoulder. "Why is everyone running?" he shouted.

Michael looked at him, unsure how to answer. Before he could utter a word, they heard a thud against the glass door, making everyone flinch. Cynthia instantly panicked.

CEO loomed, plastered against the pane, its white, chalky face peering through the glass.

Cynthia sank to the floor, shaking her head at the vile thing while her husband and the two store clerks stood in awe. No one said a word. Michael backed up and knelt beside his wife, his eyes locked on the anomaly.

CEO leaned to one side for a better view of the store.

"It's looking for something," Steven said, voice low with unease.

Christian put his hands in his jacket and moved to block the dummy's view. The mannequin responded by leaning in the opposite direction, focusing on something behind the young man.

Michael stood sharply and pulled free of Cynthia's grasp, his eyes taking swift inventory of the store. The souvenir shop specialized in handmade Japanese crafts, including knives and fans, antique coins, and a variety of ninja darts. A display of beautifully crafted swords hung on the walls, but none stood out like the mannequin in full samurai regalia. It held a polished sword over its shoulder, poised to strike.

Christian gasped when he made the connection. "Are you thinkin' what I'm thinkin'?"

The glass door rattled.

Cynthia cried out in despair.

CEO struck the glass with its pale hands, then backed up and bashed into the door. It rattled on its hinges but held.

Cynthia covered her ears and shook her head. "Make it stop! Make it stop!" she screamed, rocking back and forth like a helpless child. "Just let it in and give it what it wants!"

Steven crouched in front of her. "Listen," he said, forcing her to look at him. "There's nothing we can do! Do you hear me? We don't know what that thing is, and I'm sure as hell not gonna let *it* in so we can have coffee and cake!"

"No shit, Sherlock." Michael pried Steven away from his wife. "The least we can do is push *that* counter against the door!"

Surging with adrenaline, Steven seized on the idea. *He's right. If we work together, we can haul the counter against the door to stop the mannequin from gaining entry.* The fire left his eyes as he nodded, ready to leap into action.

Christian grabbed one end of the counter and heaved, his curly hair bobbing as his muscles strained. Before they could swing the counter, the dummy slammed into the door, launching Cynthia into another fit of hysteria.

CEO backed up several feet, then surged forward, crashing through the door and scattering shards of glass. Steven and Michael immediately tackled the mannequin when it hit the floor. They punched and jabbed relentlessly, but there was no resistance. No cry for help. No surrender. Instead, CEO inched toward the samurai, pulling the two men along with it. Steven jammed his elbow into the dummy's spine, punishment no ordinary man could withstand. And yet, CEO crawled forward, undeterred.

"Out of the way!" Christian shouted feverishly.

Michael and Steven looked up just as Christian swung a Japanese sword overhead. The blade swooshed through the air as the two men scrambled off the intruder. Christian plunged the single-edged sword into the mannequin's neck, severing its head with a single, brutal stroke. He struck the creature several times with fierce determination, cursing with each slice into its synthetic body, shredding the expensive suit. The katana, now streaked with grime and synthetic fibers, quivered in his hands. Body parts wriggled briefly before going still.

Christian's face twisted in anger, sweat drenching his body. "Your mama! You hear me?" He pointed the sword at the mangled mannequin and repeated, "Your mama!"

"You need to take a chill pill, man. Can't you see he's already dead?" Steven said as he pushed him back.

"Your mama!" Christian had to get the last word in, his hand trembling from adrenaline. He spat at the dummy and shouted, "¡No juegues conmigo, puto!"

* * *

Westwood Lakes, seven miles northwest of Nautical South Mall.

Hunting lodge relics adorned the dark wood paneling of an outdoor supply store. Among them, a massive moose head with a 48" spread, a deer with an impressive eight-point rack, and numerous vintage rifles and handguns from the turn of the century. Behind the busts, a towering mural of a hunter aiming at a charging moose cemented the store's identity. The sharp scent of cedar, leather, and pine filled the air as framed photographs lined the south wall. Each captured a frozen thrill: past hunts, shared stories, and camaraderie. They turned the shop into more than a storefront. This was a gathering place, an altar to the outdoor life.

Frank Irving, who preferred to hunt deer in Jackson County, Florida, stood behind the old wooden counter proudly demonstrating his favorite big-game rifle.

"This is my most popular firearm, a standard bolt-action rifle available at a reasonable price. It's the kind of rifle serious hunters go for: clean design, dependable build, and real presence."

The client glanced at his wife, nodding his stamp of approval. After a stealthy look at the price tag, he said, "I'd expect it to be more expensive."

"The rifle has an aluminum floor plate, instead of steel. Aluminum alloy is lighter and less expensive. Plus, this model lacks the adjustable trigger on pricier models. I can give you an exceptional deal if you purchase the scope, bipod, and cartridge today."

What the fucking hell was that?!

He saw it out of the corner of his eye.

It was unusual for a mannequin to jog into the shop, especially one with its head thrown back and mouth wide in laughter. Blonde twin ponytails bobbed above slender shoulders as thin arms swung in stiff, robotic arcs. Tiny feet pumped with relentless energy, mimicking a thorough workout.

Frank jumped back, his salt-and-pepper eyebrows lifting. The two customers followed his gaze, and their mouths fell open in unison.

Gliding with unnatural grace, the artificial woman power-walked through an array of rods, reels, and tackle boxes, eyes locked on the lone male mannequin perched on a white riser, decked out in camouflage and gear. It lifted a finger and tapped the other as if playing a children's game of tag: You're it! No tag backs! A simple flick of its tiny finger was the only requirement. Then the creature jogged out with mincing steps and that silly laugh plastered on its face.

"I think we'd better go now," the customer said with a tremor in his voice. He grabbed his wife's arm. "We'll come back when you're not so busy."

Long frozen in a crouched position, peering through the scope of a rifle, the hunter moved its egg-shaped head. Beneath the pulled-up hood, there were no eyes or mouth, just dents where eyes should be and a slight mound for a nose. With mechanical focus, the figure surveyed the area, registering the rifle. Its gaze landed first on the wall-mounted moose, then drifted to the big game mural, a sprawl of sunbaked colors and wilderness shadows. The mural evoked a legacy the dummy seemed born to reenact. Then the connection formed: the camouflaged man, the rifle, the antlered moose. It was learning.

Still in hunting pose, the mannequin aimed at the North American bull mount and fired a single shot. No loud bang. No recoil. The mounted beast remained still without even flicking an ear. Mystified, Hunter tilted its head and hurled the weapon to the floor.

The proprietor and his two customers stood frozen as they watched the mannequin shift its legs, separating from the metal bracket that held it in place. It stood clumsily, teetered, then tumbled off the riser, crashing to the floor with a loud, hollow thump. Fumbling, it brought both legs in and pushed to its knees. Slowly, the creature placed one foot on the floor and stood precariously.

"Oh, my goodness," the woman cried, her knees buckling under her weight.

Hunter suddenly lunged forward like a child learning to walk. It knocked over several boots from a shelf, momentarily hindering its advance. But once it grasped the mechanics of balance, it surged forward.

The husband was the first to sprint across the floor, followed closely by his screeching wife. Frank Irving was left to face the unnatural being. In his adult life, he had faced charging bears and moose with antlers as wide as five feet without so much as a shiver. Today, he was afraid for the first time.

He snatched up the box of cartridges and ripped it open, scattering the bullets across the counter. With a trembling hand, he loaded a single bullet, slammed the bolt shut, and cocked the rifle with a sharp metallic snap. Before he could raise it, the unnerving figure stood before him and gripped the barrel with both hands, attempting to wrestle the firearm away. Its strength was unexpected, but Frank held on grimly through the bizarre tug of war. With one hand on the rifle, he struck the mannequin on its bulbous nose with the other. The creature staggered back, still holding the rifle.

No surprise registered on its blank face, but it learned quickly. Hunter planted its left foot and pulled its right arm back, delivering a devastating blow to the proprietor's face.

Frank's body slammed into the shelf, sending binoculars and a hidden bottle of Scotch crashing to the floor. The bottle shattered, spilling the whisky he had enjoyed after closing hours. Blood dripped from his nose onto his deer-print shirt as he watched helplessly. The shop bell jangled with unnatural cheer as the mannequin fled with the rifle.

* * *

Minutes later, two officers responded to Frank's frantic 911 call. They found the proprietor holding a blood-stained tissue to his nose.

"You've got to hurry! Don't let it get away!" His eyes were wild, as if his life had become a bizarre dreamscape.

Officer Morgan lowered the volume of his handheld radio. "Can you tell us what happened here?" he asked.

"I'm telling you. It's the most incredible thing I've ever seen," Frank said excitedly. "The thing grabbed the rifle right out of my hands and took off running!"

"Sir," the officer said firmly, "you need to slow down. You're not making any sense."

Frank rolled his eyes, biting back a retort. He paused to wipe his nose and grab another tissue, then said more calmly, "It all started when a laughing female mannequin ran into my shop—she wasn't really laughing, just had her mouth open like she was. She touched a mannequin that was kneeling on that display." He turned and pointed. "And when he came to life, he walked over to me, took my rifle, and ran out of the shop!"

Curiously, the second officer asked, "Did you say . . . a mannequin?"

"Yes!" Frank yelled, his voice strident. "A man-ne-quin. How much plainer can I be!"

"What is your name, sir?" the first officer asked.

"Frank Irving," he said matter-of-factly. "I'm the owner."

"Have you been drinking today?"

"No, I haven't been drinking! Do I sound like I've been drinking?"

The two officers gazed at each other, confirming identical thoughts.

"Why do I smell alcohol?"

"Because the thing struck me. It busted my lip and bloodied my nose!" Frank lowered the tissue from his face, revealing a swollen upper lip and a bloodied nose. "When I hit the shelf, several items fell, including a bottle of whisky," he shouted, waving at the mess.

The second officer scribbled notes, trying not to snicker at the implausible story. *Other officers have submitted strange reports*, he thought, *but this one takes the cake*. He looked up from his pad to ask, "How was the mannequin dressed?"

"He's wearing an expensive hunting outfit," Frank said, his expression begged: *Who will pay for that?*

Suppressing laughter, the officer asked, "Did he happen to say his name?"

Frank saw the officer smirking as he scribbled. His annoyance was palpable as the officer's flippant attitude pressed on. Frank's eyebrows shot up, his face contorting with a cascade of emotion. "As a matter of fact, he did! His name is Johnny Hunter!" he scoffed, his head jerking with each word.

* * *

Approaching Gables by the Sea.

The emergence of hundreds of mannequins unleashed a flood of terror across Miami, but none as horrific as the massive pileup on the southbound Palmetto Expressway, State Road 826, where thirty-four mannequins ran into traffic going the wrong way. They scattered into four lanes, their arms pumping as they ran, never tiring, never faltering. No heart to overwork. Their eerie eyes were fixed on the horizon, never blinking or shifting under the rush of the wind.

Horns blared and tires screeched as confused drivers swerved to avoid the pack of oncoming dummies, leading to twisted metal and shattered glass, audible from blocks away. The destruction worsened when a diesel truck plowed into the stalled cars, exploding in a huge fireball. Within minutes, the pileup left eighty-seven vehicles wrecked, fifty-seven injured, and nine dead before traffic came to a stop.

Southeasterly winds raced under a sweltering noon sun as seagulls hovered in a cloudless sky. They glided in looping circles, riding the wind. Drawn by curiosity, they lingered until thick black smoke twisted skyward and drove them off.

With the wild calls of seagulls fading, the mannequins navigated the chaos of mangled vehicles and injured passengers. The throng climbed over the twisted metal, deftly jumping from one crumpled car to another. After clearing the half-mile devastation, they ran between the lanes of motionless cars, white-lining with the precision of seasoned motorcycle riders. Their plastic faces and robotic movements stunned onlookers as they sprinted by. People scrambled out of their vehicles to watch as thirty-three mannequins sprinted north on the southbound highway.

"Hey, everyone," cried a woman at the forefront of the accident. Her hands flew to her cheeks in shock. "There's someone pinned underneath this car!"

Several men ran over and positioned themselves. On the count of three, they strained together to lift the front end as two others freed the injured man. Their faces buckled with disbelief as more people crowded around. The injured man lay crumpled beside his severed leg. His black leather shoes and suit were scuffed and torn after being dragged forty-five feet.

But the most gruesome detail wasn't the blood or bone. It was the headless image that lingered, as if time refused to move on.

The woman who had cried out for help fainted.

Unexpectedly, the body moved. Muttering ran through the crowd as everyone took an involuntary step back. The maimed figure felt the road with a white hand, scraping its fingertips against the rough asphalt. The tension thickened around them. Astonished, the crowd watched as the mannequin pushed up from the ground with both arms. After a moment's strain, it managed to stand on one leg, balanced like a pink flamingo in its natural habitat.

"What the heck?" someone said, backing away from the inexplicable specter.

Even though it had no head, just a stump of neck, the mangled figure recognized the presence of the people around it, clustering together to see the freak. It meant no harm. It merely wanted to seek out more of its kind and give life.

Attempting to run, the mannequin plunged forward onto its torso like a doomed science project, sparked into motion by crossed wires. With difficulty, it stood again, fearing nothing and aching to resume its mission, only to fall yet again. It failed to comprehend why it couldn't run with just one leg.

"Don't let him get away," someone yelled. "He's the cause of this accident!"

Two men lifted the mannequin to its feet and began pummeling it. With each blow, it jerked violently, but even on one leg, it learned to lash out. Mirroring its attackers' clenched fists, it swung forcefully, knocking one man into the others with an unexpected hook. Several other men jumped in to restrain its arms. Using their grips as anchors, the mannequin lifted its only leg and hurled a man with a swift kick to his chest, leaving him wheezing for breath.

"He's too strong!" someone shouted, his chest heaving. "Get fuel, now!"

Within seconds, the mannequin was engulfed, spasming in fire until nothing moved but smoke.

* * *

Miami International Airport.

A solitary dummy bolted down the curbside pickup area, startling a cluster of jet-lagged passengers still dazed from recent landings.

One woman inhaled sharply, clutching her purse. "What is that thing?!"

Their astonishment rippled through the crowd as the mannequin whizzed by in stonewashed jeans and a sports shirt. Many watched in wonder, as if seeing an extraterrestrial. Little did they know how right they were.

Caught off guard by the commotion, a taxi driver craned over his shoulder and rear-ended the car ahead. Oblivious to the fender bender, the second driver stumbled out, his bulging eyes tracking the disturbing figure.

"The white zone is for immediate loading and unloading of passengers only," the overhead speaker droned. Automated doors slid shut behind the mannequin as it disappeared into the terminal. Drawn by the spectacle, a large crowd trailed the unholy one at a safe distance. People jostled and shoved like paparazzi in pursuit of an international superstar. Women and children shrieked, and men stepped back with bewildered expressions as the tardy dummy sprinted past like a late traveler chasing a gate.

Retrieving their luggage from the conveyor belt, a couple peered toward the rising chaos. Like everyone else, they were astonished to see a mannequin flash past them.

"You see," the husband grumbled, hiking up his pants. "I told you vacationing in Miami was a bad idea. This kind of thing only happens in Florida."

"Shut up, Howard."

* * *

Hundreds of mannequins surged through the city streets, flexing synthetic limbs like marathon sprinters, driven to multiply. Their heads bobbed with each step, eyes locked in narrow tunnel vision, never flinching or blinking. Except for a few dummies sporting forged smiles, their expressions were stone-hard, giving no hint of what bizarre thoughts might be going through their minds.

Then, like spores caught in a seismic wind, they multiplied. What began in the downtown veins spilled into highways and suburbs, with thousands streaming faster and farther, emitting a low hum that tunneled into civilians' minds. The farther they spread, the quicker they bred, spreading like the perennial wildfires of Southern California.

Shopping centers and malls across Miami succumbed to a paralyzing outbreak of living mannequins. They emerged in grotesque variety: some clothed, some bare; some with heads, others topped with smooth neck stumps; some ambled on full-length limbs, while others staggered on truncated arms. A spectrum of synthetic hair: painted, curled, braided, and bearded, adorned their molded scalps. Dummies in business suits mingled with models in sleek evening gowns and teenagers in tight blouses and designer jeans. From the lingerie departments emerged the most provocative figures: mannequins clad in sheer teddies, chemises, bridal sets, and bustiers. Rather than triggering terror, they stirred catcalls and whistles from gawking onlookers.

A brave man had the temerity to accost a lingerie mannequin from the South Nautical Mall. It stood before him in a black see-through teddy, shameless and bold, as licentious thoughts ran through his head. For a moment, he swore its sapphire eyes stared back, unblinking. His eyes gorged on its long, feathered blonde hair and succulent, rosy lips, but it gave no response to his leers. His fingers trailed down its face and lingered on the smooth breasts, enjoying the silken texture. Though the flesh wasn't soft like a living woman's, it was still luscious. His eyes traced the sensuous curve of its inviting thighs before focusing on its virgin nipples.

Practically drooling, he fondled the lacy fabric and asked, "What are you doing tonight?"

* * *

Doral, Miami-Dade County.

A mannequin with large, sad eyes under a brown bob that played in the wind exited the Palmetto Expressway at NW 36th Street and turned left on NW 72nd Avenue, causing a stir as it ran through the intersection. Dressed in black yoga pants and a sleeveless striped top, Cute Cindy headed east on NW 51st Street into an industrial district.

Curious pedestrians followed at a safe distance until it stopped in front of a mannequin manufacturing plant.

A pedestrian door stood ajar beside a closed dock door. Cindy jogged up the ramp and stepped confidently inside, unfazed by the turmoil unfolding in the parking lot. Standing still by the metal door, it observed hundreds of skin-toned dummies, naked and aligned in rows of ten, stretching as far as its olive-green eyes could see. Each row held five expressionless females and five equally impassive males, all devoid of facial features.

Ashanti wore her glasses low on the bridge of her nose, pushing them up only to read. She stepped through the office door into the warehouse. "What the?" she mumbled, noticing the solitary dummy standing by the dock door. Her eyes scanned the area. "Okay, who's the practical joker?" she shouted, her brown eyes narrowing. No one answered. No one ever did. Ashanti exhaled sharply, shaking her head. *What a bunch of witless wonders!* Clipboard tucked under her arm, she stalked toward the meticulously dressed mannequin, wig and all. She scrutinized its facial features, scrunching her nose at the shoddy craftsmanship. "This isn't one of ours."

The mysterious figure flexed its fingers surreptitiously.

Sweeping her gaze over the crowd in the parking lot, Ashanti wondered whether it was safe to leave the door open. She could see the crowd gesturing and shouting, but couldn't make out their cries over the clanking and pounding on the production floor. She slammed the door shut and locked it, missing the subtle tilt of the dummy's head.

Balancing the figure under her left arm, Ashanti strode across the floor until Cute Cindy wriggled against her grip, its plastic body writhing like an Alaskan salmon swimming upstream.

She froze, her grip slackening as the mannequin twitched again.

Cute Cindy turned to face Ashanti with a cold, lifeless stare that sent shivers down her spine. Her breath caught. "Aaagh!" she screamed, instinctively releasing her hold. The large doll clunked on the floor.

Several workers in navy jumpsuits ran over.

Tall Jackson was the first to reach her. "Are you okay, Ashanti? What happened?"

"The mannequin . . . It came to life in my hands!" she cried, the hairs on her arms standing on end. Her hands shook as she backed away, unable to tear her eyes from the lifeless figure on the floor.

They looked at one another, baffled, and then their gaze fell upon the mannequin. The doll lay on its side, its head turned toward Ashanti as if listening. There was nothing unusual about it except that it wore the latest fashion and a short brown wig.

Then the creature jerked.

Its legs pumped in place, running but getting nowhere. The three warehousemen jumped back in surprise while others kept their distance. Ashanti's breath caught in her throat before she screamed again.

Tall Jackson said through hysterical peals of laughter, "That's a mechanical mannequin!" He patted her shoulder, comforting his trembling supervisor. "I've heard about these battery-operated dummies." His eyes watered as his tall frame shook with mirth. The other two workers joined in, laughing at Ashanti's expense as she began to feel small and insignificant. She smiled meekly, avoiding her coworkers' mocking eyes.

Before anyone could speak again, the mannequin twisted. Setting both hands against the cement floor, it pulled its legs in and stood flawlessly.

There's nothing mechanical about that! T.J. thought.

They held their breath, seeing but not believing, until Ashanti couldn't take the strain any longer. She shrieked and bolted for the exit door, clipboard tumbling away, arms flailing like an inflatable tube man. Her hands shook as she fumbled with the rusty handle—a long overdue OSHA violation. After ramming it repeatedly, she gave up and struck the large red button, causing the dock door to roll up. Drenched in sweat, Ashanti burst through the opening, barreling down the ramp toward the crowd in the parking lot.

T.J. gaped. The doll he had called mechanical crept forward, its arms reaching out as if to carry him across the floor like the supervisor had.

"Get your hands off me!" he screamed. Jackson bashed the female mannequin in the face several times. Learning from this predicament, Cute Cindy struck back with equal precision, pounding his face and driving him back with explosive blows.

"¡Apártate!" A short, stocky man with a thick mustache sprang into action. *¡Ninguna máquina podría realizar tal maniobra!* He swung at the dummy with a 2x4, clobbering it across the face several times and knocking it to the floor. The mannequin lay on its left side with its right leg scissored forward, fists still clenched. Benjamin gasped, his lips quivering as his wild eyes landed on the torn jaw. The mere sight of the maimed doll gave him goosebumps. Thinking the worst was over, he dropped the 2x4.

The day crew clapped and cheered at the outcome, relieved that he had killed whatever it was. Jackson pounded Benjamin's back and shouted, "You did it, mi amigo! You killed the devil!"

Whack!

A blow to the head sent Benjamin to the floor. His jaundiced eyes focused on the perfectly aligned warehouse lights and galvanized ducts. Cindy stood over him, holding the 2x4 like a batter on deck. Its lower jaw dangled like a broken drawer, but it displayed no pain. No longer cute, Cindy did what it had been taught. It raised the 2x4 over its head and bludgeoned the convulsing man, splitting his skull until he breathed no more. Every worker stormed out the dock door and down the ramp, never looking back.

Amid the chaos, the machines roared on, hissing, cutting, stamping in relentless cadence. Conveyor belts groaned and clacked, their industrial chorus echoing the frenetic pulse of Grand Central Station at rush hour.

Still holding the bloodied 2x4 like a new appendage, Cindy turned rigidly and walked toward the first row of newly manufactured dummies, its narrow nose jutting past a dangling jaw. Five hundred mannequins stood before it. The moment Cindy touched the first one, an electric spark leapt between them, igniting a chain reaction. Daughter cells multiplied, transferring their DNA to trillions of cells, giving life to the artificial being. The naked mannequin tilted its head, taking in its surroundings. Sensing the presence of another mannequin, it grasped the other's arm. Gradually, each dummy reached for the next, until every figure had gained life.

In eerie unison, they held each other's hands for balance and placed one foot in front of the other. Tentative movements lengthened into confident strides, accelerating like a locomotive. The echo of five hundred synchronized feet reverberated through the warehouse. Within seconds, the horde of neonate mannequins surged toward the dock door where Cindy had vanished.

Neither proud nor pleased about bearing so many children, Cindy jogged down the ramp into the unruly crowd, its impassive eyes staring straight ahead.

Huddled with the rest of the crew, Jackson suddenly pointed. "There she is! The murderer is getting away!"

A mob closed in on Cindy, unleashing a flurry of blows and kicks, but nothing seemed to affect the creature. It didn't cry out or recoil from the brutality. Jackson glared at the mannequin before driving his fist into its face. With a fury, he hurled it into the chain-link fence. The 2x4 clattered to the pavement as Cindy lost her grip, rebounding into his waiting arms.

Someone from the crowd shouted, "Gawd, would ya look at that!"

With their backs to the warehouse, everyone turned to look. Their jaws dropped, disbelief shimmering in their eyes.

Unashamed in their nakedness, a host of mannequins were midway down the ramp in flawless formation, their plastic feet in perfect step like a well-trained brigade.

One, two, three, four.

One, two, three, four.

They watched Cindy's mistreatment unfold—each blow, each insult absorbed in silence. Under the beating sun, they studied technique: stance, pivot, follow-through. What had once been passive observation became preparation. Arms once molded for display curled into fists. Legs bent, ready for impact.

Then came the loud lunch whistle, slicing through the air like the bell that starts a bout. It wasn't meant for them, but they took it as a signal. A cue. A call to arms.

No longer props, but contenders entering the ring, the mannequins bolted in unison. Their movements were stiff yet purposeful, driven not by instinct but by imitation. They had learned enough.

Panic rippled through the crowd. People scattered, heedless of one another, desperate to escape the throng of living dummies. For many, it became a lesson not soon forgotten. Kicks and blows landed with mechanical precision. Several men were hurled into the chain-link fence, rebounding into fresh punishment.

Though he'd endured the sting of a naked angel tattoo on his left calf, Alden was about to discover real pain. Faced with the advancing army, he danced and dodged, showing off the fancy footwork he had learned as an amateur boxer and lashed out at the closest mannequin with a double jab, right cross, left hook, and another right cross. The figure recoiled as each strike hit home, but quickly assimilated the boxer's techniques. Then it executed its fancy footwork. Not as agile as Alden, its attempt was mediocre.

The boxer laughed. "You've got to be fuckin' kidding me," he said, lowering his guard. Without warning, the mannequin lashed out with a double jab, right cross, left hook, and another right cross to his face. It kicked Alden in the groin, doubling him over in agony. His face turned purple, eyes glazed as he gasped for air. Only a dry wheeze escaped his throat before he toppled over, unconscious.

Ignorant of their victory, the mannequins darted in different directions, searching for more of their kind. Cindy headed southeast, clutching the 2x4 it had come to rely on.

* * *

Unaware of the danger lurking outside the hotel room, Nolan sat quietly in bed wearing only a tank top, his skinny hairy legs tucked under the sheets. He stared at the cheap oil painting of the Grand Canal in Venice. As the brushstrokes blurred, his mind drifted back to the hotel lobby earlier that day, to where he stood at the front desk, Dolores eyeing the candy rack. Nolan had met her at a grocery store nearly four months ago, and he had begun to wonder how much longer he could afford their weekly rendezvous. The room on the ground floor had cost him $69.95, plus tax. "I only have forty-five dollars on me. Do you have any money?" he had asked, his voice barely above a whisper, eyes avoiding hers.

Dolores's belittling gaze cut through him as she chewed on a stick of gum like a contented cow chewing cud. "Why can't you just use your credit card?" she had said in a nasal tone.

Nolan had given her a miserly smile and paid with a card, leaving further evidence for his suspicious wife, who would eventually use the receipt in a divorce case.

"After this, I want you to take me to the supermarket to get some groceries," she had said, sliding into bed naked. She gave him an insincere peck on the cheek to soften the financial blow and reached for the remote control.

Now, with Dolores flipping through the channels beside him and laughing at smidgens of *I Love* Lucy reruns, Nolan caught sight of her 15-millimeter mole on her thigh that he found repulsive. It was dark and lumpy, with a single hair sprouting from its center.

A scuffle outside the hotel room caught his attention. It was nothing new in this part of town, mainly since the hotel was next to a bar. He sat up in bed, turning his left ear toward the window and furrowing his brows in concentration. As the scuffle grew louder, the thin canvas shook after someone or something slammed into the wall, and based on the commotion, Nolan guessed three or four people were struggling outside their window.

Dolores lowered the television volume.

A crash shattered the calm, scattering shards like glittering, deadly confetti. Someone landed with a thud at the foot of the bed. Dolores screamed, shielding herself with the sheets as Nolan yanked the covers over his head like a frightened child. Outside, retreating footsteps echoed as the perpetrators fled after flinging some poor soul into their room.

Flapping wildly like an angry goose, the vertical blinds settled into eerie silence. Nolan peered out from the bed sheet with Dolores painfully still next to him, her knuckles pale and rigid, pleating the sheet with silent panic.

A hand appeared at the foot of the bed, groping for a hold like a ghoul clawing its way out of a grave. Using the mattress for leverage, a male figure rose, the broad brim of a ten-gallon hat shading a pale, unreadable face. He wore an embroidered shirt, jeans, and a black leather belt with "America" engraved on the gaudy bronze buckle. The man lifted his dimpled chin, revealing plastic-coated features, and moved its head mechanically like an industrial robot. Through fiberglass eyes, it saw the lovers bathed in an orange tint, its stare cold and indifferent.

When Dolores lifted her gaze, her pupils dilated, and her hands began to tremble. At first, she remained silent. But when she realized the man was a walking mannequin, she screamed in terror. She yanked the sheets off and dashed out of the room, wearing nothing but a terrified look.

Nolan hunched on the bed, languishing in a pool of hot urine. Blood dripped from the knuckles of his right hand, where his teeth had gouged the skin.

After watching Dolores bolt for the door, the cowboy turned and jumped out the window in search of more mannequins, sending the blinds flapping wildly again.

* * *

Evelyn dragged her son out of the car, her grip firm with urgency. The keys jingled in her trembling hand as she unlocked the apartment door. Herman shouted in protest when she yanked him inside—an uncharacteristic burst of desperation she didn't have time to explain. It was only a matter of time before the plastic plague consumed Miami, its chaos spilling outward, infecting neighborhoods, igniting panic, poised to engulf every state and, in time, the globe.

After ensuring she hadn't been followed, Evelyn slammed the door shut, letting out a sigh of relief. It was the first time she could catch her breath, but her heart still burned.

Herman gave her a puzzled look. His innocent mind had seen no trouble. It was all fun and games to him. He had no clue what he'd set in motion, and there was no way to scold him or make him understand he'd just changed the world forever.

Before he could say a word, Evelyn was off and running again. She scrambled between their bedrooms, flinging clothes and toiletries into a large suitcase. The Mr. Cow photo and letter he'd written last Christmas, still tucked in the drawer, stayed behind. After thirty minutes, she hauled the bag out into the living room, where Herman stood with a blank expression. Not letting up, she opened the closet door and tugged the string. Light spilled into the room, catching the twin dolls as they strolled out of the shadows. They looked up at her, their arms reaching for affection. "I'm afraid there's no time for that now," she said, grabbing the dolls and making the voice mechanism squeak. She stuffed them between two pairs of jeans and zipped up the suitcase.

Evelyn glanced at her watch, the ticking second hand sharpening her urgency. "Did you use the bathroom?"

Herman nodded, but anchored himself to the spot, pulling back against her grip on his arm. With her free hand, she dragged the suitcase to the door.

"Hat." He pointed at his toy chest.

"Not now, Herman," she said impatiently. "We have to go!"

"Want hat."

"But you already have a jester hat!" she raised her voice.

Herman's eyes were glassy and his lower lip quivered. "Want other one," he sniveled.

Evelyn breathed in slowly, aware now of her harshness. "All right then. Go get one." Her voice softened, and she smiled. It was something she hadn't done since the incident at the department store. *It wasn't his fault. None of this would have happened if I had kept a closer eye on him.*

Herman ran to the toy chest and rooted through its contents. Action figures and board games tumbled out, creating a cheerful mess. The squeak of a rubber ducky echoed playfully against the tinkling notes of the jack-in-the-box. A grin spread across his face when he found the hat he wanted.

In a fresh panic, Evelyn seized his wrist and stormed out, locking the door behind her. The suitcase rattled down the stairs, its uneven cadence merging with the sounds of the bustling street.

She reached the car and threw the suitcase into the trunk. Moments later, Evelyn sped out of the driveway, sweat beading on her brow as she cut off a red sedan. The driver slammed the brakes, and though she couldn't hear his words, his obscene gestures made his frustration clear. Determined to fly out of Fort Lauderdale, she tightened her grip and pressed harder on the gas.

Driving north, she saw signs of chaos: shattered storefronts, upturned mannequins tangled in seaweed, the distant wail of sirens echoing through salt-thick air. Sadly, street gangs also took this opportunity to loot and vandalize establishments. The glare of brake lights snapped her attention back to the road.

"Great," she said, jamming her foot on the brake pedal. "Now what?" Her car stopped behind other vehicles.

Excited, Herman leaned forward in his seat. "Crash!"

Two cars had collided at the intersection ahead. *Probably caused by a mannequin*, she thought. Evelyn exhaled hard, realizing she might be stuck for a while. She hit the horn. "Come on! Move it!"

A group gathered on the sidewalk, gesturing wildly, their voices sharp with alarm. They were pointing at something down the street, where sirens had begun wailing. One by one, they crouched. Hands scraped the pavement, snatching up rocks, bottles, chunks of crumbled asphalt. Debris arced through the air, whipping past Evelyn's car.

Herman's head tilted back, following the rocks' trajectory. "Beautiful people," he said softly.

Evelyn's heart skipped a beat. Her frightened eyes stared into the rearview mirror and saw three mannequins sprinting up the street.

A rock hurtled through the air and struck one on the head. The impact left a small dent, but the dummy didn't flinch. Dressed in khaki and a red shirt, it bent down, grabbed the offending stone with its smooth, flesh-colored hand, and hurled it back.

Evelyn screamed as the rock shattered her rear windshield. She threw the gear into reverse and glanced over her shoulder just as her son's fingers knotted in her hair.

"Herman, no!" she yelled in pain.

"Beautiful people!" he yelled, afraid she wouldn't let him play with his friends.

Evelyn pried at his fingers, the car jerking as her foot wavered between the accelerator and brake pedals. Herman clawed at her face with one hand.

"Stop it, Herman!" she begged, her voice cracking. "We need to get out of here!" She slapped his hands away and pushed him aside, guilt clawing at her.

The tires squealed as Evelyn slammed it into drive and punched the accelerator. Fueled by raw determination, she cut into a driveway and barreled down the sidewalk, horn blaring. Pedestrians scattered, diving into bushes as she tore past.

"Play with beautiful people!" Herman's tantrum escalated, his fists pounding on the door panel as he kicked the dashboard.

When Evelyn careened back onto the street, the bumper scraped the asphalt with a grating noise and a shower of sparks. Air whipped through the window, tousling Herman's hair as his fury faltered—blown thin like smoke. Her grip tightened as she spotted a crowd beating a lone mannequin. The crack of plastic limbs hitting concrete triggered a queasy twist in her gut.

"Herman, close your window," she said firmly.

Pressing the button, Herman watched the window ascend, his gaze climbing with it.

As Evelyn turned left onto Flagler Street, a surge of people spilled into her path. Heart racing, she slammed the brakes. The tires screeched just inches from the mob. She exhaled slowly, thankful no one had been hurt.

"That's odd," she murmured, scanning the sea of faces. Evelyn leaned forward, locking eyes with her suspicious neighbor, Olivia Sanders. She offered a polite smile, but something in Olivia's demeanor made Evelyn's skin crawl.

"That's him! He's the one!" Olivia shouted, pointing at Herman, who sat clueless in the passenger seat. She grabbed the man next to her and pushed him forward. "Do something! He's the one who gave life to the mannequins!" Olivia exclaimed, thinking back to when her son had told her about the two walking dolls.

Evelyn couldn't believe what she'd heard. Her neighbor betrayed her, barely blinking. *How could she have known?*

Already in a murderous frenzy, the man marched toward the car's passenger side, the threads of his torn-off denim sleeves brushing against the wind. He slammed his face against the window, shouting profanities and pounding his fist into a cupped palm.

Facing a new threat, Evelyn locked the doors and shifted the car in reverse, but the crowd had already swarmed around them. She gasped as the man yanked on the door handle, his fury mounting with each failed attempt.

After he kicked the window to no avail, another man put a restraining hand on his arm. "Taylor, you're taking this too far! Just let them be, for goodness' sake!"

An unexpected shove sent his friend hurtling to the ground. "I'm not going to sit around and let this happen to my town!" Taylor shouted. He whirled around and kicked the window with brute force. Glass burst into glittering shards, spraying the seat and slicing Herman's cheek. His violent display incited others to join the mayhem.

Several people began rocking the car, their hands gripping the frame as they tried to flip it over. The vehicle groaned under the strain. Evelyn's head knocked against the window. She winced, searching the crowd for a sympathetic face.

"Help us," she called out, voice cracking as she clung to the steering wheel. "Someone, please help!"

Herman whimpered beside her, pawing at the cuts on his face. A man leaped onto the hood, denting the metal with each step. Then, out of the corner of her eye, she saw Taylor reach through the shattered window and unfasten Herman's seatbelt. Her breath caught. She lunged forward, arms outstretched, trying to pull her son back.

"Stop!" she cried, voice raw.

Herman's legs slid through the window as her fingers grazed his ankle, then nothing. Just the blur of movement and the sting of tears clouding her vision.

Olivia continued to incite the crowd, her face flushed with rage. "Don't let them get away!" Her voice boomed through the melee as she steered them toward the blocked car.

Evelyn jumped out to retrieve her son, ignoring Olivia's cries for justice. She chased Herman's cries, yelling, "Leave my son alone!" No one listened.

Herman cried out, fists pummeling Taylor's grip as he was dragged up the courthouse steps.

"So, you're the one who brought the mannequins to life!" Taylor shouted, his gaze sharp and unflinching.

Herman tried to explain. "Beautiful people," he moaned through his tears.

To the crowd, Herman's tears were just anguish—but they were a beacon for help. Some mannequins were hours away, others mere minutes, but they all felt the immediate pull. From Leisure City to Cooper City, every mannequin paused in its mission and responded to the lifegiver's distress.

The crowd, growing louder and rowdier, chanted, "Burn the freak! Burn the freak!"

Her hair in shambles, Evelyn ran up the steps and stood on the landing, overlooking the frantic crowd. She held her arms out, beseeching the mob to see reason. "My son is not a troublemaker! He's simply curious!" Her voice, ragged and thunderous, crashed against deaf ears as the crowd surrounded Taylor and her son, vitriol spitting from their angry faces.

As Taylor raised his fist to strike, a sharp wooden thud cracked against the back of his head. The world spun as he stumbled backward, collapsing onto the stairs, eyes fixed and face twisted in a grimace of pain.

Disfigured Cindy stood over him with the same bloodstained 2x4 that Benjamin had used. Its face was blank, showing no emotion for having saved its lifegiver. The tear in its jaw had widened from the crowd's clawing fingers, and the protrusion jiggled like a loose bicycle fender with each step.

For one suspended beat, silence reigned. Then a young man with a bucket hat tackled Cindy, and a surge of bodies followed, fists and boots raining down. The hat flew off as he seized Cindy by the torn jaw and forced it to stand.

"Stand back, everyone!" someone shouted. The 2x4 sliced through the air and struck the pummeled dummy in the head, ripping it off and sending it tumbling down the steps like a rogue bowling ball veering across multiple lanes.

Fifteen or twenty mannequins lay motionless, already fallen in their attempt to rescue the boy who gave them life. Seeing the defenders unresponsive, the crowd turned their attention back to the helpless boy. Evelyn, clutching her frightened child, fell to her knees. "Please don't hurt my son!" she cried, shielding him with her arm. "He meant no harm!"

The crowd refused to listen. They converged again, intent on retribution. A man pointed at Herman. "We need to end this right now!"

But before the crowd could act, a ripple of unease ran through them. Their voices faded, one by one, until no more cries of hatred lingered in their lungs. A blanket of confusion settled over them as they stood alert, ears perked like meerkats in the grasslands of southern Africa.

They heard it . . . and so did Evelyn.

It sounded like an approaching locomotive or the feet of ten thousand marathon runners coming from every direction. Fear washed over the crowd as they twisted and turned, scanning the streets for the source of the noise—until it was too late.

They appeared everywhere, bursting at the seams in the fabric of life. Showing no fatigue, thousands of mannequins stampeded through the streets toward the courthouse steps. Many were dressed in the latest fashion, while others were stark naked, attracting stupefied expressions from civilians. Within seconds, the crowd found itself encircled. No exits, no mercy.

On Flagler Street, mayhem erupted under a clear sky.

Maybe the raging bull on Ethan's T-shirt drove him to charge in without thinking. It cost him his life. Grabbing the 2x4, he battered a few mannequins. With every swing, the board sliced through the air. He ducked to avoid a punch, letting the 2x4's momentum guide his next move. The board arced upward, smashing a mannequin's face and dropping it cold. Ethan had the upper hand, but his mouth dropped open in disbelief when he turned to face his next assailant.

Before him stood the mannequin from the Japanese store. It wore Japanese armor from the Oda Nobunaga era, with vertical plates across the torso and a crest on its helmet. Ethan flinched as the samurai showed off its footwork and newly acquired one-handed techniques. How it had learned kenjutsu remained a mystery, but the blood on its blade spoke of violence in a martial arts school. Emulating the moves of a legendary samurai master, the mannequin swiftly drew a sword and aligned its wrist behind the blade handle. At the last instant, its elbow joint snapped forward, the blade dragging in a brutal arc designed for maximum damage . . .

The automated Metromover 15 had just pulled away from Government Center Station, where a large crowd stood quietly. Nearby, the escalator hummed as Johnny Hunter emerged from its depths. First came the gleaming tip of its rifle, piercing the earth's surface. Then, slowly, the mannequin's hooded head rose into view. As Johnny fully appeared, it deftly stepped off the moving staircase, its boots gripping the comb plate. Several people recoiled at the sight of a rifle. But when they realized it was a walking mannequin, panic erupted. They screamed and rushed into the station, pressing behind the glass doors, huddling for safety as a crowd of stunned onlookers gathered.

Johnny Hunter stood at the edge of the landing beneath a waffle-iron ceiling. With nowhere else to go but down, it scanned both directions before leaping off the 3-foot ledge, its camouflaged boots gripping the Brickell Loop tracks. It stepped over the guide rail and ran south on the Downtown Loop tracks without wasting time. Passing several Metrorail support pillars, it felt the rumblings of the northbound train braking to a stop above it. Johnny could see the skyline ahead, but it meant nothing. The sun's warmth—a distant cousin—was more appealing than anything this world offered . . .

For the first time in Miami's history, mayhem flooded Flagler Street and spilled into surrounding neighborhoods with a vengeance. People and mannequins clashed in a frenzy, fists flying without pause.

In frustration, a man wearing a guayabera grabbed his short, curly hair and tried to calm the mob, "¡Señoras y señores, no se asusten! ¡Mantengan la calma!"

"¿Qué demonios es esto?" someone else cried before fleeing.

A swarm of forty mannequins quickly surrounded the lifegiver, shielding him from the mob, their blows landing with eerie precision. Herman danced in the center of his safe zone, elated to be among friends instead of being dragged around by that nasty man who wanted to hurt him. He writhed and jerked to imagined music. Each time he jumped, he snorted like a wild beast. The antlers on his moose hat bobbled with each ecstatic leap, mimicking a sparring buck in rut.

Johnny Hunter stopped running. Remembering the massive hunting mural, the mannequin thought it saw the greatest prize of all.

And sure enough, there it stood, about three hundred feet away. A bona fide, gorgeous moose bucking ecstatically and making beautiful grunting sounds! It was just like the mural. The pose. The distance. The thrill. The hunter aimed, peered into the riflescope . . . and fired.

It was the shot heard across Miami. When the lifegiver hit the ground, the mannequins dropped with him, from the outer reaches of the city to the concentrated center where Herman's body lay. The streets fell silent, as if the city itself had gone dark.

Then came the high-frequency yawp, undetectable to the human ear. Each mannequin released a final shriek that echoed through empty alleys and high-rise towers. The sound threaded through every mind, bursting the protective bubbles with mannequin-related memories. Every trace of this historic day dissolved, leaving a void of confusion.

Evelyn had built her life around contingencies, but losing her son had never been part of her plan. "No!" she wailed. Her son lay lifeless, his legs bent out of shape and his eyes appallingly still. Huddled on the rough concrete steps, she gathered his limp body, rocking him as her voice trembled with endearments and grief.

One could bend pain, twist it out of shape, and alter its perception, and it would still register as agony. Add deep colors, dark red and raven black, and it becomes torment. Evelyn's torment was captured on canvas with splashes of grief. In that haunting spectrum, the universe lost a son.

The last mannequin toppled over, landing on an endless sea of fiberglass bodies. Flagler Street had become a cemetery of lifeless forms stretching into the distance. The bond between Herman and the mannequins had vanished. No yearning remained. No urge to flourish or seek others of their kind. The passion had extinguished.

As the confused crowd stood on the courthouse steps, scratching their heads and scanning the chaos, a grim realization began to settle: civilians had been injured, some brutally murdered. They looked to one another for answers, wondering how they'd ended up here, in the heart of downtown Miami. No one could remember a thing. Where had the mannequins come from? Why were they scattered across the streets, so many of them battered and broken? These and other unspoken questions churned through their minds.

* * *

One perk Governor Arthur J. Townsend enjoyed was reading the next day's headlines before they reached the public, streamed in real time through the steady clatter of his office teletype. But at 5:30 that afternoon, he sighed heavily as a frown formed. Now in his second term, Arthur sat back in his swivel chair, tapping his upper lip as he savored a Dominican cigar. Through his half-rim glasses, he peered at the thin paper curling out of the machine beside him, each line stamped with outlandish headlines: "City of the Dead," "Invasion of the Mannequins," "The Dead Walk Among Us," and "Are Friends Fiberglass?" Every outlet had picked up the story, clueless about what had happened.

Sure, Florida was known for weird and unusual stories, but Arthur never remembered seeing anything like this. Editorial pages brimmed with requests for the public's help to explain the phenomenon. Despite dozens of interviews and countless reporters out on the beat, no one could unravel the mystery. Even with the promise of being named a state hero and given the keys to the city. One person did know the answer to all the questions. Evelyn Sinclair. And she wasn't talking. Not for fame, not for safety, not for anyone.

Arthur had called an emergency meeting in his Tallahassee office. Puffing furiously on his cigar, he turned his irate gaze on each staff member in turn. He waved a stack of teletype headlines. "Are you telling me not one fuckin' idiot can remember what happened in four hours?" he barked, as if they'd personally penned the cringeworthy columns. He was starving for answers, and every time he puffed on his cigar, not one cloud of smoke satisfied his appetite. "Even I remember stubbing my toe at two o'clock in the morning! Give me a break!"

Within an hour, the governor made his position unmistakably clear: every newspaper in Miami was to scrap the mannequin story. He couldn't stomach the idea of the nation thinking Florida was full of inept fools. Better to sweep the whole episode under the rug than invite national ridicule. Under pressure from the governor's office, Miami's editors folded. The mannequin story was buried. In its place, headlines spoke of a citywide festival gone awry and the massive cleanup that followed. People could dig through the archives all they wanted. They'd find no trace of the day the mannequins came to life.

After the final call, and once the staff had gone home, Arthur stood at the window, admiring the trees outside his Capitol office. As usual during crises, Lieutenant Governor Nate McFadden stood quietly behind him. His pleather shoes squeaked with each shift of weight.

Arthur couldn't stop thinking about the mannequins and the deaths that defied explanation. The questions haunted him.

Could the mannequins have come to life to cause chaos and destruction? Were they figments of imagination, triggered by a gas leak or fumes from the sewage system? Perhaps they were never alive to begin with. Only God knows how many secrets the mind holds.

The governor puffed on his cigar, exhaling from his sour mouth. "A wise man once said," he remarked, his eyes fixed on the red sunset.

"What's that?" Nate replied.

"Imagination is the secret."

* * *

Tuesday, September 30, 1980.

Knowing she and Herman had lived too little intensified Evelyn's sense of loss. Feeling the weight of a cruel and unforgiving world, she walked to her apartment, oversized sunglasses hiding her red, puffy eyes. Her cherished off-white cardigan offered fragile comfort, softening the anguish radiating from her funeral dress.

As she stepped into her apartment, a wave of relief washed over her. The door clicked shut, followed by the heavy thud of the deadbolt.

In the quiet sanctuary of her home, her son's presence embraced her. From the bronze baby shoes atop the television to the photographs cluttering every surface, his spirit lingered.

Tossing her keys onto the kitchen counter, she picked up one of her most treasured pictures. It was a snapshot of Herman dancing in his whimsical cow hat, twirling blissfully to the beat of his favorite new-wave song. His laughter rang in her mind as she relived the joy of jumping and dancing beside him. His memories were like a flickering flame—offering warmth even in her darkest hours. *I would do it all over again, just for the chance to hold his hands and hear his infectious laughter.*

She smiled.

And now he was gone.

The aroma of stale coffee lingered, mingling with the quiet ache that filled the room. As she bowed her head and closed her eyes, a single tear slipped down her cheek. *If given the chance*, she sighed as she wiped away the tear, *I would fill his life with more laughter. And with greater vigilance, let him explore the world he so seldom saw.*

In the days leading up to the funeral, Evelyn had been thinking about leaving Miami, going somewhere far from Flagler Street and those dreadful, coldhearted steps of the courthouse. She longed to vanish, to escape to a new community where nothing strange ever happened. *Someplace,* she mused, *like Koreatown, Los Angeles.*

After slipping into her nightgown, Evelyn moved her rocking chair beside the lamp, where the dim light illuminated the sparsely furnished room. Her slippers flapped against the floor as she moved. Then she opened the closet door and beckoned. “Come here, my little ones.”

The two dolls wobbled into the light. They reached their arms up, pleading to be carried. Evelyn bent down, lifted both dolls, and cradled them tenderly in her arms.

"Don't worry, my darlings," she said, docking into the rocking chair. "No one will ever hurt you." Her feet pushed against the floor, rocking the old wooden chair. The gentle creak of the old wood soothed her grief.

The dolls stared impassively at Evelyn, their round blue eyes blinking mechanically, their faces devoid of a smile. They ran their tiny hands through her hair. Evelyn felt a flicker of gratitude that the dolls had not met the same fate as the mannequins. *Is it because they're made of rubber instead of polyethylene?* she wondered. They patted her tear-ridden cheeks lovingly, then paused. Their touch grew deliberate, as though grief had taught them tenderness. With the help of the weighted mechanism crier, they whispered, "Mama."

* * *

Thursday, October 2, 1980.

In the days following the melee, garbage trucks rumbled through Miami's streets, scooping up the mannequins like battlefield casualties. Governor Townsend had ordered their immediate removal, hoping to erase the spectacle from public memory. For weeks, the dummies sat in a cavernous recycling facility, surrounded by the groan of conveyor belts and the hiss of pneumatic arms. Fluorescent lights buzzed overhead, casting a sterile glow over the two mounds of mannequins. The first mound held mutilated dummies with torn limbs and ripped garments; the other, perfectly intact mannequins that had perished en route to the courthouse steps.

Department store adjusters and hired workers sifted through the mounds, tossing salvageable mannequins into the backs of pickup trucks. The scene was too bizarre to ignore. Workers couldn't resist snapping pictures with the dummies, grinning beside their frozen companions like tourists in a wax museum.

"Look, everyone!" shouted a man in work gloves, stumbling backward. His voice cracked as he pointed at a figure near the edge of the mound. "This mannequin is pregnant!"

The crowd converged, boots crunching over broken plastic. As their eyes fell upon the figure, chatter turned to whispers. A female mannequin lay flat on its back, its see-through teddy splayed open over its protruding belly. Its sales tag traced back to the lingerie department at Nautical South Mall. The same place where a man of flesh and blood had once interrupted its eerie stride down a corridor. Its synthetic blonde hair was swept to the side, held by an elastic headband. Pink lips and glassy sapphire eyes gave it a disturbingly lifelike expression.

The belly twitched.

In unison, they gasped. Someone fainted. Then the mannequin's belly convulsed. A kick. A thrash. A sudden rupture. A gush of amniotic fluid splashed across someone's boots.

CHAPTER SEVEN

THE CHILD WITHIN

Saturday, January 15, 2005. 4:18 p.m.

He had only stopped to grab a pack of cigarettes, but paused when the young man behind the register caught his eye. A lock of blond hair draped over half his face, veiling golden-green eyes and fair skin. The exposed eye sparkled as he moved, and that gorgeous lock swayed with each gesture, like the hem of a dancer's glowing gown.

"I can see you starring in a big motion picture, young man," the customer said, flashing a gap-toothed smile.

Hope igniting, Ethan swiped his hair from his hidden eye and shifted to make his name tag visible.

"Granted," the man continued, ignoring the people in line behind him, "you'd have to start in smaller roles, but with your looks, you could move up quickly."

"Are you a talent scout?"

"Roger Anderson, Hollywood, California," the man replied, flicking a business card into the clerk's waiting hand with practiced ease.

Ethan scrutinized the card, weighing whether the man was genuine or just another scammer. He glanced at the people in line, who were growing increasingly restless. Feet tapped. Watches were checked. Pressure coiled in his chest, rising into a lump in his throat.

"I-I-I'm sure this will cost heaps of cash, mister," he said, shaking his head.

"Truth be told, young man," Roger said, winking, his smile unwavering, "acting classes will run you around four thousand, plus my fees."

Ethan felt his hopes sink. He didn't have that kind of cash, not on a minimum-wage salary! "I appreciate it, mister. But I'd rather not," he said, brushing his hair aside. *I hope I'm making the right decision.*

Fingering his receipt, the talent scout gave Ethan another once-over. He stuffed the cigarette pack into his coat pocket and said, "No worries, chap. Give me a shout if you change your mind. But ask yourself this: Do I really want to stand behind a cash register my whole life?"

The woman next in line was seething as Ethan followed the man out the door with his eyes. Her face flushed as she rapped her car keys on the counter. "Ahem," she cleared her throat stridently. "Do you suppose I could get some service sometime today, Mr. Hollywood?"

* * *

Friday, February 18, 2005. 8:46 p.m.

Forty-seven watches and counting, all thanks to the art of misdirection and sleight of hand. Patrick had perfected the art of lifting high-end watches from unsuspecting marks in seconds. He'd find his subject and ease them into a relaxed state. Subtle physical contact was always at play: a handshake, a gentle pat on the shoulder, any small gesture to build trust. Most importantly, he beckoned them closer to witness his disappearing-and-reappearing ring trick. Then, covertly, he began working the strap and pin. Within seconds, the watch slipped free, vanishing into his pocket before they even noticed.

"Thank you for letting me use your ring for the trick," he said, returning it to his latest victim with a flourish. "That's an exquisite ring, I might add."

The man laughed. "You won't believe how many times I've lost this thing." With pride, he held the gold ring up to the light. Leaning in, he gave Patrick a stoic look and said, "I feel fortunate that my belongings always find their way back to me."

"Really?" the con artist asked, cocking his head and scratching his nose. The scent of smoke on his finger tugged at his old craving. "How so?"

The man flicked the ring into the air and caught it, then turned it over to show Patrick the engraving on the inside. He smiled at his own ingenuity and said, "I had my phone number engraved on every one of my valuables." His hearty laugh made his face flush until it almost matched his burgundy polo shirt.

Patrick ran a hand through his beard and grinned at the man's cleverness. He reached into his shirt pocket and pulled out a pack of cigarettes before bidding farewell to his unsuspecting victim.

* * *

Tuesday, March 8, 2005. 9:11 p.m.

Tabatha gently grasped her husband's frail arm and eased it through one sleeve of the sweater that reeked of pain medication. She repeated the process with his other arm before pulling the sweater over his head. Alzheimer's disease had robbed him of any quality of life, and for several years now, she had taken on the difficult role of caregiver without hesitation. Nothing else mattered. Her devotion was as vast as the sun—capable of thriving for billions of years, radiating warmth and joy into his life. It was the least she could do after he had given her the most extraordinary life imaginable.

The soft pitter-patter of rain drummed through the room, and she shivered in the increasing chill. Her hands, riddled with sunspots like chocolate-covered candies, draped a wool blanket and tucked it around his shoulders. His vacant gaze burned into her as his lips struggled to form a question. She knelt beside his chair, her joint protesting, and took his trembling hand in hers. "Yes, Papa? What do you want?"

He pulled his hand back slightly, staring at her with a flicker of fear. "Who are you?" The words straggled out, leaving his mouth slightly agape.

Tabatha chuckled. "I'm your wife," she said, peering into his disoriented eyes and patting his arm. "I've been your wife for forty-six years, Phillip." She ran her bony fingers through his unruly hair, which sprang back after each pass, and leaned in to plant a kiss on his withered cheek. "I'll always take care of you," she said, smiling. "I've loved you since the day you offered me sprinkles for my ice cream." Her gaze drifted overhead. "I was going through a rough patch. You saw my frown and came over to cheer me up." She looked back, her expression softening. "I'll never forget what you said that day: 'Colorful sprinkles get rid of the wrinkles.'"

She cherished the memory, her face glowing.

"I like it when it rains," he said in a raspy voice, indifferent to everything she had said.

Tabatha gazed out the window at a bush swaying gently in the breeze. The drizzle drummed softly against the window, forming droplets on a cobweb that glistened like tiny jewels in the dim light. Winston, the neighbor's black Labrador, ran by as if experiencing rain for the first time.

"I like it too, Papa. It's very soothing." Then added, "But it makes this rickety old house damp and cold." She rubbed her arms to warm herself. "It doesn't help that our heater is broken."

Getting him into bed took time. Once he was settled, she tucked in the sheet, her fingers stiff with pain. The arthritis gnawed at her joints, turning even the simplest tasks into quiet battles.

Phillip lay shivering, gazing at the strange woman who had popped into his life from nowhere. His lower lip quivered, and his eyes welled up. He asked through labored breaths, "What is your name?"

The question didn't surprise her—she'd heard it many times and was always glad to answer. "My name is Tabatha," she replied gently, remembering the first time he asked. "I'm your wife, silly goose. Now go to sleep and dream of me," she said, kissing Phillip before climbing stiffly into bed next to him. A warm glow from the nightlight settled over them, quiet and constant.

Phillip slipped quietly away in his sleep sometime before the morning light.

As the first rays of sunlight filtered through the curtains, Tabatha awoke. "Papa?" she called out frantically. But there was no response, only a haunting silence that filled their once-shared bedroom. Her heart shattered as she realized her husband would never again ask for her name. Weeping, she caressed his lifeless face, her fingers tracing the lines time had etched upon his features. She clung to him as she cried out loud. She wanted the world to know her pain.

"Don't leave me, Papa," she pleaded, tears soaking his chest.

* * *

Tuesday, July 19, 2005. 7:45 a.m.

In ten minutes, I'll open my bedroom door and go downstairs to tell my father my asthma is getting worse. I know this from déjà vu. It's happened four times already. Something must be wrong with the time continuum. For several weeks, I've been experimenting. Every time I deviate from my routine, I get nauseous. My head spins like a top: wild, dizzy, and out of control. I can think freely, but I can't alter my movement. A powerful current pulls me toward an unnatural course. Without those motion sickness pills, I'd be in a world of hurt. What's worse, I know that the world ends tomorrow morning at 8:15. The answer to this vicious cycle lies somewhere outside my home. I've dedicated my life to saving people. Now, I must do something to save the world.

White shelves laden with toys filled the four walls. Over the past ten years, hospital staff and friends had brought her so many dolls and plush animals that Penney had no space for posters of teenage movie idols. Lying sick in her mission-style bed, she knew the consequences if she deviated from her usual routine. But it was her only way to unlock the mystery behind a global tragedy set to strike within twenty-four hours.

Wearing her father's button-down mountain flannel shirt, which she preferred over her new pink leopard-print pajamas, Penney took a deep breath and slipped out of bed. Her body jerked as she veered toward the closet, deviating from the timeline to test her theory. Instantly overcome with vertigo, she felt a tug in a northwesterly direction, like scraps drawn to a magnet. Her snow-white hair and oversized shirt flapped as she fought against the current. Penney abandoned her experiment and resumed her usual routine. She opened the bedroom door and went downstairs to tell her father about her worsening vertigo.

* * *

9:35 a.m.

Attend Med Transport responded to an emergency call to transfer a female patient from the Norwood District to the Woodburn Center for Clinical Research in Cincinnati, Ohio. Best known for its pediatric care, WCCR also housed one of the nation's most advanced aging research facilities. Its scientists had pioneered treatments for cellular senescence, developed a vaccine to prevent genetic degradation in connective tissue, and reversed early-stage pigment deterioration, alongside numerous other breakthroughs in age-related decline. Based on this reputation, the Millers chose WCCR to continue Penney's fight against aging.

While Owen and Ingrid filled out paperwork at admissions, ambulance personnel guided the gurney into the emergency room. Julian, the EMT, and a nurse with a stethoscope slung around her neck helped Penney onto the bed. Placing a pillow under her legs, Julian listened to her labored breathing. Usually quick with a joke, he didn't know how to break the eerie silence. His discomfort was palpable; he could barely look at her. As Penney settled in, he stole glances while pretending to smooth the sheets. A liver spot on her skin resembled a cluster of stars; her pale legs, delicate reeds. The nurse noticed his confusion, but it wasn't unusual—new EMTs were often unsettled by Penney's appearance before learning her diagnosis.

As he guided the gurney back to the ambulance, Julian stopped by the doorway to confer with the driver. "I don't get it. What are we doing with this old woman in the children's wing?" he whispered.

Seeing his partner's blank stare, he said, "I've brought this poor girl here several times. She has progeria syndrome. This elderly woman is sixteen years old. She's aging so rapidly that it's as if she's living in dog years."

Julian pondered this thought. "Maybe we should've taken her to an animal hospital instead."

They laughed.

Overhearing them, Penney pulled herself up by the bed rails. "It's funny you should say that," she said, her gaze lingered on his wedding ring and the dragon tattoo peeking from under his sleeve. "I'm not the only one being treated like a dog."

Julian didn't understand what she meant, at least not yet. Embarrassed, he lowered his gaze and walked away, pushing the gurney as it squeaked in protest.

As the Millers walked down the corridor, Owen tightened his grip on his wife's hand. Rounding the corner into the ER, his heart sank at the sight of their daughter in bay twelve, awaiting treatment.

"Hello, Snowflakes," he said softly, drumming his hands against the bed's metal railing. His gentle greeting never failed to warm her.

"Here we are again," she said, a pang of guilt gnawing at her for dragging her parents through this unending ordeal. It was too much for any girl to endure—though Penney was anything but typical. The Millers were fortunate that the federal government had stepped in to assist them with their finances. Without it, they'd have plunged into poverty years ago.

Ingrid reached into a small suitcase she had hastily packed. "We brought your favorite books," she said, removing two slim hardcover books: one about adventurous dogs and the other about a little bird searching for its mother.

"Mom," Penney protested, her eyes squinting as she laughed. "You know I'm too old for kids' books."

"You're still Daddy's little girl, aren't you?" Owen teased, tickling her rib cage.

"Stop it, Dad. You're embarrassing me!" Penney laughed, brushing his hands aside before anyone could see.

* * *

2:17 p.m.

Before long, Penney's trusted physician arrived, wearing her usual warm smile.

"Hello, Penney. And how are we today?" Her quick, practiced glance took in Penney's shortness of breath, wheezing, and unsteady hands. Smoothing some loose tendrils of gray-streaked hair back into her neat bun, she put an arm around Penney's shoulders and squeezed a quick hug. "Let's get you feeling better." Without hesitation, Emelia delivered albuterol through a fast-acting inhaler, followed by dimenhydrinate and salmeterol to stabilize her condition.

Penney had built a strong bond with Dr. Barraza over the years of specialized treatments. She had even learned all the names of the doctor's boyfriends. During one hospital visit, she had seen a vision of Emelia with her first boyfriend, bouncing to the tune of a catchy bubblegum song on the handlebars of Leonard's new bike. The unexpected re-emergence of the long-forgotten memory had warmed Emelia's heart.

Meeting Dr. Barraza became Penney's salvation, though the journey was long and arduous. At age two, Penney was diagnosed with

Hutchinson-Gilford Progeria Syndrome (HHPS), a genetic mutation affecting one in four million children that accelerates aging. The Millers lived in a modest house on Jo Jean Road, located near McHopner's Manor, a renowned facility adjacent to the county museum, where Penney spent hours exploring local history exhibits. This proximity made it easier to manage her care without needing to travel out of state. But her visits ended abruptly when doctors recommended a new treatment involving a class of cancer drugs, the name abbreviated due to its complexity.

Wide-eyed and trembling, Penney watched as her father excoriated the medical staff. "I don't want my daughter to take cancer drugs!" he snarled. "She doesn't have cancer! Do you understand me?"

"Please try to calm down, Mr. Miller. We are aware Penney doesn't have cancer, and are doing everything we can to help your daughter," Dr. Brian Scott said, moving about the conference room with both hands in his lab coat pockets. "Hormsodiumregulators are a class of drugs that could potentially alleviate your daughter's symptoms. Yes, they are prescribed for cancer patients, but recent studies suggest that they might also be effective with progeria." He paused to scratch his head, grateful his silver hair concealed his dandruff.

"Dr. Scott," Owen shut his eyes and shook his head. "I'm not subjecting my daughter to something as harsh as hormeosodiate . . . harmenosodio . . . or whatever you doctors call your fancy drugs!"

"HSRs for short."

"Whatever! You can take your HSRs and shove them up your A-N-U-S!" Owen stormed out of the conference room, followed by his astonished wife and daughter. That was the last time they stepped into McHopners Manor. Penney was proud of her father for stepping up to bat for her. She, too, did not think HSRs or any cancer drug would cure her "spiritual" advancing age disorder. Because of this embarrassing outburst, the Millers turned to the Woodburn Center, where they first met Dr. Barraza, for support.

* * *

5:35 p.m.

After dropping Penney Miller off at the research center—and fielding several other calls—Julian arrived home to the same draining routine he and Lilli had settled into. A blast of arctic air greeted him as he entered, but the chill wasn't in the air. It lingered in the silence, in Lilli's eyes. For nearly two months, their home had felt hollow, a void born of his infidelity. He believed it was easier to uphold the facade of a happy marriage than risk losing the single-story home he cherished. Meanwhile, Lilli had no one to turn to. Her entire family, and even her best friend Natasha, were in Hamburg, Germany, far from the moral support she needed most.

Lilli suspected her husband of cheating with Debbie, an EMT he worked with, back in May. After Julian repeatedly came home reeking of cheap perfume, she followed him like a private detective tracking cheating spouses. Watching through a zoom lens from an empty second-story office, Lilli snapped pictures of the lovers in the back of the ambulance during a fabricated emergency call. Later, she trailed Debbie to her apartment and discovered that she, too, was married; that discovery was the final blow.

On Memorial Day, Lilli had waited long enough. She seized her chance to speak with Debbie's husband, Eugene, a muscular 257-pound, 6′4″ killing machine.

"It breaks my heart to see these pictures," he said, anger mounting. He scrawled his cell number and handed it to her. "I want you to call me the next time they meet. I'll take care of it." With a fierce nod, he slammed one fist into his palm—the crack a promise of violence.

Lilli nodded quietly, as if sealing a pact.

Like clockwork, the lovers met again the following Monday. Now armed with evidence to match her courage, Lilli had her answer to the emotional abuse she'd endured. Jaw clenched, she punched Eugene's number into her cell phone. Twenty minutes later, Eugene was at hand to lambaste Julian and Debbie. She watched the ambulance rock violently, listening, unmoved to the sounds of smashing and caterwauling. After a long silence, the rear door flung open with a reverberating thud. Eugene leaped out with such force the vehicle's rear end bounced like a toy truck on a trampoline.

"Donkey!" he spat. He left his wife moaning beside the unconscious Julian and drove off in his red gas guzzler. Lilli stood on the corner, replaying Eugene's words on the phone: *I don't want to alarm you, Lilli, but I'm going to kill that donkey!* It was the last she heard from Debbie and Eugene.

Julian changed out of his sweat-stained shirt and sat at the table, hunger gnawing at his belly. He didn't expect a reply, not after everything. From the kitchen, drawers slid open and shut. A wooden spoon scraped the pot, making his mouth water. "I hear the city's finally repaving our street next week," he said, attempting casual conversation.

Lilli said nothing. She walked briskly out of the kitchen, her face a mask of stone, and set his plate on the table: spaghetti with meat sauce, a side salad, and several pieces of toasted garlic bread. She hadn't spoken to him since the beating, but she maintained the home and cooked dinner with a gleam in her eye. Her psychiatrist reveled in her therapeutic instincts.

"Might want to leave your car on Pine or somewhere off the block. Once they start, you won't be able to get out," he said, shoveling a forkful of pasta in his mouth and savoring the beef as it went down. Lilli ignored him as she prepared the trash for tomorrow morning's pickup. She hefted the bag and slipped out the side door, the weight pulling at her shoulder. Outside, the garbage bag slipped from her fingers and hit the concrete, spilling two empty cans of dog food—odd, since they didn't own a dog.

Given the state of things, Julian knew he was in the doghouse for life.

* * *

8:20 p.m.

Penney's battle with rapid aging made her the most popular kid at the Woodburn Center. The other children quickly warmed up to her peculiar laugh and snow-white hair. Though she had her own room, it rarely stayed quiet—kids often slipped in, drawn by her psychic stories and strange charm. That night, six children clustered around her, two of them lucky enough to ride shotgun on her mattress.

"Tell us another story, Auntie Penney," said a young girl dealing with cystic fibrosis. Her hair was brushed back under a red bandana, and her round glasses gave her a vintage charm.

"I know a good one. Let me tell you about the FBI coming to visit me one day," Penney said with a mischievous grin. Even the nurse who sat quietly in a corner straightened in her seat to listen.

"Oh no!" the girl said. "Did they come to take you away?" She stared at Penney in awe.

Amusement touched the corners of Penney's lips as she softly cackled. "They came to take me away, but not to jail. Listen . . ."

Saturday, September 11, 2004. 1:37 p.m.

Penney was ten years old and already an accomplished cellist, thanks to her studies at the music conservatory. Her lessons were funded by people she had aided with her psychic ability. She dreamed of performing with a symphony in Cincinnati, near her hometown of Fort Shawnee, just outside Lima.

She was mid-phrase in Saint-Saëns' "The Swan" when the doorbell rang. Hoping to get through the movement uninterrupted, her father rose with annoyance. When Owen opened the door, two men in well-tailored suits stood patiently on the porch, one with a duffel bag slung over his shoulder and the other holding a leather portfolio. The heavy one presented a badge before clipping it back onto his belt.

"Mr. Miller, I'm Randall Brunelle. This is my partner, Chris Lin." He jerked a thumb at his companion, who smiled and waggled his fingers. "We're from the Federal Bureau of Investigation. May we come in?"

Owen hesitated, knowing where this interview was going. These visits always led to the same conclusion. *They're users! Always wanting something, never thinking about her condition.* Nevertheless, out of respect for the badge, he let them in and offered them something to drink.

"Bottled water would be great, thank you," the first agent said.

As Owen went for the drinks, Randall approached Penney, still attuned to the melody. Her andante rendition, with its unique twist, was divine. Surprised by her seasoned appearance, he kept his composure. "That was sensational, Miss Miller," he said, clapping his hands. "My name is Randall Brunelle." He shook her spindly hand with a gentle grip.

Young Miss Miller's penetrating gaze locked onto Randall's. "Don't buy that new car," she warned. Her words hung in the air. "There will be a worldwide recall to fix the oil consumption problem caused by faulty pistons."

Randall gaped at Penney's ability. With just one touch, she saw straight into his mind, unmasking desires and fears he barely acknowledged. The fact that she knew he was in the market for a new car was extraordinary. Unable to contain himself, he let out a nervous chuckle.

Chris elbowed Randall aside and extended his hand. "Hi, I'm Chris," he said eagerly. Penney took his hand. With a knowing smile, she shook her head. "If you want to propose, you'd better do it now," she murmured, her eyes twinkling with mischief. “Otherwise, your best friend will beat you to it.”

Dumbfounded by the revelation, Chris was torn between disbelief and amazement. Before he could gather his thoughts, a voice broke the tension.

“Gentlemen, I see you’ve met my daughter, Penney,” Owen said, handing each of them a bottle of water. He knew she’d read them from the glazed look in their eyes.

“Mr. Miller, I’ll cut to the chase,” said Brunelle, twisting off the bottle cap and taking a long swig. “We’ve hit a wall on a stubborn case. We’d like your daughter to help us solve it.”

Owen’s face tightened, and he rubbed his neck. “Gentlemen, we would love to help every Tom, Dick, and Harry who knocks on our door. As you can see, my daughter is not in any condition to—”

“Dad, I don’t mind,” Penney interjected, her voice resolute. All eyes turned to the girl who looked sixty.

“Honey, you know what happens when you look into the future,” he said, his eyes pleading with her to reconsider.

“I know, Dad. But if I’m going to die of old age, why shouldn’t I die knowing I helped people along the way?”

Owen smiled at his charming daughter. She always thought of others, even at the expense of herself. Her genuine motives made him proud. Reluctantly, he stepped aside.

Penney clasped her hands and asked, “Well then, what can you tell me about this case?”

“It involves a missing person named Alexander Blackwell,” Chris said, digging into a battered brown portfolio he treasured for its leather aroma. He produced a snapshot of Alex with his father, Hunter, in a sparring match. Alex looked no older than fifteen and was extraordinarily handsome. Penney studied his blue eyes, the window to his soul, but felt nothing stir inside her.

"Do you have something that belongs to him, maybe a handkerchief or a tie?" she asked, her tone flat with quiet defeat.

Chris rummaged through the duffel bag. "All we have is this shoe left at the scene of a jewelry store robbery. The guard dog managed to pull it off the perpetrator's foot, and we believe it belongs to Alex. Unfortunately, the dog didn't survive the encounter."

Penney reached for the black loafer and fingered its tassel. She read the manufacturer's name, examined the sole's markings, then raised it to her nose to sniff for lingering scent. After a moment of silent concentration, she murmured, "I smell . . . a corpse."

Randall and Chris exchanged a look. They were onto something—and anything was better than nothing. Chris opened his laptop and clicked on a file. "There's been a significant number of robberies near Long Island over the past decade, totaling $3.5 million." Owen leaned in at the mention of the losses. "This is surveillance video of the bank in Massapequa, Long Island. Similar videos from high-end department stores and jewelry stores all show the same flaw."

Grainy footage played, date and time blinking in the corner. Monochrome rows of safe deposit boxes lined the walls, each metal door bearing a combination lock that guarded the vault's treasures. Dim lights cast secrecy over the room, broken by the faint hum of the air conditioner. Suddenly, an object appeared out of nowhere.

"What is that?" Penney cried, leaning forward to see better.

Chris hit the pause button. "*That* . . . is the top of someone's head with a black ski mask."

"I believe this guy knows where the power switches are at each location," Randall said.

"Or he knows how to shut down the surveillance cameras," Chris interrupted. "We have yet to see a break-in."

Randall rewound to just before the thief appeared. "Other surveillance videos show the same hiccup. First, there's nothing, and then he just appears."

"What makes you think the thief is Alex Blackwell?" she asked.

Randall leaned forward, shoulders hunched. "We got a partial fingerprint from a tool he left at a jewelry store. We're certain it belongs to Alex; it matched prints from a shoe entered as evidence in a 1970s case, when he was a stock boy at a convenience store."

Penney looked up in surprise. "You mean there's another shoe involved in this case?!"

The two agents chuckled.

"Whoever he is, this guy must have an extensive shoe collection," said Randall, shaking his head. "Unfortunately, his family knows nothing about his whereabouts; he was a very private individual. To stop his spree, we've set up battery-powered cameras at several jewelry stores. However, these sophisticated burglaries have mysteriously halted in the last week. If at all possible, we'd like you to help us bring him in for questioning." His eyes narrowed, watching Penney for hesitation.

Penney focused on the screen again. The man in black moved toward the lockboxes and took some tools from a pouch on his belt. Someone entered the vault and startled him before he could punch the lockbox. The man in the mask dropped both tools and bolted, elbowing the bank teller against the steel wall.

"I need those tools!" Penney jumped to her feet, pointing at the screen. The FBI agents laughed and high-fived each other. From the duffel bag, Chris pulled out the hammer and steel punch abandoned by the burglar.

Matching the agents' excitement, Penney stepped forward. Her dry, slow-healing hands traced every nook and cranny of the tools. She closed her eyes and breathed in the scent that all living creatures emanate. "This man is eight feet under." Chris and Randall looked at each other, baffled. "I don't believe he's dead," she continued. "He's been crying out for help for the last four days. If he's alive, he's not in good shape."

“Where can we find him?” asked Randall.

“Gentlemen,” Owen said, jumping into the conversation in his characteristically blatant manner. “What kind of silly-ass question is that? It’s not as simple as you think!”

Randall could see the investigation was beginning to wear Penney down. “I’m truly sorry if we’re being pushy, Mr. Miller. I just got excited about getting a break in this case.”

Penney appeared weak, and her voice began to quiver. “I can only tell you what I see,” she said, breathing hard. “This place is the most beautiful cemetery in the country.” Owen helped his daughter toward the sofa and planted a tender kiss on her forehead. She gave Randall a feeble smile. “It’s not your average cemetery. It’s an arboretum.”

Chris was already on the line when Randall yanked the phone from his ear. “This is Randall! I want a list of every cemetery in the nation, east to west, including cemeteries that are no longer operational, and don’t exclude Indian Reservations! . . .

“I don’t *care* how long the list is! I want a file emailed within the next couple of hours! . . .

“Well, then tell them to get off their asses and get started on it! . . .

“And make sure you get pictures of them, too!” Randall handed the phone back to Chris.

“I couldn’t have said it better myself,” Chris said with a sarcastic smirk.

Randall shook Owen’s hand vigorously. “Mr. Miller, you and your daughter have been a tremendous help. Chris and I are heading back to the hotel to do some research.” He shifted his weight and stroked his chin, carefully considering how to pose his question. “Once we zero in on the location, would it be possible to take your daughter with us for additional help? Of course, you’re welcome to come along as well. My department will cover all expenses.”

Owen looked to Penney. She nodded. "There are some mounting medical bills," he hinted.

"What are you talking about, Mr. Miller? As of today, you no longer have any medical bills," said Randall, smiling broadly. He'd risk a reprimand from his department captain to solve this case.

Owen smiled.

Early next morning, Randall, Chris, Owen, and Penney boarded a private plane bound for Republic Airport on Long Island. The two agents had sifted through thousands of potential locations. Randall was about to call it a night when he read about White Blossoms Cemetery. From the internet, they learned that it was a woodland garden sanctuary crafted to recreate the ambiance of a natural forest. With this significant information, Randall and Chris felt confident they had the right site: a beautiful cemetery that wasn't a cemetery. Randall called the Millers with the exciting news shortly after 3:30 a.m. and arranged transportation to the airport.

It was a hectic morning for Brunelle and Lin. While the Millers enjoyed breakfast at a café, the two FBI agents hastily made plans to exhume the most recent burial, a well-to-do entrepreneur named Kathryn Foster. Randall tracked down the deceased's next of kin, two children named Erik and Stacey Foster, who were stunned to learn that the FBI had requested a disinterment. Stacey put up a big fight over the phone, claiming it was sacrilegious to disturb a fresh tomb and ranting about how the coffin was encased in steel. Randall sensed she was hiding something.

When Erik and Stacey arrived in a sleek, high-performance sports car, Chris Lin planted his hands on his hips and said, "Will you look at that? We're in the wrong business."

Randall flicked away the toothpick he had been chewing on. "Wrong business, my ass. That's blood money."

By two o'clock, the same excavator that buried the massive casket was reclaiming it from the earth. It gently set the oversized metal casing onto the ground with a long hiss.

Stacey hooked a wayward lock of hair behind her ear. "Mr. Brunelle, what you are doing is wrong. Let the dead rest in peace!" she hollered.

Randall's eyes skimmed her wrist, noting a dozen gold bracelets of assorted designs. Her arched eyebrows and angelic face recalled a classic Hollywood starlet. "Miss Foster, please don't interfere with government work. We believe a robbery suspect is inside this tomb with your mother, may she rest in peace. You have two choices: make it easy for us, or we'll make it difficult. What's it going to be?"

As Stacey stepped aside, the striker sparked, igniting the acetylene with a pop and a hiss. A yellow flame flared on the torch. Several minutes later, six men lifted the metal lid. Randall and Chris stood by the coffin, handkerchiefs pressed to their noses as they recalled a previous exhumation of a young man found near railroad tracks—and came prepared. Randall nodded for the men to open the lid. Everyone held their breath, with the agents anticipating the end of a long search.

Stacey jammed her purse under one arm and craned her neck, her silver pendant swaying against her ivory silk top. Her heart ran double time, evident in her fidgeting. Penney had focused on her from the start, intrigued by the peculiar agitation no one else seemed to notice.

The workers stood at each end of the coffin and lifted the lid. At the sudden rush of fresh air, a body lunged upward, gasping for air. With arms flailing, Alexander Blackwell unleashed a horrifying moan born of the dead. His arms flung around Chris, and everyone gasped and stepped back in horror, including Erik, who fell on his buttocks. Owen pulled Penney in close to shield her from the macabre scene of the dead returning to life. One assistant wet his pants. "Santo Dios!" his partner cried before darting away.

"Get it off! Get it off me!" Chris bellowed. His eyes were wild and panicked, and his face went chalk-white.

Despite his racing heart, Randall struck the corpse until it collapsed back into the coffin. Alex's body twitched and jerked in his own filth. As the reek of Kathryn's decaying body wafted over the small crowd, Chris let out a strangled cry, fell back, and scurried away on all fours to escape from the damned coffin.

Randall whistled sharply at the waiting ambulance, then turned to the dispersing crowd, arms raised. "Remain calm, everyone! This is a natural reflex. The body's been confined in a tight space for five days!"

Stacey glared at her brother, the only one chuckling after everyone else had been spooked. She leaned in, her voice low and hostile. "Can you at least try to act like a grown-up?" Her stare lingered until his smirk faded. But even as she silenced him, fear clenched her stomach. *How had Alex survived? Days sealed inside a coffin, no air, no light—how was he still breathing? Considering his state of mind and health, can he still clear?*

With all the focus on Erik, Randall jumped at the opportunity to interrogate him. "Mr. Foster," he said, escorting him to one side. "Would you mind telling me how you got Alexander Blackwell into the coffin?"

Erik stopped snickering. "You're out of your fuckin' mind if you think I'm responsible for this debacle," he replied, yanking his arm out of the detective's grasp.

"I think you know more about this than you'd like to admit," Randall insisted.

Erik ground his teeth. "I see why you and your partner haven't cracked this case," his left eye twitching.

Oblivious to the escalating dispute, Chris called out, "Randall, come check this out!"

Randall broke away from Erik and approached the coffin, handkerchief pressed to his nose. Between Alexander and the deceased lay a large sack—one Chris had just pulled from beneath Alex's torso, its fabric smeared and crumpled. "Jewelry?" he asked, bewildered.

"Very expensive jewelry," Chris said, lifting a necklace. "Do you think it's our stolen gems?"

Randall turned to him, perplexed. "That doesn't make any sense."

"That's because you're not one of the family," Stacey said contemptuously. "My mother's wish was to be buried with her jewelry. I'll never understand why, but we honored it nonetheless. That's why the coffin was encased in metal, as a way to deter burglars from disturbing the dead."

3:07 p.m. The emergency medical technician jumped out of the ambulance and quickly helped his partner lower the gurney. They took hold of Alex Blackwell, whose ghoulish face sent a chill through them, and gently placed his convulsing body onto the stretcher. Unbeknownst to them, an empty 3-liter oxygen canister remained in the casket, along with a hollow flashlight that slipped deeper behind the white silk pillow during the transfer. After strapping Alex down, they pushed the gurney into the rear of the vehicle and locked it into place.

"This is EMT Michaels calling in from ambulance twenty-four. We are transporting a convulsing male patient, mid-forties. Skin is pale, pupils are unresponsive, blood pressure 78/40, heart rate 110. He seems to be extremely dehydrated. IV fluids will be administered. ETA is fourteen minutes. Requesting immediate assistance upon arrival. Over."

"Copy that, EMT Michaels. A team will be ready to receive the patient for immediate care. Please proceed directly to the trauma bay. Over."

On the way to Saddle Rock Hospital, the medical technician was preparing an IV when he inadvertently dropped the needle packet. He bent to retrieve it, and when he rose, his breath caught. Alex's body had vanished! Only the wrinkled, soiled linen remained, cradled by the limp stretcher straps. Michaels popped his head through the divider and shouted, “He’s gone!”

The ambulance screeched to a halt, sending loose items cascading to the floor.

When Randall answered the call from the ambulance driver a few seconds later, his face turned several shades of red. “What do you mean you lost the body?!”

Stacey froze; her mouth parted in disbelief.

The little girl with cystic fibrosis scrunched her nose. “Didn’t the dead body stink?”

Penney pinched her nose. “It sure did,” she sang. Teasingly, she leaned in close and whispered, “It stunk like your butt.”

The children laughed. Even the nurse gave an indulgent smile.

“Tell us another story, Auntie Penney!” said a young boy, surreptitiously rubbing the patch over his left eye.

“My butt doesn’t stink,” the little girl pouted, crossing her arms and sticking out her bottom lip.

“I will tell you the last one for tonight. The story involves the television night show host Craig Lennox, which occurred one week prior,” said Penney mysteriously.

“My butt doesn’t stink,” the soft voice insisted.

New York City. Friday, September 3, 2004. 1:00 p.m.

Three . . . Two . . . One . . . Cue.

Talk show host Craig Lennox tapped his prompt cards on the mahogany desk and beamed at the camera. “We’re back,” he said. “Our next guest is a genuine psychic, hailing from Fort Shawnee, Ohio.”

The audience applauded, and a few locals from her hometown cheered aloud.

"Fort Shawnee, Ō-hī-ōōō," he repeated, plastering a smile across his face. "That's a funny word, isn't it? Ō-hī-ōōō. Who comes up with these names?" Craig shrugged and chuckled. "I'll never understand people. Do you understand them, Melvin?"

His sidekick, Melvin, sporting a gray porkpie hat and vintage black shades, laughed good-naturedly, holding his hands up in protest. "Don't get me involved in politics, Craig. I have enough problems," he said, playing a flat, out-of-tune note on his saxophone.

The audience laughed on cue.

"Seriously, folks, our next guest is from Fort Shawnee, Ohio. She's a psychic who has helped many people make the right decisions. Tonight, she'll put her psychic ability to work live on stage! Please give a warm round of applause for Penney Miller!"

Prompted by the off-camera sign, thunderous applause filled the studio. The camera crane swooped down to zoom in on Penney, who looked stunning in a short mauve beaded jacket dress and matching ankle-strap shoes. Craig Lennox rose, shook her hand, and gestured to the seat beside his desk. Despite her million-dollar smile, traces of tears shimmered in her eyes.

"Penney?" he asked, noticing a shining droplet on her cheek. He leaned forward and studied the network of delicate creases on her face, like the intricate lines on a well-worn map. "You've been crying. Was it something I said?"

Penney tugged a tissue, wiped her eyes, and said, "You crack me up, Craig. I couldn't stop laughing backstage."

"You love laughter, don't you, Penney?"

"Laughter makes the world a better place." She smiled at the audience. "I love comedy. I wish I were a comedian with a show and a desk like this one."

Penney caressed his desk like a game-show prize model, provoking another round of chuckles.

This woman is trying to take my job, he thought. A flicker of concern crossed his face. With a playful smirk, he reached into his desk drawer and pulled out a folding fan. He tapped her shoulder lightly and teased, “Back! Back!”

Laughter echoed like applause.

Craig waited for the crowd to simmer down before turning to Penney with a grin. “You know how some people have signature catchphrases?” he said, gesturing to the audience. “Well, Penney here has a signature laugh.”

Penney’s peal of laughter rang through the studio: “HAA-HAA-HAA-haa-haa!” It was akin to a diminishing sequence of tones, a true decrescendo. “Are you happy now?” she asked, wiping away more tears. “You’ve got me laughing in front of these people. You couldn’t get enough backstage, could you?”

In response, Melvin blew a riff on his saxophone that perfectly mimicked her cackle, and the audience again erupted into hysterics.

Craig Lennox directed his attention to the audience and said, “Let me tell you what happened backstage. I’m in my dressing room when I hear this loud, strange cackle.” He shook his head as he tried to contain himself, his fist pounding the desktop. The crowd bubbled with excitement. “I run out in my underwear.” He paused for comedic effect, and a new wave of laughter erupted from the crowd. “And I ask, ‘Who brought the goose?’”

The audience roared. Penney released another signature goose call while Melvin followed along with his saxophone. Craig pounded on his desk with unbridled mirth and allowed a commercial break.

Three . . . two . . . one . . . cue.

“We are back with Penney Miller, a well-known psychic from Fort Shawnee, Ō-hī-ōōō. Hey Penney, Penney,” said Craig, tapping her shoulder and then plucking a wooden duck call from his drawer. He blew five times, and she followed suit.

Tearing up, Craig laughed and jiggled in his seat like a bobblehead on a bumpy joyride. Melvin chuckled, shaking his head, his teeth gleaming above a graying soul patch. "You're crazy, Craig."

The host's demeanor shifted, urging the audience to settle down. "Penney, how long have you been a psychic?"

"I've been getting mental images since I was five," she said, crossing her legs. "And making predictions since I was seven."

"I see."

"At that age, I had no idea what the visions meant, nor could I explain them to my parents."

"So, you've been getting mental pictures over the last ten years?" he said, arching an eyebrow, knowing the crowd would react.

The audience buzzed. Penney, who looked nearly seventy, claimed she'd been psychic for just ten years. She started at age five! The math didn't add up!

"That is correct, Craig."

He shot her a sidelong glance. "How old are you, Penney?"

"I'm fifteen years *young*," she corrected him.

Gasps echoed as Penney revealed her age. Silence fell, then a rising tide of murmurs. It took minutes to settle. The host watched, unmoved, as the crowd absorbed the shock.

"Tell the audience about your condition," Craig finally said, resting his chin on his fist.

"The doctors diagnosed me with progeria, a rare disorder that causes rapid aging. But my parents and I believe my condition has nothing to do with genetic defects. Instead, we think my rapid aging is due to my dipping into the spirit world, or timeline, something like that."

"That sounds reasonable to me. If I saw a ghost, I'm sure I'd go from fifty-five to eighty in about two seconds!" The crowd laughed on cue. "Let's select some audience members to participate in today's fascinating topic, extrasensory perception. Penney, why don't you pick someone who could use your help?"

Half of the audience raised their hands in response.

"It would be my pleasure, Craig. Let's start with the woman in the burgundy sweater in the fourth row," she said, pointing toward the center section of the studio. Camera one panned and zoomed in on the woman's pleading expression.

"Thank you, Miss Penney. I got two tickets for this show weeks ago, but my daughter wanted to spend some time with her father instead."

Craig gawked and did a double take for the camera. "How is that possible? What could be better than spending an afternoon with Craig Lennox?" The audience cheered.

The woman gave an embarrassed smile. "This morning, I woke up petrified. In fact, I'm still shaking." She lifted both hands, fingers twitching slightly. "It feels like something awful is going to happen to my daughter. I was so nervous I couldn't eat breakfast."

Cameras two and three followed Penney offstage, the microphone crane hovering overhead. The woman made her way toward the center aisle, where they met at the same precise time. Penney clutched her hand and asked, "What is your name, my dear?"

"Raelynn. Raelynn Hawkins."

Penney saw the terror in her eyes. She knew everyone possessed some degree of clairvoyance, enough to sense danger. Determined to put her mind at ease, Penney skipped the pleasantries and focused on locating her daughter through remote viewing, which oftentimes gave her a clear mental image minutes before the event itself unfolded. Her head swayed slowly from side to side, eyes blinking rapidly. Then she smiled; she had found the little girl. But the smile quickly faded, replaced by sorrow, and a ripple of alarm ran through the audience.

"I am sorry, Ms. Hawkins," said Penney, wiping her tears. The woman began to weep, sensing something terrible. "Your daughter passed away at 12:20 today, about an hour ago. She was trampled in a panicked crowd."

Raelynn screamed, "No, NO! Not my baby!" Her legs buckled, but someone from the aisle seat leapt forward, catching her as she sobbed into his arms. Tears streamed down her face, silencing the room with a grief so palpable it soaked the air.

"Do you know where your husband is right now?" asked Penney softly.

After a deep, trembling breath, Raelynn gulped, "Abilene, Texas. My daughter, Mary, is spending the week with my ex-husband, and today they went to the circus." She buried her face in the stranger's shoulder, sobbing anew.

"Abilene, Texas?" Penney leaned forward, raising an eyebrow and puckering her lips. "Did you say Abilene, Texas?"

Raelynn nodded, unable to speak.

"That's Central Standard Time!" Penney whooped, startling the crowd with her sudden burst of joy.

Raelynn looked up, confused. "I don't understand," she said, swiping at her tear-streaked face.

"Ms. Hawkins, *we're* on Eastern Time!" Penney checked her watch. "We've got seven minutes until 12:20 Central time!"

A shocked silence fell over the audience as this new revelation unfolded. For the first time, a palpable sense of urgency filled the air, electrifying the atmosphere. With bated breath, they perched on the edge of their seats, gripping the armrests. Raelynn's daughter may yet be saved! Hope lit her face as the woman in the burgundy sweater fumbled for her phone.

After several rings, Raelynn wailed, "She's not answering! Mary, answer the phone!" She redialed with a trembling hand. Around her, the audience stirred in their seats.

Pointing at her watch, Penney reminded her that six minutes remained. Owen emerged to accompany his daughter, whose face was pale and weak. The phone rang again, and someone finally answered!

"Mary!" Raelynn shouted.

"Mom, is that you?" Mary said, her words barely audible over the circus noise.

"Where are you?" implored Raelynn.

"I'm with Dad," replied Mary, confusion and alarm creeping into her voice.

"I know you're with your father, but where are you?"

"We're at the circus, Mom. Is everything all right?" asked Mary, reflecting the fear in her mother's tone.

Ms. Hawkins, who had switched her name from Hennessey after the divorce, repeated her daughter's response to keep Penney in the loop.

Penney hushed the audience with a wave of her hand, then directed her attention back to the distressed mother. "What is she doing now?"

"Honey, what are you doing now?" Raelynn asked. Her pulse quickened as the seconds pressed on.

"I'm in the bleachers at Milagro Circus. Dad went for popcorn about two minutes ago, so I couldn't answer the phone earlier. Mom, why are you repeating everything I'm saying?" asked the bewildered girl.

"Mary, listen to me. Do exactly what I say. Do *not* do anything else. Sit still and *do not* leave your seat. Do you understand?" After receiving an affirmative but perplexed response, Raelynn said, "Honey, tell me what is happening now."

"Two men are forcing an elephant to sit in the center ring. Oh no! The pole is too close!" cried Mary.

"Mary, what is going on?!" No answer. "Mary!!"

"The tent pole is breaking! It's caving in!" she screamed, her voice cracking with panic.

"Honey, stay in your seat! Promise me you won't move, no matter what! Do you understand? Don't leave your seat . . . Mary!!"

"I promise!" Her terrified cry crackled over the speaker . . .

Panic spread like wildfire as the tent collapsed. Screams filled the air, blending with wood snapping. People abandoned their seats, turning the joyful crowd into a panicked, shoving mob.

"Mom, everyone is getting up and running away!" Mary squawked. She hesitated. "I think I have to leave now."

"No! Mary, don't run with the crowd!"

Beneath the collapsing tent, faces etched with fear as the crowd trampled one another in their haste to escape. In vain, the performers tried to restore order, but their cries for calm went unheard.

Mary's phone plummeted to the floor when someone bumped into her, then it skittered away when someone else kicked it. At first, she didn't know what to do, but then she stood . . .

Raelynn heard a trumpet blast, wild and furious, like an enraged elephant, followed by splintering wood, screams, and pounding feet. "Mary!" she cried again, her face contorted. She heard the familiar sound of shotgun fire, the shock in the crowd, and then an eerie silence. Smoke and dust curled in her mind's eye, blurring the chaos. "Mary," she whimpered into the cell phone.

"I'm here, Mom." Mary sounded shaky and out of breath. "I dropped my phone when somebody bumped me, and I grabbed it as soon as the crowd settled."

Delighted to hear her daughter's voice, Raelynn looked at Penney and yelled, "She's all right!"

Tears streaming, Penney hugged Raelynn, knowing she'd saved another life. Her watch read 1:20 EST. Overwhelmed with emotion, her legs weakened, but Owen caught her before she could strike the floor.

Due to its intense nature, this episode of "The Craig Lennox Show" never aired.

* * *

Wednesday, July 20, 2005. 12:05 a.m.

Mr. Miller was the only one left after the tales and had requested to stay the night. As he dozed in the recliner, his breathing slowed into a gentle rhythm, and a soft snore escaped his lips, filling the room with calm. His fingers twitched once, then stilled.

Penney flipped through channels and paused on a news station. The anchor for WPND-TV wore a chic three-button pinstripe jacket and brown slacks, tailored to flatter her full figure. That night's segment, prerecorded two months earlier, was titled: *"The Origins of American Phenomena."*

> "Ann Marie Johnson here. Today, I'm standing beside what might be the most amazing grandfather clock ever built. This floor clock, as it was known in the early 1800s, has a fascinating history. Joining us today is the proud owner of this timeless piece, Fazal Hickaby."
>
> "Zitcaby," Fazal corrected meekly.
>
> "Mr. Zitcaby, enlighten us about this wonderful mechanism, now on display at Fazal's Dry Cleaning on Ardmore Street in Richmond, Indiana."
>
> He cleared his throat. "Well, the story, as told by my maternal grandfather, begins in New Brunswick at the start of the nineteenth century. Seventeen men died at the hands of a deputy of the king's court for illegally cutting down trees."
>
> Fazal held out one hand as if gripping the barrel of a gun and curled his finger around the imaginary trigger with the other. "Hezekiah Coopers and his militia surrounded the illegal loggers and let them have it! Rat-tat-tat-tat-tat!" he said,

narrowing his eyes and sweeping the fictitious weapon around the room.

"Sounds like they were using machine guns," said Ann Marie, her forehead creasing.

"Yup." Fazal nodded, running a finger around the inside of his too-tight collar. "Thompson submachine guns, to be exact." Seeming more at ease, Fazal leaned forward and peered into the camera, his left eye looming large in the frame. "Legend has it," he said, lowering his voice as if the clock might overhear, "a group of *fifty* men were massacred on the stockpile of timber." He lifted his hands into monster claws to spook the viewers. "Blood and guts splattered across the freshly cut timber like a lawn sprinkler."

With a confident nod, he directed his attention to the clock and tenderly rubbed its side. "After crafting the clock with scraps from the cursed timber, death and destruction followed like an evil omen. British ships built with the cursed wood sank, and the warehouse where this clock was built burned to the ground. The only relic to survive the fire is this gem before me."

"She's certainly bewitching," Ann Marie said, stepping closer to admire the intricate woodwork.

"I wouldn't get too close," the dry cleaner warned, extending one arm to shield the clock. "The poor fool who bought this clock died the day it was delivered. You wouldn't want to be the next unfortunate fool, would you?"

Ann Marie quickly shook her head. "So, how on earth did you end up with the clock?"

"My grandfather purchased the piece after the death of the . . . unfortunate fool. It remained inoperative for many years, but he had hoped to fix it someday. Unfortunately, he never did. It wasn't until I came along that this masterpiece came to life."

"You mean, it just started working on its own?" the cameraman asked.

A flabbergasted look crossed the dry cleaner's face. "You see these two hands?" he asked, wiggling his short, stubby fingers at the camera. "I fixed it!" said Fazal, his voice rising. "I brought it back to life with my own two hands! You know, many people believe this old clock is still haunted." Fazal's eyes spread as wide as his tall tale.

"That was a spellbinding story," Anna Marie said. She smiled at the camera.

"That's it!" Penney shouted.

Owen snorted, startled out of sleep. His stomach churned aggressively, and soon, nausea took residence. Panic widened his eyes as his clothes and hair fluttered around him. Lunging forward from the recliner, he hit the floor with a hard thud while his body continued to pull in one direction. Scrambling, he clung to the bed railing, bracing against the invisible current that clawed at his body.

Penney felt it too, but the motion sickness pills she'd taken earlier dulled the edge.

"What's happening to me?" Owen cried, his eyes bugging out. His shirttails flapped like a tattered flag on a blustery day. Then he puked.

Groaning, Penney rose, trembling as she reached for a cup of water sitting undisturbed on the overbed table. The water spilled onto the floor as she lifted the cup. Undeterred, she crept toward her father, careful not to slip on the vomit. Now that they had entered the time drift, it was imperative to bring her father up to speed.

"Dad, take two of these. They'll help with your nausea," she said, handing him two motion sickness pills.

Owen popped the pills into his mouth and then downed the sloshing water, soaking his chin and shirt. Penney helped him to his recliner before revealing what she understood about the world's drift and probable destruction.

"Dad, don't speak. Just listen," Penney said. He looked ready to lose his stomach, again. "Something catastrophic has disrupted the time continuum. Time has been repeating," she said, letting the empty cup drift. "We've already made this journey four times. It resets at 8:15 this morning. I've been working on a theory, but couldn't say anything until I was sure. I believe a grandfather clock in Richmond, Indiana, is causing these time loops."

Owen shut his eyes, but the nausea lingered. "Is the rest of the world feeling this strange effect too?"

"We're the only ones crossing the line, but it won't be long before the rest of the world is affected. It's a domino effect. Once we alter someone's path, it pulls them into the temporal slip, and the disruption spreads."

"I still don't understand," he said, unable to meet his daughter's eyes.

Penney took her father's trembling hand. "We should be asleep. Instead, we've slipped out of sync with history. Think of it like a river; we're fighting against the current. That's why our hair, skin, clothing, or anything we move out of place pulls with it."

Owen looked at her, eyes unfocused like an inebriated man. "Are you sure about this, Penney?"

"Dad, I'm going on my gut instinct. Have I ever been wrong before?"

She's right. She's never been wrong.

"What will happen if we do nothing?" he asked, shifting uncomfortably.

"Now that the ripple effect has begun, I'm afraid the universe will cease to exist at 8:15. There'll be no more loops."

Owen was silent, letting the gravity of her words settle. He knew they might be out of hope, but he felt a moral duty to try. "Life is precious. No matter how difficult it seems, we must set things right. How can we fix it?"

"You must drive me to Richmond, Indiana, without being seen. Even a slight distraction will cause someone to deviate from their course, affecting hundreds, then thousands, and eventually millions of people. Once there, we must dismantle the grandfather clock."

"That's impossible!" He shot to his feet, his shirt whipping behind him. "We can't possibly get to Richmond without crossing someone's path!"

"We have to try, Dad," she pleaded, her eyes weary but resolute. "It's our only hope."

"If we're going to do this, we need something to hide our hair and cheeks. The fluttering will attract attention." He struggled to his feet and said, "Wait right here."

12:35 a.m.

Owen peeked out the door, checked the hallway, and slipped into the corridor. He was gone only minutes, but it felt endless. When he returned, he held several items in his hands.

"Where did you get those without being seen?" Penney asked.

"From an unattended supply cart at the other end, away from the nurse's station." He held out a hand. "Here. Put it on."

* * *

12:50 a.m.

"I can't believe we're doing this," Owen said as he peered around the door. One nurse sat at the station with her back to them, absorbed in a phone call. He guessed the other nurses were making their nightly rounds. Whatever the case, their timing was perfect.

Wearing a green surgeon's cap and mask to conceal his flailing hair, Owen, followed closely by a similarly dressed Penney, hurried past the station and turned left toward the elevators. The change in direction caught them by surprise as they found themselves walking with the current, their steps quickening to keep up with the flow. Owen felt like a kid running down a steep hill, unable to stop.

Penney struggled to keep her bare butt covered as the hospital gown fluttered ahead of her. She was losing a prodigious amount of integrity. Owen jabbed the elevator button. Moments later, the doors vibrated open, groaning against their guide rails. "Come on, come on, come on!" he shouted, hammering the button to hurry the close.

Footsteps echoed down the corridor.

"Hold the elevator, please," a woman shouted.

Owen slammed against the steel wall, shooting Penney a concerned look. As the doors slid shut, they heard an empty bucket hit the floor and roll in a clanking loop. "She's drifting, isn't she?"

Penney nodded, her voice low. "She should've been on this elevator. Now she's caught in the ripple."

"We knew this would happen, sweetheart."

Her finger hovered for a moment before she pressed the STOP button. The elevator screeched and jerked violently before coming to a halt, prompting a light panel to drop from its casing and swing precariously above their heads. Dust rained down, clouding the air.

"What are you doing?" asked Owen in alarm, watching the light panel swing.

"We have to help her," Penney said, her eyes reflecting her pain.

"Honey, we can't save every person who crosses our path. You don't have that many pills! Besides, the best way to help everyone is to stop the grandfather clock from destroying the universe!"

She knew he was right. If only she could give the woman a pill, but time was slipping away. Fighting back tears, Penney pressed the lobby button. The lift shook side to side, fighting the drift's impressive pull as it continued its descent. Owen feared the cable might snap under the strain; not until they reached the lobby did he breathe freely.

When the doors finally slid open, Penney led the way down the long, sterile hallway, struggling to keep her balance. As they approached the lobby, she heard voices from around the corner. Fear clawed her throat as she nudged her father behind a tall palm. In haste, he bumped the planter, nudging it out of place. The plant's fronds thrashed to life. Owen felt a rush of adrenaline as they pressed their backs against the wall. Penney placed a finger to her lips, turning to hush the plant. In response to her silly gesture, Owen pushed the rustling branches back against the wall to suppress the noise.

Two janitors strolled by. One steered the wringer by the mop handle, its rubber wheels gliding smoothly over the tiled floor, while the other carried a bright yellow CAUTION: WET FLOOR sign. They walked past, immersed in chatter, unaware of the strangers flanking the quivering palm.

Owen watched them disappear around a corner and turned to see Penney staring cross-eyed at a lock of hair that had slipped from under her cap. Together, they breathed a sigh of relief.

"That was close," Owen whispered, a nervous smile easing a little of the tension on his face.

Penney twisted the lock of hair back under the cap. Retaking the lead, she inched along the wall and slowly peered out into the lobby.

At the reception desk, a weary security guard hunched over a crossword puzzle. His back was turned toward Penney as he tapped his pencil in a steady rhythm, grappling with a clue. Getting past him unnoticed was impossible. Though she hated putting him in danger, Penney led her father through the lobby, sprinting like carpet clowns chasing a tiny runaway car. As they passed the desk, she plopped a motion sickness pill on the counter and called over her shoulder, "This'll help with your nausea!"

Caught by surprise, the security guard looked up. Vertigo struck before he could utter a word. His pear-shaped body quivered. The crossword slipped from his hands, pages rattling as it drifted northwest with the current. His comb-over slapped against his prominent forehead, fluttering like ribbons in the breeze, while his cheeks bubbled like a pot of pea soup.

Owen and Penney's escape briefly stalled when the airlock doors refused to open. Glancing at his watch, he noted that regular operating hours had ended. But he wouldn't let that stop him from saving the world. He pried the sliding doors apart enough to let them through, then did the same with the exterior doors. Owen took the lead, wobbling across the empty parking lot. Grateful that no patients were around, they moved carefully, trying not to draw attention.

Penney giggled. "Dad, do you know the theme song for *Impossible Missions*?" she hollered.

"Yeah, what about it?" he called back.

"I can't get the blasted tune out of my head!"

* * *

1:30 a.m.

Owen helped Penney into his trusty truck and shut the door with a firm click. Sliding behind the wheel, he fumbled for the key, then turned the ignition. The engine hesitated, once, twice, as if resisting the time fissure itself. Then it roared to life with a sharp backfire, coughing out a plume of black smoke from the exhaust.

In the bed, wood studs and chunks of drywall jounced with each vibration. Owen shifted into gear and pulled away, deliberately leaving the headlights off. The truck jittered down the oval driveway and came to a stop at the flagpole.

"We need to stop by the house first, Dad," Penney insisted.

"What? That'll take too long." He shook his head. "Not a chance. What if your mom wakes up and sees us? What do you even need from the house?"

"Dad, I am butt naked. I need clothes! It's impossible to run in this gown."

"Really," he teased.

Penney gave him a grave look. "Yes, really! *You* try running without mooning everyone!"

"That wouldn't be a pretty sight," he agreed with a chuckle.

"Precisely!" She rolled her eyes.

Owen groped behind the seat and found Penney's discarded gown from a previous hospital visit. "Here, put this one on backward."

Penney couldn't believe her eyes. "Great, another hospital gown!"

* * *

Northbound US Route 27, 2:30 a.m.

It took an hour to reach the highway out of Cincinnati toward Richmond. Owen and Penney had to pull over several times and duck to avoid hurling innocent people into the drift. The fewer they affected, the better. Although the chain reaction had already begun at the hospital, she knew the drift was spreading like a contagion.

Nearing Liberty, Indiana. 4:30 a.m.

"Thank you for trusting me," Penney said, placing her bony elbow on the armrest to stifle the door's squeak.

Owen remained silent as the truck jittered along the highway. Unsure what to say, he was just grateful the nausea had passed. Everything felt surreal, happening far too fast. He wished he could close his eyes and make this nightmare disappear.

"We're on our fourth loop," Penney continued. "My decision to step out of our normal paths has caused this drift. Our bodies, and everything we touch, begin to flow against the current of life." She paused to take a deep breath. "Life has been looping from an unnatural force. It is linked to a grandfather clock in Richmond, at Fazal's Dry Cleaning on Ardmore Street. At 8:15 this morning, the clock will malfunction. It will force time to retreat, then surge forward, only to arrive at the same fate: Wednesday, July 20, 2005."

Owen nodded. "At what moment in history does the loop begin?"

"I'm guessing it will resume after the grandfather clock is built."

He considered this carefully, then said, "If the grandfather clock is an antique, it could have been built in the early 1800s!"

"According to the TV interview, it *is* an antique. That could only mean," Penney said, pausing briefly to calculate in her head, "the world has lost eight hundred years due to the four loops." A moment of silence fell between them. Fearing the unknown, Penney felt responsible for the world's impending destruction. She looked at her father, who was busily digesting the revelation. "To undo the loop, we need to stop the clock before it strikes 8:15."

"And if we don't?" he asked, even though he already knew the terrible fate about to occur.

"Think of the truck's tires. They rotate smoothly—until misaligned. Then they wobble, and that wobble causes damage. The universe works the same way. Wobbling leads to chaos. Chaos breeds instability."

Owen swelled with pride at his daughter's grasp of such complex ideas. A warm smile spread as his eyes shone with affection. "If we manage to undo the loop," he said, "would *we* jump ahead eight hundred years to make up for the lost time?"

"No," she said with certainty. "Think of a river with a dam. If you remove the dam, the water doesn't leap eight hundred miles ahead. The flow will continue from where it was blocked. We just need to remove the dam."

Owen threw his daughter an impish grin. "You mean, we need to remove the damned!"

"Look out!" Penney screeched.

Owen swerved to avoid what looked like a dog darting across the road. The tires skidded into a trench with a bone-rattling thud. The truck bucked violently, missing a black locust tree by inches. The impact jolted Owen forward, slamming his forehead against the steering wheel.

Dust and gravel erupted skyward, pelting the hood with a staccato clatter like distant gunfire. His right hand brushed against the radio dial, causing it to crackle to life. A searing pain shot through his leg.

Penney sat rigid, shaken but uninjured, watching pebbles dance on the hood to a disco song blaring from the speakers.

"Dad!" She rushed to his side and turned off the radio.

"I think my leg is broken," he said, grimacing.

"Don't worry, Dad. I'll help you!" Penney jumped down and eased Owen out of the truck, stopping whenever he cried out. She grabbed two shivering 2x4s from the bed, then rummaged in the cab for a flannel shirt stuffed under the seat. After several minutes, she had fashioned a crude splint for his leg.

"You must continue by yourself, Snowflakes." Owen winced, shifting his weight as his fingers dug into the dusty ground. "If I ride in the truck, it will hurt my leg too much. Just drag me behind those bushes. I'll be okay. You can come back for me after you've saved the world." He felt awful for screwing things up. *If I'd just paid attention, kept my focus on the road, we wouldn't be wasting all this time!* The Millers had been averaging 25 miles per hour and were on the outskirts of Liberty. After two exhausting hours, they had just nineteen miles to go and only a little more than two hours left before 8:15. It can be done! She just couldn't afford any more unexpected delays.

Penney's heart skipped a beat. "I'm not sure about going solo, Dad," she said, her stomach churning at the idea.

Owen grabbed her shoulder and squeezed. "You're sixteen years old, sweetheart. You can do it. Now take me to those bushes!"

Penney knew her father was right, again. Wasting no time, she grabbed her father and dragged him through the dirt. Shrubs undulated as they brushed past. "I'll be back as soon as I can, Dad. Hang in there," she said, reluctantly leaving his side.

Owen watched with immeasurable pride as she sprinted back to the truck. "Snowflakes," he called after her, "if you don't make it in time . . ."

"I know, Dad. I love you, too." She forced a small, doleful smile.

* * *

5:46 a.m.

Fog delayed the break of dawn, fooling crickets into a chorus of mating calls well into the morning. Their chirping saturated the air with fragile tranquility.

Only fifteen minutes had passed since Penney drove off. Owen leaned back, thinking about the joy she brought to their lives. He often wondered how they could live without her. Though he knew her death was inevitable, he clung to the hope that a miracle might save her.

Owen shifted his weight slowly, careful not to worsen the strain. *If all goes according to plan*, he thought, *Penney should return in two or three hours to rush me to the hospital*. He nodded, trying to reassure himself.

Huh, the crickets have stopped chirping.

The sudden silence was like an alarm bell—nature's way of keeping everyone on their toes.

A sharp glance up. Eyes in the dark, penetrating.

Someone, or something, was sneaking up on him. Owen leaned forward and listened carefully, his heart starting to race. He realized staying alone by the roadside might not have been prudent. In the cover of darkness, something lurked in the bushes. The rustling grew louder and closer. Three shapes prowled in the dark, maybe four. The uncertainty clawed at him.

"Stay back! I have no intention of—" Without warning, a gray wolf lunged from the bushes, baring its 2-inch fangs. Two smaller wolves immediately followed the alpha male. Though wolves hadn't claimed Indiana in decades, these three moved as if they remembered it. They were a transient northern pack, seeking new territory.

Owen collapsed, a raw scream tearing from his throat as agony ripped through his shattered leg. He was oblivious to the transformation unfolding before him. Instead of fangs tearing into flesh, the wolves twisted and writhed—his presence disrupting their natural flow. They yelped and hit the ground with loud thumps. Their cheek ruffs and bushy tails vibrated independently, fear blooming in their moon-shaped eyes. The wolves snapped and howled at the wind, attempting desperately to shed whatever had invaded their furry bodies. The alpha darted away, whimpering as it collided with bushes that seemed to leap from nowhere. Alone and trembling, Owen realized he was lucky to be breathing.

* * *

2 miles north of Old Indiana 122. 6:34 a.m.

Wisps of moisture coalesced into fog as Penney pushed the truck to its limit; every muffler clack and rear panel rattle rang in her ears like a doomsday clock. Determined to stay invisible, she pulled off the road and ducked below the dashboard at the first sight of an oncoming car. Her luck ran out when she reached Endsley Road.

A small car pulled onto the highway behind her, accelerating aggressively before swinging out to pass. The driver blared the horn, then veered recklessly into her lane without warning. As the vehicle slipped into the drift, its control faltered. It swerved hard to the right, shot over the berm, and plunged into a ditch, rolling violently across the shoulder. Dust and pebbles exploded, clouding her view and holding her frozen as chaos unfolded.

Penney slammed on the brakes and jumped out, praying the driver was alive. She staggered down the slope to the groaning car, each step an effort against the time drift. Wrenching the door open, she peered inside and found a young man, mid-twenties, unconscious and dangling upside down in his seat belt. Vomit streaked the dashboard and steering wheel. He reeked of alcohol. Penney got one arm around his shoulders and managed to pop the buckle out, letting her body break his fall as she heaved him out of the car. She dragged his twitching body a safe distance away. Spurred into action by his inebriated state, she pulled the key from the ignition and flung it into the bushes. Even if he could right the car, she wouldn't let him behind the wheel again. *If he had any sense, he'd have a spare key at home.*

* * *

7:46 a.m.

US Route 27 cut through downtown Richmond, where morning fog rolled in like a stealthy predator. Tulip poplar trees, their crowns shaped like giant broccoli heads, poked through the mist. Penney breathed a sigh of relief as the truck sputtered over the railroad tracks. Driving past the fork onto 9th Street, the vehicle triggered a snowball effect that led to the most destructive day in Richmond's history.

The truck stirred the air, rippling unnatural energy through the tulip trees. Leaves trembled, branches jerked with eerie resonance. A flock of song sparrows erupted from the foliage, careening skyward in panicked disarray before spiraling down, cloaked in a suffocating sickness. On the ground, fox squirrels convulsed in desperation, clawing at their fur as if beset by a plague of unseen insects.

The unusual disturbance caught the attention of Lindsey and her two daughters, who were the first Indiana family to experience the drift. Sitting outdoors at Mingo's, where the pancakes were fluffy and the pastrami savory, Lindsey glanced over her shoulder. A sudden convulsion seized her. A lock of sandy hair tumbled from behind her ear, immediately springing to life and dancing in rhythm with her ponytail. Her frame quivered as her blouse fluttered wildly, as if stitched from jubilant butterflies.

During her spasms, Lindsey's hand smacked the coffee cup into her lap. She bellowed and, in her panic, struck her head against the patio umbrella as she leaped to her feet. Her sudden, erratic movements caught her daughters' attention. Their eyes rolled back as vertigo took hold, their bodies trembling violently. The youngest vomited across the table, narrowly missing her sister's pink vinyl jacket.

A sparrow veered into the café's massive window and struck with a sickening thud that smeared crimson streaks down the glass. The diners froze at the bloodied pane, but their reprieve was brief. They trembled feverishly, and anything moved out of place vibrated against the tables. Cries of despair filled the air, and gravity slipped away.

The panic spread to the kitchen, where the staff found themselves enveloped in a shroud of sickness. One by one, they drifted together, drawn helplessly into the undertow. Their bodies quivered as they struggled for control.

Juggling a stack of ceramic plates, the dishwasher bellowed, "Look out!" The load slipped from his hands and crashed to the floor, shattering into jagged shards that skittered across the tiles. The young man's wavy hair surged to life; it whipped and recoiled like the tentacles of a sea anemone. At the grill, a cook squawked in agony as his palm met scorching metal, never noticing his chef hat drifting weightlessly into the airstream . . .

At M Street, a biker roared past the vibrating truck and lost control after veering off his natural path. The motorcycle careened through shrubs and straight into a glass repair shop, crumpling against the bulkhead as its headlight burst like a flashbulb. Time slowed as the biker sailed headfirst through the display window. With a shattering explosion, shards of glass erupted in a glittering arc around him. His US Army Retired cap stayed firmly perched on his head, absurdly dignified amid the chaos. He hit the floor with a loud thump and was knocked unconscious. The patriotic suspenders unraveled over his shoulder and instantly whipped the air. Slivers buzzed across the floor, and his leather boots twitched, tapping out Morse code against the tile . . .

A blur of fur—that's what Arpita saw dart in front of her car. The final notes of a Hindi song left her lips as she gasped. Instinct took over. She slammed the brakes. The car shuddered to a screeching halt, and her hair, a river of black oil, slickened the air with lashes, whipping like tendrils of tar. Fear struck her Cleopatra eyes as her stomach sloshed and her limbs quivered like windblown reeds. Then, in a panic-fueled surge, her foot slammed the accelerator. The car lurched forward, its engine roaring like an unleashed wild beast. A bloodcurdling scream tore from her throat as the sedan veered uncontrollably into a building, where the airbag deployed with a forceful burst . . .

You could be next! Screamed the vibrant posters of past theatrical performers adorning the walls of the spacious dance studio. Thirty young actors moved before floor-to-ceiling mirrors that reflected bodies in motion, self-doubt, and the hunger to be seen. The polished hardwood floor gleamed beneath them, though its scuffed patches told quieter stories of missteps, breakthroughs, and the long ache of repetition.

Ethan stood front and center, ready for the spotlight. Despite the cost, he couldn't resist Roger Anderson's proposal, joining the class soon after signing. A lock of hair draped over half his face as he smiled, knowing the next hour could change everything.

Clad in black tights and a bright teal headband, the instructor exuded infectious enthusiasm. He led the group through the basic choreography for a scene tailored to an upcoming zombie movie. "Keep in mind that you've risen from the dead," he barked, voice sharp with theatrical fervor, hands clawing like the undead. His gaze scanned the eager faces before him. "The producers are looking for authenticity here, people. I want fatigue, distress, *agony!*"

With a wave, he cued the sound technician in the rear of the room. An eerie soundtrack sent a shiver of excitement and fear through the group. The instructor turned on the camcorder and, in a booming voice, said, "Let's take it from the top. Five, six, seven, eight—"

The car's impact was cataclysmic. Glass doors exploded inward, shards erupting like confetti from hell. The storefront frame buckled and twisted like a tin can. Smoke billowed from the crumpled hood, filling the studio with an ominous haze. Behind the deployed airbag, Arpita lay unconscious, her head lolling to the side.

Everyone fell into the drift, bodies contorting to the eerie music blaring in the background. Smoke from the radiator thickened, curling through the room like morning fog. Overwhelmed by vertigo, several aspiring actors vomited and slumped to the floor. The camcorder captured the dead slithering and moaning across the floor, in what could have been an Oscar-worthy performance of distress.

Ethan's eyes snapped open. His breath, a sudden vacuum, escaped his mouth. He fluttered toward the wrecked sedan, each step advancing with uncertainty. A violent shudder sent him falling forward, striking his skull against the unforgiving panel with a clunk. Pain shot through him as stars bloomed behind his eyes.

Somewhere in the haze, the line between rehearsal and reality had vanished . . .

Watching the destruction in her rearview mirror, Penney despaired for the world, but kept driving.

Then, on Oyster Street, the unthinkable happened.

Patrick rubbed his scraggly beard, irritated by the rash but proud of his scruff. While pumping gas with one hand, he took another drag of his cigarette with the other, the end glowing like amber. He watched the fog curl and wisp overhead. Exhaling a long plume of smoke, he nodded and said, "A little misty, but it'll be another glorious day."

A backfire from a pickup truck pierced the silence, twisting his gut into a knot. The sound jolted Patrick into a panic, sending the cigarette tumbling from his quivering lips into the rising fumes.

BOOM!

The blast seared the air with a mushroom ball of fire, scattering debris hundreds of feet. Patrick's body was instantly obliterated, devoured by the flames of wrath. All that remained was a severed hand, squelched against the side of the payment booth. Still dangling from the wrist was a gold watch, its case back engraved with a haunting inscription: **If found, call 765-555-0176**.

The explosion stopped Penney dead in her tracks. Her face pale, eyes wide as silver dollars. She longed to jump out, pull him out of the fire, and smother the flames. That is, if he even existed. Instead, she could only cover her ears to deaden the sound of ensuing blasts. "Stop!" she shouted, pounding futilely on the steering wheel. Her heart ached for the helpless man and for the world unraveling around her.

The chain reaction is spreading faster!

Alone and powerless, she choked back a sob and gripped the steering wheel with renewed determination. Fog thickened, curling in dense wisps that made her squint. Headlights flared to life, slicing through the haze as she pressed forward.

Destruction followed as she clattered past a senior community where several older adults sat at picnic tables. One by one, they fell prey to the time shift, their bodies jiggling like bowls of peach gelatin, their clothing and silver hair twitching in unseen eddies, as if time had turned against them.

Bereft of purpose, Tabatha Pratz sat in her wheelchair, one claw-like hand curled around an open bag of colorful sprinkles—the last bright thing she refused to surrender in her descent into despair. Her eyes stared out from the abyss, a place no rope could reach and no hand could pull her free from.

As the wheelchair began to tremble, Tabatha's frail body quivered with it. She remained unfazed as her lovely gingham dress bubbled to life. Slowly, she leaned forward until gravity claimed her. Like a marionette with its strings cut, she tumbled sideways, her legs tangled in the footrests, her head striking the edge of a concrete planter with a dull, final thud. Confectionery toppings scattered across the pavement in a bloom of color. A single sprinkle bounced once, twice, then arced into the air and landed in her slack, dreadfully open mouth. It melted on her tongue. The sweet taste triggered one final, dying thought—

Colorful sprinkles get rid of the wrinkles.

She breathed her last with a smile on her face.

* * *

Turning left onto Main Street, Penney passed a young man with skin as smooth and dark as polished ebony, dressing a mannequin in a window display. She wished she could sneak past him without attracting his attention, but the truck's rattle was enough to make him turn his head. Instantly, his body quivered uncontrollably as an invisible wave knocked him off balance. Though his close-shaven hair and fitted clothes offered no leeway for fluttering, Eric flailed. His arms sliced through the air, desperate to stay upright. With a helpless cry, he fell backward through the pane of glass. It exploded over the sidewalk, arcing through the air before clattering into a thousand bright shards. Then silence fell. His eyes squeezed shut, and his mouth opened in a breathless scream.

The accident triggered a silent alarm at the police station, where a young dispatcher leaned forward to respond. But Linda's chair had begun to inch away across the wooden floor, and she could no longer reach the radio. "What the fuck!" she said, looking around for the practical joker. Her blond hair thrashed, and her eyes were enveloped in shock. Though trained to deal with emergencies and unusual circumstances, Linda couldn't process this surreal situation.

"Help!" Her cry fractured the room's composure, sending the department into a spiral of panic.

Officer Charles Freeman had finished cleaning and reloading his gun when he doubled over and vomited. His short gray hair fizzled, and the long sleeves of his uniform twisted unnaturally along his arms. Mid-spasm, his trembling hand nudged the gun. Charles's eyes flared, pupils dilated, locking onto the weapon as it drummed against the metallic desk, its hammer and trigger twitching like nerves beneath skin. The clanging reverberated throughout the room, growing louder with each strike of the barrel and butt.

Bang!

The room convulsed in unison, each officer seized by the same invisible force, until a collective gasp tore through the air. Groaning, Charles fell to the floor, blood staining his navy pants.

Officer Ira Wright had just called his wife to say he was on his way home after another long night. As their conversation veered, the shift in reality registered in their home.

Hailey was frying thick slices of ham for breakfast, her hand gripped around the pan's handle when the shaking began. Her legs trembled, knees buckling as panic flooded her bleary eyes. The vibration surged through her limbs. The pan jerked violently, sloshing hot oil until it ignited. The result: a charred wife, a house gutted by flame, and a devastation that licked through the neighborhood.

Penney veered onto Ardmore Street, nearly missing the turn in the thickening fog. Her heart pounded as she glanced both ways, grateful that no cars materialized out of the mist. As she drove under the pedestrian overpass, her eyes finally locked onto Fazal's Dry Cleaning. For the first time that morning, she felt a glimmer of hope. At last, the chaos would soon end.

Pulling up to the shop, the tires bumped the curb and jarred the glove compartment open. Several items spiraled out like space junk, drifting as orbital waste. Feeling the oppressive heat and the sticky dampness, Penney allowed her surgical cap and mask to float freely with the rest of the clutter. Her hair thrashed, and her cheeks and lips fluttered with excitement, as if a blow-dryer blasted her face. She slid out of the truck without bothering to turn off the headlights and stumbled for the door . . .

After discovering that his clock could repeat time, Fazal had manipulated it to address certain ignored obligations. However, when his wife unexpectedly passed away a few days later, he attempted to revive her by turning back the hands of time. Tragically, Agnes died thirteen times—each death more gruesome than the last. Despite his efforts to prevent her demise, destiny always found a way to sink its talons into her soul.

Fazal Zitcaby clenched his teeth and jabbed an arthritic finger at the clock, howling, "What do you want from me?!" Saliva sprayed, and the veins in his temples pulsed. In a fit of wrath, he kicked the floor clock, almost losing his balance. The pendulum swung violently, and the delicate chimes erupted in a cacophony of discordant notes. The glass door rattled, threatening to shatter under the weight of his fury . . .

Emerging from the ethereal glow, Penney trudged forward like a walking corpse, her shadow stretching unnaturally long under the piercing headlights. The hospital gowns whipped around her gaunt frame like a ship's tattered sail in a storm. Her heart raced. Each labored step drew her closer to Fazal's shop.

Tarnished brass met her palm, its cold metal awakening her senses. The shop bell chimed overhead as she opened the door. Penney stepped inside, extending her arm in a desperate attempt to get the proprietor's attention . . .

Fazal grabbed the sledgehammer he had placed on the counter and swung it over his shoulder. He steadied himself, his eyes fixed on the still grandfather clock as its minute hand moved another notch. With a deep breath, he raised the hammer high, ready to bring it crashing down.

"Stooop!" Penney shouted.

The sound shattered Fazal's concentration, freezing him mid-swing. With a startled jerk, the sledgehammer slipped from his grasp, clattering to the floor with a metallic thud. The instant he disturbed the fabric of reality, a jarring sensation ripped through him, causing his body to convulse violently. Like the others before him, nausea struck like a rogue wave, and he fought to steady his stomach. His frightened eyes settled on the specter in the doorway, sending an unsettling chill prickling across his skin. Shaking his head incredulously, Fazal stepped back in horror.

The truck's headlight silhouetted Penney's body, creating a halo that accentuated her hair's uncanny resemblance to writhing tentacles. She fought to stay upright as both gowns flapped, exposing glimpses of her wrinkled, naked body. The shop's fluorescent lights flickered, casting eerie shadows on the walls. Before she could utter a word, her left cheek ripped and flapped like wet parchment caught in a fan, blood trickling down her neck.

"Please don't take me!" Fazal shouted, shielding his eyes from the truck's glaring light. He slumped to his knees and said, "I'm not ready to go, Agnes."

Penney inched forward. "The key to the clock," she rasped, cringing as pain tore through her outstretched arm. The clock's gravitational pull slid Penney across the floor against her will. Images surged through her consciousness: glimpses of a not-too-distant future in which humankind lived in peace and harmony without currency, of beautiful cities accommodating everyone, of efficient cars that didn't poison the air, of a world full of happy, smiling faces! *How could a world of grief, hunger, and despair change from one extreme to the other overnight*? It was hazy, but she sensed the world was awakening to love and respect, a place where everyone lived for the benefit of humankind. *If only I could receive a sign confirming it! Even if it's just a song!*

Penney thrust her hand at the proprietor. "Give me the key," she said in a raspy voice.

As Fazal retched onto the floor, the Grim Reaper's voice echoed through his skull. He blinked hard, struggling to focus. Then, with frightened eyes, he met the specter's gaze.

"Give me . . . the clock key!" Penney demanded, her voice throbbing with urgency. More skin unraveled under the force, each inch a toll paid to time. Blood splattered on the clock's glass door as she fought against the current.

Still vibrating, Fazal staggered toward the counter and dragged the drawer open. Its contents, including the clock key, erupted in a maelstrom. With a desperate lunge, Fazal snatched the key from midair just as the drift hurled his body into the cash register. The impact knocked the register to the floor, scattering coins and bills into the current. Fazal lay sprawled across the counter, unconscious, the key clenched tightly in his hand.

Penney's time was slipping away. From the farthest reaches of space to the smallest atom known to science, life on Earth had mere moments before a fissure ripped through the time continuum, collapsing the universe. The tug-of-war between reality and her altered life was causing irreparable damage to her fragile body. With forty-five seconds before a universal catastrophe, she fought desperately against the grandfather clock's pull. Through bloodshot eyes, she saw the key in the unconscious man's grasp. His head lolled, slack and senseless, neck bent at an unnatural angle. If the universe had any hope of moving forward, she had to get that key!

Penney glanced at the clock and gasped: 8:14. *I've got maybe twenty seconds to spare.* The pendulum swayed, ticking away time. Suddenly, the skin on her left arm ripped, exposing bone and surrounding tissues. Eyes brimming, Penney pushed away from the clock and stumbled toward the key. She could almost feel its metallic shape in her quivering hand. The wind slashed around her resolute face as she took one more strenuous step.

"I've had enough . . . of your fuckin' games," she said, her voice rising confidently. With her teeth clenched, she looked like the Grim Reaper without her scythe. Only ten seconds remained. She lunged for the key, yanking it from his grasp. Holding it triumphantly, a sigh escaped her trembling lips. Instead of struggling back toward the grandfather clock, she allowed the gravitational pull to draw her in.

Her body was whisked across the floor. She struck the clock and cried out. Penney jammed the key into the lock, twisted hard, and flung open the glass door.

Five seconds.

She turned to face the pendulum, its arc slicing through time.

"Time's up!" she rasped.

The minute hand began to shift . . .

With a twist of her wrist, she seized the pendulum mid-swing, and the universe held its breath.

The fluorescent lights stuttered, then steadied. Penney Miller collapsed.

Silence filled the room.

Fazal Zitcaby, stirring from unconsciousness, opened his eyes in time to see objects spiraling in midair plunge to the floor. His thinning hair and crumpled suit stilled.

"Hello?" he called, peering over the counter. Straightening up, he spotted the nightmarish figure draped in what looked like hospital gowns. Unable to resist, Fazal steeled himself and crept toward the creature. "Are you alive . . . or dead?" he called. No reply. *With my luck*, he thought, *the Grim Reaper will whisk me away into the darkest pit imaginable, where I belong for putting my wife through thirteen horrible deaths*. Still, the urge to see its face fascinated him. He nudged the body with his foot, moving the deadweight slightly. Satisfied it was dead, he kicked the mound harder.

"Hey, that hurts!" the Grim Reaper yelped.

Fazal staggered back. A shiver ran down his back as the bloodied mound shifted slowly, its movement disturbingly human.

To his astonishment, a pair of skinny arms emerged from beneath the fabric, groping for purchase. Instinct screamed at him to flee, but his feet felt rooted to the floor. A lump rose in his throat as the creature sat upright and turned toward him. With a delicate hand, it brushed aside the tangled hair from its face.

"Holy shit!" Fazal's eyes lit up.

Instead of the Grim Reaper, a young girl sat innocently before him—an image so wrong it made his breath catch. Her angelic face, streaked with red scars where the skin had healed, held a quiet grace, like moonlight on broken glass.

"Well, are you going to help me up?" Penney asked, tucking her feet under her for leverage.

Rushing to her side, Fazal took her hands and helped her to her feet, her hospital socks gripping the floor. "You're . . . just a little girl," he stammered. He blinked rapidly, trying to convince himself he wasn't imagining things.

Puzzled, Penney raised her hands. She, too, was shocked to see soft and youthful arms, those of a young girl! Her fingers trailed over smooth skin dusted with peach fuzz. Some girls would die for smooth, hairless arms, but not Penney. She loved her hair. Running her fingers through the peach fuzz, an indescribable joy filled her heart.

With excitement coursing through her, she rushed to a full-length mirror next to the fitting room and gasped. Her brown eyes sparkled with a mix of joy and disbelief as she stared at a teenage girl with shimmering sandy hair, rosy cheeks, and a perky upturned nose. The thinning hair, aching bones, age spots, and wrinkles were now distant memories. Ecstatic, she lunged forward, slid down the cool mirror, and collapsed to her knees.

I've been given a second chance at life!

Penney wept.

Stepping closer, Fazal asked, "Can I do anything for you, miss?"

"My name is Penney," she said softly, wiping her eyes. "You can help me find my father. I left him alone beside some bushes on Old 122. He's hurt."

"Absolutely," he said with a nod. "But first, let's get you into some clothes."

While Fazal rummaged through a pile of unclaimed clothes, Penney explained how her father ended up alone in Liberty.

"Here," he said, breaking her train of thought. "What do you think about this dress?"

"That's perfect!" she beamed. "I like flower prints! It reminds me of Spring, my favorite season." She grabbed the dress and disappeared behind the dressing room curtain. "It all makes sense now," she called, peeling off the shredded gowns. "When I saw you with a sledgehammer over your head, I realized your action is what set the time loop in motion."

Fazal lowered his head. "What you don't know is that my wife, Agnes, died thirteen times," he said, his eyes welling up. "I manipulated the clock to revive her, but each time she met the same fate."

He brushed the countertop, lost in memory.

Silence hung between them, heavy with truth.

Penney brushed the curtain aside and stepped out. Though the dress radiated cheer, her face remained solemn. "I'm sorry to hear about your wife." Her eyes met his, offering quiet solace. "I truly believe Agnes is in a better place. You must accept reality to find peace." She smiled, then said, "Live life to the fullest, even when it's hard."

They lingered in silence, honoring Agnes. Then, without another word, they set off for Liberty.

Fazal drove south on US Route 27 in his restored '57 classic, its engine purring like a contented kitten beneath the hood. The new leather squeaked as he shifted. An old-fashioned AM radio with push buttons that moved the pointer gleamed like the car's front grill.

"I still can't fully grasp how today always ends at 8:15. How did you determine the universe was infinitely looping?" he asked.

"Déjà vu," she answered boldly.

"But why couldn't I, or anyone else, detect the loop?"

"You might say I stepped outside the box," she said, eyeing him. Fazal badly needed a shave, a bath, and clean clothes. The circles under his eyes were as deep and dark as caverns. "This is our fourth loop. I was in my hospital room when I decided to break the cycle. When I saw your interview on television, I immediately knew the grandfather clock had something to do with the phenomenon. Now that the loop has been broken, you mustn't destroy the grandfather clock. That might reset the vicious cycle," Penney added, her voice unsteady. "It must be carefully dismantled."

Fazal reached for his short-brimmed hat and squeezed it onto his balding head, just as he would a cork into a freshly opened bottle of wine. His face was triumphant. Finally accepting his wife's death, he knew she was in a better place. Not because Penney had said so, but because he felt it. Turning to face the teenage girl, he gave her a genuine smile. "You can trust me, Penney," he said, then patted her knee and flicked the radio on.

The familiar sound of Louis Armstrong's deep, raspy voice filled the air, bringing comfort and solace. "I see skies of blue . . . clouds of white, bright blessed days . . . dark sacred nights. And I think to myself . . .

What a wonderful world."

ESSENTIAL CIRCUS LINGO

beat back— The trapeze performer who swings back above the pedestal board.

big top— The main tent used for performances.

boss canvasman— The man whose job is to decide exactly where and how the tents should be put up at a new circus lot.

bull handler— Circus employee working with the elephants.

bullhook— A tool used by elephant handlers to manage and discipline them.

carpet clown— A clown who works either among the audience or on the arena floor.

cast out/force out— The far end of the first swing on a trapeze.

catch bar— The trapeze that the catcher swings on.

clown alley— Backstage area where clowns put on their makeup and store props.

cutting up jackpots— Swapping tall tales about the circus.

first of May— A novice performer in his first season on a circus show.

flag— A vaulting exercise where the performer extends one arm and the opposite leg while facing forward with the chin higher than the shoulders.

fly bar— The bar the flyer (flying trapeze) uses.

guys— Heavy ropes or cables that support poles or high wire rigging.

harlequin— A diamond pattern with elongated shapes arranged vertically.

hep/hup— Trapeze signal meaning "go."

king pole— The central pole that supports the main canvas of the big top.

lista/listo— Trapeze signal meaning "ready."

lunge line— A long, single rein and the primary means of communication between the handler and the horse.

lunge whip— A training device with a cord and pole that allows the equestrian to send the horse forward without needing to be on their back.

main guy— Guy rope that holds up the center pole in the big top.

off—In equestrian language, off refers to the right side of the horse. Traditionally, people mount horses from the left (near side), so the right (off side) is considered the opposite.

remount— To return to the platform after swinging on the fly bar.

ring horse— A horse that performs in the center ring and is trained to maintain timing despite distractions.

surcingle— A surcingle is a broad strap that goes around the horse's body, typically just behind the front legs. A vaulting surcingle is used in the sport of equestrian vaulting. These feature sturdy handles to assist vaulters in performing gymnastic moves on a moving horse.

towners— Townspeople, any outsiders.

withers— Part of the spinal column that projects upwards between the shoulder blades of a horse.

ESSENTIAL MEDICAL JARGON

albuterol: A quick-relief medicine that helps people breathe easier when they're having trouble due to asthma or other lung problems. (The Child Within)

apoplexy: A sudden and often fatal loss of consciousness, typically caused by internal bleeding in the brain. In early 19th-century medicine, apoplexy referred broadly to strokes, seizures, or any abrupt collapse without external injury. (A Vicious Cycle)

atrophy: A gradual weakening or shrinking of muscles, organs, or body parts when they aren't used or don't get enough nourishment. (House of Broken Bones)

Brushfield spots: Small, white or light-colored spots that can appear on the iris, which is the colored part of the eye. They are often associated with Down syndrome, but they can also occur in people without this condition. (Lifegiver)

cannula (nasal): A soft tube with two little prongs that sit in your nostrils to deliver oxygen. (House of Broken Bones)

capsaicin: The compound that makes hot pepper spicy. Eating something with capsaicin, like a chili pepper, activates certain receptors in your mouth that send signals to your brain, which is why you feel a burning sensation. (La Bruja Maldita)

cellular senescence: a biological process in which cells permanently stop dividing but don't die. Instead, they linger in the body and can release inflammatory signals that affect surrounding tissues. (The Child Within)

cimetidine: A medication that helps reduce the amount of stomach acid. It's commonly used to treat conditions like heartburn, stomach ulcers, and gastroesophageal reflux disease (GERD). (House of Broken Bones)

cirrhosis of the liver: A condition where the liver becomes severely scarred and damaged over time. Various factors, including excessive alcohol consumption, chronic viral infections, or fatty liver can cause this scarring. (The Clown and the Caregiver)

decompensation: The failure of an organ or system in the body to function properly after it has already been weakened or stressed. (House of Broken Bones)

demyelination: The damage or loss of myelin, which is the protective covering surrounding nerve fibers in the brain and spinal cord. The myelin sheath helps electrical signals travel quickly and efficiently along the nerves. (House of Broken Bones)

dextran: A complex carbohydrate made up of many sugar molecules linked together. It is often used in medical settings to help increase blood volume or improve blood flow because it can attract water. (House of Broken Bones)

dimenhydrinate: Used to prevent and treat nausea, vomiting, and dizziness caused by motion sickness. It's also sometimes used to relieve symptoms of vertigo and dizziness associated with inner ear problems. (The Child Within)

dysrhythmia: Any irregularity or abnormality in the rhythm of the heartbeat. A normal heart rhythm is crucial for effectively pumping blood throughout the body. (House of Broken Bones)

epicanthic: A type of eyelid fold that covers the inner corner of the eye, giving the appearance of almond-shaped eyes. (Lifegiver)

esomeprazole: A medication that helps reduce stomach acid. It's often used to treat conditions like heartburn, gastroesophageal reflux disease (GERD), and stomach ulcers. (House of Broken Bones)

glioma: A malignant tumor of the glial tissue of the nervous system. (House of Broken Bones)

glottic carcinoma: A type of cancer that affects the glottis, part of the larynx (or voice box) that contains the vocal cords. This cancer usually starts in the cells of the vocal cords and can lead to symptoms like changes in your voice, difficulty swallowing, or pain in the throat. (The Clown and the Caregiver)

hetastarch: A synthetic starch-based solution used primarily in medical settings, especially for fluid resuscitation. It's designed to help increase blood volume in patients who have lost a lot of fluids due to injury, surgery, or certain medical conditions. (House of Broken Bones)

hormsodiumregulators (HSRs): A fictitious drug name made up to fit the narrative.

Hutchinson-Gilford Progeria Syndrome: A rare genetic condition that causes rapid aging in children. It is characterized by symptoms such as growth failure, aged-looking skin, stiffness of joints, and cardiovascular problems. (The Child Within)

hypoperfusion: A condition with insufficient blood flow to a specific body part. This can happen for various reasons, such as low blood pressure, blockages in blood vessels, or severe dehydration. (House of Broken Bones)

ibuprofen: a drug that reduces pain and fever. (A Vicious Cycle)

intravascular: It is often used in medical contexts to describe processes, treatments, or conditions related to the inside of blood vessels. (House of Broken Bones)

iodopropynyl butylcarbamate: (IPBC) A preservative used in many personal care products such as lotions, shampoos, and cosmetics. It helps prevent the growth of bacteria, mold, and yeast in these products, which in turn helps extend their shelf life. (As clear as night)

ischemia: A condition that occurs when there is not enough blood flow to a part of the body, which can lead to damage or dysfunction of the tissues. (House of Broken Bones)

lacrimatory agent: A substance that causes the eyes to produce tears. These agents are often used in crowd control situations, like tear gas, where they make people cry and temporarily impair their vision. (La Bruja Maldita)

lactulose: A type of sugar that is often used to treat constipation. It helps draw water into the bowels, which makes it easier to have a bowel movement. It can also help treat a liver condition called hepatic encephalopathy by helping lower certain toxins in the blood. (The Clown and the Caregiver)

lentigo: A type of skin mark that appears as a small spot. It's usually brown or black and can vary in size. These spots often develop because of sun exposure over time. (The Child Within)

lung crackles: Also known as rales, are sharp, crackling sounds that can be heard during inhalation. They are often associated with fluid in the small airways of the lungs. Lung crackles can signify various medical conditions, such as pneumonia, heart failure, or chronic obstructive pulmonary disease (COPD). When a healthcare provider listens to your lungs with a stethoscope, they may hear these crackling sounds, which can help diagnose the underlying condition. (House of Broken Bones)

misophonia: A condition where certain sounds trigger strong emotional or physiological reactions, such as irritation, anger, or anxiety. These sounds, often referred to as "trigger sounds," can be everyday noises like chewing, tapping, breathing, or repetitive clicking. (The Clown and The Caregiver)

myelin sheath: A protective covering that surrounds the nerve fibers in the body. Think of it like the insulation around electrical wires. It helps speed up the transmission of electrical signals between nerve cells. (House of Broken Bones)

perfusion: The process of blood flowing through the body's tissues. Think of it as delivering oxygen and nutrients to different body parts while carrying away waste products. (House of Broken Bones)

progeria: A rare genetic condition where a child's body ages much faster than usual. Kids with progeria often look older, have hair loss, and develop health problems typically seen in elderly people. (The Child Within)

pupillary sphincter: A tiny muscle in the eye that controls the size of the pupil, which is the opening in the center of the eye. When the muscle contracts, the pupil is smaller, letting in less light. (The Clown and the Caregiver)

salmeterol: A long-acting beta-2 adrenergic agonist (LABA) commonly used to manage asthma and chronic obstructive pulmonary disease (COPD). (The Child Within)

(single) transverse palmar crease: A specific type of line that can appear on the palm. Typically, people have two main creases across their palms, but some individuals have one continuous line that runs across the palm instead. This feature is often associated with certain genetic conditions but can also occur in people without health issues. (Lifegiver)

thyroxine: One of the main hormones produced by the thyroid gland. It plays a crucial role in regulating various bodily functions. (Lifegiver)

triethanolamine: A compound used in various cosmetic and personal care products. It serves as an emulsifier, pH adjuster, and surfactant (a substance that, when added to a liquid, reduces its surface tension, thereby increasing its spreading and wetting properties), helping to blend and stabilize different ingredients in creams, lotions, and other skincare products. (As clear as night)

triiodothyronine: One of the primary hormones produced by the thyroid gland. It is more potent than thyroxine and plays a vital role in regulating various physiological processes. (Lifegiver)

zero porosity: A material or substance that has no pores or voids. There are no gaps for liquids or gases to pass through. (La Bruja Maldita)

GOING FORWARD

(Taken from A Vicious Cycle)

The Twin Towers erect out of rubble in a matter of seconds and expel two airplanes into the sky. Iraqi troops run backward out of Kuwait. The US exits Panama and frees Noriega while the Berlin Wall is erected with broken pieces of cement lying on the ground. Somoza overthrows the Sandinistas in Nicaragua. Neil Armstrong is the last person not to leave footprints on the moon. The Soviet Union retrieves Sputnik with an R-7 rocket, which lands in Kazakhstan. Hiroshima rises from the rubble in a matter of seconds when the atomic bomb ejects from the ground and floats into Enola Gay's bomb bay doors. Amelia Earhart is the last woman to fly solo across the Atlantic backward. The last talking film, The Jazz Singer, gives way to silent movies. The US exits World War I, and three years later the war ends. The dismantling of the Panama Canal ends, and a year later Orville and Wilbur Wright successfully fly a powered airplane backward. King C. Gillette scraps his idea for the safety razor, and two years later Karl Benz dismantles his four-wheel car. The last skyscraper of ten stories is dismantled in Chicago. Alexander Graham Bell ditches his idea for the telephone. Abraham Lincoln comes back to life after a bullet exits his body. Isaac Singer dismantles his sewing machine, and The New York Times disappears forever. The rush to put gold back in California ends. Texas becomes dependent of Mexico. The last printing of An American Dictionary of the English Language by Noah Webster becomes blank paper, then a pulp, and then timber, which is planted back into the ground with repairing saws. The first words that Ellis Amspoker says after returning to life on the stockpiled timber are words of damnation. His hand lifts from a lifeless position and points at Hezekiah Coopers while the life drains back into his body. Blood seeps out of the white pine and into the bodies of the group of seventeen illegal wood cutters formed by Ellis Amspoker.

BIBLIOGRAPHY

About Our Scrap Metals, ABC Recycling Scrap Metal Recyclers, accessed August 2, 2024, abcrecyclingga.com/ about-metals.

Deffeyes, Kenneth S. *Hubbert's Peak: The Impending World Oil Shortage* (Princeton University Press, 2001), 1.

Einstein, Albert, "The Need for an Ethical Culture," a speech given at the Ethical Culture Society, New York, NY, January 5, 1951.

Einstein, Albert. As quoted by William Miller, "Death of a Genius," *LIFE Magazine*, May 2, 1955, 64.

Einstein, Albert. Quoted in "Einstein Is Terse in Rule for Success," (Short title) *New York Times*, June 20, 1932.

Food Waste FAQs, USDA, accessed August 2, 2024, https://www.-usda.gov/foodwaste/faqs.

Mori, Masahiro (1927-2025), "The Uncanny Valley," Energy 7, no. 4 (1970): 33-35.

Torrella, Kenny "We raise 18 billion animals a year to die — and then we don't even eat them," *Vox*, December 12, 2023, https://www.-vox.com/future-perfect/22890292/food-waste-meat-dairy-eggs-milk-animal-welfare.

ACKNOWLEDGMENTS

I would like to extend my deepest gratitude to Geoffrey Chaucer, whose timeless work, the Canterbury Tales, served as a profound source of inspiration for this book. His masterful storytelling continues to influence writers across generations, and I am deeply honored to be one of them.

House of Broken Bones was written between 2006 and 2008, long before the emergence of AI-assisted writing tools. In 2024, the author embraced these innovations to enhance the manuscript through selective drafting and editorial refinement. Scenes involving Senate debates, visionary methods for a currency-free society, scientific developments related to age-related diseases, and medical dialogues beyond the author's expertise were enriched using AI-generated suggestions. This manuscript reflects a collaborative process between the author and Microsoft Copilot, an AI-powered writing assistant, with all final decisions and narrative direction remaining solely the author's.

I want to thank my beta reader and copy editor, Carissa Schlafer, of Carissa's Editorial Services, and my line editor, Ginny Ruths, Touchstone Publications, whose constructive feedback strengthened the story. In addition, any shortcomings that remain in the book after the editorial process are my own.

Witch's pulley, futuristic cityscape, and cover characters generated by AI. Cover design by Tea Jagodić.

A NOTE FROM THE AUTHOR

While a 3-liter oxygen pocket-sized canister was not available in 2002, I have chosen to include it in this story for narrative purposes. The first public release of this product occurred in 2021.

One section is set in the early 1800s. Great care has been taken to reconstruct the historical context accurately while minimizing sensitive issues. However, some minor sensitive dialogue remains to authentically reflect the era. My utmost respect goes out to all as we collectively strive for a brighter future.

I fought hard to keep my list of 230 nations in the story, but in the end, my two editors won—and that's a good thing. Thank you, ladies.

This book was born from a love of storytelling and a desire to thrill readers with outrageous adventures that keep them on the edge of their seats. If it left you breathless or grinning, I'd be honored if you shared that excitement with others.

Edgar J. Hern

ABOUT THE AUTHOR

Edgar spent the formative years of his life in Southern California, attending private schools. As a teen, he enjoyed reading horror and science fiction novels that explored utopian and dystopian ideas. He often wondered how a utopian society would come about. As a young adult, he noticed that most utopian and dystopian novels introduce readers to an unknown future without explaining its origin. Inspired by this, he wrote a story about a pre-utopian society on the cusp of becoming a great nation. Combining his love for fantasy, action, and suspense, he brings you an action-packed story that paves the path to a utopia. "Pay close attention," he says. "My book is a puzzle."

Edgar now lives in Ontario, California. He is retired and enjoys traveling and meeting with social clubs for karaoke, dining, and other fun activities.

X: @EdgarJHern12748

www.ingramcontent.com/pod-product-compliance
Lightning Source LLC
Chambersburg PA
CBHW022242020726
47496CB00004B/1027

* 9 7 9 8 9 9 2 8 8 4 0 1 2 *